MONSTERS OF THE EARTH

MONSTERS OF
THE EARTH

DAVID DRAKE

TOR®

A TOM DOHERTY ASSOCIATES BOOK
NEW YORK

MONSTERS OF THE EARTH

A Tor Book
Published by Tom Doherty Associates, LLC
175 Fifth Avenue
New York, NY 10010

www.tor-forge.com

Tor® is a registered trademark of Tom Doherty Associates, LLC.

Library of Congress Cataloging-in-Publication Data

Drake, David, 1945–
    Monsters of the Earth / David Drake.—First Edition.
        p. cm.—(Book of the Elements ; Book 3)
    "A Tom Doherty Associates book."
    ISBN 978-0-7653-2080-3 (hardcover)
    ISBN 978-1-4299-4884-5 (e-book)
    1. Magicians—Fiction. 2. Monsters—Fiction. 3. Romans—Fiction. 4. End of the
world—Fiction. 5. Europe—Fiction. I. Title.
    PS3554.R196M66 2013
    813'.54—dc23

                                                                    2013022127

Tor books may be purchased for educational, business, or promotional use. For information on bulk purchases, please contact Macmillan Corporate and Premium Sales Department at 1-800-221-7945, extension 5442, or write specialmarkets@macmillan.com.

First Edition: September 2013

To the late
HANK REINHARDT,
hoping that he would be pleased with the way I've used some of
the information he provided me with over the years

ACKNOWLEDGMENTS

Dan Breen continues as my first reader. He has summed up our different approaches to editing as, "You want to make it better. I just want to
make it right." We went over about two-thirds of this novel in a single
five-hour session, which gives you a notion of how extensive his help to
me is.

Dan doesn't just point out missing words or typos (and I can be very
creative with typos). He and I can discuss the place of Vergil in the
Middle Ages or the reason for a seeming digression in my text or a hundred other matters that interest the two of us more than they're likely
to interest anybody else. Readers like Dan stretch me, and there aren't
many readers like Dan.

Dan, Dorothy Day, and Karen Zimmerman, my webmaster, archive
my texts as I complete them and occasionally answer my panicked que-
ries about what I said in an earlier chapter. Things not infrequently
(very frequently!) go wrong with my hardware when I'm working on
a novel. I feel better knowing that my work is safe in three widely
separated locations even if something horrible happens to my entire
network.

Speaking of which: my base unit (the desktop) failed just as I finished the rough draft. As it turned out, the on/off button had stuck.
This was the second time I'd had trouble with the same button. This
time my son Jonathan fixed it by swapping the computer internals into
a new case.

A few days later my printer died. Jonathan researched the options,
ordered me a replacement printer, and guided me through installation.

(Fewer things are plug-and-play if you're me than they might be for other people.) My friend Mark Van Name backstopped Jonathan by offering to print the draft out if I needed it sooner than UPS could get the printer to me. I've got the best IT support structure in the world.

I have a homegrown geek, as the preceding shows. Mark's daughter Sarah helped in a different fashion. Her photograph of and paper on the tombstone of Quintus Coelius, Signifer of the 11th Legion, in the Uffizi Gallery gave me valuable contemporary information that I would not otherwise have had.

My generation can be proud of raising offspring like Jonathan and Sarah. The future is better for having people like them in it.

And my wife, Jo, kept things going while I was writing *Monsters of the Earth*. Coincidentally, we were building a major addition to the house (which is also my workplace). She handled the stress a lot better than I did and kept as much of it off me as possible.

Thank you all, and thanks to the many others who helped me. Writing is indeed a lonely business, but the life of a writer doesn't have to be lonely, if he has family and friends like mine.

I intend individual volumes in The Books of the Elements to be self-standing (though I also hope that they add up to something greater than the sum of their parts). This note will therefore repeat some things that I said in *The Legions of Fire* and in *Out of the Waters*.

The most important of these repetitions is that my fictional city of Carce (KAR-see) is not the historical Rome of A.D. 30. (Neither is it the fictional city of Carce in *The Worm Ouroboros*, a novel by E. R. Eddison, which I urge you all to read.)

Here in *Monsters*, the most important difference is that the historical poet Vergil is also the mythical magician Virgil. In the Middle Ages, the idea grew that the author of the *Aeneid* was a powerful magician. The most pervasive aspect of this myth was that his name began to be spelled "Virgil" rather than the correct "Vergil."

A magician's wand in Latin is a *virgilla*, the diminutive of *virga*, a staff or branch, so the mythical magician became Virgil to make the connection clear. The poet's name is still generally spelled "Virgil," especially in America, because the myth became so widespread. This has occasionally caused me problems with copy editors who are sure that I'm wrong in referring to Vergil.

Speaking of possible problems with copy editors: the Old World sycamore tree is quite different from the North American sycamore. The Egyptians often built ships out of sycamore wood for want of anything better, though it wouldn't ordinarily be recommended for such a purpose.

Which leads me to a further point: I make mistakes, but they're usually not careless errors. I try to avoid reading reviews, because I get unreasonably angry at seeing a reviewer, for example, state that Romans didn't really behave in some fashion that I describe.

Everybody has a right to an opinion. My opinions are based on extensive reading of Latin literature in the original, from Plautus to Macrobius. The folk who seem most determined to correct me appear to base their opinions on Hollywood—or perhaps on the Natural Wisdom that Plato claims Socrates believed in. Take your pick.

Most of the spells in *Monsters* are translated or paraphrased from the *Sibylline Books*, the *Aeneid*, and a West African (Yoruba) folktale. There are also snatches of Ovid, Diogenes Laertius, and goodness knows who else. We are what we eat, and I devour classical literature for pleasure.

In passing, I reread my OCT volume *Vitae Vergilianae Antiquae*, but that was mostly to refresh myself in the rhythms of Latin prose rather than use it as source material. I mostly read and translate verse nowadays.

Roman society was based on slavery, which I regard as an unspeakable evil, and was extremely class-conscious even by later European standards. My dad was an electrician, and I am well aware of where I would have been placed in the Roman class structure. I know exactly how that feels, because I was a junior enlisted man in Vietnam. I much prefer an egalitarian society.

That said, I describe the society of Carce as I understand the society of Rome in the 1st Century A.D. to have been: as a reporter, not an advocate. I shouldn't have to mention this, but thirty years ago I was repeatedly pilloried for describing war as horrible by people who honestly thought I was advocating the horrors.

A final note on the dedication. My son is aware that I've been in correspondence with Arthur C. Clarke and that I've known and even been friends with many famous SF and fantasy writers. I don't think he's paid much attention to that.

Some years ago, however, he saw a picture of me at dinner with Hank Reinhardt. He immediately asked, "Is that *the* Hank Reinhardt?" I assured him that it was.

For the first time, Jonathan was impressed at the fact that his dad knew somebody.

DAVE DRAKE
www.david-drake.com

MONSTERS OF THE EARTH

CHAPTER I

G aius Alphenus Varus looked back over his shoulder. There were
only a dozen servants ahead of him and his friend Corylus as they
wound through the streets of Puteoli to the wharfs on the Bay itself.
Behind, however, there must be a hundred people. More!

"We look like a religious procession," Varus muttered. He tugged the
shoulder of his toga, a square of heavy wool with the broad purple stripe
of a senatorial family, to settle it a little more comfortably.

Varus had no taste for pomp, but he was polite, so he couldn't treat
this occasion as though he were merely a scholar who needed only a
tunic and at most one servant to carry his satchel of writing and reference materials. That would be insulting to the friend of Corylus' father
whom they were visiting—and to Varus' own father, Gaius Alphenus
Saxa: senator and recent consul of the Republic of Carce.

Corylus chuckled. He said, "We look like a train of high officials
going to consult the Sibyl, you mean? That's a good five miles from
here, though, farther than I want to hike, wearing a toga on a day this
warm."

He and Varus were the same age, seventeen, but Publius Cispius
Corylus was taller by a hand's breadth and had a bright expression that
made him look five years younger than his companion. Corylus had
gotten his hair, reddish with touches of gold, from his mother.

He had been born on the Rhine frontier where his father had commanded a cohort. His mother, Coryla, was a local girl who had died
giving birth. Soldiers couldn't marry while on active duty, but Cispius
had acknowledged his son as legitimate.

"Saxa wouldn't be in the best shape after a five-mile hike," Varus said mildly, pitching his voice so that only his friend was likely to hear the words. "Let alone Hedia."

Hedia was Saxa's third wife and therefore by law the mother of Varus and his sixteen-year-old sister, Alphena. Hedia was twenty-three, beautiful, and sophisticated to the point of being, well, *fast*.

In most senses, one could scarcely imagine a less motherly woman than Hedia. In others—in all the ways that really mattered—well, she had faced demons for her stepchildren. What was even more remarkable was that the demons had been the losers.

Varus was a bookish youth who had almost no interests in common with his stepmother. He had nevertheless become glad of the relationship, and he was very glad that his father had a champion as ruthlessly determined as lovely Hedia.

"It's not something I need, either," Corylus said. "Especially not in a toga. I told Pulto—"

He nodded to his servant, who had been the elder Cispius' servant throughout his army career.

"—that he needn't bother wearing one unless he wanted to impress somebody."

Though Corylus kept a straight face, Varus knew the servant well enough to chuckle. He said, "How did Pulto respond to that?"

"He said that if he needed to impress somebody, he'd do it with a bloody sword," Corylus said, grinning again. "Like he'd done a couple hundred times before, he figured. I told him I hoped that wouldn't be necessary on a visit to an old friend like Marcus Veturius."

Pulto was a freeborn citizen of Carce, unlike the other servants and attendants accompanying the nobles and dignitaries present. That said, Pulto had spent his army career keeping Publius Cispius as comfortable and well fed as was possible in camp, and alive when they were in action.

Since Corylus' father believed in leading from the front, "a couple hundred" Germans and Sarmatians probably *had* met the point of Pulto's sword. Pulto had accumulated medals over the years, but his real honors were the scars puckering and crisscrossing his body.

An animal screamed in the near distance, meaning they were nearing the compound where Veturius stored the beasts he imported. From here he shipped them to amphitheaters—largely in Carce, but all over Italy.

Varus felt his lips tighten. His first thought had been that the cry had come from a human in pain, but it was too loud.

"An elephant, perhaps?" said Corylus, who must have been thinking the same thing.

"Loud even for that," Varus said. "Well, we'll know soon enough."

The spectators lining both sides of the street shouted, "Hail, Lord Saxa!" and similar things. Balbinus, the steward who ran Saxa's home here on the Bay of Puteoli, must have planned extremely well.

This district housed sellers of used clothing and cookware whose booths would normally fill the street. A detachment of husky servants had cleared them back before Saxa and his entourage had tried to pass through, but the squad leading the procession itself was flinging little baskets to the crowd.

The gifts—sweet rolls, candied fruit, or a few copper coins—changed the residents' mood from riotous to a party and led them to cheer instead of finding things of their own to hurl. Buildings in Puteoli didn't reach four or five stories as they did in Carce, but even so bricks thrown from a rooftop would be dangerous.

"Varus . . . ," Corylus said, his voice suddenly husky. "I, ah . . . That is, my father feels greatly honored that former consul Saxa has accepted his invitation to visit the compound. I don't think Father cares greatly for himself, but it raises him in the eyes of his old friend Veturius. I, ah . . . I thank you on behalf of my father, and on my own behalf, because you've so pleased a man whom I love."

"I accept your thanks," Varus said mildly. "I believe that's your father waiting in the gateway, isn't it? And I suppose that's Veturius in the toga beside him."

Corylus already knew that Varus hadn't encouraged Saxa to come with him to the animal compound, so there was no need to repeat the statement. Indeed, the whole expedition had grown of itself, the way a rolling pebble might trigger a landslide.

The importer Marcus Veturius had told his friend Publius Cispius that he had brought back a group of unfamiliar animals from deep into Africa. Cispius had suggested he send for his son, Corylus, a student in Carce, who was learned and might be able to identify the creatures.

Corylus had asked to bring along his friend and fellow student Gaius Varus, whom he said was even more learned. After a grimace of modesty, Varus could have agreed. Corylus was himself a real scholar as well as being a great deal more; but dispassionately, Varus knew that his own knowledge was exceptional.

All that would have been a matter of academic interest, literally: a pair of students visiting an importer's compound to view exotic animals. Everything changed because Saxa, Hedia, and Alphena were spending the month nearby at the family house on the Bay.

Saxa was not only a former consul—which was merely a post of honor since all real power was in the hands of the Emperor and of the bureaucrats who had the Emperor's ear—but also one of the richest men in the Senate. Anything Saxa did was done—*had* to be done—on a grand scale.

Saxa had no political ambition, which was the only reason he had survived under a notably suspicious emperor, but he did desperately want to be seen as wise. Unfortunately, although he loved knowledge and knew many things, Saxa's mind was as disorderly as a jackdaw's nest.

Varus, however, *was* a scholar. Despite his youth, he had gained the respect of some of the most learned men in Carce—including Pandareus of Athens, who taught him and Corylus. Instead of being envious, Saxa basked in his son's successes.

Saxa hadn't been a harsh father, but he had scarcely seemed to notice his children until recently. Now he was making an effort to be part of his son's life and so had asked to accompany Varus to view the strange animals.

Varus hadn't even considered asking his father to stay out of the way, but his presence had turned a scholarly visit into a major social undertaking. A younger senator named Quintus Macsturnas had bought the whole shipment of animals to be killed at a public spectacle in Carce to celebrate his election as aedile. When Macsturnas heard that Saxa planned to visit the compound, he had asked to accompany his senior and even wealthier colleague.

Varus smiled, though his lips scarcely moved. Courtesy aside, how could he—or his father—have denied Macsturnas permission to view the animals he himself had purchased?

Besides which, the even greater pomp was certain to please Cispius and his old friend. The aedile's attendants were added to those of Saxa and the separate establishments of Hedia, Alphena, and—because this was now a formal occasion—the ten servants accompanying Varus himself.

"I wonder . . . ," said Corylus, looking at the following procession and returning Varus' attention there also. "If there'll be sufficient room in the compound, what with Veturius just getting in a big shipment?"

He shrugged, then added, "I don't suppose it matters if the servants wait in the street, though."

Varus consciously smoothed away his slight frown, but he continued to look back. *Corylus will stop me if I'm about to run into something.*

A dozen servants walked directly behind the two youths. They were sturdy fellows who carried batons that would instantly become cudgels if there was a problem with local residents. Next were the two senators and their immediate family—in Saxa's case—and aides.

Varus faced front again. "The old man behind Macsturnas?" he said. "The barefoot old fellow. Do you recognize him, Publius?"

Corylus looked back and shrugged. "Can't say that I do," he said. "Is there something wrong with him?" He coughed and glanced sidelong at Varus. "That is, he seems pretty harmless to me."

"There's nothing wrong that I can see," Varus said, feeling embarrassed. Because he was speaking to Corylus, however, a friend with whom Varus had gone through things that neither of them could explain, he added, "I caught his eyes for a moment when I looked back. He either hates me, or he's a very angry man generally. And I don't recall ever having seen him before in my life."

"He may be the aedile's pet philosopher," Corylus said equably. "Though Macsturnas strikes me as too plump to worry much about ascetic philosophy. And the fellow doesn't have a beard."

"If he were the usual charlatan who blathers a Stoic mishmash to a wealthy meal ticket," Varus said, "he *would* have a beard as part of the costume. Which implies that whatever he is, he's real. And I agree that Macsturnas doesn't appear to be philosophically inclined, though we may be doing him an injustice."

Varus found comfort in his friend's comfortable acceptance of present reality. Corylus didn't worry about every danger that could occur, but he was clearly willing to deal with anything that did happen.

Corylus' father, Publius Cispius, had started as a common legionary and been promoted to the rank of knight when he retired after twenty-five years in service. Corylus also intended an army career, but his would begin as an officer: a tribune, an aide to the legate who commanded a legion as the Emperor's representative.

That was the formal situation. Informally, Corylus had been born and raised on the frontiers and he'd spent more time on the eastern bank of the Danube—with the scout section of his father's Batavian squadron—than most line soldiers did. Corylus didn't talk about that to Varus or to other students, but sometimes Varus listened while Pulto talked to Saxa's trainer, Lenatus, another old soldier.

There was a great deal Varus didn't understand about his friend's background, but he understood this: Corylus might be frightened, but fear would never stop him from doing his duty to the best of his ability.

He was, after all, a citizen of Carce. *As am I.*

"Eh?" said Corylus.

I must have spoken aloud. "I was thinking that we have duties as citizens of Carce," Varus said. "As well as our rights."

Corylus said, "That had occurred to me, yes."

Part of Varus' mind considered that a mild response for a soldier to make to a civilian who was talking about duty. His consciousness was slipping into another state, however, in which the Waking World flattened to shadow pictures like those on the walls of Plato's Cave of Ideal Forms.

Corylus had joked about them being a royal procession visiting the seeress whose temple was nearby at Cumae. Varus in his mind was climbing a rocky path to an old woman who stood on an outcrop above all things and all times.

She was the Sibyl, and during the past year she had spoken to him in these waking dreams.

HEDIA SAW VARUS GLANCE in her direction from beyond the squad of attendants. She smiled back, but almost in the instant she saw him stiffen as his eyes glazed.

Varus faced front again. He was walking on, his legs moving with the regularity of drops falling from a water clock. Hedia had seen the boy in this state before. Seeing him now drove a blade of ice through her heart.

Smiling with gracious interest, Hedia looked past Saxa and said to the aedile, "If I may ask, Lord Macsturnas—why did you decide to give a beast show in thanks for your election instead of a chariot race?"

In a matter touching her family, Hedia would do whatever was proper. Not that poor, dear Saxa was capable of thinking in such terms, but it was possible that one day he would need a favor from Macsturnas. If on that day the aedile remembered how charming Saxa's lovely wife had been—well, courtesy cost Hedia nothing.

Aedile was the lowest elective office, open to men of twenty-five; Macsturnas was no older than that and seemed younger. An aedile's main duties—even before the Emperor began to guide the deliberations of the Senate and therefore the lives of every man, woman, and child in the Republic—were to give entertainments to the populace.

"I thought it was more in keeping with my family's literary interests to offer the populace a mime when I was chosen consul," Saxa volunteered. "My son is quite a poet, did you know?"

Hedia had no more feeling for poetry than she did about the defense of the eastern frontier: both subjects bored her to tears. Varus had assured her, however, that his one public reading had proved to him that he had no poetic talent and that he should never attempt verse again.

Saxa, in trying to become part of the life of the son whom he had ignored for so long, was resurrecting an embarrassment. Well, that was easy to cover.

"Though of course we're great fans of chariot racing also," Hedia lied with bubbly innocence. "After all, some of the most illustrious men in the Republic are. We follow the White Stables in particular."

Hundreds of thousands of spectators filled the Great Circus for even an average card of chariot racing; it was by far the most popular sport in the Republic. Hedia didn't care about that, though charioteers tended to be more lithely muscular than most gladiators and thus of some interest.

The Emperor was a racing enthusiast. Hedia cared about *that*. And because the Emperor backed the Whites, Hedia would swear on any altar in Carce that her husband did also. She didn't have any particular belief in gods, but she felt that any deity worth worshiping would understand that the survival of the Alphenus family was more important than any number of false oaths.

"Well, you see . . . ," said Macsturnas, his tone becoming more oily and inflated with every syllable. "My family were nobles of Velitrum. Our house was ancient before the very founding of Carce."

He gestured with both hands, as though flicking rose water off his fingers as he washed between courses of a meal. A more prideful man than Saxa might have taken offense at the implied slight; and though Saxa's wife, also a noble of Carce, didn't let her smile slip, this bumptious fellow might one day regret his arrogance.

"To Etruscans of *our* rank," Macsturnas continued, "gladiatorial games are not a sport but a religious rite. I therefore expected to hire pairs of gladiators for my gift to the people. But then the agent I sent to Puteoli learned that Master Veturius was back from Africa with a number of unique animals. I ordered him to purchase the whole shipment and came down to look at them myself. My gift will be unprecedented!"

Varus' sister, Alphena, was out of sight. She and Hedia had been getting along well since recent events had forced them to see each other's merits, but the relationship of a sixteen-year-old with her stepmother was bound to have tense moments.

Today Alphena had planned to walk with her brother and Corylus at the head of the procession; Hedia had forbidden her to do so. Instead of joining Hedia and the two senators, Alphena had flounced back to the very end.

Hedia hadn't objected; the girl wouldn't get into any trouble surrounded by her personal suite of servants and the roughs of the senators' households who formed the rear guard. Alphena probably wouldn't have gotten into trouble in the company of Varus and Corylus, either, but Hedia knew too much about taking risks to allow her daughter to take a completely unnecessary one.

Varus, of course, wasn't a problem; nor was even Corylus, not really. Varus' friend was a very sensible young man. The attitude of a sixteen-year-old girl toward a youth as brave and handsome as Corylus *might* become a problem, though, if they spent too much time together.

For all his virtues, Corylus was a knight and therefore an unsuitable husband for a senator's daughter. After Alphena was safely married, of course, her behavior was a concern for her husband, not her mother.

Hedia smiled faintly. She had been sixteen herself not so very long ago. Alphena didn't have the personality required to make a success of her stepmother's lifestyle.

Macsturnas laid his hand on Saxa's shoulder and leaned across the former consul to bring himself nearer to Hedia. In a conspiratorial tone—though a rather loud one in order to be heard over the cheerful banter of spectators—he said, "The man accompanying me, Master Paris—he's a priest of great learning. He honors you by asking to join us, Lord Saxa. Paris is the recipient of the wisdom passed down from the great founders of the Etruscan race."

If Etruscan wisdom is so remarkable, Hedia thought, smiling softly toward the pudgy little man, *then why is Velitrum a dusty village in the hills and Carce the ruler of all the known world?*

"Is this soothsayer helping you plan your gift, Quintus Macsturnas?" Saxa asked, glancing for the first time at the Etruscan who walked behind them. "Choosing the day for you to give it, that is?"

Paris glared at Saxa, and at Hedia, who turned with her husband. She hadn't paid any attention to the scraggly old man until now. He was barefoot, wearing a simple tunic and a countryman's broad-brimmed hat. His appearance made him unusual in a nobleman's entourage—but not interesting, at least not to Hedia.

And what an odd name. Surely he can't be a freedman whose former owner gave his slaves names out of Homer?

"Oh, no, nothing like that," Macsturnas said, lowering his voice to where Hedia was as much reading his lips as hearing the words. "He, ah . . . I knew of Paris, of course, but I haven't had actual dealings with him. As some of my fellow Etruscans have. He asked to come along today to see the scaly monkeys. I, ah . . . I really don't know why."

There was a look of nervousness on Macsturnas' pudgy features, as though he actually cared about what the old man thought. Even if Paris was freeborn, the opinion of a poor commoner was no proper concern for a noble of Carce.

"Well," said Saxa expansively. "I'm more than happy to have your little priest get the benefit of my son's wisdom. Varus is an exceptional scholar, you know. Marcus Atilius Priscus assured me of that when we were last chatting. Do you know Priscus? He's the most learned of our senatorial colleagues, in my opinion. He's head of the Commission for Sacred Rites and a great friend of my son's teacher, Pandareus of Athens."

Hedia almost giggled. That sort of patronizing boast would be alien to her husband under most circumstances. Apparently Saxa hadn't been quite as unmoved by Macsturnas' tone as she had believed.

On the other hand, everything Saxa had said was quite true. Varus was quite a remarkable youth . . . as in different fashions was his friend Corylus. Corylus was a respectable scholar himself—that was how a noble like Varus had become friends with a youth of only knightly rank—but he was also an accomplished athlete and a *very* handsome young man.

Unfortunately—Hedia smiled ruefully at herself—Master Corylus also had better sense than to chance an affair with a senator's lovely young wife. Well, that was probably for the best.

She was glad that Saxa was taking an interest in Varus. Though Saxa was anything but a social manipulator, his wealth allowed him to give dinners at which his son would be introduced to the sort of people whose help he would need while steering his future course through society. Hedia had recently begun to craft guest lists that suited that purpose, and her husband acquiesced to them happily.

She wished she could find some more worldly fellow to give Varus a grounding in the more earthy aspects of life, though. All the men Hedia knew were rather *too* worldly, unfortunately. The last thing she wanted was to turn her son into a hard-drinking wastrel like those with whom she had whiled away her time during her previous marriage, to Gaius Calpurnius Latus.

She still met them, though more discreetly since she married Saxa. Saxa was a very sweet man, but Hedia had needs that her husband couldn't satisfy. Saxa had known he wasn't marrying a Vestal. She suspected that he was secretly proud of her and her reputation, but it wasn't a subject they discussed.

The procession was about to reach the entrance to Veturius' animal compound. The walls were masonry—coarse volcanic tuff from the beds layering all the land overlooked by Mount Vesuvius—and over ten feet high.

Hedia had never visited a beast yard before, but she often toured gladiatorial schools when she was summering here on the Bay. The schools
were fenced off—the gladiators were slaves, after all, and under a stiff
training regimen—but she hadn't seen any barriers so impressive as this.

"I wonder why Veturius has such walls?" Hedia said aloud. "Do you
know, Lord Husband?"

"Why, no," said Saxa, frowning. "You'll build a wooden enclosure
in back of the Temple of Venus for your gift to the people, won't you,
Quintus Macsturnas? Or have you engaged the Great Circus? You'd
need several thousand animals to justify that, I would think."

"My gift won't be that extensive, no," Macsturnas said with a flash of
good humor. "Not for the aedileship, at least. If I gain the honor of the
consulate like you, Gaius Saxa, perhaps I can manage something on a
greater scale."

Hedia pursed her lips in silent approval. Macsturnas had asked to
accompany Saxa to curry favor with his senior colleague, after all. He
must have belatedly realized that boasting about his lineage wasn't the
way to accomplish that.

"Well, when we're inside, we can ask my son," Saxa said. "I'm sure
Varus will know why it's built this way."

"Better that we ask Veturius himself, my dear heart," said Hedia,
patting her husband's hand to take away any suggestion of sting in her
rebuke. "See, there he is in the gateway to receive you."

The servants leading the procession had fallen away to either side.
Varus and Corylus waited with two older men. The elder Cispius would
be the one wearing the toga whose border was dyed with the two narrow stripes of a knight.

The other man must be Veturius. The beastmaster's toga was plain,
and he looked as though he'd been used very hard.

Hedia consciously avoided a frown: been used and used himself. The
broken veins in Veturius' nose were surely the result of wine.

"Welcome, noble Senators Gaius Alphenus Saxa and Quintus
Macsturnas!" Veturius said. His voice was strong, though it reminded
Hedia of rusted metal. "You are most welcome to my establishment,
Your Lordships!"

Corylus had a hand on Varus' shoulder, a silent direction to his
mentally distant friend. Hedia relaxed slightly. Corylus would prevent

her son from injuring himself in his present state. If Varus suddenly shouted an incomprehensible prophecy, as he had done before, that would be easy enough to brush from the consciousness of social inferiors, Macsturnas included.

But it didn't remove Hedia's deeper fear. When Varus had fallen into waking dreams in the past, it had always been a warning of some event that was about to occur.

Some *terrible* event.

CORYLUS TOUCHED THE FRAME of the gateway, feeling the dryad still present though the wood came from the ancient keel of a broken-up trading vessel. She stirred faintly. Though the sycamore sprite was aged, she managed to smile at him; her eyelids were shadowed with kohl.

Corylus was worried by Varus' state and still more worried at what his waking dream might mean this time, but there was nothing to be done about those things at the moment. His present duty was to act as intermediary between his father and the pair of senators facing him.

"My lord Gaius Saxa . . . ," Corylus said in a clear voice. He and the two veterans were all braced to attention. "Allow me to present my father, Publius Cispius, and his friend Marcus Veturius."

Instead of bowing—they were freeborn citizens of Carce—Cispius and his friend each saluted by striking his clenched right fist on his chest. If they had been equipped for battle, that gesture would have banged their spear shafts against their shield bosses.

Saxa had stepped down from the consulship after the usual month in office, but he remained Governor of Lusitania and nominal commander of the troops there. Saxa had the right to the salute, though it probably startled him to receive it.

Lusitania was on the rocky Atlantic coast of Europe, closer to Britain than to Carce or to civilization generally. Saxa would never visit it: a younger, fitter, hungrier Knight of Carce was acting as the governor's representative. Saxa had an antiquarian's knowledge of Carce's history, though, and enough patriotism to feel the honor of a salute from two of the men who had held the Republic's borders against barbarism.

To Corylus' surprise, Saxa returned the salute. The new aedile, Macsturnas, blinked at the scene.

Of course. Saxa probably couldn't draft a dinner invitation in an orga-

nized fashion, but he would have read lengthy monographs on the forms of military protocol. Varus' father wasn't a stupid man, though he was a profoundly silly one.

"Marcus and I had the honor of serving under your cousin Sempronius Mela," Cispius said. "When he was Legate of the Alaudae, that is. It's a real pleasure to meet a kinsman of Mela."

Corylus didn't let his mouth drop open in amazement the way Macsturnas was doing, but he was certainly surprised. Instead of creating an awkward situation, Cispius—the third son of a farmer in Liguria—was handling the wealthy senator perfectly.

Corylus suddenly realized that his father wouldn't have risen through the ranks as he had without meeting many noble officers. Some would have been as foolish as Saxa and a great deal less pleasant personally.

"Master Cispius, I'm pleased to meet you," Saxa said. "And to meet your friend, of course. You've a fine son in Master Corylus, a very fine son."

"We are here to view the scaled monkeys from Africa, are we not?" said the old farmer who had come with Macsturnas. His tone was querulous.

"And who would that be, lad?" Cispius asked, quietly but in a voice that sounded like the growl of a big cat. Corylus might not have understood the words if he didn't know his father well enough to expect them.

Cispius didn't have the vinewood swagger stick he had carried as a centurion, but as a child Corylus had met his father's calloused hand enough times to remember its weight. Cispius had grown plump and softer in retirement, but he could still deal with the likes of Macsturnas' hanger-on without help or a weapon.

"I'm sure we all wish to see the strange animals, Master Paris," Macsturnas said nervously, glancing between Saxa—who wasn't the sort to take offense—and the farmer. "As soon as Lord Saxa is ready to, of course."

"The aedile's pet philosopher, I guess," Corylus said quietly to his father. "And the aedile's not a particular friend of Saxa's, but he's footing the bill for this load of animals."

"Right," said Veturius, relaxing. "Not the business of a poor working soldier like me."

"Till they tell us it is," Cispius added, but he had relaxed also.

"Well, if you're ready, Macsturnas," Saxa said. He nodded to Veturius. "Take us through, my good man. I'm quite interested in what my son thinks of the creatures."

"Why do you need such walls, Master Veturius?" Hedia asked. "Are your animals so dangerous as that?"

Corylus flinched minusculely. He'd been so focused on Varus that he hadn't noticed Hedia was at his elbow until she spoke.

The servants had stepped aside as they neared the gate, allowing the principals to come together for the first time since they stepped out the front door of Saxa's house in Puteoli. Alphena, who must have been at the end of the procession, had joined her parents also. She wore a stony expression.

"Well, they're dangerous enough, Your Ladyship," Veturius mumbled, refusing to meet Hedia's eyes. "But the cages that held the bloody creatures all the way to here ought to hold them now. The problem's the boys here in the port—aye, and some of the girls too. They'd creep in at night for a lark, don't you see, if we didn't have walls like these—"

He slapped the coarse tuff with his right hand. It sounded as though he'd laid into it with a harness strap.

"—to keep them out."

Macsturnas had leaned close to Paris and was whispering urgently, presumably to forestall another impatient outburst. The aedile had no intention of letting a boorish associate turn Saxa into an enemy.

"Does it matter if a few kids look at the animals before they're shipped to Carce?" Alphena asked. Varus' sister was a fairly good-natured girl underneath, though half the time she seemed determined to prove something. She drove herself and everybody around her to distraction when she got frustrated. For now, at least, curiosity seemed to have drawn her out of her earlier bad temper.

"Well, it's not that, mistress," Veturius said. "You see, we just keep the rare stuff and the carnivores in here. I've got pasture outside the city for the bulk animals, the deer and wild asses and bulls, that sort of thing. Even the ordinary elephants. But when there's a big load like now, the aisles between the cages here are pretty tight."

Corylus had seen his father wince, but there was no harm done.

Cispius sold perfumes and unguents to upper-class households and thus knew not to call a senator's daughter "mistress," instead of "Your Ladyship." An importer whose clientele was brokers—slaves and freedmen—who handled beast hunts and gladiatorial bouts didn't normally need to worry about forms of address.

"I don't see . . . ," Alphena said, letting her voice trail off as she apparently realized that interrupting a man like Veturius wasn't going to get information out of him more quickly. "No, no, just go on."

Cispius had been the Alaudae's First Centurion, the legion's highest permanent officer—directly under the legate whom the Emperor appointed. At that time Veturius had commanded the tenth company of his tenth cohort. In the Alaudae the Tenth of the Tenth was the Special Service company rather than being a posting for the legion's most junior centurion. It handled raids and patrolling, the sort of jobs that the Scouts did when Cispius became prefect of the 3d Batavians on his final posting.

Scouting and the things that scouting requires take a toll on a soldier even when he retires with all his limbs and not too many physical scars. Corylus was only ten when he moved with his father to the Batavians on the Danube, but even then Veturius drank enough to be noticed in a community of professional soldiers.

"Well, some kid would be poking a stick at the baboons, but he'd jump back when they banged into the bars and a lion would reach out a paw and grab him from behind," Veturius said earnestly. "Or it might be the other way around, you see? And when there's a fresh kill like that and blood all over, hell, why, the whole compound screams and carries on all night."

Veturius surveyed the crowd, noticing the number of attendants for the first time. "Say, Your Lordships," he said in concern. "You might want to leave most of this lot outside. I don't mind the trouble, I don't mean that, but I guess some of these slaves are pretty expensive, right? Believe me, they won't be pretty anymore if they lean close to look at a leopard and he claws their faces off."

"I think that's a fine idea," Hedia said briskly. "Leaving the servants outside, that is. My daughter and I—

Hedia nodded regally toward Alphena.

"—are both wearing new garments—"

Hedia extended half of her short cape like a blue silk wing. Alphena wore a similar garment in white, appliquéd with symbols of the zodiac.

"—which we don't want splashed with blood. Syra"—Hedia's maid, listening at her mistress' side—"you'll stay here with Balbinus and the others."

"Yes, ladyship," the girl said. Her face relaxed from its previous look of blank horror. Corylus wasn't sure that Hedia was *really* that callous, but her maid obviously found it possible.

Hedia made a gracious gesture with her left hand. The men in the gateway turned together like drilling soldiers and led the way into the compound.

Veturius was that callous: he couldn't have done his job with the Alaudae if he hadn't been. After Cispius retired, he had dried his friend out and set him up in this importing business, which had become very successful. But that hadn't made Veturius the man he might have been without twenty years on the Rhine.

Corylus kept his right hand on Varus' elbow, using light pressure to direct him. With his left hand he motioned Hedia and Alphena to follow the two senators. The man Paris stepped in front of them.

Paris flew aside just as quickly. The servants of both senatorial households were waiting in the street, but Pulto didn't take the direction as applying to him. He'd grabbed the old man's wrist, bent his arm behind his back, and pushed him away sharply enough to spill him in the dust with a squawk.

"Thank you, Master Pulto," Hedia said, nodding pleasantly. She swept into the compound behind her husband.

What an empress she would make! Corylus thought, then felt a chill in case he might have spoken aloud. That sentiment would mean a number of executions if it reached the Emperor's ears—and the youth who voiced it would be on the first cross.

The roadway from the gate to the harbor was wide enough for loaded wagons, though the paths between rows of cages were much narrower. Cages of birds and smaller monkeys were stacked two and three high.

Pulto walked beside his master and Varus, whistling something cheery between his teeth. He had obviously reacted badly to hearing some scraggly farmer be disrespectful to his betters. Veterans like Cispius and Veturius, let alone the senators, were Paris' betters in Pulto's opinion.

Well, in the opinion of Pulto's master, also.

The animal Corylus had heard as they approached now screamed again, louder by far without walls of the compound to muffle it. Corylus looked toward the sound. To his amazement the head and trunk of an elephant were fully visible beyond wheeled lion cages that were eight feet high.

"What's that?" Corylus said—directing his question toward Veturius but speaking to anybody who might have an answer. "It looks like an ordinary elephant, but it's bigger than even the ones they bring from India sometimes."

Everyone in the group looked at him. Saxa's face went blank, then melted into concern: he must have noticed that Varus wasn't in a normal state. At least he didn't blurt something out.

"Your son's got a good eye, Top!" Veturius said, referring in army slang to his former superior. "Come on over here and I'll show you. We leave plenty of room around him, though he hasn't been a problem since we got him off the boat."

The visitors dutifully followed Veturius past hyenas held four to a cage. There wasn't room for the beasts to pace, but they watched the humans with hatred that was almost palpable.

Paris didn't make another attempt to hurry the process, but the look he fixed on Pulto was as angry as that of the hyenas. Pulto was used to civilians hating him; one more wouldn't be a concern.

Corylus suppressed a smile: like Veturius, he'd formed his sense of humor on the frontier. Paris might feel ill-used, but he'd actually been lucky. Pulto wore hobnailed army sandals, which he would have used if the farmer had actually touched Master Corylus in stepping past.

The elephant's hind legs were chained to bollards sturdy enough to tie up a giant grain ship; the area in front of him had been left clear. He was huge, more like a building than a creature of flesh and blood.

Though the elephant had the build and large ears of his African kin, Corylus had never seen one of those that was much more than seven feet tall at the shoulder. This monster was well over eleven feet tall, bigger even than the Indian elephants like Syrus, which Hannibal had ridden over the Alps.

"You see . . . ," Veturius said. His voice was strong and animated now that he was discussing his importing business instead of wondering how to deal with noblemen. "The ones you're used to, the elephants we mostly get, they come from near the African coast. South of that's desert, so of course you don't get elephants there, there's nothing for them to eat, right?"

The elephant curled its trunk, raised its massive head, and screamed louder than any living thing Corylus had heard in the past.

"But south of the desert, then there's more grass and more forest and Hercules *knows* what kinds of animals," Veturius resumed as his visitors lowered their hands from their ears. "They've got elephants like this as was floated down the Nile from way beyond the First Cataract. And if you come here with me, I'll show you what else we got, the things I asked my friend Cispius to bring his son to see."

Veturius, limping as he walked more quickly than he had done earlier in the afternoon, stepped around the elephant's plaza to a cage on a cross street wide enough for a wagon rather than an aisle. Corylus followed with the others, guiding Varus as he had been doing since his friend went into his dream state.

"Stand well clear, if you will," Veturius said. "They've got a reach that'll surprise you. They came down the Nile on a barge same as brought the elephant there, straight out of the dark heart of Africa!"

Corylus moved to his father's side, directly in front of the cage where he got the best view through the close-set bars. They were welded iron, not the usual wood pinned or lashed.

"Here they are, Your Lordships," Veturius said. "Scaly apes like nothing seen before in the Republic!"

Corylus looked at the four creatures; they met his gaze calmly.

Those aren't apes, and they sure *aren't men,* he thought.

But they might very well be demons.

THEY LOOK LIKE THEY stepped out of a nightmare, Alphena thought as she stared at a lizardman. A membrane flicked sideways and back across the creature's left eye; then the same thing happened to the creature's right. The lizardman seemed very patient . . . and amused, though Alphena couldn't have explained why she felt that.

"How did you capture the creatures, Veturius?" Saxa said, leaning toward the cage. Cispius grunted; Corylus stepped sideways to put his body between the senator and the lizardmen.

"Father!" Alphena said. *Did I ever call him that before?* She pulled Saxa back by the wrist and elbow. "You'll be killed if you're not careful!"

Saxa looked startled, then understood what had happened. "Oh!" he said. "Well, I don't think I was really in danger, do you, my child? But thank you."

He looked at the lizardmen again. "Their arms really are very long, aren't they?" he said in a reflective tone. "Though their bodies aren't the size of ours. Thank you very much, my dear, and—"

Saxa looked at Corylus, who had slipped to the other side of Varus, concealing himself as much as possible behind his shorter friend. For a commoner—even a knight—to physically interfere with a senator was potentially very dangerous, but Corylus hadn't hesitated when he saw the risk to her father.

"—thank *you*, Master Corylus. I'm afraid I was very foolish."

Alphena looked at the lizardmen again. They were creatures of nightmare, all right, but they weren't from the particular nightmare that had been torturing her for the past three nights.

She'd dreamed of three short Nubian women dancing in a circle, naked except for a belt of iridescent stones around the waist of each. They weren't frightening, nor was anything else that Alphena remembered from the dream, but she woke every night sweating and a cry choked in her throat.

Whereas the lizardmen were merely interesting, the way an ancient bronze sword would interest her. And speaking of bronze, what were those collars they were wearing?

"Strictly speaking, I don't capture animals," Veturius said. "Ordinarily, I mean, I hire local Nubians to do the catching and bring the beasts to where I set my camp. If I went south with enough men to do the whole job myself, I'd need an army. You go march into Nubia with an army and the tribes'll treat you the same way they would a Prefect of Egypt who decided to advance the Republic's boundaries some."

"There were periods when Egypt was ruled by Nubians," said Corylus, nodding. "I was wondering how you managed to bring animals back from that far south."

He and Varus knew lots about that sort of thing. Alphena didn't resent the education her brother and his friend had gotten: *she* didn't care who ruled Egypt, let alone making formal speeches about whether a stepson or the wife's steward was guilty of her murder. But she resented that she hadn't been given the choice.

"Yeah, that can be a tricky business," Veturius said, bobbing his head like a sparrow drinking. "I don't take so many men that I look like I figure to stay, but I need enough that the locals, they figure it's cheaper to take my pay for the animals they bring me and as porters."

He lifted his hands, palms up. He was missing his left little finger, and the fourth finger stopped at the first joint.

"Nowadays, the chiefs know I'm coming back, so they'll make more trading with me than just trying to take it," Veturius said. "Also, they know that taking it wouldn't be so easy as it maybe seemed first off. I hire pretty good boys, you see. Most've 'em decided that Nubians'd be a nice change from Germans or Sarmatians. And I've got Parthian archers who can shoot over a shield or through it, whichever they choose. But early on, I tell you, there was times I wished I was back on the East Bank of the Rhine."

Cispius snorted. Veturius met his old friend's eyes. Alphena was suddenly aware of a kinship like nothing she had ever had with another human being. It went beyond shared danger: it was a shared *trust*.

They'd trust Corylus! And they would, because Corylus had been on the East Bank too; he'd proved himself.

I will make myself worthy of trust. Whether or not anybody else knows it, I will know.

"Anyway," Veturius said, "we'd just set up down below the Third Cataract; that's way south. I put out the word to the tribes to bring us animals, pretty much anything."

He knuckled his nose as he frowned in concentration. A scar ran from below his right eye to the base of his jaw on the left; his nose dipped in a saddle where the line crossed it.

"We pay in cloth and glass beads and brass wire," he muttered, gathering his memories. "The Nubians like them better than silver, which they can't do much with. Pound for pound, it'd be easier to carry silver, but that's not a choice. Anyway."

Veturius gestured with both hands again. "We just set up, like I say, and here comes a couple Nubians with these apes, neck-yoked like slaves, each one to the one ahead and walking on their own. They asked what we'd pay for 'em—they'd never seen the like before. And I said, same as for baboons, since that's what they likely were. Only they weren't baboons. And I don't bloody know what they are!"

"My friend Varus and I are also at a loss, Veturius," Corylus said, speaking clearly and with his voice raised. He was focusing all attention on himself—and away from the youth at his side. "Now that we've seen these lizard apes—lizardmen, I should say—we'll be able to enlist the aid of greater scholars than ourselves."

He's covering for my brother. Varus and Corylus hadn't discussed the creatures or anything else since Varus slipped into his present state. By speaking for both of them, Corylus concealed the fact that his friend was only physically part of the world around him.

Instead of coming to Puteoli with the rest of the family, Varus had remained in the town house in Carce while he took classes in speaking and argumentation from Pandareus of Athens. Varus had sent a messenger to inform the family as a courtesy that he and Corylus would be visiting Puteoli to view some unusual animals. Saxa had decided to join his son and his friend.

Whereupon Alphena had announced she would go also.

She hadn't known then why she said it, and now in reflection she didn't have any better notion of what had been going on in her mind. She had just said it; and once it was said, there was no taking the decision back. Not for her.

Hedia's decision to join the group as soon as Alphena spoke was as certain as sunrise: she thought her daughter was too interested in Publius Corylus, and she didn't trust anyone else to chaperone the girl effectively. Hedia's attitude *infuriated* Alphena.

The possibility that there might be some truth to her mother's opinion made Alphena even more angry. She had learned by experience that Hedia was extremely perceptive. That was true whether or not Alphena liked the things that Hedia perceived.

"Lord Macsturnas, may I ask . . . ?" Corylus said, turning from the beast catcher to the aedile. "If these lizardmen will be going to Carce for your show with the rest of the consignment of animals?"

"Why, yes," Macsturnas said, looking puzzled. "That is . . . I mean, is there some reason they shouldn't?"

In a tone of rising agitation, he went on, "Is there something you're not telling me? There *is* something you're not telling me!"

"No, my lord, there is not," said Cispius, stepping between his son and Macsturnas. Cispius didn't raise his voice, but he was suddenly in control of the situation.

Alphena realized that she was seeing the difference between rank, which her father and the aedile had by birth, and command, which Publius Cispius had gained on the frontier. She felt suddenly ashamed, though neither she nor her family was a part of this unexpected confrontation.

"No, Your Lordship," Corylus said calmly, moving again to his father's side. Nothing in Corylus' tone suggested that the man to whom he was speaking had seemed to be on the verge of panic. "I was hoping that if you sent the creatures to Carce, there would be an opportunity for Master Pandareus to view them himself."

"Oh!" said Macsturnas, suddenly embarrassed. "Why, yes, of course, what a good idea, Master—"

His mouth opened and shut for a moment without further words coming out.

He doesn't remember Corylus' name. Aloud Alphena said, "I'm sure Corylus and my brother will take care of that for you. You'll see to it that the attendants in Carce are instructed to allow them and anyone they bring with them to view the animals. Won't you, Quintus Macsturnas?"

Corylus glanced at her. His smile and the jerk of his chin in approval were minuscule, but Alphena noticed them.

"Why, yes," the aedile said, his words running over each other. "Why, yes, of course, and—"

He returned his attention to Corylus.

"—I'm very appreciative to you both for your help."

Veturius and Corylus' father had been whispering while the others discussed what would happen in Carce. Now the beast catcher cleared his throat loudly enough to get attention. He said, "Your Lordships? Since the subject's come up, there's some other stuff I might ought to mention. I don't know what it means or if it means anything, but if I have your permission?"

"Certainly, my good man," said Macsturnas. "With my lord Saxa's permission, of course?"

Father mumbled in surprise and some confusion. *So long as they're maundering about due deference and that sort of thing, there's no danger,* Alphena thought with relief.

She was sure that Hedia would have protected Corylus if the aedile had completely lost his head, as might have happened. But Alphena preferred that . . . well, she preferred that Corylus not feel obligated to her mother. Not that it was any of Alphena's business what Hedia did, or what Corylus did!

"I bring my catches down the Nile instead of marching them cross-country to Mios Hormos like most suppliers do," Veturius said. "It's a harder trip than sailing up the Red Sea and then the canal and down to Alexandria, but I get different animals my way."

He nodded toward the caged lizardmen. "Not usually this different, but different. And I don't have competition, because nobody else in the business can put together teams like I do to get past the tribes on the Upper Nile, you see?"

Veturius and Cispius smiled at each other. Corylus was smiling also. Alphena turned her head quickly so that she wasn't watching the men exclude her from the experience they had shared and she never would.

A pair of leopards stared fixedly between the bars of their divided cage. *At me!* she thought. But the cats were looking past her, toward the lizardmen.

Alphena had never been in an animal compound before, but for years she had visited the gladiatorial schools on the Bay when the family came to Puteoli for the summer. She had fancied fighting in the arena herself.

She'd have assumed a name like Victrix or Nike or Atropos, something romantic like that, but it would have been scandalous even so. She'd been sure that she could cow her father into pretending he didn't know what his daughter was doing, however. Saxa liked a quiet life, and Alphena had found that she could get her way in the end if she screamed and carried on loudly enough.

Then her father remarried, and Alphena didn't rule the household anymore. Hedia didn't care about scenes. She was rumored to have been involved in scores of scandals. As Alphena got to know her step-mother better, she learned that this time the rumors were less than the truth.

The result was oddly comforting. Not being able to shock Hedia meant that Alphena didn't have to try. She could do things because they pleased her, not because they would displease those around her. And when Alphena accepted that she couldn't ever compete as a gladiator, she found that she actually didn't want to.

"The lizards weren't a problem while we were in camp," Veturius said. "The Nubians who brought them in said they'd never seen monkeys like them before. They'd caught 'em in a box trap they'd set for a leopard, which seemed funny—getting all four in the same set, I mean—and they'd been feeding them meat like they would leopards. They've got sharp teeth, so I did the same. And like I say, no trouble."

The creature who had been watching Alphena ran its forked black tongue around its lipless mouth, then yawned. The teeth in front were pointed, though those farther back in the jaws had shearing edges. The leopards caged behind the visitors both shrieked in response to the lizard's display.

The cats' cries made Macsturnas squeeze his arms close to his chest as though he were hugging himself; his eyes darted from Veturius to the leopards and back. Saxa simply looked interested as he turned toward the sound. Alphena was ready to stop him if he tried to get close to the cats, but Hedia had already put a restraining hand on her husband's shoulder.

When the aedile twitched, Alphena got a good view of Paris, who was examining the lizardmen in apparent satisfaction. The old man had ignored the leopards, but when he noticed Alphena's attention he glared at her with hatred.

Alphena stared back, mimicking Hedia's look of scornful contempt. Paris grimaced and turned. *I'll never be as good as she is, but I'm learning.*

"The locals aren't the only problems in the south," Veturius said. He'd waited for the cats to fall silent, but the screams hadn't otherwise affected him. "There's fevers and skin rot and Mithras knows what all else. Though—"

He grinned at Cispius.

"—I never lost a man to frostbite, I'll say that for the posting. Anyways, I got a fever and couldn't do aught but sweat and moan the next three days. Now, the barges were ready and we pretty well had a load, so my number two, that's Tetrinus, he decides it's time to head back."

Veturius knuckled his nose again. "You remember Tetrinus, don't you, Top?" he said. "Brave as you could ask, but maybe not the best on details."

"Especially if he was drinking," Cispius agreed grimly. "Which I'd guess he was if you were flat on your back."

"Yeah, that's so," Veturius admitted. "Not so much he wasn't in charge and no mistake about *that*, but Pampreion, the attendant who was supposed to be feeding the lizards, it turns out he wasn't when I wasn't around to watch. He really hated them. He was an Egyptian and I think there was some sort of religious thing going."

Alphena eyed the creatures again. Their hides were dusky with dark green hints, but one was noticeably paler along the spine and seemed older than his fellows. All four wore collars of coppery hoops and spikes, but the old one also had around his waist a loop of chain made from the same dark metal.

She was losing interest in the creatures. In truth, she had never been very interested in animals. These could be dangerous, no doubt; but so were leopards, and the cats were much more attractive to look at.

And even leopards weren't dangerous at a staged beast hunt in the arena like what Macsturnas was planning to stage. The "hunters" would be archers and javelin throwers standing behind a metal fence. They could shoot through it, but the animals couldn't get to them.

If elephants were to be killed, the hunters stood on stone stages higher than the great beasts could reach. Sometimes a hundred arrows would feather an elephant before it died.

If cats were to be the victims, netting would extend for ten or twelve feet above the fence. These lizardmen could probably climb, so they would be shot from behind nets also.

There was no skill to killing animals in the arena and therefore nothing of interest to Alphena. A well-matched pair of gladiators, on the other hand, was like a dance with an added thrill of danger.

"Three nights downriver the whole flotilla was anchored in the current, as usual," Veturius said. "It's safer than tying up to the shore that far south. There was the god-awfulest scream I ever heard, and I've heard a few, let me tell you."

A thought made his face scrunch and look momentarily uglier than usual. "You know, I hadn't thought about that," he said. Though everyone could hear him clearly, he was speaking to Cispius rather than addressing the whole group. "That brought me out of the fever. The boys, they'd pretty much given up on me, you know."

"If a scream in the night doesn't wake you," Cispius said with a grin of sorts, "then you're likely to be the one screaming yourself in the time it takes the next German to get to you."

"Aye," Veturius agreed. "Well, I got up anyhow. The cage with the lizards was on the same barge as me but none of the other animals. When we got torches lighted, there was Pampreion inside the cage and the lizards were eating him."

He grinned at the memory. "Starting with the liver and lights," he said. "Just like a leopard."

"The lights?" said Hedia coolly. "Do you mean the eyes?"

"Huh?" said Veturius. He thumped his chest. "Oh, no, ma'am, the lungs."

Veturius took a deep breath as he collected his thoughts. "His head wasn't touched," he said. "Just spattered a little from when they opened up the ribs. And the old lizard, he looked at me like what was I going to do about it? And I figured, well, there wasn't any helping Pampreion now and the lizards were worth something, so, Hercules . . . Not like the first time I lost a man, you know?"

Alphena looked at her stepmother and wondered about tomorrow night. Hedia had told her that they would be going to a dinner party—a real dinner at the house of one of Hedia's fashionable friends. Alphena knew that it wouldn't be the sort of wild party she heard whispered about on the rare occasions that she socialized with girls of her own age; but still.

A few months ago she would have been horrified and disgusted if someone had insisted that she attend such a gathering. Now she was willing to admit that she was a little apprehensive . . . but a little excited also.

She had come to understand that Hedia wasn't interested in making her submissive but rather in teaching her to know how to behave decorously according to the rules of whatever society she found herself in. Behaving like a lady did not, in Hedia's judgment, always mean behaving like a Vestal Virgin.

"How had Pampreion gotten into the cage?" Corylus asked. His father looked at him in approval.

"Well," said Veturius, "what I told the crew must've happened was that he swam over to my barge during the night and was going to tease the lizards. He was a nasty piece of work, Pampreion, though he was smart enough to be useful if you kept an eye on him. Anyway, one grabbed him and dragged him through the bars. Only . . . well, Pampreion couldn't swim that any of us had ever heard. And there was his head, like I told you."

Veturius shrugged. "I wouldn't have said there was room enough between the bars for his head to fit through," he said. "But there it was, ears and all, and the only other way it could've got there was if somebody picked the padlock, brought Pampreion in to eat, and locked the door behind him."

"Master Veturius and I thought that was an interesting story, Lord Macsturnas, that you might want to know," said Cispius. "To add to the interest of the gift you're preparing for the Republic."

"Veturius?" said Hedia as though she were addressing a servitor at dinner. "What did you do about the creatures after that experience?"

"Do, ma'am . . . ," Veturius said, his face twisting again. "Well, I'll tell you the truth. I made sure the lizards always had food and water. I handled it myself because the rest of the crew didn't fancy being around them much. And we never had another lick of trouble from them, not a lick."

Silence followed as those present digested the story they had just heard. Then Varus straightened and opened his mouth to speak.

"GREETINGS, LORD VARUS," the Sibyl said.

She glanced around to acknowledge his approach, then returned her attention to the scene below. Varus stepped to her side and looked down from the cliff. Increasing mist shrouded the rock, but the scene on the valley floor was as sharp as the lines of his own palm.

"Greetings, Sibyl," Varus said. "Why have you called me here?"

The Sibyl of his visions never changed. She was an old—unthinkably old—woman wearing a white linen tunic and a cape the color of a summer sky. A fold covered her head in Greek fashion. She always seemed pleased and somewhat amused at his presence.

She laughed, a sound more like the chirping of insects than anything from a human throat. She said, "I cannot summon you, Lord

Magician! Who else has powers like yours? Certainly not me, a wraith who exists only in your own mind."

Varus grimaced. *If you're a part of me, then how do you know things that I do not? You know the past and the future, and things completely beyond time.*

But experience had taught him that asking such questions aloud would bring him no answers of any use. He focused on the scene at the bottom of the valley.

Often when Varus looked from the Sibyl's vantage point, he saw himself and his companions below, as though his soul were using the eyes of a raven perched on a high crag. This time, though, he watched scaly swordsmen battling with seven-foot-tall giants with mottled hides and heads like horses. They fought on a neglected field, trampling goldenrod and blooming thistles in their struggles.

"I recognize the lizardmen," Varus said. In this vision the creatures wore bronze armor, but there was no doubt that they were the same race as the ones in the cage in Puteoli. "But who are the giants they're fighting? Are they from Africa too?"

"They are the Ethiopes," the Sibyl said. "A very long time ago the Ethiopes came to Africa from India. In Africa they fought the Singiri, whom you call lizardmen. As you see."

Below, the lizardmen had been retreating to keep from being surrounded, but they now stood back to back in a circle. There were only a dozen of them standing, though six or eight more armored bodies lay as lumps on the flattened meadow.

At least a hundred Ethiopes had fallen, dead or too injured to advance farther, but hundreds more pressed the surviving lizardmen. The weapons of the horse-headed giants were crude, heavy-shafted spears with flint points, but they thrust with enormous power.

Repeatedly Varus saw a lizardman flung backward by a blow that his shield had stopped. Sometimes the stone point shattered; the metal looked like bronze, but it blocked spears that would have penetrated an infantry shield's two-inch thickness of laminated birch.

Even so, the lizardmen tangled with one another, then fell and were battered to death. Corylus—or Alphena—would understand better what was happening, but even Varus could see that the fight would be over shortly.

"You say this was long ago," Varus said. "The Singiri . . . that is, *do* the Singiri still live in Africa?"

He had started to say that the lizardmen still lived in Africa, but that was an assumption that the fact that Veturius had found four of the creatures in Africa did not prove. Veturius himself had been in Africa too, and he certainly didn't live there.

"The Singiri could not stand against the Ethiopes," said the Sibyl. She spoke dispassionately, as Pandareus had done two days ago in explaining why the unvoiced letter *h* remains in the written form of the noun "honor." "But their princess was a magician and created a haven for her race within the Earth."

Two armored lizardmen fell simultaneously, opening a gap in the defensive circle. Then they were all down, dead or dying as the Ethiopes pounded them like grain in a mortar.

The Sibyl moved her left hand as though wiping the surface of the air. The battle blurred away. In its place was the image of a distant hillside on which thousands of Singiri stood. In front were armored warriors while behind them sheltered slender females and offspring as supple as trout.

Ethiopes in tens of thousands and hundreds of thousands poised below the Singiri. There were males and females alike, both genders armed, both savage. The horse-headed giants swept forward with a great cry, a pitiless tide.

The hill behind the lizardmen gouted rock like a cold volcano. The spray rose and continued rising. The Singiri warriors continued to face their opponents, but the Ethiopes paused to view the wonder.

The column of rock slackened, then stopped. An Ethiope stepped forward and shouted back to her fellows; the onslaught resumed. The ranked Singiri faded and vanished like wraiths of gossamer on the wind. The Ethiopes continued to advance because only those in the front of the mass could see what had happened.

Varus looked at his companion. "Why have the Singiri returned, Sibyl?" he asked.

There was movement in the corner of his eye. He turned quickly. The rock that had blown skyward now cascaded out of the sky. It buried the hillside and the valley below in a churning, thunderous torrent.

Clouds swirled even after the dust ceased to fall. It formed images and dissolved and re-formed again and again. As it settled, a mountain slowly emerged where the valley had been. There was no sign of the Ethiopes.

"The Singiri have lived for a thousand ages in their place, complete in themselves because of the magic of their princess," the Sibyl said. "But they are safe only so long as the Earth is safe. And driven by a great magician, the Earth—"

She gestured again with her open palm.

"—has turned against all life."

In front of Varus was the image of a ball on which movement glittered. *Caterpillars on a globe of fruit*, Varus thought. *Crystal caterpillars on a plum or a—*

"You see the Earth," the Sibyl said. "And you see the Worms of the Earth, her children. They will scour the planet bare to its molten core, Lord Varus."

Varus suddenly appreciated the scale of what he was seeing: two serpents of crystal each a thousand miles long writhed over the world, devouring rock and sea alike. As the Worms ate, they grew from the substance of the world that shrank beneath them.

"Sibyl, how can I stop them?" Varus said.

"When the Worms have hatched, no man can stop them," the old woman said. She turned and met his eyes. "Not even you, Lord Magician. And the Worms have hatched!"

Varus felt himself falling back into the Waking World, his soul rejoining his body and his friends in Puteoli. The Sibyl's mouth opened, but he knew it was his own voice shouting, "'A *terrible snake breathing war against all life will kill every human and destroy the world!'*"

CHAPTER II

Alphena started protectively toward her brother, because he was always disorganized after one of these spells. Embarrassment aside, Varus could be badly hurt if he stumbled the wrong way among these cages.

"A snake!" said Macsturnas, rising on tiptoes and trying to look in all directions at once. "Where's the snake? *Where is it?*"

"There's no snake, Lord Macsturnas," said Alphena, turning to face the aedile. Corylus was already holding his friend's arm, and Pulto had come from somewhere to stand on Varus' other side. "That was just a line of poetry. My brother is a poet, and he's always working on new verses."

She smiled, and she had managed to keep her voice soothing. *Hedia will be pleased.* "And even without snakes, your gift to the people of Carce will be marvelous, unique. I've been entranced by even this short glimpse of your animals."

If Macsturnas had been Alphena's servant, she would have slapped him instead of burbling flattery. That would probably be the best way to settle even a senator who was sniveling with fear, but it wouldn't be decorous. Her first concern had to be her brother.

Paris, the old man who had come with Macsturnas, started past his patron to get closer to Varus. Alphena looked at him sharply. Either that or the way Pulto hunched caused Paris to change his mind and slip back behind the aedile.

"A poem?" said Macsturnas. He relaxed visibly, though he still kept his arms closer to his sides than he had done before the fright. "Oh, I see. I wasn't expecting . . . that is, I didn't realize that Lord Varus was quoting poetry."

Alphena wasn't sure, either, though it seemed likely enough. It was a good excuse to offer a stranger like Macsturnas, so she had offered it.

Varus was standing straight again. Corylus had loosened his grip, though he still kept his hand on his friend's shoulder.

Saxa looked almost as disturbed as the aedile had, though his concern was for Varus. He hesitated, unable to choose between going to his son's side and leaving him to Corylus and his servant.

Varus was probably better in their experienced hands. From the way Hedia shifted her body, she would have stopped Saxa if he had tried to join Varus.

"Brother?" Alphena said, speaking clearly and louder than would have been necessary for Varus alone to hear her. "I was just telling Lord Macsturnas that you often call out lines when you're composing poetry. The way you did just now."

Varus grinned at her. He moved his shoulder gently out from under Corylus' touch.

"Why, yes," Varus said. He dipped his head toward the aedile. "I apologize if I startled you, Your Lordship. A muse like mine is a hard taskmistress, you will appreciate."

If Alphena hadn't known that her brother had given up writing poetry after the humiliating failure of his first public performance, she would have taken his statement as his real feelings—just as Macsturnas did. The aedile now saw Varus as a ninny with illusions of talent, a self-important fool, and, above all, harmless.

Hedia had been whispering into Saxa's ear. Her smile hadn't slipped, but Alphena was close enough to hear her mother's urgent tone though not the words themselves.

Saxa nodded three times as though settling a jumble of ideas into order in his head. He turned to the aedile and said, "Quite an interesting collection, Macsturnas. You've done well, very well for a young man. I shouldn't wonder if your gift isn't the standard against which all beast hunts in the future will be measured."

Since her parents had the aedile's attention, Alphena moved without haste to join her brother and Corylus. Varus was fully himself again, adjusting the folds of his toga.

It was a single piece of cloth. Despite its quality—the son of Alphenus Saxa wore the best Spanish wool woven so fine that it was relatively comfortable even on a day as hot as this—the toga had begun to loosen while Varus sleepwalked through the compound. Tradition forbade a gentleman of Carce from pinning the ancient garment in place.

"I just asked your brother . . . ," Corylus said. He spoke in a calm voice that wasn't a whisper but couldn't be heard beyond the three of them. "Whether he was quoting the *Sibylline Books* again."

"And I was about to reply," said Varus, "that I can't very well say because I've never even seen the books. But judging from what Commissioner Priscus said when I had one of these spells before, I suppose I was."

He made a moue of embarrassment and added, "At any rate, I was dreaming of the Sibyl again. Having a vision, at least."

Pulto had joined Cispius and Veturius. They stood shoulder to shoulder, far enough from the cage behind them that the six wolves within couldn't scrabble far enough through the bars to reach the veterans' legs.

The three veterans were stiffly alert, scanning the entire scene but staying safely clear of whatever was going on. It was an affair of their betters. Until one of the nobles directed an order toward them, they weren't going to get involved.

Cispius glanced toward his son more often than his companions did, but his face was expressionless. Alphena wondered what he was thinking.

She grinned. Varus and Corylus both noticed the expression, but neither responded with anything more than a frown.

"I'm not sure what *I* think just happened," she said, answering her own unspoken question. A combination of humor and hysteria almost tipped her into wild laughter. "So I shouldn't be worrying about other people, should I?"

"The Sibyl showed me lizardmen like these," Varus said, nodding. "They may be called the Singiri."

"Are they a danger?" Corylus said. "Is there an army of them marching out of Africa?"

"I don't think so," Varus said, dipping his chin in denial. "No, I'm sure that's not it—not what the Sibyl was warning me about. But there are Worms coming out of the Earth and devouring it as though it were an apple. Great, glittering Worms, devouring the whole surface and all life with it."

"I wish Pandareus were here," Corylus said quietly. "We should have brought him with us from Carce, Gaius. He would have come if we'd asked him—and the rest of his students wouldn't have cared; they'd have been pleased at a day or two more holiday. You *know* they would."

Alphena looked from one youth to the other, waiting for either of them to come to the obvious conclusion. When neither spoke, she said, "Well, we'll bring him here now and he can look at the lizardmen himself. I'll send a messenger to Carce and have one of the stewards at the town house engage a mail coach for him. He can be here by tomorrow night."

Her brother and Corylus were babbling agreement to her back as Alphena strode toward the servants waiting outside the compound.

HEDIA MADE A POINT OF WALKING on her husband's right with her fingers on his elbow. In the tight alleys of the compound that meant that Macsturnas occasionally had to wait for them to go on ahead.

"Why are the horns of that deer so twisted, Master Veturius?" she called to the owner just ahead, as he and Corylus' father led the procession out.

Cispius muttered something to his friend. Veturius showed surprise, then looked over his shoulder and said, "Your Ladyship, I mean—"

He hadn't actually called her "mistress" before his friend warned him, but the word had obviously been on the tip of his tongue.

"—that's a desert antelope, an oryx. And I don't know why the horns are that way, but the reason he's here and not in the pasture is that this particular one's a bloody son of a bitch. Those horns aren't just for show: he spiked a zebra through the lungs on the crossing from Alexandria. That's fine in the arena, but I don't get paid for animals I don't deliver there."

"Thank you, Veturius," Hedia said. Under other circumstances, she would have dropped back and let the senators walk together. She hadn't done so this afternoon because, despite her smile and the cheerful tone with which she discussed the animals as they passed, she was angry and perhaps a little frightened.

Certainly a little frightened.

Hedia wasn't afraid of the priest whom Macsturnas had brought with him, Paris, but neither did she want the old man directly behind her. He was an unpleasant sort who clearly disliked her and Saxa. Paris might not be the reason Varus had had his spell, but there was probably a connection with the fact that the priest had appeared just before it happened.

"Ah, there's Alphena," Saxa said when he saw their daughter waiting for them at the compound's gateway. "I saw her go off, but I didn't want to say anything while—"

He leaned his head close to finish in a whisper, "—I was talking to Quintus Macsturnas."

"Yes," Hedia said. "She had some direction to give one of her servants, I suppose."

Hedia didn't have the faintest notion of why Alphena had rushed out of the compound. Her relief at seeing the girl standing decorously at the gate was greater than her husband's, though no one watching her would have guessed she had been concerned.

"I say, Lord Saxa?" Macsturnas said as he came abreast of Hedia and her husband again. "I'm giving a small dinner tonight. I would be honored if you and your son could join me."

Hedia glanced back to see if Varus and Corylus were with them now. They had been talking with Alphena, but they hadn't joined the girl when she strode off.

Perhaps they were still viewing the lizardmen. At any rate, they weren't visible for as far as Hedia could look back along the road into the compound. Four burly men were moving a cage of baboons down a cross aisle. The laborers looked as savage as the beasts, and the ridged scars of old whippings covered the back of one of the nearer men.

"My premier cook remains in Carce," the aedile was saying, "but my man here at my house on the Bay is quite good, especially for seafood. His Lucrine oysters in a sauce of cheese and giant fennel are wonderful, wonderful. And the oysters won't be more than an hour out of the water, of course!"

"Well, I don't know about Varus . . . ," Saxa said doubtfully. He looked around anxiously: he didn't seem to have noticed that Varus was staying behind.

"Our son is continuing to examine the creatures, Lord Husband," said Hedia over her shoulder as she walked to Alphena's side. "And I believe Master Corylus is with him."

"We thought Pandareus should be told about the lizardmen," Alphena said quietly when Hedia joined her and they turned to go out into the street. "And about my brother's vision, since he already knows that Varus has them. He said he saw the Sibyl again and there were Worms."

"Master Pandareus is a very sensible man as well as a learned one," Hedia said calmly. "I shall be pleased to hear his advice in this instance, as before."

She spoke in a normal voice, but no one outside the household would be able to overhear the conversation. The attendants had kept a considerable space clear for the return of the senators and their closest associates, but of course the attendants themselves were a crowd.

"Our lord is discussing dinner with Lord Macsturnas tonight," Hedia said. Her index finger made so slight a gesture toward the senators that only someone who knew her well would notice.

She smiled with an almost professional brightness and continued, "Are you looking forward to our own dinner tomorrow with my friend Bersinus? It may not be as learned as a senator's table, but I have reason to hope it will be more interesting."

"I'm going," Alphena mumbled toward her hands. She raised her eyes to meet Hedia's with conscious effort—and blushed. "That is, I'm a little nervous, but I realize I must learn about . . . about this sort of thing."

Syra and Florina, Hedia's chief maid and her daughter's, stood at arm's length from their mistresses, as silent as the rolled awning of the jeweler's stall behind them. Florina was the first permanent servant Alphena had had since she outgrew her nurse.

Until recently, the duty of serving Saxa's willful, contrary daughter had been assigned as a punishment rotated among the members of the household who were out of favor with the majordomo. Alphena had resented more or less everything, so far as Hedia could tell. Saxa could avoid her tantrums, but the servants could not.

Hedia could have kept away from Alphena—and Varus—also, but she took her duties as their mother by law seriously, as she took seriously everything to do with family. She smiled; a stranger might have said that the expression would cut glass. Alphena had been making a real effort to behave like a lady since she had learned—been forced to learn—that though this was a man's world, a proper lady was by no means powerless in it.

"You have a charming face," Hedia said, "and you move as gracefully as any woman of your age. It's time that polite society learns to appreciate your beauty."

"If I'm really graceful . . . ," Alphena said. She was trying to sound cynical, but Hedia heard an underlayer of pride. "Then it's because of the swordsmanship training I get from Master Lenatus. You should thank him."

"I *have* thanked Lenatus for his many services to the family," Hedia said, though the words weren't precisely agreement. The trainer, an old soldier and a friend of Corylus' servant Pulto, had been very circumspect in giving the lessons Alphena had demanded and her father was unwilling to forbid. "And you certainly are graceful, though I think the more usual sort of deportment teachers would have been able to bring out your natural gifts as well."

Lenatus was a freeborn citizen of Carce, but the gap between an ex-soldier and a senator's daughter was as great as the distance between the soldier and a slave. A weaker man might well have allowed Alphena more leeway—sparring with her or even arranging secret bouts and praying that they wouldn't come to the attention of his employer.

As they would certainly have done. Even Saxa would have had all those involved in the business executed; and if Hedia was on the scene, they would have been tortured to death. It would have brought disgrace to the family.

Still, wearing armor as she danced about the post she was hacking at with a heavy wooden sword probably had made Alphena more graceful. Clumsiness spilled her in the sawdust of the exercise yard, after all.

Recent events had taught Hedia to respect her daughter's merits as well as teaching Alphena to respect her mother. Swordsmanship wasn't a common accomplishment for a polite lady, but Alphena's skill had saved her life; and it had saved her mother's life as well.

Alphena shifted into a marginally stiffer posture. Her lips pursed as she formed the words she intended to say next. Hedia noticed the hesitation, but her pleasant smile didn't slip.

"I think I'll go shopping by myself this afternoon, Mother," Alphena said. "Rather than going straight back to the house."

The girl was trying to keep her statement from being a challenge, but she obviously felt that any attempt to assert her own will was going to be examined by her mother before it would be allowed to take place. Alphena was correct in her understanding, of course.

"I'm sure you'll be quite safe with your own escort, dear," Hedia said. "Though if you'd like to borrow some of my servants, I can easily spare them as I'll be with Lord Saxa."

Hedia offered the additional attendants to show gentle interest instead of brusquely sending Alphena on her way. They would be quite unnecessary unless the Germans raced over the Alps and began pillaging Puteoli.

A few weeks earlier, when the Alphenus household had been in an uproar because of the way Hedia had vanished, Alphena had kept her head and managed to right the situation. Ten of the male servants had coalesced around her, because she was fearless and her crisp orders convinced others that she was in charge of whatever was happening.

Those servants had since become Alphena's escort. They had come from various divisions of the staff: footmen, kitchen staff, groundskeepers, and even one of the hairdressers. They weren't in their original positions, but Saxa's house in Carce had a staff of over two hundred, so there was no reason they couldn't assign themselves to escorting the daughter of the house.

They weren't the biggest servants in the household man for man, and they weren't even the ugliest and most threatening, which was the usual way to select personnel for public escort. The fact that they had volunteered themselves into what looked at the time like a dangerous job outweighed—in the opinion of Lenatus as well as in Hedia's own—any amount of muscle.

"Oh, I'll be all right, I'm sure," Alphena said, looking relieved that Hedia hadn't made a fuss. Alphena took a deep breath and said, "I thought, I'd, ah, look for jewelry. Not for swords or armor or something. Not today, I mean."

"I'm sure that will be very nice, dear," Hedia said, also relieved. "Something to wear to Bersinus' dinner?"

She had forced herself not to ask what kind of shopping her daughter had in mind. Hedia's real concern had been that Alphena planned to buy not a sword but rather a gladiator or two. Hedia would have had to prevent that, which would have undermined her recent months of building trust between her and her daughter.

"Not really," Alphena said, looking unexpectedly concerned. "Well, I mean I suppose if I find something that I think. . . ."

In a burst of candor she met Hedia's eyes and said, "Mother, I've been having dreams and I don't know what they mean and I just felt that I ought to go shopping!"

Hedia lifted her chin in approval. "We could find a dream interpreter here in Puteoli, I'm sure," she said. "And in Carce I know the names of several. Caelia Rufa has a very fine one, she says. He's in her household if you'd prefer to avoid public practitioners."

Hedia didn't ask what Alphena had been dreaming, for fear of frightening the girl into silence. Talking to her about serious matters— about anything, really, because who could guess what the girl would find serious?—reminded Hedia of watching a servant feed barley meal in honey to a baby sparrow. Anything more than a tiny droplet offered gently would throw the bird into a wild panic.

"No, no," Alphena said with a touch of anger, quickly suppressed. "It's nothing scary. I just thought I'd like to look at jewelry."

Which made no sense at all, but perhaps it didn't make sense to Alphena, either. Hedia merely smiled and said, "Of course, dear. Have a good time."

The aedile and his separate entourage were leaving, going to his house on the Bay. Saxa joined Hedia, but his eyes followed their daughter. "Alphena isn't coming back with us, my dear?" he said.

"She's gone shopping on her own," Hedia said. "I think it's good for her to develop her own taste."

She paused, then added, "I believe our daughter is excited to be going out to dinner at the home of Julius Bersinus tomorrow night. She's becoming quite a lady, Lord Husband. Which I'm glad to be able to say."

After a period of doubt on my part, Hedia thought, but she chose not to say that aloud to Alphena's father.

As it was, Saxa frowned uncomfortably and said, "My dear wife, I'm a little concerned about Alphena going into, well, public while she's still unmarried. It seems to me that society here on the Bay has a reputation of being, well, fast?"

He risked glancing toward Hedia's face as he finished by twisting his intended statement into a question. She touched the back of Saxa's hand and said, "Your paternal concern does you honor, Lord Husband, but I believe it's better that our daughter learn to navigate the reefs of polite society while you and I are still present to guide her."

"Well, you to guide her . . . ," Saxa said, making a face. Muttering, he went on, "If you think that this is really something she ought to be doing, my dear."

"I think it is necessary, Lord Husband," Hedia said. Her words were courteous and her tone deferential, but she spoke with the cold certainty of an executioner's axe falling. "I promise you that the party will be decorous. Master Bersinus has assured me of this."

And I promised Bersinus that if it wasn't, I would geld him myself, Hedia thought. Saxa wouldn't be reassured to hear that, however, so she didn't speak the words aloud.

Her husband sighed. "Well, I'll leave it to you, little heart," he said. "I'm sure you know best."

Hedia patted his hand again. "On my honor, Lord Husband," she said. "On my honor."

Movement deeper into the compound drew her attention. "Ah!" she said with deliberate brightness to jolly Saxa out of the brown study into which concern over his virgin daughter had thrown him. "Here comes Varus now! You can ask him about joining you at the aedile's dinner tonight."

Mention of Macsturnas brought the priest Paris to Hedia's mind. *I wonder if he'll be at the dinner too,* she thought. She would prefer that he went back to some distant Etruscan city like Caere or Praeneste.

It would be better yet if Paris drowned in Macsturnas' eel tank and was eaten by the morays.

"I'M ALL RIGHT NOW," Varus said to his friends. At least he thought he was. His visions came on him without warning, but it would be unusual for another episode to follow the previous one so closely. Another fit it must look like to those who weren't standing with the Sibyl on the peak in Varus' mind.

Corylus nodded and lowered his hand. He'd been ready to grab if Varus suddenly toppled over while babbling gibberish. Pulto watched them both from a polite pace away.

Varus shook his head, trying to make sense of the vision he'd just seen. His parents had gone back toward the entrance, vanishing behind the cage of a pair of hyenas that jutted into the street a little way up.

"I suppose," he said, "that the snatches I quote from the *Sibylline Books* aren't precisely gibberish, but neither do they give us a clear prescription of how to deal with the danger. Which are crystal worms, from what the Sibyl showed me."

Am I correct in using the word "quote" when I haven't actually read the Books?

Varus grinned sadly at himself. Because he was frightened and uncertain, his mind was taking him into the familiar territory of grammatical puzzles. That was harmless, but unfortunately it was also useless for preventing the very real danger that threatened the Republic.

"If we know there's a problem," said Corylus with a smile of sorts, "then at least it isn't as likely to slip past the sentries and slit our throats in our sleep."

His smile grew broader as he added, "Though I suppose we could hand the problem to the Commissioners for Sacred Rites, since they have the duty of examining the *Sibylline Books* in event of a crisis. Then we could return to Carce and put the final polish on our rhetoric studies."

Varus considered the proposition. He knew that his friend was joking, but Varus knew also that treating the suggestion as a real question of logic was exactly the right way to bring his mental focus sharply into the here and now.

As Corylus realized. He's a very perceptive friend as well as a good one.

"I somehow doubt that ordering the construction of a temple to, say, Jupiter the Slayer of Giants is going to cure the problem quickly enough," Varus said with a deadpan expression. "Besides which, so far as anyone but me knows, there isn't a crisis on whose basis to assemble the Commissioners."

Corylus snorted. "I accept your report as accurate," he said, using military terminology. In a tone of very careful unconcern, he went on, "I wonder about your mother, Gaius? That is, should we tell her what you've seen? I'm sure Hedia knew you were, well, *weren't* with us from the time we entered the compound."

Varus suddenly realized that he was turned toward the cage of lizard-men. He hadn't been looking at them—but they were looking at him with interest of varied sorts. The old one seemed to be smiling. The same look on the face of a crocodile wouldn't be a friendly greeting, though.

Instead of answering his friend immediately, Varus said, "They call themselves the Singiri. At least the Sibyl called them the Singiri."

If she exists outside my mind.

"They're soldiers," Pulto said unexpectedly. "The old one's the officer, but he was on the line too when he was younger."

Varus turned to the man in amazement but didn't speak. Corylus said, "Why do you say that, Pulto?"

The soldier-turned-servant shrugged uncomfortably. "Why do you say the sun's in the sky, master?" he said. "Look at the lizards, the way they hold themselves and the scars they got. And—"

He gestured with his left hand. Varus noticed that the pattern of scars and puckering on Pulto's arm was not dissimilar to the ridges and discolorations visible on the lizards' pebbled skin, particularly that of the old one.

"—they're keeping quiet now, but they're listening to every bloody word we say. I wish the army got recruits who paid attention so well. And I mean legion recruits, not the auxiliaries where you're lucky if they speak enough Latin to know 'right foot' from 'left foot.'"

The younger Singiri held themselves very still. The old one smiled more broadly.

"Corylus?" Varus said. "Look at their collars."

"Hercules," Corylus murmured. "Those are thumb knives. Well, ring knives. There seems to be one for each finger."

What Varus had first thought were ornate necklaces of dark bronze were, when viewed the correct way, loops from which short, curved knife blades protruded. The points were needle sharp; Varus supposed that the sharpened inner curves were razors, though he couldn't tell for certain without coming a great deal closer to the Singiri than he had any intention of doing.

"How d'ye suppose they get the links apart?" Pulto said, frowning deeply.

He had edged back, as had Varus and Corylus. Varus didn't know what his companions were thinking, but for his own part he remembered what Veturius had described happening to the attendant who shirked his duties on the voyage down the Nile.

"Like a conjuror, splitting and joining rings right in front of you, I suppose," Corylus said. He looked at Varus and went on, "Gaius, this isn't a monkey jabbing a stick into a bee's nest to get out the honey. These are tools. Your Singiri aren't animals."

"No," said Varus, "they're not. Which makes me wonder why they stayed locked up except to solve the problem they had coming down the river. And even then they came back as soon as they'd found their dinner."

The points of the ring knives could turn the wards of the massive padlock fastening the cage. That assumed the person using the points knew what he was doing, of course, but Varus didn't have any doubt that the Singiri—these Singiri, at least—were competent.

"Let's head back to the entrance," Corylus said, nodding up the passageway.

Varus lifted his chin in agreement and stepped off. Corylus matched him stride for stride, and Pulto brought up the rear.

When the hyena cage was between them and the lizardmen, Varus said, "Do you think we should do something? I mean, the Singiri aren't animals. They shouldn't just be shot in the arena."

Corylus chuckled. "I don't imagine they will be," he said. "They've proved they can get out anytime they want to, so unless they *want* to be killed. . . ."

He shrugged.

"I saw Singiri fighting big horse-headed men that the Sibyl called Ethiopes," Varus said. "In my vision."

The images he'd seen were sharper than they could have been if he were watching with his real eyes as far away as the battle had seemed to be. "The Sibyl didn't say that they were a danger to us."

"And they aren't the sort that make me think I'd like to fight them if they aren't enemies already," Corylus said in a reasonable tone. "Besides—"

He looked back over his shoulder to formally include Pulto in the conversation.

"—Veturius isn't stupid, so I don't think we'd be telling him anything he didn't know already. If the lizardmen wanted to come to Italy in a cage, then nobody seems to have lost anything by it. Except that Egyptian attendant, I guess."

The entrance to the compound was in sight. Corylus' father and Veturius were just inside the open gate. They spoke to each other occasionally as they watched what was going on. Cispius saw his son and they exchanged nods. Hedia and Saxa were in the street; Alphena wasn't with them.

Varus took a deep breath. He'd finally answered the question he had been deliberating ever since his friend had asked it.

"If Mother asks me what happened," he said, "I'll tell her. It may be that Alphena has talked to her or will; that's fine. But I'm not going to volunteer what I saw because I don't really *know* anything. And she makes me uncomfortable. I don't know what she's thinking, ever."

"Your mother is very self-contained," Corylus said, looking toward the gate instead of meeting Varus' eyes. "She's as closed as a block of stone."

From the odd undertone to the words, Corylus was thinking something quite different about the lovely Hedia. Every man past puberty except for her stepson probably did at one time or another.

That Varus did not was less a virtue than a flaw. He respected Hedia; he even liked her for her quick intelligence and a sense of duty that would have done credit to Cornelia, the Mother of the Gracchi.

But he didn't think of Hedia as any more human than the splendid statue of Venus in Caesar's temple was. And he wasn't sure that he was really wrong.

"My mother would sacrifice anything to preserve what she considers most important," Varus said, speaking as much to himself as to his friend. "I'm not sure what is most important to her, though. It certainly isn't her own life."

Corylus stopped to talk with his father. Varus walked through the gateway to greet Saxa and Hedia.

The life of her stepson isn't of first importance to her, either, he thought as he nodded to his mother. *But the survival of Carce may be.*

A WEIGHT, THOUGH NOT THE whole weight, had lifted from Corylus' shoulders when he turned toward home with Pulto. Corylus suspected that the servant was even more relieved. The tavern a few doors up from Wharf Street wasn't prepossessing, but it would do.

"Let's get a table," Corylus said, leading Pulto past the counter facing the street where two sailors were drinking wine. The bartender had probably been a sailor also until an accident had crushed his left hand and forearm into a distorted flipper.

All three were small, dark men with short goatees, born on either the African or Spanish shores near the Straits of Hercules. They continued their conversation without taking notice of the newcomers. Corylus didn't recognize their language.

"Whatever you like, master," Pulto said. "I was only planning to have a jar of wine, anyway. Ah—if I *was* hungry, this isn't a place I'd want to trust the sausage."

"None of my relatives have died lately," said Corylus with a grin, "so at worst I'd be spared that sacrilege. But I'm here for a drink too. I just wanted to sit down."

"Shouldn't mind that myself," Pulto said. "My knees being what they are."

"This one," Corylus said as his servant started to slide behind the nearer of the two tables. Neither was occupied, but the farther one had a wooden top while the other—like the counter—was a slab of marble.

Corylus ran his fingers over the tabletop, seeing in the foggy distance an elm sprite, hunched and very old. She looked back at him with sad eyes, but there was nothing he could do for her now.

The wood had been a door panel, cut down to cover the table after the marble original was broken. Before it became a door, however, it had been decking on a ship that sailed out of Massillia to Gades on the Atlantic for fish sauce, to Cyrene in Africa to load giant fennel, and finally to Puteoli with a load of fine pottery.

Some of the cargo had been salvaged when a violent storm drove the vessel ashore. The hull had been broken up for reuse when possible, for firewood when the scraps were good for nothing else. Corylus thought of the sprite and wondered whether it might not have been kinder to shovel these planks too into the ovens of a public bath.

He rubbed the wood gently. Looking across the table at his servant, he said, "Do you ever wonder what you'll be a hundred years from now, Pulto?"

Pulto snorted and said, "That's an officer-type problem, master. No business of mine, thank Mithras."

The bartender left his fellows and walked over to the table without speaking. Corylus looked up and said, "Two mugs of house wine, mixed one to one."

"House wine," the bartender repeated in a brittle accent. "Like we have any other kind here."

Then, hopefully, he added, "You want sausage rolls? I could heat the sausage rolls up again."

"Just the wine," Corylus said, trying to keep his anger at a human-sized problem in check. *If he doesn't shut up and bring the wine, I'll stuff his head into one of those wine jars!*

Though of course Corylus wouldn't. He was worried about the lizardmen—worried because he didn't know what the presence of the lizardmen *meant*—and he was worried because Varus had gone into one of his waking trances again. When that had happened in the past, it meant something very bad was threatening the Republic and the world.

Corylus had chosen not to interfere with the lizardmen until they gave him a reason to, and there wasn't a thing in the world he could do about giant crystal worms if they crawled over the Alban Hills on their way to Carce. The bartender, though, was a problem on a human scale; Corylus could solve it very easily.

But he wouldn't. Growing up in an army camp, Corylus had too often seen a centurion who was having a bad day take out his anger on a trooper whose main sin had been to be seen at the wrong time, and seen a trooper, angry about being put on punishment detail and maybe a little drunk as well, break his girlfriend's face to pass the misery along.

The bartender came back with a generous carafe of wine and two mugs of tarred leather, all in his right hand. He thumped them down on the table and glared at Corylus. "You want water in your wine, you go somewhere else!" he said belligerently.

Pulto shifted slightly, waiting for his cue. The sailors at the counter heard the tone if not the words; their hands dropped below the level of the counter, reaching for the knives in their belts.

Corylus laughed. "We're in a gourmet joint, Pulto," he said. He raised the carafe—it was stoneware and would make a useful weapon if needed—and poured a mouthful of wine into each mug. "Be sure to treat the vintage with the respect it deserves."

Corylus and his servant drank, watching the bartender over the tops of their mugs. Pulto's right hand was hidden at belt level also.

"Not bad," Pulto said, putting his mug down and filling both properly. "Pretty bloody good, in fact."

The wine was local and hadn't been aged for long enough to reach full strength, so mixing it with water would have thinned it more than Corylus had intended. The tang of tar was slight but blended better with the new wine than he would have guessed.

There'd been so much Greek colonization in southern Italy, especially here on the coast, that some called the region Larger Greece. Wine to the colonies was carried in jars waterproofed with tar; many people thought the resin stabilized the wine against the ships' violent shaking as well.

The locals had turned necessity into a style by blending pitch into the local vintages. Corylus drank resined wine generally when he was on the Bay, and he'd come to accept if not precisely to favor it.

The bartender suddenly grinned. "My father, he got a vineyard right up on the mountain," he said, meaning Vesuvius. The volcano wasn't the only hill in the vicinity, but its steam and rumbling made it the only one people on the Bay thought about. "You guys are all right."

He turned and walked back to his friends at the counter. Corylus thought about what had just happened. His left hand was flat on the table; to his surprise, the dimly viewed elm sprite was smiling at him.

"That could've gone another way," Pulto said. "I was about ready to pick this table up and start swatting wogs with it."

"I'm glad it didn't come to that," Corylus said mildly.

An old man came in from the street. Instead of sitting at the empty table, he stepped toward Corylus. He was holding a scrap of parchment.

"Excuse me, master," he said.

"If you're a beggar," Corylus said, "get out of here."

"If he's a beggar, I'm going to help him out!" said Pulto, getting to his feet and reaching for the old man's neck.

"No!" said Corylus, jumping up also. The stranger looked like a bundle of sticks, scarcely a threat. Further, he was well-groomed and wore a clean tunic of good quality.

"I am not a beggar," the old man said. He had flinched when Pulto reached for him, but by effort of will he had managed not to turn in terror toward the threat. "My name is Lucinus and I own a farm on the Nola Road four miles out of Puteoli. I just want you to read this."

I wonder how old he is? Corylus thought. *His face has wrinkles on wrinkles.*

Lucinus set the scrap of paper on the table and stepped back slightly. He added, "It's a line of verse which my uncle wrote some five or six years before he died."

Corylus picked up the document and tilted it to catch the light through the front of the shop. It was a palimpsest: a used sheet from which earlier writing had been rubbed off with a block of pumice, leaving a blotched surface that would do for notes and scribbled drafts.

Aloud to make Pulto part of the discussion, Corylus read, "'Someday, my brethren, even these things will be pleasant to remember.'"

He looked at Lucinus and said, "Your uncle wrote this?"

"That is correct," the old man said.

"Then your uncle was a plagiarist," Corylus said, more sharply than he had intended. He'd detected a hint of smugness in Lucinus' voice, and that offended Corylus as a scholar. "This is by Vergil: from the first book of the *Aeneid,* to be more precise."

"My uncle was not a plagiarist," Lucinus said in the same half-mocking tone. "My uncle was Vergil. You know that he was a poet, but he was also a great deal more of which you may not know."

Corylus picked up the document again, frowning at it. "Vergil died fifty years ago," he said. "Longer than that, even."

"Yes," said Lucinus. A tiny smile cracked his Stoic calm. "And though you haven't asked why I brought the draft to you—"

That would have been my next question.

"—I did so because I could talk to you and you can talk to your friend Gaius Varus. If I were to have attempted to accost him in the street today . . ."

Lucinus turned up one of his hands and gave Corylus a wry smile.

"You'd have been pushed aside by the attendants," Corylus said, completing the thought.

"No," said Pulto. "There's three different squads on duty—Daddy's, Mommy's, and the lad's. Between them all, they'd have beaten the crap out of this fellow"—he nodded—"and tossed what was left into an alley."

"Yes," said Corylus. He tapped the palimpsest on the table as he considered the situation. "I'll show this to Varus, yes. Then what?"

Lucinus shrugged. He said, "Then it's up to Lord Varus, whether he wishes to join me in saving the world from disaster. If he is willing to help, then the sooner he visits me at my farm, the better. Time is very short, even with the help of so great a magician as he is."

Lucinus turned and walked out of the tavern, moving briskly despite his apparent age. The bartender and his friends continued to talk, apparently oblivious of the world around them.

"Do you believe him, master?" Pulto asked, his eyes on the street into which Lucinus had turned.

"I believe this," said Corylus, waggling the scrap of papyrus. He stared at the line of verse again, then said, "Pulto, go back to the house and tell Father that I may be late for dinner tonight. If he asks—"

Cispius wouldn't ask. He might assume that Corylus had met an interesting girl, but he trusted his son's judgment in that sort of thing.

"—tell him I needed to see Varus immediately."

"Right," said Pulto, dropping bronze coins to the price of the wine on the table. He drained the carafe without bothering to pour the remaining contents into his mug.

Corylus clapped his old servant on the shoulder as they parted in the street. He set off northward toward the house of Senator Saxa.

Was Varus so great a magician or a magician at all? Corylus had no way of telling: he wasn't a magician himself.

The fact that Lucinus felt he could judge implied that he was something more than a frail old man himself.

CHAPTER III

Because of her mother's training over the past two months, Alphena was able to recognize that though this arcade was small by the standards of Carce, its shops catered to a very wealthy clientele. The Bay Region contained Italy's main commercial ports, but it was also the summer resort for senatorial families and their hangers-on. There was more real wealth per acre here than in any district of Carce.

A striped linen awning, tan on the natural off-white, threw a golden shadow on the interior of the arcade. "There aren't any hawkers," Alphena said in surprise as her eyes adapted.

The central open space was crowded, but the crush mostly consisted of attendants waiting while their mistresses were being served in the shops. In most arcades there were barrows and small traders dealing in inexpensive goods. Many people came to admire gold and silk but bought the brass and linen that they could afford.

"Much chance any cheapjacks would have getting into *here*," said Florina with a sniff. She had taken to her new role as the maid of a fine lady with much more enthusiasm than Alphena had to becoming a fine lady. "The doormen would sort them out before they had time to take a breath!"

Besides the usual shutters to close and lock up for the night, many shops in this arcade had bronze grills. The attendants standing outside wore expensive tunics, embroidered and fringed with silk or precious metals, but they were all impressively big men. Florina was certainly right that they had the secondary duty of keeping the arcade clear of cheap goods—and very possibly clear of the sort of people who shopped for cheap goods.

"Who does Your Ladyship choose to first honor with your custom,

Your Ladyship?" Florina said. She coughed, realizing as the words came out that they didn't sound as cultured as she had meant them to be.

"I don't know," Alphena said, looking about the arcade. She was standing with her escort just inside the western entrance archway. Because she was short and the plaza was crowded, she couldn't see very much. She started down the long side to her right, walking slowly.

She didn't have any reason for coming to this arcade or for going anywhere at all. She had been dreaming of three plump, dark-skinned women—not the tall purple-black Nubians whom some wealthy people bought as showy attendants, the way they might keep a leopard with a jeweled collar as a pet.

The women she dreamed of were naked except for bits of rainbow-colored glass strung on twine, and in their midst was a foggy egg that rippled with the same colors that their belts did. They turned their heads toward Alphena when they danced close. Though they didn't speak, they left Alphena with an urge to find *something*. She had the same dream every night of the past three, and today the urge was even stronger after she awakened.

Florina slowed and turned her head as they passed a clothier's; she was eyeing the vivid yellow cape being displayed by three boys dressed as cupids complete with gauze wings. The proprietor sat on a low stool, personally offering slices of candied fruit to the severe-looking female customer who reclined beside him. The customer's maid stood behind the couch, intent on her mistress' face rather than on the cape.

"Not there!" Alphena snapped, quickening her pace. The ten men of her escort wore matching blue tunics with a white stripe down either side. The four in the lead jumped to stay ahead of their mistress, while the remainder sprinted a moment later to keep up.

Hedia didn't have this problem. Hedia was always in the place she wanted to be, doing the thing she wanted to do. Or at any rate, that was what it seemed like to watch her.

Hedia's maid Syra would *never* try to guide her mistress while shopping!

A thought struck Alphena and made her half-step, almost falling. Her escort was in a thorough jumble because of her changes of pace. *I don't have experience being a fine lady, so I'm hard for my escort to follow. But Florina doesn't have experience being a fine lady's maid, either.*

Florina had just been purchased when she was assigned to serve Alphena. She had done well in difficult circumstances. Because Alphena was trying to learn to act like something other than a screaming harridan, she had made Florina her chief maid. It might have been better to appoint a girl who'd been serving Hedia for long enough to know the details of deportment, but . . .

On thinking about it, Alphena realized she didn't want a servant who sneered at her mistress's ignorance. That was even more true if the scorn was silent and the servant was a model of decorum in all public fashions. *Florina's the right attendant for me, though I might ask Hedia to lend me a more experienced servant to coach her.*

Alphena said, "Stop now! We're all stopping!" and did so herself.

When they stopped, most of the escort turned their backs to Alphena and watched the crowd. That was their *duty*. They didn't know that their mistress wanted to talk to them, so they continued to look for threats.

"Right," Alphena said, suddenly sure of herself. "I'm going into this jeweler's right here."

She turned. *It's the right place!* Pulto's wife, who was Marsian and a witch, had told Alphena that she was a witch also. Alphena knew that she couldn't control anything consciously . . . but this *was* the right place.

It was one of the fancier shops, even in this arcade. The grill of gilded bronze was closed though not locked. The attendant standing before it wore a red tunic on which Mars and Venus were embroidered with gold thread. They reclined to either side with their feet intertwined in the center.

The attendant didn't move aside as Alphena started toward him.

For a moment, Alphena didn't understand what was—what *wasn't*—happening. Florina strode forward and said in a clear, cutting voice, "Make way for the Lady Alphena, daughter of Gaius Alphenus Saxa, senator and former consul!"

I'm dressed to visit an animal compound, not to shop in a store like this!

In the past Alphena had worn short tunics and heavy boots suitable for fencing exercises. As a senator's daughter she had gotten away with eccentricity; and if her behavior reduced her desirability in the marriage market, so much the better.

Recently she had begun to wear more ladylike garments, at least when she went out in public. That was partly at Hedia's urging—not orders; Alphena knew how stubbornly she would have resisted an order to dress in a different fashion, and Hedia knew also.

But it was also Hedia's example, and Hedia's insistence that Alphena could look pretty if she tried. She didn't really believe she was pretty—certainly not as pretty as Hedia was!—but she had begun to *half*-believe; and anyway, it made Hedia happy to see that her daughter was trying.

Today Alphena wore a plain linen tunic and a short cape of fine Spanish wool that had been bleached white and appliquéd with signs of the zodiac. Though she wasn't wearing army boots, her sandals were thick soled and suitable for walking rather than creations of silk and glove leather that demanded that the wearer be carried in a sedan chair rather than depending on her own legs for any distance over cobblestone streets. She was properly dressed, but she didn't look like a customer for *this* shop.

Florina's shrill direction made the doorman stiffen, hiding his obvious uncertainty. Alphena noticed that the fellow's left forearm had been broken and his face was slightly asymmetrical. She stepped forward and said, "You're the Macerator, aren't you? I saw you box the Seven-Foot Thracian in Carce last year. You were paired directly below our seats in the senatorial loggia."

"I was indeed, Your Ladyship," the boxer said, bowing as he opened the grill behind him. His Latin was as cultured as that of Agrippinus, majordomo of Saxa's town house in Carce. "You honor the premises of Syenius."

Alphena was glowing with pride at having overcome an unexpected obstacle in her own way. *I wonder if Mother would be pleased?* Hedia might feel that if Alphena had been better dressed, there wouldn't have been a problem to begin with. . . .

No, Hedia would be pleased. She made her own rules when she believed she had the power to force them on society. She wouldn't object to Alphena doing the same—so long as she was successful, as she had been this time.

Instead of sweeping straight into the jewelry shop, Alphena paused and said, "I was impressed by that fight, Macerator; the Thracian had the reach on you as well as fifteen pounds, I would have said. But you put him down with the last blow when I thought you were finished."

"Thank you, Your Ladyship," said the boxer. "It was twenty pounds, actually, and that was my last bout. In the third round he broke my arm—"

He held his arms out in front of him, so that kink in the left ulna was obvious.

"—but I had to keep blocking with it. After that, well. . . ."

He shrugged. The Macerator had seemed small to Alphena when she watched him fight the Thracian, but his shoulders were like a bull's.

"I had a bit laid by, you see, betting on myself, and my brother-in-law Syenius had been asking me to come in with him anyway. After the fight it was ten days before I stopped having spells where the pain made me dizzy and I'd see double, so I took him up on it."

The doorman cleared his throat and added, "Your Ladyship? I'm proud you took notice of me like that, but the Macerator's gone this past year. My name is Theodromus now, if you please."

Professional boxers wrapped each hand with a caestus, a bullhide strap with bronze studs on the outside and a bar of lead to grip, weighting the blow. Alphena looked at the doorman and said, "Certainly, Theodromus."

She entered the shop, accepting the bow of the fat Egyptian merchant who had waited for her to conclude her conversation with his doorman. Theodromus had earned the right to be called by any name he pleased.

The merchant bowed and said, "I am Syenius, Lady Alphena. How may I serve Your Ladyship?"

"I'm looking for something," Alphena said. Her mouth had gone dry with embarrassment because she didn't know what to say next. In a burst of inspiration she went on, "Something special, that is, *unique*. I want a gift for my mother, the Lady Hedia."

"Ah, the Lady Hedia," Syenius said in evident satisfaction. "Your mother patronizes Pompilio in Baiae when she's visiting the Bay. Pompilio is all right for ordinary wares, but I feel that you were wise to come to me. If you'll just relax on the couch, I'll see how well I can suit you."

He looked past her with a slight frown and said, "If you'll tell your servants to wait outside, we'll have more room. I assure you, Your Lady-ship, you'll be quite safe without them."

"She'll be bloody safe with us inside too, buddy," rasped Drago, who, with his cousin Rago, led Alphena's escort. They had entered behind Alphena and her maid.

Drago and Rago were Illyrians, probably former pirates. The best that could be said of their Greek was that it was better than their Latin; but they were quick-witted, fearless, and had demonstrated that they were willing to face death on their mistress's behalf.

Alphena considered the situation for a moment. The Illyrians were unnecessary, and their presence would irritate the jeweler. On the other hand, Syenius would serve her to the best of his ability regardless, and she had no reason to care about his opinion. She might need the cousins to face a gang of bandits—or demons.

"They will stay," she said, reclining on the couch covered in pale green silk. "Show me what you have that would be worthy of the Lady Hedia."

Two young men came from the curtained rear of the shop, carrying a small, round table of desert cedar, waxed and polished to a luster that brought out the grain. The servants mixed wine one to three with wa-ter at Alphena's direction. They poured it into a cup with a stag hunt in gold pressed between two layers of clear glass.

Servants brought out wonders on trays or cushions. Alphena exam-ined them, sipping wine and feeling satisfied with herself.

It was meaningful that Theodromus hadn't stopped her Illyrians from entering. Alphena didn't imagine that he was afraid of them or of her whole escort together: they might well kill him, but the man who had battered the Seven-Foot Thracian unconscious wouldn't back down for a pack of scruffs.

By letting Rago and Drago inside, Theodromus had avoided a scene in front of the shop, whether or not his brother-in-law realized it. There was another possibility too, though Alphena might be flattering herself to consider it: the Macerator was no longer fighting, but Theodromus might make allowances for a knowledgeable fan whose escort didn't have all the polish of some noble entourages.

Syenius began with polished jewels—he claimed the seven large emeralds set into a gold breastplate had come from lands beyond the

Indies—but he quickly realized that his customer wasn't particularly interested in them. Close up, Alphena could see that a ruby was far more brilliant than a bit of red glass and that diamonds really did have an internal fire like nothing else. She could see those things—but she didn't care.

Syenius, who was as observant as a good salesman has to be, murmured to an assistant who returned a bracelet of pearls and sapphires on gold to the back room. Another man bustled in with a cushion on which was spread a necklace of seven gold plaques, each embossed with the winged figure of the Mother Goddess flanked by rampant lions.

"This is very old," Syenius murmured. "It came to me from Rhodes, but I cannot say with certainty that it was made there. Is the Lady Hedia perchance a devotee of the Great Mother?"

Alphena examined the necklace carefully. Hedia didn't have any religion that her daughter knew about: she believed in the gods, but she trusted them to keep to their own spheres while human beings—Hedia herself, at any rate—dealt with human affairs.

Alphena didn't want to be insulting about religion, though: Egyptians were notoriously superstitious. The necklace interested her. Either its age or the goddess images whispered to the secret places in Alphena's mind, but this was not the piece that had drawn her to the shop.

Syenius made a hand gesture toward the service area. Alphena leaned back from the necklace, frowning. The attendant carried the cushion away, and another slim youth swept in with a diadem on a tray of mica in a silver frame.

That's it. That's what I've been dreaming of.

"The work is of Tarantine style," Syenius said. "The piece came from Egypt, from a tomb in Egypt, one of the later Ptolemies. Many craftsmen came to Alexandria to suit their taste and that of the Greek mercenaries they hired as well."

Alphena didn't know history, *certainly* not Egyptian history, and didn't care. What she cared about was the stone gripped in the jaws of the two gold lion heads at the front of the diadem. The remainder of the piece was a simple gold band with a clamp at the back for adjustment.

A fragment of Alphena's mind noticed that the gold lions were well crafted, but her consciousness was focused on the jewel the lions were holding. It was a flat—well, slightly convex—plate of pulsing color the size of her thumbnail. The edges were irregular but rimmed with heavy gold foil to which the lion jaws were soldered.

It wasn't a color; it was all colors. When Alphena turned her head, she remembered the stone as blue; but under close scrutiny bands and bubbles of color rippled up from deep inside it.

Alphena blinked and looked at Syenius. *There is no inside. It's as thin as the foil of the setting.*

"What is this jewel?" she snapped. "And where did it come from?"

Her voice sounded angry in her own ears. In truth she was more frightened.

"Your Ladyship," Syenius said, "I know no more than I've told you: the diadem, including the stone, was found in the tomb of a pharaoh who died during the One Hundred and Thirty-second Olympiad. I have never seen or heard of another stone of its type, nor has any other dealer to whom I have shown it."

Alphena *had* seen this sort of stone before. The Nubians who danced in her dreams strung chips like this one on lengths of twine to make their belts.

Syenius had stiffened slightly at the initial edge in Alphena's voice. As she relaxed from her initial surprise, the jeweler did also.

He coughed and said, "You'll notice that the edges are irregular. I wondered at that when I purchased the piece on a buying trip to Alexandria, but I've been unable to cut it myself. One of my most skilled workmen tried the edge under the foil with a diamond drill but was unable to scratch it."

"But . . . ," said Alphena as she considered what she had just been told. "How could naked savages pierce them to string?"

"They could not pierce a stone like this, Your Ladyship," Syenius said, gesturing toward the diadem with his left hand. "No more than they could fly. So far as I know there is nothing harder than a diamond, and a diamond could not mark this."

Syenius wore no jewelry, and hanging from the door to the service room was a peaked "Phrygian" cap, the mark of a freedman. That a man so obviously successful and cultured would openly admit his former slavery made him suddenly more impressive to Alphena.

"I see," she said, but she didn't really see. It had been a dream, but it seemed utterly real in memory. "I. . . ."

Alphena rose from the couch, suiting her action to the sentence she hadn't completed aloud. The shop assistant swung the tray back as though he and the customer were parts of the same mechanical device, one acting on the other like a lever.

I wasn't going to knock it to the floor! Alphena thought, but she controlled the flash of anger before it reached her lips. She was . . . *disturbed* . . . by the situation, and therefore ready to take her mood out on whoever was closest.

Hedia had taught Alphena the value of bridling her temper. If people liked you, they were apt to treat you better. That was as true of the servants who fed and dressed her as it was of her father's senatorial friends.

Alphena didn't think she would ever be as smooth as her mother. She had seen Hedia calmly direct that a maid be sold to a dockside brothel for stealing a lace mantilla; she hadn't raised her voice or shown anything harsher than ironic amusement. But Hedia's daughter was getting better than the frustrated child who screamed more often than she smiled.

"I will take the diadem with me," she said. "Send the bill to Balbinus at my father's house here."

She realized as she spoke that she had given Syenius a license to rob her father. The money didn't matter, not measured against Saxa's wealth, but the thought of being imposed on hardened her expression.

As though he had read her thoughts, Syenius said, "Thank you, Your Ladyship. I think that your steward will consider the cost to be very moderate."

An assistant was wrapping the diadem in red silk brocade. The other assistant held ready a polished wooden box to hold the item. Florina joined the assistants to take the completed parcel.

Syenius smiled faintly. "To be honest, Your Ladyship," he said, "I find the piece disquieting, though I couldn't give a reason for that. I actually considered taking the gem from its setting and disposing of it in the sea."

He shrugged. "It was a unique piece, though," he said. "I wasn't willing to do that for . . . antiquarian reasons, perhaps. It's so much easier to destroy things than to create them, is it not?"

"Yes, I suppose it is," Alphena said. Her throat was dry.

Florina had the package. Alphena turned; Theodromus pulled open the grill and bowed.

"I'm glad it's going to a good home," Syenius said to his customer's back.

I hope you're right about that, Alphena thought. But for now at least she would trust her instinct.

HEDIA KNEW FROM THE BUSTLE among the servants that something was happening. "Something" might not be very interesting to her, of course.

The house here on the Bay had eighty servants. That wasn't exceptional for a senator's household: Saxa had some two hundred in his town house in Carce, and some of his colleagues had larger staffs yet. Nevertheless, most of what any one servant of eighty did during the day was nothing. They were likely to find excitement in matters that made their mistress yawn.

At the archway between the loggia where Hedia sat and the house proper, Syra whispered to an understeward, then returned purposefully to her mistress.

"Speak," Hedia said. There was no point in trying to conceal the news from the six additional servants with her in the loggia.

Two held trays of snacks and drinks; Hedia occasionally sipped diluted wine poured from the carafe that sat in a water-filled basin of earthenware to keep cool, but she always directed Syra to carry out that duty. Two more held ostrich-plume fans; Hedia disliked the fans' repetitive motion at any time, and the sea breeze this afternoon was delightfully sufficient.

The last two carried saffron silk sunshades, which would be useful only if Hedia moved to the corner of the curved bench touched when the sun slipped under the marble roof. There was no chance of her doing so on such a warm day.

Even if Hedia would prefer that a message be kept secret, it would have been impossible. The understeward would babble to somebody. Balbinus, who had sent the understeward, would babble to somebody. And in the order of a dozen other babbling servants had been present when the message was delivered to Balbinus.

Also, the message was probably completely unimportant.

"The Lady Alphena has returned from shopping," Syra whispered. "She will shortly come to see you with the piece of jewelry which she purchased this afternoon."

Hedia lifted her chin slightly in acknowledgment. She had received messages even more inconsequential—but not many. Regardless, it would be interesting to see what Alphena's taste in jewelry was when she was on her own.

Almost with the words, Alphena appeared in the archway. She was followed by her new maid—who seemed to be working out, Hedia was glad to see. She would not have interfered with her daughter's choice of a chief maid, but Hedia might have interfered—discreetly—with the maid herself if she had turned out to be unsuitable.

Hedia rose, smiling with cool pleasure. "Greetings, Daughter," she said. "I hope you had a successful outing? Here—"

She patted the cushion on which she had been sitting. A second cushion appeared beside it, winged by the hands of a servant who disappeared as swiftly as he had arrived.

"—won't you sit with me and tell me all about it."

Hedia really was glad to see Alphena. The girl was Saxa's offspring by blood, but she was quickly becoming Hedia's daughter in spirit if not tastes.

Alphena turned and took the flat wooden box her maid was carrying. Hedia noted the dovetail joints at the corners and the swirling grain of the lid. *Very upscale,* she thought.

Hedia had a great deal of experience judging the quality of a gift without seeming to more than glance at it. While she didn't do anything simply for the money, the amount of money an admirer spent on her was certainly a factor in judging the man himself. You could never know too much about people with whom you might shortly find yourself in intimate contact.

She saw Alphena's eyes drift out to sea past the pink-flowering branch growing over the loggia's railing from the almond tree planted below. The air was hazy this afternoon, muting the blue water and softening the lines of the ships on the water. Many were pleasure craft, but there were working vessels too: motionless fisherman, and freighters tacking on a breeze that was strong enough to spare their crews the backbreaking work of the sweeps.

Hedia found the sea restful to watch, though she didn't care to get it on her body. Seawater made her feel sticky when it dried, and sand had a way of getting into delicate places that salt made even more uncomfortable.

Smiling, she said to Alphena, "It's even prettier at night, when the fishermen's lamps reflect on the water."

Alphena swallowed and sat down beside her. "I was thinking of someone else, I suppose. Sorry."

Hedia lifted her chin, barely enough to be called a motion. There had been a man in Alphena's life, not so very long ago. Well, Hedia knew that feeling also.

When Alphena didn't immediately bring up the subject that had brought her out to the loggia, Hedia said, "Our lord Saxa and your brother are dining tonight with Senator Macsturnas. Would you care to join me, or would you prefer to be on your own for dinner?"

The words jolted Alphena out of her thoughts. She looked startled, then forced a smile and said, "I haven't been thinking. . . ." Then, "I'd like to eat with you, Mother. I'm sorry that I was—"

She fluttered her free hand with a grimace.

"—missing, there."

"Not at all," Hedia said. On instinct, she touched the back of the girl's wrist. "Now, what is it that you've purchased? Something to wear tomorrow night to dinner with Bersinus?"

"Well, I . . . ," Alphena said. *She seems embarrassed. Surely it's not a dil—*

"Here!" the girl said abruptly, thrusting the box toward Hedia. "Mother, I got it for you. I just . . . well, I just did."

Hedia was embarrassed in turn for the direction her thoughts had taken. She did not, she was sure, show any sign of that as she took the box.

Pausing, she let the kneeling Florina hold the bottom with one hand and remove the lid with the other. Hedia unfolded the silk wrapper inside. She kept her eyes on the gift rather than the giver, because staring would embarrass Alphena even more.

Hedia hadn't known what to expect. The diadem was beyond anything she could have imagined.

"This is beautiful," Hedia said. "And—"

She met Alphena's eyes.

"—it's a terrible thing as well, as beautiful and terrible as standing in the middle of a lightning storm. How did you find it?"

"I went into a jeweler's shop and asked for something unusual for my mother," Alphena said, her voice carefully controlled. "The jeweler said it was Tarantine work, but it came from Egypt."

She held Hedia's eyes, but that was obviously a trick to make it appear she was being more candid than she really was. *Don't think you can lie to me, missie!* Hedia thought, but that was unworthy. The girl was learning how to handle difficult discussions, a skill that every woman needed to perfect.

"Gold is gold," Hedia said, her voice chilled to the edge of harshness. "What is the stone and where did it come from?"

"He didn't know," Alphena said. Her hands were clenched tightly together. "Syenius didn't know. He said he'd never seen anything like it. And I think it frightened him. He wasn't a man easy to frighten, I think."

She reached for the box again, saying, "I'm sorry; I'll—"

"You will *not*," said Hedia, lifting the diadem. "I don't so easily give up things that so impress me, my dear. Although—"

Her smile was suddenly mischievous.

"—I'm generally willing to share them. But that in good time."

She fitted the gold band onto her head. The bedchamber servants had appeared in response to quickly relayed hand signals from Syra, but Hedia chose not to let them place the diadem for her.

When Hedia tipped an index finger toward her, a maid—a specialist—held the mirror in place. It was a circle of bronze, polished as smooth as sunlight and then silvered. The face blazed momentarily with the presence—it was more than light—of the jewel; then the image settled back and Hedia viewed herself wearing the diadem.

"Your jeweler was right to be frightened," she said, smiling again. It was the sort of smile she might wear while watching an execution.

I look like the Queen of Heaven. Or perhaps of the Underworld, a queen worthy of Hades . . . as the mewling Proserpina of myth is not.

"I like it very much," she went on, removing the diadem and placing it back on the silk wrapping. "I will wear it tomorrow. Syra, remind me to choose a dinner gown that goes with it. Gray, I think, but I'll want to try it against pure white before I decide."

The closed box and the bedchamber staff vanished with exemplary lack of incident. Hedia wasn't a petty tyrant, but she expected her servants to do their jobs quickly and unobtrusively. There was nothing petty about Hedia's anger toward those who failed to meet her standards.

Alphena rose to her feet with a grace that equaled that of the most sophisticated ladies of Carce, her stepmother among them. Relief evident on her face, she said, "Then it's really all right?"

"Yes," said Hedia, rising also. "It makes me look like a queen."

There was a bustle among the servants again. It was like watching birds in the shrubbery when a cat is prowling, though of course the servants were much quieter in their excited twittering.

"I'm going to choose a dress now, dear," she said to Alphena. "Would you care to join me? And perhaps you could show me what you're planning to wear, so that we don't clash too badly. Though—"

She gestured toward the doorway through which a maid had carried the diadem.

"—your gift has its own logic to which we both must bow."

"I think . . . ," Alphena said. She paused to consider, then went on, "I think the jewel will go with any color. If it wants to. And you did look like a queen. Like a goddess."

"I'll try to be worthy of your gift," Hedia said, giving no hint of how surprised she was at her daughter's perception. This wasn't the resentful brat of a few months ago.

Though Hedia knew better than to take all credit for the change. Various things, most particularly the threat of imminent death, had brought Alphena to a more useful approach to life.

The girl flashed an unaffected smile. "Thank you, Mother," she said. "I'm feeling a little dizzy now, though. I believe I'll take a nap."

She went off with her entourage of servants. The cudgel men didn't escort Lady Alphena within the house, of course, but she had collected a considerable coterie of maids and attendants in the past few weeks. Ambitious servants used the status of service to the daughter of the house to lift them from the general mob of their fellows.

That said a great deal about the change in the girl's behavior. She had become Lady Alphena, who reflected glory on those who served her, and who, however terrible she might be to her enemies, was just and generous to those who served her well.

"Syra," Hedia said, following the girl with her eyes. "Has someone just arrived?"

"Master Corylus came to see Lord Varus, Your Ladyship," Syra said. "They're speaking in Lord Varus' suite."

Hedia gestured minusculely to indicate she had received the information. She did not otherwise move.

Corylus had left them at the animal compound to return to his father's house; there had been no suggestion at the time that he would be back today. This visit must have something to do with Varus' vision at the compound and perhaps with the lizardmen . . . but perhaps not.

"I will look at dresses now, Syra," Hedia said, starting back into the house.

She was a successful woman, which in this world meant a woman who could turn the plans of men to her own benefit and the benefit of her family. The plans here might be those of demons or worse, but the principle was the same.

And if things didn't work out in her favor this time . . .

Hedia smiled. *It's time that the Underworld had a real queen.*

CORYLUS WAS A FREQUENT visitor to Saxa's town house in Carce. The household staff knew him well.

Normally Corylus came in company with his friend Varus, though occasionally he used the excellent gymnasium and had no dealings with the family unless Varus—or less often and less comfortably Alphena—chose to join him. Senator Saxa had probably approved the arrangement, just as he would have approved any request his son made, but it wasn't a matter of great concern to him.

Corylus hadn't visited this beach house before, however, and Varus wasn't expecting him. The doorman was a tall Thracian who spoke Latin better than the Germans whom Agrippinus, the majordomo in Carce, purchased for that duty.

The Thracian looked at Corylus in his plain—dusty and somewhat sweat-stained by now—tunic. "Lord Varus is not at home to your like, sirrah," he said. The tone would have gotten him kicked where he'd feel it if Pulto had been present: a slave didn't speak that way to the son of Prefect Cispius.

Fortunately, Manetho, an understeward from the Carce establishment, was in the entrance hall and had started toward the doorway as soon as he heard Corylus' voice. Manetho burst into the guard kiosk and shrieked, "You barbarian! Was your mother a sow! This is His Young Lordship's closest friend and you would send him out into the street?"

The doorman's expression went from supercilious toward the under-dressed stranger to fury at a fellow servant—and then to uncertainty. His face finally settled into cringing fear as he took in the plump Egyptian understeward's words.

"Who hired such an untrained buffoon?" Manetho said, capping his rant.

Corylus smiled faintly. *Now* he understood what that was all about.

Publius Cispius Corylus was a friend of the family and particularly of Varus, so he had expected that any member of the Carce establishment would vouch for him at least to the degree of sending a message to Varus saying that a man of that name, claiming to be a friend, was at the door. He hadn't expected this sort of violent endorsement, though.

But if Manetho thought he should have been appointed chief stew-ard here on the Bay or if the Carce establishment and the local estab-lishment were mutually hostile already, the outburst made sense. It wasn't about Corylus, except to the degree that Lord Varus' friend made a useful club with which to pound a rival.

"Please forgive these clowns, Master Corylus," Manetho said, bowing—which he never would have done to a mere knight had they been back in Carce. "I've sent a messenger to alert Lord Varus, who is in his apart-ments. I'll take you to him now."

"You have no duties in this house save for those I choose to give you," said a tall man whose austere face contrasted with his tunics of green layered over red, both trimmed with gold embroidery.

"Look here, Balbinus—," said Manetho.

Three additional servants formed in front of the Egyptian and forced him back without actually pushing him. Corylus felt a degree of sympa-thy for the fellow, but he'd clearly overplayed his hand. He thought about the human need to create rivals out of fellows. It was no different in the army, except perhaps that there deadly weapons were readily to hand.

Balbinus bowed, though not as deeply as Manetho had, and said, "If you'll please come with me, Master Corylus, I'll take you to Lord Varus. I've informed him of your arrival."

"Publius," said Varus, walking toward him around the pool in the center of the reception hall. "I'm very glad to see you. My suite is on the second floor here. It's supposed to catch the evening breezes better."

He wore a very fine silk tunic and sandals with gilded straps. Corylus had caught Varus dressing for dinner, but at least he hadn't wrapped himself in his toga yet.

"I came across a literary puzzle," Corylus said, lifting the scrap of paper to call attention to it. "I realize the timing isn't good, but I'd like to discuss it with you now."

"Yes, of course," Varus said, turning to the staircase concealed by a wall frescoed with a scene of Bellerophon on the back of Pegasus. "There's no library here, but my room should be literary enough to suit our purposes."

He glanced over his shoulder at the top of the stairs and added, "I have my own loggia, so we'll sit there since you prefer the outdoors. The light will be better anyway."

"You don't care where you are," Corylus said, voicing a sudden realization about his friend. "So long as you have a book."

Varus laughed as he led the way into his own suite. The walls were rich yellow with cartouches painted to look like alcoves holding statues. "True enough," he said. "Though I'm trying to become a better-balanced man and therefore a *true* philosopher."

Servants stood at attention within the suite; they bowed as the young master and his friend passed through. Corylus counted eight. Enough to fill a squad tent, though they wouldn't be much use if the Germans came across the border.

They probably weren't much use here, either, even when the family was in residence. Varus didn't care about food and luxuries—save for books. He could have lived on army rations as easily as a soldier who grew up on a farm in the hills, though he drank a great deal less wine than that soldier.

The loggia had masonry benches to either side, protected by a sturdy roof that supported part of the open-air dining area. The location wasn't private, but it was as close to private as a house full of servants could be; and the light was good.

Varus sat, gesturing Corylus to the place beside him. Servants started to crowd onto the loggia. Varus looked up, frowned, and said, "I will not need you. Scillio, see to it that I'm left alone."

A servant whom Corylus recognized from the town house, one of the copyists, immediately said, "Out! Out! The master is in the process of creation!"

Corylus looked at his friend, trying to control his surprise. Varus smiled wanly and said, "Even when I *was* writing poetry, I didn't deserve that kind of effusion."

He held out his hand. "Let me see this literary puzzle, if you will."

Corylus gave him the palimpsest. He said, "A man brought it to me in a bar near the harbor. He said it was scratch paper used by his uncle, Vergil. I recognized the line from the *Aeneid*."

Varus read it, then looked at Corylus and said, "It's not quite the *Aeneid*. This says 'my brethren.' The poem—the completed poem—reads 'my lads.'"

He turned the document at ninety degrees and tilted it to catch the sun at a raking angle. He was reading the original message, which had been rubbed off with pumice to allow the sheet to be reused.

"I noticed that it was very good quality papyrus," Corylus said. "The edges were smoothed and painted red with henna."

Varus chuckled and lowered the document. "Yes," he said. "If we're to believe that this sheet—"

He wiggled it; Corylus took it from his fingers and examined the original himself.

"—really came from Vergil's study, then I would guess that a senator with literary pretensions sent Vergil his epic, hoping that the great man would approve of his efforts. The great man made the same decision I would have, unless I decided to wrap fish in the sheets instead."

"'Then Hannibal, raving like a demon, leaped the wall into the midst of the defenders,'" Corylus read, then set the palimpsest on the bench between them. "Yes, it's pretty bad, all right."

"If anything," Varus said, his tone losing some of its cheerfulness, "it's worse than my own verse was. Which is not a thing I say lightly."

"The man said his name was Lucinus," Corylus said. He was changing the subject, but he was changing it back to the real purpose of his visit. "He gave me the page because he wouldn't be permitted to see you. He said you are a magician who can help him defeat the danger which threatens the whole world."

"I'm not a magician," Varus muttered with a grimace.

The servants who had retreated from the loggia were still more or less within hearing, but there was little chance that any of them were listening to the master and his friend. A high-level literary discussion was possibly the most boring subject on earth to most people. Certainly to most of the servants who catered to a nobleman's grooming.

"All I'm telling you is what this Lucinus told me," Corylus said. "But I've seen you send demons back to the fires they sprang from. That may not make you a magician, but you're certainly someone I'd want to have close by if I thought I might be facing demons again."

Varus' laugh was wistful rather than bitter, but it sounded as though it might turn bitter very easily. He said, "I don't know what I am. Other than that—"

He met Corylus' eyes.

"—I'm not a poet." He pursed his lips in thought, then said, "What do you think, Publius?"

"I think that Lucinus looks as though he's about fifty, but Vergil died fifty years ago," Corylus said, marshaling the facts as he—as both of them—had been taught to do by Pandareus. "He should be older, even if he was quite young when he became his uncle's apprentice. Apart from that, though—"

He touched the palimpsest.

"—such evidence as we have suggests that he's telling the truth. This is precisely the sort of draft that Vergil might have made. There can't be many other people who would have had access to scrap papyrus of such quality."

"No," agreed Varus with the same wan smile as before. "I burned all my manuscripts. I didn't want to inflict my verse even on dead mullets."

His face sharpened suddenly to that of the most learned pupil in the class of Pandareus of Athens. "We know that there is some danger approaching the Republic, since I have prophesied as much."

He smiled; Corylus smiled back. They both remembered just how accurate Varus' previous quotations from the *Sibylline Books* had been.

"It therefore follows that Lucinus' warning is trustworthy. That doesn't prove that he, or that he and I together, can overcome the dan-

ger, but there seems very little reason not to discuss the matter with
him. Given that the alternative is that we allow the world to be destroyed without making an effort to avoid that result."

A servant standing near the arch to the loggia cleared his throat
loudly. Corylus placed a hand on his friend's arm, then nodded toward
the entrance.

Saxa diffidently stepped onto the loggia but hesitated there. He
wore his toga and was otherwise groomed for dinner.

"Ah, Master Corylus!" he said, blinking. "Ah, you're very welcome.
In fact, would you care to join us for dinner? I'm sure that Quintus Macsturnas would be glad to add a place for a man of your accomplish-
ments. Ah, and I'm sure that Balbinus can find you a toga."

Could Balbinus find a toga with the two narrow stripes of a knight?
Corylus wondered. But given Saxa's wealth, it was just possible that he
could. Indeed, it was possible that the chief steward had sent out for
suitable dinner clothing as soon as the unexpected visitor arrived with
such a flurry.

"No thank you, Your Lordship," Corylus said, bowing. "I'll be dining
tonight with my father. I don't see him very often since I've been studying under Master Pandareus and, well, we have a lot to catch up on."

On an impulse, he offered that palimpsest to Saxa. "Your son and I
were discussing a variant reading of the first book of the *Aeneid*, Your
Lordship. Or rather, Lord Varus was explaining the variation to me."

"Really?" Saxa said with delight. He bent to look at the document but
did not touch it. "Really, this is marvelous! Are you sure that you can't—"

He brought himself up short. "But what am I doing?" he said in
horror. "Trying to corrupt a son who is carrying out his filial duty
according to the traditions of the people of Carce! Pray forgive me. Ah!
Unless your father would perhaps care to join us also?"

"He'll be flattered at the invitation," Corylus said. "But not tonight,
I fear. I'll be going off now."

He wasn't wholly certain that Cispius *would* be flattered. He treated
all members of the nobility with the deference due their rank, but he
had served under too many noble incompetents to be impressed simply
because a man was a senator.

On the other hand, Alphenus Saxa had proved himself unexpectedly
worthy of respect during the past difficult months. Courage was a virtue

that made up for most things in the mind of a soldier. Varus' father had in his dithering way proved himself as brave as Horatius holding the Tiber Bridge.

"Well, I understand that, of course," Saxa said, which, from his puzzled tone, was unlikely. "I'll be in the office until, ah. . . ."

"Master Corylus?" Varus said. "I want to discuss one more aspect of that text, if you will. And Father, I'll join you downstairs in just a moment. All I need to do is put my toga on."

As Saxa turned, Corylus said in an undertone, "I'll pick you up in a cart at dawn if that's all right. I think just the two of us and a driver who knows the way. I won't tell Father much, but he can find me the cart and a driver who knows where this Lucinus lives on the Nola Road."

"Yes, that seems right," Varus said. "We don't want to make a production of this, at least not until we know more."

Corylus quirked a grin at his friend. "Lucinus didn't say I should come," he said. "But I intend to come anyway."

"If you didn't, *I* would ask you to come," Varus said with a similar grin. "And if it's appropriate, thank your father for his help."

"Yes," said Corylus. "We're going to need his help while we're here."

"We're going to need it," Varus said, "and it appears that the world will need it."

They clasped arms. Corylus turned to go out, still holding the palimpsest. Four servants held a toga ready to wrap around His Lordship Gaius Alphenus Varus.

Behind Corylus, Varus mused, barely audibly, "I only hope that all we have and the world has will be enough."

"WELCOME, VERY WELCOME, Lord Saxa!" Macsturnas cried as he met Varus and his father in the entrance hall. "And you, Lord Varus. Until your messenger arrived, I feared that the press of business had detained you and you wouldn't be able to join us after all."

"I was responsible for the delay, my lord," Varus said, following his father and their host through the house as servants bowed or ducked out of the way—or both. "My friend Corylus arrived with what purports to be the draft of a portion of the *Aeneid*. I've summoned our teacher Pandareus of Athens here to the Bay to examine it."

That was a minor falsehood: Alphena had summoned Pandareus,

and the purpose of the consultation was only tangentially literary. *Though if Pandareus knew of an example of Vergil's handwriting that they could use for comparison—by the Holy Wisdom, if I have really touched a document written by Vergil himself!*

"The *Aeneid*, you say," Macsturnas said. "Would that be a poem, then?"

Saxa missed a step and stared at their host in horror. Varus caught him by the arm.

Before he could say something that might be taken as insulting—or even be meant as insulting, though Saxa was a truly gentle man—Varus laughed as cheerfully as he could manage and said, "That's right, Your Lordship. I'm such a bookworm that I forget that not everybody shares my tastes."

They entered the garden. A summer dining room was set in one of the back corners. Three men were already reclining on the U of masonry benches built out from the walls. The fourth side was open to allow servers to reach the table in the middle. One guest, placed on the left bench, wore a senatorial toga; the man on the cross bench was also in a toga, though his had the twin stripes of a knight.

On the right-hand bench was Paris. If the Etruscan priest had been invited to dinner with two senators besides the host, his connection with the aedile was unexpectedly close. Paris watched without expression, but there was certainly no affection in his eyes when they rested on Varus.

Varus was feeling rather pleased with himself, though he knew a true philosopher should be above pride. Still, if one didn't take some notice of good behavior, one would be unable to duplicate it.

He had prevented his father from launching into what would at best have been a lecture on Vergil and his importance to world literature. That would have been desperately boring to their host and presumably to the other guests of a man who had to guess even that the *Aeneid* was a poem.

Varus had grown from the recent crises. He would always have known that Saxa was making a mistake, but in past years Varus would merely have cringed in silent embarrassment. Being around Corylus—and Hedia and Alphena!—had shown him how to act in the fashion he knew was correct.

The guests had plates in front of them, still holding the remains of dormice in honey, though the serving platter had been removed from the small central table. *They must have started the first course before our messenger arrived,* Varus realized.

"Our colleague, Trebonius Haltus," Macsturnas said, indicating the other senator. "He has a home in Baiae also. And my brother-in-law, Collinus Afer. And of course Paris, whom you've met."

The walls behind the benches were painted with scenes of wild bulls running and leaping. The bulls were blue, though, causing Varus to wonder if they were religious art.

He had been daydreaming during the exchange of pleasantries. He realized this when he heard his father say, "And my son Varus greets you also, gentlemen."

His skin suddenly hot—*am I blushing?*—Varus bowed to the company, which certainly wasn't called for. "Your pardon, sirs," he said. "I was lost in a literary problem."

That was a very useful excuse. There were advantages to having everybody think you're a cloth-headed intellectual. Which wasn't far from the truth, he supposed.

"Lord Varus," the aedile said, "would you take the head of the right bench, above Master Paris? Paris said he was looking forward to meeting you. I suppose you intellectuals will have a lot to discuss that would go right over the heads of us simple folk."

There were chuckles from others, Saxa included. Paris didn't crack a smile.

"And Gaius Saxa," Macsturnas continued, "please honor me by taking the couch to my left. Indeed, your presence honors the whole gathering."

Varus and his father settled themselves onto the indicated couches. Paris looked over his shoulder at Varus. With two instead of three on each cushion, they weren't so close that avoiding contact during the meal would be next to impossible, but they were certainly close.

The Etruscan priest said, "I was told that you would identify the specimens from Africa, Lord Varus. If you did so, I failed to hear you."

The tone was flat, not sneering, but the question was a sneer nonetheless.

Varus looked at the fellow. Close up, Paris was older than he had seemed in the crowd in the compound. Even granting the natural querulousness of the old, and perhaps a poor old man's equally natural resentment of a rich youth, it took a great deal of philosophical resignation not to respond more sharply than would be polite to the host's hanger-on.

Varus smiled at the thought. His expression, probably misunderstood, turned out to be the perfect response: Paris went tremblingly white with fury. *Score one for philosophical resignation. . . .*

Servants brought in finger bowls with rose water and linen napkins for the guests who had eaten the first course. As they did, little girls in pastel tunics—meant to impersonate Hebe, the cupbearer of the gods, Varus supposed; in other settings, Hebe was the Goddess of Youth—poured wine to the guests.

Varus tasted his cup cautiously, because he hadn't been present when the host decided the dilution. He guessed it was two measures of water to each measure of wine, which was moderate if not ascetic.

Paris *was* being ascetic, drinking from a clear glass tumbler to emphasize that it contained only water. The plate in front of him held nut meats, slices of peeled apples and peaches, and a wedge of bread without even a bowl of olive oil to dip it in.

"My bout of sunstroke at Master Veturius' compound prevented me from stating the little I know about the lizardmen," Varus said in a cool tone. "I will hope to learn more in good time, but for now all I can say is . . ."

He let his voice trail off as servants brought in a richly carved bronze platter—true Corinthian Bronze, Varus suspected—cast with six hollows in which nestled what seemed to be miniature hares, skinned but otherwise complete. Varus took one and nibbled carefully, finding it to be a paste of hare meat cooked on a skeleton of rye bread and stuffed with a rich pork sauce. He caught the juice in his napkin before it dribbled onto his toga.

When he looked up, he saw that his father and the aedile were both staring intently at him, waiting for the answer. Their attention had drawn that of Macsturnas' two friends as well, making Varus the center of all eyes. That was a regular thing when it was his turn to declaim in class, but he wasn't used to it happening at formal dinner parties.

I'm not used to formal dinner parties.

Varus revised the answer he had been about to give. "Honored sirs," he said, nodding to bring the other guests formally into the discussion.

"I'm only familiar with one written account which might have bearing, that of Herodotus. In discussing the tribes of Africa, he says that in ancient times the Garamantes battled serpents and finally drove them deep into the desert. It's at least possible that this is a garbled memory of lizardmen like those Master Veturius brought back from the depths of the continent."

"Ah!" said Macsturnas. "Very interesting. Will you contact this Herodotus, then, young man?"

Varus managed not to blurt, "No, because Herodotus has been dead for five hundred years." *Though perhaps the Sibyl could put me in touch with him.* He said instead, "The historian himself is deceased. I intend to search libraries and discuss the subject with scholars who are more learned than I, however."

Did Macsturnas really find this interesting? Varus had felt . . . not contemptuous, exactly, but patronizing about the bird's nest of information cluttering his father's head; but Saxa was well read, though not an intelligent or critical reader. The aedile appeared to have no more literary knowledge than one would find in a pig farmer in the Alban Hills.

I should talk to a pig farmer before I use that simile in a declamation.

Varus lowered his eyes and returned to the fake hare. He dabbed his fingers in the rose water and then wiped them before he realized that Paris was still staring at him.

"Do you have something to say to me, fellow?" Varus said. *What would Corylus do? What would—*

He giggled at the sudden vision of his sister taking the "hare" remaining on the platter—Paris hadn't eaten the one set out for him—and mashing it into the priest's face. That was the sort of response that worked for Alphena. In her brother's case, it was better to act as a gentleman and a scholar.

Before Paris could reply, Varus sobered his expression into a mere grin and said, "Forgive me, Master Paris; I was curt. A man like me who spends his life among books may show himself to be sadly lacking in social graces."

"Books!" Paris said as though he were cursing. "You can talk about books to these others—"

His voice was pitched low enough that the remaining diners probably couldn't hear the words, but it seemed to Varus that the hissing tone should have aroused attention. The host, Saxa, and Haltus were discussing governorships, while Afer was giving his attention to the meal. His cup was being refilled—not for the first time since Varus sat down—and he'd taken the leftover hare.

"—but *I* am not a child in the art myself. What have you learned by reflection in your mirror of art, Magician?"

"By reflection?" Varus repeated. He found he had eased back slightly, repelled—literally—by the priest's venom. Varus deliberately leaned forward and shook out his napkin between them. "I told you that on reflection, I remembered the passage in Herodotus. And I'm not a magician, Master Paris. I am a scholar."

"You know that the Singiri were driven from this world in the far past," Paris said. "You *know* they are demons."

"I do *not* know that," Varus said. *And your saying so doesn't make me more likely to believe it.*

Servants brought in the next course. Varus deliberately turned his head to watch the platter on which what seemed to be a miniature bull hunched, its legs drawn up under it. Varus wasn't any more interested in food than he was in clothing—or in trees, if it came to that—but if he didn't look away he would give the advantage in the contest to Paris.

Varus didn't let his smile reach his lips. His sister watched gladiators cut and thrust with edged weapons. The law courts had a similar dynamic. Varus didn't *like* the competitive declamations by which Pandareus prepared his students to conduct trials, but he had analyzed and practiced the necessary skills with a depth of understanding that few of his fellows could match.

"Why do you lie to me?" Paris said. "I tell you, I too am one of those who *know*."

"This is a fetal calf from one of my own farms," Macsturnas said proudly. "The mother was brought here and slaughtered in the kitchen this morning so that the meat is perfectly fresh! The horns and hooves are pastries made with the mother's brains!"

Varus felt an urge to jot down that datum as he had begun doing with anything having to do with sacred rites. When he gave up verse—he couldn't claim to have given up poetry; he had never been more than a versifier—he had decided to become the historian of the religion of the Republic. Even now many of the meanings that underlay traditional rites had been lost, even to the priests who carried them out by rote.

Presumably the butchering took place in the outdoor kitchen behind the garden rather than in the house proper. Even so, it was the sort of task Varus would have preferred to be taking place at a butcher's shop a few streets distant rather than in the immediate vicinity of where he was eating.

A philosopher is above concern for blood and feces. Perhaps he should thank Macsturnas for giving him a chance to demonstrate Stoic resignation.

A servant used the blade of his knife to lay a thin slice of the meat on Varus' plate, then broke off a piece of a "horn" to go with it. As Saxa's son, he was being served second, immediately after his father.

"What I don't know is why the Singiri have returned at this time," Paris said. He was ignoring even his fruit and nuts. "But you do know, don't you? Are they here to destroy the Earth this time instead of fleeing it?"

Afer was holding forth on the use of cauls to cover puddings; his mouth was full. The others present were listening with apparent interest; Saxa had contributed an anecdote out of Hegesander. Whether or not the conversation on this bench was of a higher plane, it was certainly different from that of the remaining company.

Varus washed and wiped his fingers; he waved away the servant ready to offer another slice. There were surely more courses to go, and the remainder of the calf wouldn't go to waste. Even the servants waiting for the broken meats might be shorted with Afer at the table.

"I do *not* know what the lizardmen intend," Varus said, meeting the priest's eyes. He didn't use—but didn't comment on Paris' use of—the name Singiri, which agreed with Varus' vision of the Sibyl. "Presumably those which Veturius captured intend to enter the arena as part of our host's gift to the Republic. I have seen no more reason to believe they intend to destroy the Earth than I do to believe they intend to fly to the table of the Olympian gods and drink nectar."

The priest's face worked angrily. "Faugh!" he said. He took a slice of apple. "You pretend to be wise, but you act like a clown. Clown your way to the tomb, then! And to your world's tomb!"

Varus rinsed and dried his fingers again, thinking. Occasionally one had to make a decision instantly. He had learned how to do so, how to *force* himself to react at once. It didn't come naturally to him; but like most other problems, hesitation could be overcome by training and willpower.

When Varus had time to think, however, he did so. The priest had started a second slice of apple when Varus said, "I have answered your questions, Master Paris. Now tell me: What is *your* place in this? Why did you invite yourself along to view the lizardmen?"

A servant bent to fill Varus' cup; he waved her off. A male servant topped off the priest's tumbler of water, but he had drunk very little. *Perhaps he's fasting as well as ascetic. He's not much of an advertisement for a simple life, though.*

Paris twisted his head to face Varus again. "I advise Lord Macsturnas and other members of my race on matters of religion and omens," he said. "I regarded the return of the Singiri to this world to be as worthy of consideration as a statue speaking or the birth of a two-headed calf."

I wonder whether our host would consider the calf fetus to be even more delectable had it been found to have two heads, Varus thought.

It was the sort of consideration he could share with Corylus alone of his acquaintances. Thoughts that to Varus were whimsically humorous struck ordinary folk—and the other diners here were ordinary in that sense—as signs of madness, or perhaps of extreme eccentricity, given that he was of the senatorial order.

"You say your race, Master Paris . . . ," Varus said. Servants were bringing in a platter of six squabs, each surrounded by pigeon eggs. "I gather you mean Etruscans?"

"The doves are stuffed with a forcemeat of asparagus and chickadee bosoms," Macsturnas announced. "While the 'eggs' are pastry shells in which oysters from Lake Lucrinus swim in a sauce of sea urchin eggs. So fresh that the oysters are still alive!"

How in the name of Holy Wisdom do you tell a living oyster from a dead one? Varus realized that his ignorance didn't mean that no one knew the answer, but he was permitted to have doubts.

"Yes, Etruscan," Paris said bitterly. "The race which brought civilization to Italy in ancient times, before the Greeks came with their debased version—and long before Carce sprang up like a mushroom on a dung heap. Not that there are real Etruscans remaining, even in the best houses. Lord Macsturnas—"

He gestured to the host with his free hand.

"—has an Oscan mother, and his father's mother was Sabine—and even then her lineage was far from pure Sabine."

Varus took an egg and popped it whole into his mouth. The sauce was tart and unexpectedly good with the oyster. He suspected it contained giant fennel. Under other circumstances he might have asked, but he was sure that in the present company the question would drag him into all manner of discussion regarding a subject in which his interest was very slight.

"I've always believed that the reason Carce has been so successful," Varus said in measured tones, "is that from the beginning we have been open to all races. Latins and Sabines and Greeks . . . and of course to Etruscans, including our last three kings."

He took another egg, though he decided to pass on the squab itself. He wondered if Afer would manage three, assuming that the priest continued to ignore his portion.

"The success of mongrels!" Paris said. "A city that is open to all men is like a woman who is open to all men!"

Varus paused, then lowered the egg from his lips. "Master Paris," he said. "I am a philosopher, willing to give a hearing to any idea no matter how coarse or coarsely phrased. I suggest, however, that you learn to moderate your language in the presence of your betters. I believe you've already met Marcus Pulto, who serves my friend Corylus?"

Paris didn't respond, but his expression was suddenly guarded.

"Pulto's criticism is apt to be of a robust variety," Varus said, letting his smile spread. It wasn't his nature to use the term "betters" in that fashion, but here it was called for. "And in this particular instance, neither his master nor I would attempt to moderate it."

Varus swallowed the second egg. It was as good as the first, and in this case was further spiced by a feeling of triumph.

The remainder of the meal passed without further comment by Paris.

CHAPTER IV

The delivery cart Corylus had borrowed from his father had neither springs nor cushions, but the driver's bench where he and Varus sat with the driver was mounted ahead of the axle. The location moderated both the jouncing of the two large wheels and the racking pace of the mule drawing the vehicle.

Varus grinned at his friend. "I'd probably develop blisters if we walked the four miles," he said. "And although it's sometimes uncomfortable, I'm coming to enjoy life that involves more than reading books and writing them."

He coughed. "That is, I'm enjoying living life as well as reading and writing. If I had to pick one or the other, I wouldn't be riding in a mule cart even on what I believe is a very good road."

"I prefer it to being at sea," Corylus said. He felt queasy on shipboard, even when the ship was tied up to the dock. "And it's quicker than walking."

The cart had a trough for the feet of those on the bench. A narrow-bladed spade lay in it. It was an ordinary nurseryman's tool, but it was a little surprising to find it on a vehicle that was ordinarily used to carry jars of floral extracts in bulk from Cispius' factory to the retailers—mostly in Carce—who would blend it with olive oil or lanolin into dropper bottles for the use of the fashionable and well-to-do.

Some would be applied directly to the bodies of women who expected to entertain—in one sense or another—men, but more of the perfumes went into dinner wreaths. There were mixed dinners that women of the faster set attended, but most dinners were exclusively male except for flute girls and the like. No young buck cared what a flute girl thought of his appearance.

Corylus reached for the shovel. The driver, Lycos, beside him on the bench, turned to watch what was happening. Lycos said nothing, but his gaze was disconcerting. A scar started at his hairline and ran down the left cheek, destroying the eye in its track. The scar turned a coarsely unattractive face into something out of nightmare.

Corylus held the spade upright between his legs and let his fingers run along the oak shaft. The sprite was a dim memory deep within the wood. She had been young when the tree was cut for its present use, but that was a long time ago.

Suddenly, as unexpected as nearby lightning, Corylus was in the midst of a scene in late evening: two men coming from in front of a cart that was stopped on the right side of the road and grabbing the harness of the mule; two more men with cudgels appearing from the ditches on the other side of the road.

The spade—Corylus was watching through the sprite's eyes—rising; the blade punching through the face of a man as though cutting a turf in gritty soil; the tool reversed and the T-handle crushing the temple of a second man before he could block the stroke with his cudgel.

The man trying to clamber onto the seat from the right taking the side of the blade; the bone of his upper arm *cracking*, the knife in his hand flying free. The last man dropping the mule's reins and turning to run, then twitching like a pithed frog as another thrust of the spade crushed his lower spine.

Corylus set the spade down again exactly as he had found it. The driver was still looking at him. Varus, on Corylus' other side, kept silent. He clearly knew that something was going on, but he was clueless as to what it was.

"A load of floral extracts would be valuable," Corylus said, speaking to Lycos in a deliberate tone. "Worth stealing, I should think."

"There's been some who thought so, yeah," the driver growled. The few words he had offered previously during the drive had been gruff; now he sounded bestial. "If there's trouble, you leave it to me, boy."

"If there's trouble," Corylus said, the tone of command coming naturally, "then I'll be glad of your company, Master Lycos."

Lycos began to chuckle and faced forward again. "You know," he said, "I had my doubts with your posh talk and school manners. But I guess you're the Old Man's son, all right."

"Glad to hear it," Corylus muttered. He coughed to clear the constriction from his throat. *I've been praised in more florid terms. But I've never had a compliment that meant more.*

Cispius hadn't offered questions when his son asked to borrow a cart and a driver who could find the estate that had belonged to the poet Vergil on the Nola Road. He wouldn't have survived on the frontier, however, if he hadn't been able to see more than bushes in a seemingly neutral landscape.

"Are you expecting trouble, Publius?" Varus said with a deadpan expression. "Because if you are, I'm afraid you brought the wrong sibling."

He paused, then added, "Unless perhaps I was able to put the miscreants to sleep by declaiming some of my verse."

Corylus had let his mind wander into darker passages, so though he heard his friend's words, they didn't register for a moment. When Corylus *did* understand, he snorted with laughter.

"Thank you, Gaius," he said. "I don't foresee anything more strenuous than a literary discussion, but I'm glad that you're prepared to do your part if necessary."

There was a blockage ahead. A man and woman with a girl of no more than eight were leading their three donkeys abreast so that they could chat on the way into town with panniers of vegetables. Almost all the traffic at this hour of the morning was of goods and produce headed in from the country for sale—or directly to the tables of noble households.

Lycos murmured to slow the mule, then ticked the man—presumably the husband—under the nose with his twelve-foot switch. The fellow shouted in surprise and anger, but he dragged his wife's and daughter's donkeys into line ahead of his to give the cart room. Corylus had half-expected the man to want to discuss the matter, but apparently his first sight of Lycos' face had left him with no desire to spend time shouting into it.

"When I first saw the cart . . . ," Varus said. "I wondered why the driver had such a long switch. I now have the answer through direct observation, a technique which I prefer to that of deduction."

"Socrates may have been able to draw abstruse knowledge from the mind of an unsophisticated youth," Corylus agreed, "but I sure can't do that from my own mind. And with all honor to Aristotle, I *know* a heavy weight doesn't fall faster than a lighter one. When I was ten, I made a clay pellet the same size as a lead sling-bullet; they both hit the ground at the same time when I tipped them from the barracks' roof."

The wall on the right was in bad repair. Ground shocks this close to Vesuvius could crack masonry, let alone shake apart a wall made of fieldstones stacked on one another.

"Does your father know anything about this Lucinus?" Varus said, also looking up the road ahead.

"He knew the property," Corylus said, recalling their conversation during the previous night. "It'd been vacant for years, but a new owner moved in about the time Father bought the perfume business here before he retired. The owner keeps to himself and doesn't even have servants living on the property. A farmer on the road just this side sends men over during daytime to take care of the few crops and goats. And the farmer's wife sends a maid to cook and do housework."

Unexpectedly Lycos turned his fierce eye on them. He said, "Nobody human lives there but the old wizard himself. At night, though, there's lights and there's things moving and there's sounds too. I've been by after dark myself, coming back from a delivery, and I didn't like what I heard. I didn't waste any time getting past, for all that you can't see the place from the road."

"Well, we're going there in daylight," Corylus said. He was making an observation aloud, not trying to quell his own fear or that of his companions.

He *wasn't* particularly afraid. He'd faced demons and he'd faced Sarmatian warriors. He didn't look forward to repeating either experience; but if he had to, he would do his duty as a soldier's son and a citizen of Carce.

Varus didn't have the kind of hot courage that sent a legion uphill into a mass of tall, screaming Germans, but Corylus had never seen him flinch at any danger. If Corylus hadn't known Varus so well, he might have thought his friend had no emotions. In fact, he was as sensitive as he was observant, but he relied on his intellect in a crisis. The fact that Varus was afraid—as he was surely afraid many times, because he was far more aware of possible dangers than most people were—simply didn't affect his behavior.

Corylus hadn't met Lycos before they got into the cart together this morning. There were very brave people—Pulto was one of them—who were afraid of magic though they feared nothing in the natural world. If Lycos had been such a man, Cispius wouldn't have chosen him to drive the cart this morning.

Corylus turned toward his friend and said, "Did you have any trouble getting out? That is, getting out without an army of attendants?"

Varus smiled. "I wouldn't have been able to do it back in Carce," he said, "but the staff here doesn't know me well enough to be contemptuous. I told Balbinus that I would be going off with you at dawn wearing simple clothes—"

He tweaked the collar of his plain white tunic. He wore a cape of coarse blue wool over his shoulders; the hood was back. Except that both garments were new, he might have been a farmer dressed in his best.

"—and he saw to it that I was wakened in time and had suitable garments. Instead of telling me it was impossible, as Agrippinus would have done in Carce. Or rushing to Father with the news that I had gone mad, because obviously no nobleman in his right mind would wish to do such a thing."

Varus spoke without apparent resentment. Most servants didn't have the education to appreciate his virtues, and the fact that the son of the house was diffident and polite—particularly by contrast with his sister, Alphena—had made him an object of contempt rather than affection to the staff in Carce.

Perhaps Varus understood the expression on his friend's face, for he added with a smile, "We don't live in a philosophical paradise of the sort Plato visualized, Publius."

"Given the state that Plato created when his student Dion was Tyrant of Syracuse," Corylus said, his tone sharper than he had expected it to be, "I believe we can be thankful for that."

They were passing a farmhouse on the right; it was of some substance though not a nobleman's villa. The walls had been stuccoed white at one time, but patches of plaster were missing. Lycos nodded toward it and said, "That's the farmer who hires out at the place we're going. And here's—"

Two men watched from the veranda in front; several others working in the yard followed the cart with their eyes as Lycos turned it up a little-used track to the left.

"—the drive we take," Lycos concluded.

The road twisted through fields overgrown into a tangle of brush and saplings. Occasionally an umbrella pine rose to fifty feet, but for the most part the growth formed a tangled screen twelve or fifteen feet high.

"Hard to imagine this being owned by the man who wrote the *Georgics*," Varus said sadly. "He loved his land."

The cart turned another kink in the road. Ahead of them was what *had* been a proper villa but was well on the way to becoming a ruin. Part of the roof had fallen in; a pair of black goats munched grass, which was growing among the remaining tiles. They watched the vehicle, their jaws still working.

A man sitting on the front steps rose. He moved in tiny jerks as though his limbs were controlled by strings.

"This . . . ," said Corylus, reaching into the bed of the cart for his cornelwood staff. "Is Master Lucinus. We'll see what he loves."

VARUS WAS SHOCKED to see the ruin of Vergil's property, much more so than he would have expected to be if someone had suggested it ahead of time. The *Eclogues* had been juvenile work, mere imitations of Theocritus and of Greek imitators of Theocritus, interesting to be sure, and a window onto the development of the greatest Latin poet—and perhaps greatest poet without limitation—of all time.

The *Georgics*, though, were love lyrics not to fanciful shepherd maids but rather to the land itself and to the life on it. Even a scholar like Varus with no personal experience of farming could read that love in every line of the four books. To come upon Vergil's house half-roofless and his fields abandoned to brush was like seeing the smoldering remains of a district in Carce after a fire.

The man walking toward them from the porch was dressed like a field hand rather than as the owner—or even manager—of a villa, but it was in a cultured accent that he said, "Welcome, Lord Varus. And thank you, Cispius Corylus, for bringing your friend to me. You and the world may benefit by continuing to exist."

"I did not *bring* my friend, Lucinus," Corylus said. "I described the situation and he made the decision to come with his own fine mind. Because I'm not sure myself that his choice was the correct one, I have accompanied him."

He patted his staff into his left palm with a *whap*. It was made of dogwood, which was tough and heavy beyond any other wood Varus was familiar with. *I could ask Corylus if there's any wood that is tougher—but if there were, that would be what he was carrying.*

"If we choose to leave, we will do so whether you and your servants wish that or not."

"Come into the house, young gentlemen," Lucinus said, giving Corylus an amused smile. "I sent my gardener and housekeeper home immediately when they arrived this morning, because my art had told me you were on your way. You will remain—or you at least will, Lord Varus—because of your sense of duty to Mankind, not due to any compulsion from me."

A half step behind Lucinus, Varus walked toward the house. Without trying to hide his cold disgust, he said, "If this is really Vergil's farm, then I'm distressed to see its present condition."

"My uncle lived and worked here for many years," Lucinus said calmly. "For the last eight of those years, I was his student and his assistant. I learned much, but no other human will ever be my uncle's equal in his true art."

On the veranda, two steps up from the bare yard, Lucinus turned to face his visitors. He said, "My uncle understood that things merely of this world are of little concern. He wrote his verse for eternity, but his true work was beyond time and space. I attempt to carry on his *true* art. I need your help now to do so, Your Lordship."

"Is it poverty which prevents you from maintaining the property?" Corylus said. He glanced toward Varus and added, "Because I'm sure there are wealthy men who would willingly contribute to the maintenance of an estate of such significance."

Gaius Alphenus Saxa among them, as Corylus knows, Varus thought. *Even without his son begging that he do so.*

"Money!" Lucinus snapped. "What do I need of money?"

He stalked into the villa's reception room—the upper hinge of the front door was wobbly, causing it to hang askew—and around the pool in its center. The basin was cracked and empty except for a slime that managed to survive on rainwater funneled through the opening in the roof. On the bottom was a mosaic picture, possibly of Triton and Thetis; the green shadow of algae was too thick for Varus to be sure.

Lucinus took an earthenware jug from a wall niche that was probably intended for a bust or wax mask of one of the owner's ancestors. He tipped it onto the floor; gold and silver coins spilled out. Or were they . . .

Varus squatted, completely forgetting about the reason he had visited Lucinus, and picked up a gold piece the size of his thumbnail. It was stamped with a man's head in relief, surrounded by writing. The script wasn't Greek or that of any language he was familiar with.

Lucinus smiled down at him and said, "I think that one's Carian, but it doesn't matter. I trade them as bullion for necessary supplies, and of course as rent to Charax for the use of his slaves."

Varus set the coin back on the pile and straightened. Many questions roiled in his mind, but he wasn't sure that asking any of them would bring him more wisdom than keeping silent would—so he kept silent.

"I do not have my uncle's skill in the art . . . ," Lucinus said. Varus thought he heard a hint of pride, though the older man seemed at pains to hide it. "Nevertheless, I have some skill. If gold could buy silent attendants, I would have them. But I cannot allow the details of my researches to become known to the wider world."

He shook his head and went on bitterly, "The common people—laymen, *all* laymen whatever their rank—would burn me and everything of mine! Though it's for their own benefit and for the survival of the world that I succeed."

"How did your uncle maintain the property?" Corylus said. "Since you claim he was a magician also."

"A magician?" Lucinus repeated. "Yes, but so far beyond what you mean by the word that you can't fathom the difference. My uncle could not buy trustworthy servants, so he *made* them. He built twelve automatons. Their bodies were silver, and quicksilver blood ran in their veins. They lived in a shed by day and worked the farm by night, and they vanished when he vanished."

He shrugged. "I do not have that power in the art. I live in three rooms here—"

He gestured, not to the habitable portion of the villa but to the doorway on the left. The ceiling beyond had collapsed. Broken timbers stuck up above the tiles, and a ground squirrel scampered from its hole and out of sight.

"—and let the rest go, as my uncle would have done if he had been in my circumstances."

Lucinus walked through to the garden in back of the building. The house was of an old design without an interior courtyard; old even in Vergil's day, Varus would have thought, though at this distance from Carce fashions probably didn't change as quickly as they did in the capital.

After a moment to adjust to the fact that there were no flowers, Varus saw that the garden was in better condition than any room of the house proper. The rows had been weeded, and the apple and peach trees flanking the vegetables were heavy with still unripened fruit.

Varus heard tapping behind him and turned. The goats looked down from the roof at him. Their jaws rotated sideways, which he found to be disconcerting.

Lucinus bent and picked up a clod from between a pair of bean vines climbing poles. The trenches between rows had been recently watered, but the soil of the mounds on which the beans were planted was dry and crumbled easily under his thumb.

Mumbling, *"Their eyes glow and their tongues lick the air like hissing fire,"* Lucinus tossed the dust into the air. For a moment the loose soil was a smear in the morning sunlight; then an image gripped Varus' mind and drew him into it. He felt his breath catch, but he was a disembodied viewpoint hovering above horror.

A familiar horror: he was looking down on the great crystal serpents that he had watched from the Sibyl's side. Now they gouged across the landscape like rivers in flood, devouring their banks and whatever was before them.

"These are the Worms of the Earth," said Lucinus' voice. *"They are Earth's revenge for the destruction of her children, the Titans. If they are released—"*

For an instant, Varus watched from the porch of the Temple of Jupiter

Best and Greatest in the center of Carce. People in the Forum below were foreshortened, moving dots rather than human beings, while beyond to the east spread the familiar thousands of houses and apartment blocks in which he and his fellow citizens lived.

"—*they will destroy life and the land on which life exists.*"

Filling the far horizon, red with the setting sun, advanced a wall of crystal. Houses and hills and the bedrock itself vanished into its blazing, jewel-like facade. People were too small to matter on such a scale, but Varus' mind echoed with screams that his ears could not hear, the deaths of thousands upon thousands, the deaths of all men and all things.

"*And a wizard named Melino, who was human when he went to the Otherworld but is human no more . . . ,*" continued the voice of Lucinus, "*will release the Worms, for he is mad and a demon.*"

The blazing crystalline maw swelled over Varus' viewpoint; then the vision shattered into blackness. Varus was in Vergil's garden again. The goats had vanished and Corylus, his face impassive, stood with his left hand flat against the trunk of the peach tree. The staff was in his right.

Lucinus gave Corylus a superior smile and said, "You're a soldier, aren't you, Master Corylus? How do you like the Great Art?"

"I intend to become a soldier," Corylus said. He didn't sound angry, but there was no give in his voice. "I didn't like what your magic showed me. How do we stop it, Lucinus?"

Varus had first thought his friend was supporting himself against the tree. Closer attention showed that his hand was caressing the bark lightly, as if it were the peach that needed comfort.

"You have no part in the matter, Master Corylus," Lucinus said. He sounded noticeably more polite than he had a moment before. "Your friend and I are students of the Art, are magicians, if you prefer. Between us, Lord Varus and I may be able to retrieve Zabulon's *Book* from where my uncle placed it when he found that his fate was near. With the *Book*, it may be that we will be able to prevent the release of the Worms."

Corylus gave the tree a last pat and straightened. "What precisely do you expect Varus to do?" he said in the same calm, humorless voice.

Lucinus turned to Varus to protest. Before Varus could tell him to answer the question, the older man's scowl cleared. He nodded to Varus, then faced Corylus.

"Zabulon was the first astrologer and the first master of the Great Art," he said. "He put his wisdom and his soul into a book, which he took with him to an island separate from this world and from the Otherworld. My uncle journeyed to Zabulon's Isle and took the *Book* from Zabulon."

"Zabulon is still alive?" Varus said. He had never heard the name before; he wondered if Pandareus had.

"Zabulon's body is not alive," Lucinus said, looking at him. "But Zabulon's *Book* lives. My uncle returned the *Book* to its owner's hands."

"You believe that you and Varus together can use the *Book* against . . . ," Corylus said. He turned his right palm up, as if looking for a word in his palm. "Can defeat the Worms with it?"

"I need the help of a second magician to reach Zabulon's Isle," Lucinus said. "I need the help of Lord Varus. Then perhaps I can use the *Book*—but more important, I can keep the *Book* away from Melino, who was my uncle's assistant before me. My uncle sent Melino to the Otherworld, but Melino betrayed him and stayed for a hundred years."

"Why?" said Varus. "Why did Melino stay?"

Varus had entered the Otherworld himself. It was not a place for those born in the Waking World; it was not a place for humans.

"He sought power," Lucinus said. "He sought a ring which holds a demon, and found it, but he became a demon himself. Now Melino has returned to release the Worms. If he gains Zabulon's *Book*, he will release them, and the Worms will destroy everything."

"You say Vergil was a great magician," Varus said, voicing the question he had turned in the silence of his mind until he was comfortable with the words. "He chose to return the *Book* to the place he had found it. Why should you reverse the decision of a greater magician? And why should I help you?"

"Because the world will end!" Lucinus snapped. "Isn't that enough?"

"Even so," Varus said calmly. "Your uncle was greater than you, and I believe he was wiser than you. Why should I act against the decision of Vergil, whose pen case I am not worthy even to carry?"

Corylus smiled. Lucinus must have seen the expression—and understood it—because he immediately calmed.

"My uncle was great beyond your knowledge, and wise beyond you or perhaps any man," Lucinus said. "When he felt his fate near, he planned to rejuvenate himself. So that no one could steal the *Book* while he was weakened, he returned it to Zabulon's Isle. He planned to retrieve it when he was young and strong again. But—"

Lucinus shrugged.

"—something went wrong with his spell. He vanished, and his works vanished. And now it is up to lesser students like myself and you to save the world, because my uncle cannot."

Corylus looked at Varus. Varus nodded. This had to be his decision.

"My friend and I will discuss the matter," Varus said, "and perhaps discuss it with others whose wisdom may be greater than ours."

"There is very little time," Lucinus said. He whispered the words. "I don't know how much, but not long."

Varus gave the older man a smile not dissimilar to the expression on Corylus' face when Lucinus had raised his voice a moment before. He said, "We will arrive at a decision. If it involves you, we will inform you. Good day, Master Lucinus."

Corylus gestured Varus ahead, toward the door and the cart waiting beyond. That probably wasn't necessary, but it was simple courtesy to accept physical protection from a man as skilled as Corylus.

It was very good to have friends.

ALPHENA WAS MAKING a real effort to be ladylike, but she refused to have the curtains drawn on the way to Bersinus' party. There wasn't a great deal to be seen in a litter sliding through the streets of Puteoli at night, but she felt less confined with the sides open.

She smiled in a mixture of amusement and self-mockery. Since she was wearing a long dinner dress of silk even thinner than the gauze side curtains, she couldn't do anything but walk away in a dignified manner if some disaster beset the vehicle anyway. The fabric was so strong that she couldn't tear the skirt off with her bare hands. Though . . . she supposed she could whip the dress over her head and flee in bandeau and panties.

The thought made Alphena giggle. She wished Hedia was with her so that she could watch the older woman's face go as stiff as a smiling marble statue when her daughter explained why she was laughing.

Attendants shouted in the near distance, alerting Bersinus' servants that the wife and daughter of Senator Gaius Alphenus Saxa had arrived—and probably boasting a little as well, like gladiators greeting one another in the arena before a match. The litter rocked awkwardly as one of the four bearers lost the pace when they slowed to avoid running up the back of Hedia's vehicle.

Mother would have him flogged, Alphena thought, but on consideration she realized that Hedia wouldn't resort to physical punishment. Instead she would have the bearer transferred, probably to farm labor, and demote the lead man on the team, who had failed in his duty to properly train his subordinates.

Alphena had flown into rages when something went wrong, and often enough when *nothing* went wrong. Hedia was quieter, colder, and altogether more effective. Alphena was learning a great deal from her mother now that she had started watching events instead of simply blazing into a fury at them.

Alphena wouldn't discipline anyone this time. She would note the incident quietly to the bearer and the foreman. If it happened again . . . well, she would do something.

Maybe I'll go back to walking in sturdy sandals, but as an eccentric noblewoman rather than as a tomboy. Alphena suppressed her giggle, because the litter had stopped and settled onto the ground on its four feet.

Alphena swung her legs out and stood before the servants, her own or the host's, tried to help. She was glad to have done it gracefully this time. Through practice she was getting much better at entering and leaving a vehicle. *It's one of those tasks which a lady has to learn,* as Hedia would say.

The first litter had stopped just ahead of Alphena's. Mother had gotten out of it and was embracing a man in his late twenties who wore a scarlet tunic trimmed with cloth of gold. Though he took a great deal of trouble with his appearance, he looked soft. Alphena was accustomed to judging gladiators.

"Bersinus darling, it's so good to see you again," Hedia said, disengaging herself. "Why don't you introduce my daughter Alphena to the company?"

Hedia gestured, the motion as graceful as a wave rippling up the sand. Alphena stepped forward, suddenly unsure of herself. *I'd rather be facing a demon. Again.*

Five well-dressed men and a woman of at least thirty—the only other woman present—stood in an arc close behind Bersinus. He said, "Delighted to do anything you ask, my dearest Hedia. Lady Alphena—"

For the first time, their host actually looked at Alphena instead of being aware of her only as another figure in the entourage of the ravishing Hedia. *Which Mother is, which she certainly is. . . .*

Though when maids under Hedia's careful direction had held mirrors so that Alphena could view herself, she'd been rather pleased. *Very* pleased, though she could scarcely admit that even to herself.

Her silk dinner gown was a chestnut so dark that it looked black under most lights but was, Hedia told her firmly, exactly the color of Alphena's hair. It was tailored more closely than was usual for a dinner dress, a *synthesis*, in order to emphasize her figure in a good way. Hedia said that a looser garment would make Alphena look fat rather than trimly muscular, and that some men liked muscular.

Gold threads in the fabric gave it a luster that wasn't really a color but—again according to Hedia—perfectly complemented Alphena's gilded sandals, her earrings of gold filigree, and her half cape of cloth of gold. Finally her hair, which had required an hour for three specialists to coil, was pinned with tortoiseshell combs whose engravings were gold filled.

In any other company, Alphena honestly believed she would stand out. And even standing beside her mother, Alphena seemed to be worth their host's attention once she actually came to his notice.

"This is my wife Olivia," Bersinus said, gesturing to the woman. Olivia would probably have been a frump in most gatherings, but she was doubly unfortunate in this one. Her sour look suggested that she was aware of the fact.

"—and my brother-in-law Olivius Macer. The family has large holdings around Capua, as you may know."

Alphena eyed Macer. While his older sister looked frumpy, he had the coarse athleticism of a feral hog.

If the Olivius family were landowners, it explained the marriage. Florina had gathered information on Bersinus as her mistress had ordered. According to Florina, he was the son of a freedman who had made his considerable wealth as a building contractor. Olivia was socially a step upward even if her younger husband didn't need the dowry.

"Next is Sextus Scribonius Lantinus, who's staying in his family's house on the Bay this summer—," Bersinus said, gesturing to a languid youth closer to Alphena's age than to Hedia's twenty-three years.

"My father is Scribonius Murena, of course," the youth said with a carelessly affected gesture. "Senator Murena, that is."

"—and his friend Kurnos."

From the look Kurnos gave her, Alphena was pretty sure that the young Greek was at least as interested in women as he was in his employer. The only use *she* could imagine for the fellow was as a fencing target.

Alphena smiled: *he's eminently suited for that.* Kurnos misunderstood and smirked back at her.

"Marcus Vipsanius Castor"—a portly man nodded; at fifty he was by far the oldest guest present—"has the house beside ours here," Bersinus said. "I invited him tonight to, ah . . . I invited him tonight."

Castor smiled with amusement. "I'm in grain, my dear," he said. "I believe my friend Bersinus thought it would be as well to have the older generation represented tonight. At any rate, I was pleased to accept his invitation to meet the noble Hedia and her daughter . . . who is even more charming than I expected."

Though Castor was Egyptian by appearance and a freedman from his name, he seemed cultured and obviously had a very sharp mind. He had understood that this was to be a decorous party and that he was being invited because he was a safe guest even as the evening and the flow of wine proceeded. The fact amused rather than offending him.

"And Master Melino," Bersinus said, indicating the final guest. "He's a clever young Briton whose acquaintance I've made recently. I thought he would be an interesting companion."

Melino had been staring at Hedia—scarcely a surprise there, Alphena thought bitterly—but he immediately turned his attention to her and smiled engagingly. "I'm very glad to meet you both," he said in perfect Latin, bowing. "And yes, I'm British by birth, but it's been a long time since I've seen my soggy birthplace. At present I've rented a house in Puteoli to continue my researches."

Melino wore a white tunic under a blue dinner wrap. The garments weren't flashy, but Alphena could see that they were of the highest quality. He wasn't Castor's companion as she had first assumed; it was merely coincidence that they were two unattached men who were standing together.

What Melino *was* remained a question. Alphena felt a *prickling* in his presence. That wasn't a warning, precisely, but based on her recent experience it implied magic was at work or had been at work not long before.

Melino returned his attention to Hedia, or—

Yes, he's looking at Mother's diadem. The diadem I gave her.

"Nine, like the Muses," Lantinus said. He half-closed his eyelids, but Alphena could see that he was checking to be sure that everyone was watching him. "I'm something of a poet myself you know, though I fear that my work is too rarified for the common crowd."

"I'm so in awe of you poets, Lord Lantinus," Hedia said, sounding both soulful and sincere. *If I didn't know Mother any better than Lantinus does, I'd believe she was both those things.* "Poetry goes right over my head. Would you believe, it puts me to sleep? My poor dim mind is *such* an embarrassment in learned company."

Because Alphena *did* know her mother, she knew that what Hedia was saying was neither soulful nor sincere. But Alphena also knew that now they wouldn't be bored at dinner by the volume of verse that the young aesthete happened to have along with him.

"I believe we're ready to go in now," Bersinus said. "On such a lovely night, I've instructed my steward to serve us in the outdoor dining nook."

He turned to Hedia and placed his hands on his hips as he looked her up and down. She was certainly worth the stares that everyone, including the envious Olivia, directed at her.

Hedia had asked Alphena to join her as she chose the outfit to go with the scintillant diadem. "So that you'll have an idea about how I go about it, dear," Hedia had said. She didn't add, "Since at present you have no more fashion sense than a blind mole does," but she didn't have to. Alphena could supply those words herself.

What Hedia settled on was three layers of silk, each of which was almost transparently white, worn with a white shoulder cape that was marginally thicker, and a white sash. The only color in the ensemble was that provided by the irregular stone in the diadem flickering through numberless blue-tinged hues.

Hedia had decided to go without underwear tonight. Alphena blushed to remember that.

"My dear," Bersinus said, "you're a vision of virginal loveliness."

Olivius Macer guffawed. "Well . . . ," he said, looking at Bersinus but speaking loudly enough for the whole gathering to hear him clearly. "Maybe her left ear's still virginal, eh, what?"

There was a moment of stillness, freezing all the guests where they stood. Hedia alone moved, turning her pleasant smile toward their host. "Bersinus," she said, "I'm afraid that Macer has already had too much to drink. You'll have to limit him to water for the remainder of the evening, I expect."

Bersinus hadn't moved till Hedia spoke, but his face was already deep red with fury. "I'm very sorry, gentlefolk," he said in a wheezingly controlled voice. "My brother-in-law has decided not to join us after all, so we'll be eight for dinner."

"Say, wait a minute!" Macer said, coloring also. "All right, I was a little out of—"

"Macer, you idiot!" Bersinus shouted. "Get out of here or I'll have my footmen beat you out! *And* you'll find that every one of your mortgages has been called. *Do* you understand me?"

"Julius, you're talking to my brother!" Olivia said sharply. "And he didn't say anything that we both haven't heard—"

Bersinus turned on her in a white rage. "Listen, you dozy cow!" he said, leaning forward to shout in his wife's face. "Since you're clearly ignorant of proper dining etiquette, perhaps you'd better eat in your room. Or with the slaves in the kitchen! Is that what you want? *Is it?*"

Castor and three sturdy-looking servants—they were apparently his own attendants—were easing Macer, who wore a stunned expression, toward his sedan chair a distance down the street. The Egyptian was whispering urgently into Macer's ear. Alphena heard the word, "Saxa," and realized he was warning his former fellow guest of the consequences of making an enemy of the richest man in the Senate.

Alphena nodded with approval. The good opinion she had already formed of Castor was being reinforced.

Olivia, suddenly aware of what *she* had done, retreated from her husband openmouthed. To Alphena's amazement, Hedia stepped between Bersinus and his wife and took Olivia's hands in her own.

"I'm so sorry, dear," Hedia said in a clear, cool voice. "This is really all my fault, and I know how embarrassing it must be to you. Will you accept my apologies?"

Olivia nodded, gulped, and began bawling. She threw herself into Hedia's arms; Hedia began patting her gently on the back.

Bersinus cleared his throat. "Ah . . . ," he said. "As I was saying, I think we can start dinner now. Ah, Lady Hedia and my wife will join us shortly, I'm sure."

He started up the path to the house. Castor bowed and gestured Alphena to follow their host; she obeyed.

Kurnos had the expression of a spectator watching the slave dressed as Charon finish off mortally wounded gladiators in the arena, but his master gaped at the women.

I wonder if you'll write an epic about this? Alphena thought. It was probably too real for Lantinus, though.

Melino was staring at Hedia again. Alphena couldn't begin to read the emotion below the surface of the youth's face, but *something* was there.

HEDIA TOOK ANOTHER SIP of wine as servants carried away the remains of the platter of lampreys. The fish had been filleted before each strip was rolled around a caper and fricasseed.

"Our host told me that jellied eels are a British dish, as a special treat for me," murmured Melino from the bottom of the cross couch, kitty-corner to Hedia at the top of the right-hand couch. "Personally, I remember mostly boiled pork, but that was a long time ago. How did it strike you?"

It hadn't been a wholly successful experiment, in Hedia's opinion. She would try anything once; but in addition to her being careful of her figure, there was nothing in the texture or in the sauce of sage and parsley to urge her to have another medallion.

"I'll want to think about it for some time before I make a decision," Hedia said. She made a point of never insulting another household's cooking; not that it seemed likely that Bersinus, on the other side of the table from her and enmeshed by Lantinus in a literary lecture, would hear or care if he did. "You say 'a long time ago,' my dear, but surely not *that* long, given your youth?"

"Well, it certainly seems long ago," said Melino. He laughed, but there was a note of more than light humor to the sound, an unintended undertone, Hedia thought. "Sometimes it seems more than a hundred years since I left my home to study with masters in the greater world. And here—"

He chuckled again, this time without additional significance.

"—I have met the most charming woman in the world. Clearly I made the correct decision, and every man at this table would agree with me."

It was Hedia's turn to smile. Her lips gave a cynical twist to the expression, but she wasn't really displeased. She never minded flattery, and being flattered by a very handsome, cultured young man was piquant in itself.

"I'm afraid that the fog and drizzles you were born in have rusted your critical faculties, young man," she said, but the way she looked at him as she spoke deliberately undercut the words.

Sometimes Hedia thought she saw flames leaping in Melino's eyes. She was probably seeing the reflection of the lamps on stands around the alcove . . . but he was certainly interesting.

Melino had given Hedia all his attention during the meal, which was common enough when she was in mixed company. Under normal circumstances it would have been impolitic for a junior guest who had the host's wife on his other side (though it might well have happened), but tonight it didn't matter.

Olivia could have been replaced by a wooden statue without making a difference in the meal. She said little and ate less, though she drained two cups of wine for every one that her husband drank.

Bersinus had originally placed Melino at the bottom of the left-hand couch. When Macer decided not to come to dinner after all—Hedia smiled—Melino had asked to take the empty place at the cross couch next to Hedia. Neither she nor Bersinus had seen any reason not to grant the request.

She sipped her wine. It would have meant nothing to say that *she* drank less at dinner than Olivia did. Hedia always kept a clear head during the early stages of a dinner party. After the lamps had been allowed to dim and the guests who remained were drinking unmixed wine, well, whim and circumstance would determine her actions.

Tonight, however, she was present as Alphena's mother rather than as Lady Hedia. Alphena's mother would remain sober and watchful, whereas Lady Hedia knew how to have a good time.

Servants were bringing in the dessert trays. The fruits were in fanciful shapes—a dog's head carved from an apple with pomegranate eyes and a gullet lined with individual blackberry cells was particularly striking—and the nutshells would probably turn out to be sweet pastry or the like, but it was a relatively restrained offering. Hedia would content herself with a walnut or two.

"I've been noticing the stone in your tiara," Melino said. "It's quite unusual."

His conversation during the evening had been false, but no more false than banter between two strangers at dinner always was, two interesting, interested strangers. His tone had changed now, however.

"Is it?" Hedia said idly. *I counterfeit disinterest much better than he does.* She took a pistachio from the pannier of a camel formed from date flour. "Yes, I suppose it is, now that you mention it."

"I was wondering where you got the piece, if you don't mind my asking?" Melino said. The strain in his voice was even more obvious to an ear as well attuned to such things as Hedia's was.

She tinkled a laugh. What looked like a pistachio was actually made half from crushed hazelnuts and half from crushed walnuts, held together by a thin coating of crystallized honey.

"Really, dear boy," Hedia said. "Does anyone remember those things? I suppose it was a gift from someone, but I wouldn't choose to name names even if I could."

She swallowed the nut, then cocked her head to meet Melino's eyes. "Have you seen these stones before, then? Where do they come from?"

Melino tapped his tongue to his dry lips. The fingers of his right hand were twisting the striking ruby ring on his left.

"I haven't exactly seen pieces of this sort, no," he said carefully. "But I've heard of such stones. That's why I was wondering where you got it?"

"Oh, don't be boring," Hedia said, taking another sip of wine. Melino probably thought she was looking into her cup, but she could still watch him from the corner of her eye.

Though the young Briton had a delightful little accent, her interest in him had gone far beyond personal. *He knows something, which means he may know something we need to learn.*

There would usually be entertainment at this point in the evening. Hedia had heard of learned gatherings at which each guest would read a sample of his own verse . . . which was probably pretty deadly, since being learned and being a poet were very different things. Not that it mattered, since nobody was going to invite Hedia to such a party anyway.

At the other end of the spectrum of propriety were parties in which the guests provided their own entertainment in non-literary sorts of ways. Bersinus sometimes hosted that sort of party while his wife was at one of their country estates. Macer had been present at those; apparently he hadn't believed that his brother-in-law really meant that decorum would reign this time.

"I wonder, Lady Hedia . . . ," Melino said, his voice dropping again. "Hedia. I wonder if you would visit me tomorrow? At my home. I have some important matters to discuss with you, and I think that it's better that we keep them between ourselves."

Hedia laughed again. *He sounds so* earnest. Aloud she said, "You're a very cheeky boy, you know."

Melino looked away with an agonized expression. *My goodness, I think he's blushing!*

The servants had cleared the dessert trays and were bringing finger bowls and napkins around. Hedia dabbled her fingertips and wiped them. She and Alphena would each have a cup of unmixed wine before they left if nothing formal was planned, but from their host's air of anticipation . . .

"My honored guests!" Bersinus said. He had chosen his moment when Lantinus was taking a drink of wine. That seemed to be the only time the young man stopped talking.

"Time for me to pay for my dinner, it seems," Melino murmured. He got up from his couch, still holding his wine cup.

"Tonight I have something rather special to show you," Bersinus said. "At least if Master Melino is the wonder he claims to be."

Servants snuffed two of the three wicks in each of the lamps. It didn't really reduce the light significantly, but it changed the *tone* of the gathering. Hedia felt a thrill of anticipation.

Melino walked around the right-hand couch and stood in front of the little serving table in the center. He still held his wine cup.

"I do not claim to be a wonder," he said, surveying the other guests. He had become a different person: confident, even powerful. "But it may be that I will show you wonders tonight."

Melino smiled. Hedia imagined another hint of flames in his eyes, and his ring caught the lamplight oddly, vividly.

Melino poured the dregs of his wine onto the table. It was a terrazzo of agate chips, so highly polished that the liquid was barely a ripple against the stone.

A servant had followed him, holding a staff of black wood ready. Melino was mumbling under his breath. He dropped the cup to the pavement, not so much carelessly as because he was unaware of its presence in his hand. He took the staff.

Using his right forearm to support the heavy staff, Melino tapped the tip deliberately on the tabletop: once, twice, and a third time. He spoke at increasing volume, but Hedia still could not hear the words because of the rushing noise that filled the night.

Vaguely she saw that some of the guests were restive, looking at the sky for signs of an oncoming storm. The stars were bright and the lamp flames rose still and clear into the air. Melino's ring was a rosy lantern.

The dribble of wine swelled into a sphere of bright sunlight. On a barren landscape danced three women. They were short but not dwarfs, dark but not so dark as the purple-black Nubians whom the beast hunters sometimes brought from deep in Africa along with the animals. The women chanted as they shuffled their circular dance, but no words could be heard through the window Melino had opened.

The dancers were nude except for loose belts of jewels like the one in Hedia's diadem. The stones were strung on coarse twine. As they jiggled with the dancers' movements, iridescent light shimmered within them.

"Bravo!" Bersinus shouted, the word dimly audible over the unfelt wind. Castor, below him on the couch, wore a guarded—almost fearful—expression. Either the Egyptian knew something or he was more cautious about what he *didn't* know than his host was.

Something glowed in the midst of the dancers. It was so bright that the edges were foggy but so distant that it couldn't possibly be in the same plane as the dancers . . . but where were the dancers? Were they even real?

Slowly the scene dimmed to transparency. As Hedia started to let out her breath—she hadn't been aware that she was holding it—there was a final iridescent flash from the empty air. She gasped.

Melino wobbled and leaned against his staff. Bersinus got up from his couch and hugged the younger man close.

"Bravo!" Bersinus repeated. "Master Melino, forgive me for doubting you! I can't imagine how you accomplished that trick!"

Because it wasn't a trick, Hedia thought. *Because it was real magic.*

Melino made his way back to the couch, using his staff like an old man. He more slumped than reclined beside Hedia again. He looked as though he had been dragged behind horses.

The other guests cheered and babbled. The only exception was Kurnos, who glowered at the magician: a youth of his own age who had become the center of all attention—particularly the attention of Alphena. Melino nodded with a fixed smile, acknowledging the praise as best his exhaustion allowed.

Hedia leaned toward him. "Master Melino," she said. "I'll take you up on the invitation to visit you tomorrow."

CHAPTER V

O pen for the noble Gaius Alphenus Varus and his sister!" bellowed the leading member of their escort.

The staff based in Carce would probably have announced Alphena's name first, let alone passing her over as an adjunct to her brother. Varus winced, but Alphena didn't react with the violence he expected. She seemed . . . well, in another person he would have described her mood as one of nervousness.

Alphena noticed him looking at her and said, "I've never been to Corylus' house here in Puteoli. To his father's house, I mean."

Varus shrugged. "Neither have I," he said. He consciously smoothed the frown from his forehead, but he couldn't imagine what his sister was concerned about.

Instead of a small window, the upper third of the street door was already hinged back. The doorman was grizzled and missing half his right hand.

Not a very prepossessing fellow to have greeting your guests, Varus thought. Then he noticed the many other scars wherever the doorman's skin was exposed and realized the truth: The doorman wasn't an impressive slave in the normal fashion. He was a freeman, an army veteran, and almost certainly a man who had served under Publius Cispius in past years.

It was a matter of who you were trying to impress. It said a great deal about Cispius, but nothing that Varus couldn't have deduced from knowing Cispius' son.

The doorman swung the bottom portion of the door open and

braced to attention. "Bathylla!" he roared down the passage. "The young master's guests are here!"

A maid stuck her head out of a room. Before she could act, Corylus himself appeared at the end of the fifty-foot corridor and waved.

"Come on through, Gaius, Alphena," he called. "Pandareus and I are in the garden. Bathylla, take their escort to the outside dining room and give them something to eat. Ah—that is, how many servants do you have along?"

Varus grimaced. "Ten, I think."

"Twelve," Alphena said. "Mother said that if we came by ourselves we'd insult your house as well as *our* house."

"Twelve we can handle," Corylus said, grinning. "And trust Lady Hedia to know what propriety requires. I wouldn't want to lower our standing in the neighborhood."

"Nobody around here is going to make a crack about the Old Man," said the doorman as Varus started down the corridor. "Isn't that right, Pulto?"

Corylus' servant was standing behind him. He nodded and said, "Not unless they want to try digesting their teeth."

"Pulto, go have a drink with them and keep Dad's people from playing who's got the biggest dick," Corylus said. "Make sure everybody accepts that they're all mighty heroes, but anybody who tries to prove it will find himself wearing leg irons while he hoes a field, all right? Ah—"

He looked at Varus and Alphena with sudden concern. "That is," he said, "with your permission?"

"Yes, of course," Alphena said. Apparently realizing that Varus had been lost by the discussion, she said, "Our escorts think they're tough. Most of the servants here are veterans, I suppose?"

"Right," said Corylus, lifting his chin in agreement. "And they think they're tough too. Which of course they are."

He gestured his guests into a larger garden than Varus had expected. Marble benches were arranged in a U in the shade of the apple tree in a corner, but most of the space was given over to flowers. It was a working garden for a perfumer, not just a place to relax.

Pandareus had risen from the bench where he had been seated. He nodded to Varus, his student, with a smile, and made a slight bow to Alphena.

"You could have come to our house, Master Pandareus," Varus said. "In fact, I expected that you would. Though of course I don't doubt that Master Cispius has provided you with excellent accommodations."

He sounded sharper than he had meant to be. Corylus looked surprised, then contrite; even Alphena gave her brother a frown of concern.

"I chose to come to Master Cispius' house though the summons came from you, Lady Alphena . . . ," Pandareus said with another bow. "Because I was sure that I would be admitted to the smaller establishment and that it would be possible to send a messenger from here to Lord Saxa's dwelling. If I did wrong, I apologize, Lord Varus."

I've acted like a fool, Varus thought. The staff here in Puteoli might well have turned away a poor scholar—a beggar, they would have thought—who showed up at the door.

"I've acted like a fool," Varus said. He bowed deeply to Pandareus, then bowed again to Corylus. "I apologize."

He looked at his sister. "Alphena," he said, "if I've stupidly insulted you also, I apologize. I—"

Varus looked around the group and forced himself to smile. "Like the rest of us," he said, "I've been concerned about recent events. Apparently I've been looking for things of human scale to direct my anger and frustration toward. Fortunately, I've had an excellent education—"

He grinned at Pandareus.

"—and therefore realize that the time to correct a mistake is as quickly as possible."

"Let's sit down," said Corylus with a lopsided smile. "Gaius, I won't tell you that nobody felt insulted, because that's already obvious."

A gnarled servant had placed cushions on the stone benches. A pair of maids—of similar age and murmuring to each other in German— were waiting with wicker tables on which wine, water, and cups already rested. As soon as the young master and his guests had settled themselves, the women began mixing and pouring the wine.

Varus grinned at his teacher. "Master," he said, "I began to relax as soon as I saw you. As Publius will have told you—"

Corylus bobbed in agreement.

"—I had another vision. I don't know what to do."

Pandareus chuckled. He took a sip of wine before he said, "Since this business appears to be magical, then I must admit that I'm puzzled at the logic of a scholar who is a magician looking to a scholar who most certainly is *not* a magician for a solution."

"Gaius is right," Corylus said quietly. "Master, you bring stability to the situation. To any situation."

The servants had retreated to the portico along the back of the house proper. They might be able to overhear the discussion if they wanted to, but there was no indication that they did.

That was particularly true of Pulto. If demons attacked the garden, Pulto would fight demons as enthusiastically as he would Sarmatians, Germans, or the drunken next-door neighbor. Pulto preferred to know as little as possible about magic, however.

"I think that's a way of saying," Pandareus said with the hint of a smile, "that I'm an old man and have little fear of death."

He glanced around the gathering and smiled more broadly. "In fact, life wasn't particularly dear to me when I was younger, either. It isn't life but the opportunity to learn new things that delights me, and—"

The old man was beaming like a child offered an unexpected treat.

"—recent events have certainly brought me that. Including magic, which a few months ago I would have said was as fanciful as the existence of gryphons."

He cocked his head slightly and looked at Varus. "Eh, Lord Varus?"

Varus lowered his eyes in embarrassment. "It wasn't my gryphon," he muttered. "It was Alphena's."

Corylus began to laugh. After a moment, Varus did also.

Alphena put on a stern expression. As though she were Hedia, she said, "The gryphon was a he, not an it; and he was not my property or anybody's. I hope he's all right."

In a different, wistful voice she added, "He was a good friend. To both of us."

She glanced at Varus. He lifted his chin in agreement, remembering a place and a thing that were both out of nightmare. If he wanted to, he could almost fool himself into believing that many recent events were fragments of remembered dreams. Bad dreams.

"It appears to me . . . ," Pandareus said, setting his cup back on the serving table. "That we don't have enough information to determine a course of action. I will certainly search libraries in Carce for references to the lizardmen."

"The Singiri," Varus said. "The Sibyl called them that. In my vision."

Pandareus bobbed agreement. "The Singiri, then," he said. "But a better source of information is the magician Lucinus, who called himself to your attention, my scholars. It seems to me that you must discuss matters further with him, since he at least knows more about the situation than any of us do."

"I met a magician last night," Alphena said in a small voice. "Or anyway, Mother did. I think . . ."

She was wrestling with a phrase or perhaps even a thought.

"He seemed to like her," she said, bringing out the words at last. "Melino did."

"Melino is a magician?" Corylus asked calmly. Varus' mind was turning over the warning Lucinus had given them, that a magician named Melino was trying to loose the Worms of the Earth and thereby to destroy all life.

"He could be a clever trickster," Alphena said. "I don't think so. It's not just that his trick, the scene he showed us, was so real. . . ."

She raised her head. When she realized that her companions were staring at her, her expression hardened with embarrassment, but she didn't look away.

"I can feel magic," she said. "I felt it last night. I felt it when I met Melino."

"Lucinus said that a magician named Melino had been Vergil's assistant before he, Lucinus, was," Varus said. "Melino betrayed Vergil and stayed in the Otherworld for a hundred years. When he returned, he had become a demon."

"Oh, that can't be the same," Alphena said in obvious relief. "This Melino is a young man. Not much older than I am, in fact. Certainly younger than Mother!"

"That would not be unprecedented if one were to believe stories about men who have entered the Otherworld," Pandareus said carefully. "Time supposedly proceeds differently there."

He coughed and added, "That requires as a prerequisite that one believe in the Otherworld, of course. Which I personally am more willing to do since I appeared to enter the Otherworld than would have been the case earlier."

Varus pursed his lips. Corylus looked at him, then said to the group,

"I think Gaius and I need to visit Lucinus again. And the sooner the better."

"Yes," said Varus, getting to his feet. "Publius? Can we leave at once?"

"We can leave as soon as I borrow the mule cart again," Corylus said, rising also. "The factory's only two streets over, so that won't take very long."

"Sister, please take the entire escort back," Varus said, covering the last practical question. "And assure Mother that I'm in the care of Publius Corylus, who will keep me as safe as one can be in this doubtful world."

The others were standing also. Alphena turned to Pandareus and said, "Master Pandareus? Before I leave, might I ask you about a private matter?"

"Of course," Pandareus said. "We can stay here—that is . . . ?"

"Yes, of course," Corylus said. He started for the gate in the back wall rather than the street in front of the house. "Come along then, Gaius. And we'll find you a proper broad-brimmed hat so that you won't look quite so much out of place if we meet anybody on the road."

Varus followed without comment. He wondered what his sister needed to discuss with Pandareus . . . but there were more important questions before him just now.

ALPHENA SAT DOWN, wondering how to start. She reached for her wine cup, realized that it was empty—and noticed that the maids began gabbling to one another in consternation.

They'd started to clear the wine when they thought we were leaving. Now Pandareus and I have sat down again and they're wondering if they ought to refill my cup.

We're not here to drink.

"You may wait," Alphena said to the maids. *They do understand Latin, don't they?* "We'll let you know if we need anything further."

The women subsided onto the portico. Alphena took a deep breath. Pandareus was watching her with a smile.

"Ah, master?" she said, wondering how she was supposed to address this man who wasn't *her* teacher but whom her brother and Corylus greatly respected. "You're amused?"

"You were observant, which I would expect of the sister of Lord

Varus," the teacher said. "And you were thoughtful of a stranger's servants, which surprises me in a person of your rank in society. You were remarkably thoughtful, in fact."

Alphena looked at her hands and coughed to clear her throat. "I've been trying to behave better," she said. "Mother has been, well, explaining things. Even behaving better to servants."

She looked up and tried to smile at Pandareus. "I'm mostly around servants, after all."

"Lady Hedia is very wise," Pandareus said, bobbing his chin. "My conversations with her are always illuminating. But you had matters to discuss, Lady Alphena?"

Alphena pressed her fingertips tightly together, then folded her hands neatly in her lap. "I've been dreaming of three women dancing around an egg that hangs in the air," she said. "Last night Melino showed us—the whole dinner party—a vision of those women and the egg. I hadn't said anything about the dream to anyone. Not anyone!"

"What sort of an egg?" Pandareus asked in a quietly interested tone, much like the tone of all his other questions. Alphena realized that the teacher had been merely stating the truth when he said that he lived to learn new things.

She forced herself to breathe deeply, getting her emotions under control. *I'd be useless in a sword fight if I got into this state!* The thought made her smile, which calmed her where concentration had failed.

"I don't think it can have been a real egg because it's too big," Alphena said. "It was the size of your head—but egg shaped, I mean. And it was all colors. But I found a tiara for Mother, for Lady Hedia, with a stone that was the same color and changed the same ways, and the dancing women were wearing belts of stones like that strung on twine. And—"

Pandareus watched silently. His gaze didn't imply a threat the way similar close attention by most people—certainly by most men—would have done.

"I thought about the tiara," Alphena said, simply letting the words out to stand or fall on their own. "And the jewel in it could be a bit of cracked eggshell. And I know, it's all colors and it's too hard to scratch with a diamond, but it *looks* like shell. And—"

Blurting it, saying the thing she had said only to Hedia.

"—the dream makes me afraid and the jewel makes me afraid and there isn't any reason why they should."

"If I may correct you," Pandareus said, "as I would correct one of my students . . . ?"

He raised an eyebrow. *He really means it as a question.*

"Yes," Alphena said. "Treat me the way you treat my brother. If my brother had become very ignorant, I mean."

Pandareus smiled too slightly to be noticed by anyone less used than Alphena to reading the tiny cues on a gladiator's face. "Rather than say simply, 'There's no reason to be afraid,'" he said, "I would say that we don't yet know why you are afraid of the Egg. I have seen enough examples of your good judgment, Your Ladyship, to dispose me to assume that you're right this time too."

"Oh," said Alphena. *That means I'm right to be afraid, which should bother me. But I really knew I was right, so I'm just relieved that he believes me.*

"Tell me about this large egg," Pandareus said. "Is it in a framework of some sort? Perhaps suspended in a cage?"

"No," Alphena said, dipping her chin. "It just hung there, all moving colors with nothing else around it."

"I ask," said the teacher, "because the Etruscans used to hang the eggs of ostriches in their tombs, held in metal frames. They thought they were gryphon eggs and that the gryphon would carry the soul of the deceased to his eternal rest. We know better, of course."

"I've seen ostriches in the arena," Alphena said, thinking about a matter that she hadn't given much attention to until now. "And I've seen the eggs. Father served one to his guests one night, himself and his eight guests altogether, and I saw the shell. That could be right!"

She pursed her lips. "But the ostrich egg was just cream colored and rough. It can't be what I saw in the vision. It can't be what the diadem came from, either."

"I understand," Pandareus said in a tone that implied to Alphena that he understood a great deal more than she did. "I mention the practice of hanging eggs in tombs because recently an Etruscan landowner named Aulus Collinus Ceutus asked me to edit the letters of an ancestor who was a near contemporary of Scipio the Younger."

Either Alphena looked blank or Pandareus knew that she must *feel* blank, because he smiled faintly and added, "A hundred and fifty years ago, give or take. I looked at the letters and declined the task."

Alphena swallowed the protest that she would have shouted a few months ago. Because she was a girl, she hadn't been taught history and literature; she *couldn't* be blamed for not knowing who Scipio the Younger was.

On the other hand, Pandareus hadn't blamed her. He had just made sure that she understood what he was saying. And though Alphena would have had to fight to get the kind of education her brother had as the right of his gender, she *had* fought to learn swordsmanship. The other would have been open to her if she'd cared.

"Go on, master," she said primly. She didn't ask why Pandareus had turned down the job; he would tell her if he thought it mattered.

"The period was one of great importance—to Carce and to Greece, which joined the Republic in a junior capacity at the time," Pandareus said. Even Alphena could hear the delicate humor with which he described the way Carce's legions had conquered the Greek world from which he sprang.

"Unfortunately," he continued, "the ancestral Collinus, Sextus, was wholly concerned with his opinions on the literature of his day. There's room to differ on the merits of Pacuvius, but no room, I think, to find Collinus' opinions on Pacuvius to be anything but deadly dull."

"But they'd have paid you, wouldn't they?" Alphena said in puzzlement.

"Yes, Your Ladyship," Pandareus said. "And the public executioner is paid also, I'm sure. Given a choice, I would prefer to avoid starving by executing my fellow men to mixing my love of literature into Collinus' prose. The man had neither intelligence nor discernment."

Alphena had grown up believing that human beings outside her family—Saxa was possibly the richest man in the Senate—would do anything for money. She had already seen this wasn't true: certainly Publius Corylus couldn't be paid enough to make him do something that was against his principles.

On the other hand, Corylus was in comfortable circumstances already. Hearing Pandareus, who was poor by the standards of Cispius' free servants, bluntly dismiss money was a shock.

She bobbed agreement. "Go on," she repeated.

"Most of the documents were copies of letters, as I said," Pandareus said, "transcribed by a skilled copyist. They were on papyrus of good quality, as you would expect. I suspect Collinus intended to publish the letters himself, but he died before he did so. I do not believe that posterity lost a great deal."

A faint smile touched his lips. It vanished as he continued, "There was also a notebook made of waxed boards. The notebook was old enough that the thongs binding the boards together had rotted away, so the notebook was quite old. It would be pure conjecture to say that it was written by Sextus Collinus like the letters, however. I didn't think I'd be able to read something so old written on wax, but the bottom of the chest in which the documents had been stored was damp. That was bad for the lower margins of the papyrus scrolls, but very good for wax on elm boards."

This fascinates him the way a sword of Indian steel does me, Alphena realized. *And it would fascinate Varus. Perhaps my brother and I are more alike than I thought; we're just interested in different things.*

She giggled, surprising herself as much as she did the teacher. "Your Ladyship?" Pandareus said with a raised eyebrow.

"Varus and I are different sexes," Alphena said, swallowing. "So it's natural that we would have different interests."

Pandareus smiled so broadly that he must have understood her unstated point. "I have not heard your brother mention an interest in spinning or embroidery," he said. "But I'll begin to watch him."

Pandareus cleared his throat, then continued, "The writer was an antiquarian. The notebook is his account of opening an ancestral tomb. His slaves dug the earth away from the entrance and removed the stone panels which closed the tomb itself. He led the way into the corridor beyond, holding an oil lamp. There was an angle in the corridor, which I should note—"

He gave Alphena a sharp look, as if to see that a student was listening to the lecture. She gestured with her left hand to show that she was paying attention.

"—is quite unusual in Etruscan tombs."

Pandareus smiled, perhaps realizing that he *wasn't* in class. He duplicated her gesture in apology.

"Around the corner," he said, "was a richly dressed man seated on a stone throne. He vanished into dust the instant the writer saw him.

The writer sneezed violently and dropped his lamp, which went out. At this point, from somewhere above him—"

Pandareus grimaced and opened both hands. "The writer's script isn't good at the best of times," he said, "and he was becoming increasingly agitated the farther he got into his account. He says 'above,' but it isn't clear to me what he means. He described a rock-cut tomb, but he appears to mean something well above what should be a low stone ceiling. In any case, above him he saw a giant egg glowing in all colors. He was terrified and fled back outside, driving the slaves ahead of him."

"Why was he frightened?" Alphena said. "Was there something more than the Egg?"

"Not that he mentioned," Pandareus said, smiling again. "Just a giant glowing egg. But it frightened him. He had his slaves close up the tomb; then he sold them all to a contractor supplying labor to silver mines in Spain."

"A death sentence," Alphena said. Slaves in a large household rarely had much work to do. Slaves on small farms worked with their owners and worked very hard indeed. Slaves in a mine, particularly the deep silver mines in Spain, worked a few months or possibly a year till they died—and were replaced by more slaves.

"A death sentence," the teacher agreed. "There was no more information in the notebook."

"We can get the information ourselves, if we can find the tomb," Alphena said. "Can we find it, Master Pandareus?"

"Collinus Ceutus has a house in Baiae," Pandareus said, grinning very broadly. "I believe that if the scholar Pandareus of Athens and the daughter of Gaius Alphenus Saxa ask him, he will give us directions to his country estate and a letter to his manager there to help us."

"Then," said Alphena, rising to her feet, "tomorrow we will go there. When my brother and Corylus come back from their excursion, we'll *see* who has the more interesting information!"

"I'll be here," the driver said as he stopped the mule cart in front of Vergil's farm. Corylus knew Lycos would turn the vehicle around as soon as his passengers had gotten down. They would be ready to leave quickly—if necessary.

"Thank you, Lycos," Corylus said. He hopped to the ground, then raised his arms to support Varus as he in turn dismounted from the high seat. "I regret that you were called back to duty at such short notice."

The driver's expression was probably a grin. "D'ye think this was the first time I got waked up for an operation, lad?" he said. "You handle your end and I'll take care of mine."

He was clucking the mule into a half circle as Corylus and his friend started for the house. Lucinus stood in the doorway, but he didn't come out to greet them this time.

"Do you really think there'll be trouble?" Varus said. He sounded puzzled but not concerned.

"Not at all," Corylus said. "But there would be even less point in saying that to Lycos than there would be in trying to convince my father. And—"

He looked at Varus and grinned broadly.

"—since both of them have a great deal more experience with ambushes than I do, who am I to object?"

Midway to the house blackberries grew over the flagstones of the path, so he moved to the left. The canes were lovely earlier in spring when they were covered with white flowers, but their barbs made as good a barrier as any horse of cedar trees laid with their branches facing outward around a marching camp.

Lucinus waited with a smile. Corylus didn't want to describe the magician as looking self-satisfied—if not triumphant—but he couldn't think of more accurate terms.

He and Varus had decided that returning to Lucinus was the best choice under the circumstances, just as the magician himself had claimed it was. Corylus had no right to think slapping the expression off the fellow's face would feel good . . . but it would.

"I'm glad to see you so promptly, Corylus, Lord Varus," Lucinus said. "I fear that there is even less time to waste than I had already believed."

He turned, adding over his shoulder, "Come in and I'll show you."

He led the way through the half-ruined house again. There was no need of small talk if the fate of the world depended on quick action, but Corylus realized that because he didn't trust Lucinus, he didn't take the prediction of imminent disaster seriously. He supposed he should, since it echoed the vision Varus had described.

He smiled. Because he distrusted—and disliked—the messenger

with bad news, he was less worried than would otherwise have been the case. That was good, since it wouldn't prevent him from dealing to the best of his strength and ability with whatever *did* happen.

The garden in back looked the same as when they had seen it the day before. Varus looked around and said, "Where are the goats, Lucinus?"

"What does it—," Lucinus said, then remembered who he was snarling at, and remembered how willing the target's friend was to respond physically. The magician swallowed and said, "I had Charax pen them up before he left ahead of your arrival. I'll need them later, or one of them."

Corylus smiled faintly. Varus had struck Lucinus off-balance in a socially proper, even courteous fashion as ably as Corylus could have done by slapping the fellow. The courts of Carce were losing an effective advocate by Varus' disinclination to enter the profession.

Corylus stroked the bark of the peach tree. The dryad huddled within the trunk, a nervous shape within the shadows of his mind. *You'll be all right,* he thought. The sprite couldn't hear him, but the touch of his hand seemed to soothe her.

Corylus' mother had been a hazel sprite, or so Pulto had told him; he'd never discussed it with his father. He had been born with an affinity for trees, and the magic bathing Carce in recent months brought Corylus increasingly closer to that half of his ancestry.

"I told you about Melino," Lucinus said. He bent to pick up another clod and crushed it with his thumb. "He has returned to the Waking World with the demon ring. My uncle sent him to bring it from the Otherworld, but Melino stole it himself. The demon gives him great power, but the ring alone does not have sufficient power to loose the Worms."

Lucinus tossed the pulverized clod into the air as a yellow-gray haze. He muttered under his breath, *"Flames dance in her marrow and lust wounds her breast!"*

The vision sucked Corylus in wholly, and the world around him vanished. He was watching a dinner party. He didn't recognize any of the men, but Hedia and Alphena reclined on the right-hand couch and the handsome youth on the cross couch was in animated conversation with Hedia.

They were flirting. Corylus didn't have to hear the words to know that from the body language, from the gestures, from Hedia's flashing smiles. She looked radiant.

"*That was last night,*" said Lucinus' voice, filling the image. The words had no echo.

The vision sucked into a vortex, then re-formed as a rented sedan chair made its way down the Naples Road out of Puteoli. The curtains were drawn, concealing the female passenger's face and torso.

"*Melino has become a demon,*" Lucinus said, "*and he works through a demon. He gains power for his magic by blood and pain, and he uses a female counterpart to effect his spells.*"

The sedan chair in the vision stopped in front of a house of moderate size with a high-walled garden in the rear. There was nothing exceptional about the dwelling save for the pair of guards wearing swords and body armor who were lounging in the entryway. That wasn't strictly illegal—the armed men were on the householder's property—but it was extremely unusual and risked being reported to the imperial authorities.

The Emperor spent more time on the island of Capri, nearby in the Bay of Puteoli, than he did in Carce, and he was a notably paranoid man. Corylus for one wouldn't want to presume on what the Emperor considered sufficient evidence that someone was planning the armed overthrow of the Republic.

"*In order to release the Worms,*" Lucinus said, "*Melino must gain the Book, which my uncle replaced on Zabulon's Isle. He is enlisting a confidante to help him do this—and to destroy all life thereby.*"

The woman from the hired chair was concealed beneath a full veil, but a servant had been walking behind the vehicle. She followed her mistress up the flagstone walk. The servant was unquestionably Syra, Hedia's chief maid.

"*This will happen today,*" Lucinus said. "*In days or even hours, Melino will have the Book unless I can forestall him. That is all the time we have, and all therefore that Mankind has!*"

The vision twisted into itself, drawing Corylus' soul with it for an instant. He was back in Lucinus' garden, back in the Waking World. Gasping, he fell to his knees, then reached out to grip the rough trunk of the peach tree again. This time the touch of the wood was to settle him rather than to settle the faintly smiling sprite within.

Corylus opened his eyes—he didn't remember closing them—and

got to his feet. To his surprise Varus seemed undisturbed by the experience; he was helping to support Lucinus, who was even more wrung out by this experience than he had been by the vision he had created the day before.

"Are you all right?" Varus said to the magician.

"Yes, yes," said Lucinus snappishly. "Just let me get my balance. There."

He straightened and stepped away from Varus. Stress explained his tone, but Corylus wasn't—he realized with a smile—willing to give Lucinus the benefit of the doubt.

Though at this point—his smile faded—Corylus was furiously angry with Melino, whom he had never met. In all logic, he had even less reason for that than he did for disliking Lucinus.

Lucinus walked inside without asking his guests to accompany him. Varus looked at Corylus and raised an eyebrow; Corylus grinned—seeing the magician's exhaustion had improved his mood—and gestured his friend ahead of him.

Lucinus seated himself on a chair facing the table and apparently realized for the first time that there were only two chairs in the room. He looked startled.

"Gaius, you take it," Corylus said. He backed against the sidewall and waited, holding his staff. Plaster that had flaked off the brick core crunched under his heavy sandals. He wondered what sort of frescoes had once decorated the house of Carce's greatest poet.

Lucinus looked at Corylus. In a fierce voice he said, "Melino is using Lady Hedia to gain Zabulon's *Book*. His spells protect the interior of his dwelling from my observation, but you're a man. *You* can imagine what is going on—besides the magic."

Corylus didn't speak. He kept his face expressionless—he hoped it was expressionless—as he glanced at Varus.

"I don't believe . . . ," Varus said in a deliberate voice, "that my mother could be coerced into aiding in harmful magic. As for what else the Lady Hedia may do, that is none of my business until she requests me to become involved. As for you . . ."

He gave Lucinus a slight smile. It looked like an expression one might see on the face of a reptile.

"If you make any further comment which could be considered a reflection on my mother's character, I will have you punished. I would not dirty my own hands with you—"

"I would," Corylus snarled. *I really am angry.*

"—but I will have some of Father's servants beat you to whatever they consider a sufficient degree. Do you understand?"

"I understand," said Lucinus. To Corylus' surprise, he smiled also—much as he had when Corylus and his friend started up the walk. "Now, Lord Varus: Do *you* understand? Do you understand that unless I have your help, Melino will gain the *Book* and will have the power to do whatever he wishes?"

He paused. "You do not have to believe me that he, or at any rate the demon wearing his flesh, wishes to destroy all life, though that is true," he said. "But that Melino will have the power to do whatever he wishes—do you believe *that?*"

Corylus believed him. He didn't like Lucinus—the fellow was bumptious and patronizing—but he was completely believable, as much because of his flaws as despite them. He seemed too full of himself to see the need of lying, and he was beyond question a magician.

But it wasn't Corylus' decision. He said nothing, instead looking again at his friend.

"What do you envisage me doing?" Varus said quietly, meeting Lucinus' eyes.

"We will go to Carce," Lucinus said. "I have arranged for us to begin our real journey there. If we can leave soon—"

He gestured, apparently indicating the garden and the visions he had created in it.

"—it would be better than not."

"We can leave tomorrow morning," Varus said. "I'll inform Father that I'm returning to Carce in normal fashion. There's no reason to concern him."

"And I'm coming with you," Corylus said, his fingers tightening on his cornelwood staff. He glared at the magician.

"As you wish, master," Lucinus said with a shrug. "You may do anything you please here in the Waking World. When Lord Varus and I set out for Zabulon's Isle, however, you will have to find your own way. The boat will only hold two, so you could not join us. Not even if you were a magician greater than me."

"Gaius?" Corylus said. "Is that true?"

Varus looked at him sadly. "I don't know, Publius," he said. "I'm not a magician. At least not a magician by study; I don't know what I am now."

His face hardened. "I think it may be true," he said. "I would be very glad of your company, my friend, but just for your presence. I'm not concerned about Master Lucinus attacking me."

"There will be much to fear," Lucinus said, smiling at Corylus. "Nothing that your undoubted strength would be of any use against, however."

Varus lifted his chin in agreement. "Stay home, Publius," he said. "There's enough happening that I don't doubt you'll find a use for your talents."

"There is one thing that Master Corylus could do that is beyond my abilities and yours, Lord Varus?" Lucinus said, cocking an eyebrow at Varus.

"Speak, then!" Varus said.

"Melino has protected his dwelling and garden against spells," Lucinus said, including Corylus in his explanation. "But he has guards who live in separate housing, and he has gardeners come in to care for the herbs growing behind the house. A man of Master Corylus' sort might be able to talk to the servants when they're off-duty and learn something about his plans."

"There's an umbrella pine in the back corner of Melino's garden," Corylus said, recalling the vision. "Yes, that's something I might be able to help with."

"I'll leave our house on the Bay at dawn," Varus said to the magician. Corylus noted again that while his friend was a scholar in all senses of the term, he didn't dither in making up his mind. "I'll pick you up. Have whatever you need ready to load. If there'll be more than will fit in two carriages, tell me now."

"I will have very little," Lucinus said. "I'll need one of the goats, but I think I will take both for safety's sake."

"As you please," said Varus. He raised an eyebrow. "Publius? Do you have more to do here?"

"Let's go," Corylus said, gesturing his friend toward the door and the waiting cart.

Corylus had work to do back in Puteoli. He grinned at the thought.

He had no right to be jealous of Melino's friendship with Hedia. Hedia had made a very clear offer to Corylus when they first met, and Corylus—who had done foolish things, but never anything as foolish as becoming involved with a senator's wife, let alone the mother of his closest friend—had rejected her.

Nevertheless, Corylus *was* jealous. He was too intelligent to deny that truth even when it was embarrassing to him.

He grinned more broadly.

"YOUR DAUGHTER HAS COME HOME, Your Ladyship," Syra said quietly to Hedia. "Balbinus himself is escorting her to you, as you requested."

Hedia nodded without turning around. She hadn't directed the chief steward—or anyone else—to escort Alphena to her when she returned; she had merely said that when Lady Alphena arrived she should be informed that her mother would like to see her. Hedia hoped the girl wouldn't be offended by the servants' presumption, but it couldn't be helped now.

Realistically, someone who was determined to be upset could always find a reason. That would have been a description of Alphena a few months ago, but more recently the girl had been a pleasure to be around. She remained her own person with her own interests, skills, and opinions, but she had ceased to be a screeching brat.

Which made the coming discussion all the harder.

"Yes, Mother?" Alphena said as she walked around the marble bench where Hedia sat facing the fishpond. "Balbinus said you wanted to see me."

Hedia turned. She intended to offer a pleasant smile anyway, but the sight of the steward on the back porch of the house with an agonized expression brought her to the edge of open laughter. Obviously, Alphena had decided she didn't need an escort to find the fishpond and had made her wishes known to Balbinus in a sufficiently forceful fashion.

It serves him right for his presumption.

"Sit down, dear," Hedia said, patting the bench. As expected, two of Alphena's servants placed a red plush cushion on the marble under the direction of the girl's chief maid, Florina.

Alphena obeyed, crossing her hands primly on her lap. She was still wearing the outfit in which Hedia had sent her with her brother to the Cispius house: a rose-colored tunic with a white wrap. Her sandals were white leather and very chic, but their soles were thick enough to allow the girl to walk or even run comfortably on stone streets.

Hedia's smile turned inward. *There have been times recently when I would have been better off in sturdier footwear. Perhaps as Alphena has learned from me, I should learn from her.*

"Do you mind a little sun, dear?" Hedia asked.

"What?" said Alphena. Instead of blurting, "Of course not!" she went on politely, "No, Mother. I don't need the parasols."

At home in Carce Alphena practiced swordsmanship daily in the gymnasium at the back of the town house. Hedia hadn't objected—she knew to pick her battles—but besides the unladylike tan, the equipment rubbed the skin. Some of the calluses were obvious in a lady's daily routine; others would only be seen under conditions of greater intimacy—but that was a matter for the girl's eventual husband.

Hedia sighed internally. At least she hadn't had to worry that Alphena would refuse to sit with her in direct sunlight.

"Leave us," Hedia said. She glanced up at her chief maid. "Syra," she said. "My daughter and I wish to be alone. See to it."

Hedia didn't raise her voice. Nor did the maid—but Syra spoke with the authority of her mistress, and the urgency of her whispered demands cut like a hooked whip . . . which was what the overseer would apply in the evening to the back of any servant who hadn't responded as quickly as Syra thought Lady Hedia would have wished.

A fish had noticed her. It came to the surface; immediately several more joined it. All Hedia really cared about fish was how they tasted. It was an article of faith among fashionable cooks that no dish should resemble the creature that provided the flesh, so she couldn't even tell which of these she would like for a meal.

The servants had withdrawn into the house. That didn't mean that mother and daughter had real privacy, but it was more or less possible that they did.

"A man once told me that King Midas had the ears of a donkey," Hedia said as she watched the fish gape hopefully. "The only person who knew was his barber, whom he swore to secrecy. The barber had to tell someone, though, so he spoke the secret into a well."

She met Alphena's eyes. The girl looked puzzled.

"But the reeds around the well heard him, and now reeds all whisper, 'Midas has donkey's ears,'" Hedia said.

She smiled reflectively. "I wasn't impressed by the man," she said. "But I still remember that story. I don't remember nearly as much about most men."

"Mother?" Alphena said. *She's completely at sea . . . and I'm trying to avoid my duty.*

"I'm going to ask you to do a very hard thing, dear," Hedia said. "I want you to go back to Carce immediately."

"What?" said the girl, jerking back in surprise. "But Pandareus and I have just found something that, well, may help with my dreams and whatever Varus saw. As soon as he and Corylus get back, we're going to tell them!"

"I'm sure Master Pandareus will be able to inform them by himself," Hedia said. With no hesitation that another person would have noticed, she continued, "I'm going to be involved in my own affairs soon. I'm going to be spending time with Melino, the magician we met last night."

Alphena went from being hot with frustration to cold with disapproval. *Her face would make a study for an artist,* Hedia thought sadly.

"I'm telling you this," Hedia said aloud, "not because it has bearing on the danger that concerns us, though it does, but because I probably won't be able to pay the necessary attention to you. I won't be able to pay attention to you and Publius Corylus."

"Mother!" Alphena said. She half-stood, then forced herself to sit down again.

"I know what it is to be young . . . ," Hedia said. There was only seven years' difference between her age and her stepdaughter's, but they had been seven eventful years. "And I know that the excitement of working with an attractive man can translate into other excitement."

"Mother, I would *never* do that," Alphena said earnestly. Her voice was a hoarse whisper.

"Even so," Hedia said. "It would become known."

She looked down at the fish. A complicated system of tide pools and siphons filled the pond and changed the seawater regularly. The engineer who oversaw the work had been very pleased with it, and Hedia had found the engineer pleasing for a time.

"You might survive a fling with Corylus," she continued, "though it would harm your marriage prospects. Corylus would be destroyed. I would see to it that he was destroyed, dear, even if I suspected my daughter had been the aggressor in the business."

"You would do *that*?" Alphena whispered.

"Yes," said Hedia. "And I would regret it, because I have great liking and respect for Master Corylus. So. Will you leave the Bay at once?"

She didn't add "of your own free will," though that was the truth of the situation. An open threat would put the girl's back up, but she knew Hedia well enough by now that she had probably heard the unspoken words.

"I think . . . ," Alphena said deliberately. "That you're imagining that I'm a younger edition of you, Mother. I'm not. But I believe you have my best interests at heart. I will leave in the morning, for Carce—or at any rate, leave the Bay. And Corylus."

Hedia didn't move for a moment. She had been poised for a tantrum, and tears had seemed even more likely.

She had *not* been prepared to hear the girl analyze her motives as coolly as if she were judging the tricks and tells of a gladiator in the arena. Alphena didn't sound angry, just slightly superior. Which perhaps she had a right to be.

"Thank you, Daughter," Hedia said. She rose to her feet. "Now, I think that I'll get ready to go out. Syra?"

Alphena walked back to the house. She was going to change, probably, since she wasn't comfortable in the garments required for public.

Whereas Hedia herself . . .

She stretched in the sunlight as her maid joined her. "I will be wearing a full cloak when I go out this afternoon," she said. "But under it, I think . . . perhaps the pale green?"

"With what undergarments, Your Ladyship?" Syra said as they too started for the house.

"I'm not sure," said Hedia. She smiled. "I'm not sure that I'll wear anything at all."

CHAPTER VI

The light four-wheeled carriage was owned by the Republic's courier service, but Saxa's wealth put it at his son's disposal as a matter of course. Varus would have been perfectly willing to rent—or buy—a similar vehicle, but there was no market for them except for the government.

Varus smiled. Rich, powerful men didn't pay for things. He didn't know how he felt about that as a philosopher. He was coming to the conclusion that he grasped facts very well, but that ideology was beyond him. Every theory he heard seemed to squeeze between his mental fingers when he tried to grasp it. Yes, *but* . . . seemed to be his response to every general statement.

The driver, a government slave, cracked on the three horses—a trace horse on the right of a yoked pair. He had come with the vehicle. The baggage, including a goat, traveled behind in a heavy cart.

"When I was my uncle's assistant . . . ," Lucinus said, rocking on the rear seat beside Varus. "We crossed the sea itself on a bridge of air."

"How long were you with your uncle?" Varus asked. This sort of travel was tedium, because the carriage rocked and rattled too much for him to read. Even conversation was difficult because of the *thrummm!* of the iron tires against the stone highway.

"Ten years," Lucinus said. "He summoned me when I was fifteen—after Melino betrayed him, though I didn't know anything about that at first. I barely knew that I had an uncle. My father was a farmer, well enough off to provide for my schooling but no more than that; I was already working with him on the farm. My mother never talked about her brother. But the messenger came, and they sent me off at once."

He looked at Varus. "They were terrified," he said. "I didn't know why at the time, just that something was wrong."

Lucinus shook his head, thinking back to events that must have occurred seventy years before. "I suppose they thought my uncle might have wanted me as a human sacrifice," he said, speaking barely loud enough for Varus to hear him over the sound of the tires. "And they were afraid to object. But all Uncle Vergil wanted was an assistant, an additional pair of hands to reach things he didn't want to touch with his own."

The carriage was keeping a steady pace without having to buck traffic even in congested areas. Four cavalrymen hired from the transient barracks in Capua rode ahead, using the weight of their horses—and, when necessary, the flats of their swords—to clear the road for the carriage.

If Saxa had used his own servants for the purpose, there was a risk that he would be accused of raising a private army. Supplementing the income of off-duty soldiers was more politic.

"What did you do for your uncle?" Varus said, studying his companion. Varus and Lucinus both wore ordinary traveling garments: short cloaks over plain tunics with broad-brimmed leather hats. Varus' clothing was new, while Lucinus' was worn though not ragged.

Given the magician's jar of gold coins, that was additional proof that he wasn't interested in ordinary material things. Lucinus might be lying, but the ordinary goals of deceit—wealth, luxury, and status—didn't apply in his case.

Varus didn't think Lucinus was lying.

"I ground herbs and minerals to his direction," Lucinus said. "I spoke responses when a spell required two speakers. I read his books—all was open to me—but I . . ."

He gave Varus an angry glare.

"I am a great magician!" Lucinus said. "Even Melino would not be my equal were it not for his ring, the ring he stole. But even with my years and all my study, there is no one to equal my uncle. My uncle could have burked the Worms by himself, but now—you and I together will be able to control the Worms only if we have Zabulon's *Book*, and even then it will try our strength."

Varus thought of Vergil, and thought of his own attempts to write epic poetry. The elements were there, but the result . . .

"A scholar . . . ," he said aloud, but to himself more than to his companion. "Can have a vocabulary as great as any poet's. But he still will not be a poet, however much he might wish otherwise."

A wisp of thought touched his mind. Vergil had been a great poet and—on his nephew's telling—a great magician. Varus knew he was not a poet.

But the present situation didn't call for poetry, and the recent past suggested that Varus might be a magician despite himself.

He smiled faintly.

"Ooh!" said Syra as she followed Hedia up the short walk to Melino's front entrance. Two guards watched from the porch, their thumbs hooked in their sword belts.

Hedia frowned, though the change in expression would scarcely have been noticeable to anyone watching. There were various ways to react to the outburst. A number of Hedia's acquaintances would have had the maid whipped to bloody rags for speaking without permission in her mistress' presence.

Hedia wouldn't do that unless she were making a point to the rest of the household, but it was an unusual enough event to demand explanation. She looked over her shoulder and raised an eyebrow.

Syra flushed. "My skin tingled when I stepped onto the walk," she said in a quiet voice, her eyes downcast. "I'm sorry, Your Ladyship."

Hedia nodded minusculely and mounted the three steps to the porch. She had felt nothing, but she suspected that Alphena would have had a reaction similar to the maid's. Alphena was sensitive to magic, as her mother was not.

The guards wore helmets and body armor like soldiers on active duty. The small one was probably Greek or an Arab, but the larger guard—over six feet tall and heavily built—was more exotic. He was armored in scales of black horn sewn onto leather backing. His cap was made of boar tusks, of all things. The teeth were laid with their points upward in four alternating rows so that they described S curves from the helmet rim to the peak.

"You are expected!" he said to Hedia with a guttural accent. His black beard and moustache were so thick that she caught only flashes of his teeth as he spoke. "The servant stays outside."

Hedia considered protesting, but that would be pointless for a number of reasons. The guard would have no real authority, and the maid's presence didn't matter: not to Hedia, at least, and probably not to Syra, either.

As Her Ladyship's chief maid, Syra had more real power in Saxa's household than the majordomo of the Carce town house did. She was more than willing to pay for her status with occasional discomfort while involved in Hedia's confidential affairs.

Instead of bothering to respond directly to what the guard had phrased as a command, Hedia said, "Open the door."

The big man's expression was hidden beneath his facial hair, but the small one was leering. If she learned that Syra had had trouble with the fellows, Hedia would see to it that they were repaid.

The door valves were already squealing back, pulled not by human servants but by a pair of baboons in harness. They were big brutes, each as heavy as a well-grown man. They had large canine tusks and full manes, and they smelled overpoweringly male.

The baboons were chained to the doors and opened them by backing away. They stared at Hedia, looking more like small lions than large dogs. She walked between them, looking to neither side.

As she reached the reception hall, she glanced over her shoulder. The beasts were pushing the valves closed with their forepaws, walking on their hind legs. One of them met her eyes as he reached up to shoot the bolt.

Would you like to tear my throat out? she thought. *Or is it something different you're thinking? Perhaps one day we'll learn.*

"Lady Hedia," Melino said, walking toward her with his hands outstretched. He wore a long white robe, opaque but fluttering as though it were made of gauze. "Don't worry about my doormen. They're harmless, just there to add color."

If you believe that, you're a fool. And if you think you can fool me, young man—that's been tried by fellows who were much more clever at it than you are.

Hedia took his hands. They were surprisingly cool. "I'm glad to hear that, dear," she said. "They quite frightened me."

Still holding her right hand in his left, Melino walked with her into the office at the back of the reception room. He had left open the wooden lattice when he came out to greet her.

Hedia paused and looked around the reception room before she left it. "How many servants do you have?" she asked. She couldn't see or hear anyone else in the house.

"Inside, none," Melino said, smiling with pride. "No human servants, that is. Would you like refreshments? Of *any* sort, dear Hedia. Just ask."

Though light came through the opening above the pool just behind her, the reception room was not nearly as bright as the outdoors. In the relative dimness, Hedia noticed again that Melino's eyes glowed like a cat's. The ruby on his finger also hinted that there was a flame in its interior.

"Perhaps later, Master Melino," she said. "Perhaps you should get on to the matters you wanted to discuss with me in private?"

Because this was a rented house, Hedia was surprised to see that twelve death masks looked out through the wicker screen of an upright chest against the wall. The wax expressions were disquieting.

"Are these your ancestors, then?" she asked. Nothing in her voice showed anything but mild interest.

"My ancestors in art, so to speak," Melino said. He had knelt to open the iron strongbox against the opposite wall. He turned and pointed. "The mask on top is Zabulon's," he said. "Are you familiar with the name, dear lady?"

The answer would have been, "No," but without waiting for her to speak Melino continued, "He was the man who first brought the wisdom of the stars to Earth. He put his knowledge in a book, but the words of the *Book* cannot be spoken."

The face wasn't that of anyone Hedia wanted to know better. The features were heavy, the brow scowling. The hair and beard added to the wax image were in tight ringlets of an eastern style. She wondered if Zabulon had been a Persian or of one of the tribes that the Persians ruled.

"I've never heard of him," Hedia said with a toss of her hand. She returned her attention to Melino.

He rose, holding the hand mirror he had taken from the strongbox. The mirror's back and handle were silver, as bright as if the metal had just been polished. It was ornately molded, but because of highlights from the surface Hedia couldn't see much of the subject. From the little she could make out, she didn't regret being generally ignorant.

"Before we go on . . . ," Melino said. He smiled more broadly, which he shouldn't have done: it made the falseness of the expression even more obvious. "Has a man named Lucinus contacted you about, well, about anything? He won't look as old as he is, probably fifty or so. And it's possible that he's using a false name, but I doubt he'd bother with that."

Hedia smoothed the frown before it reached her forehead. "No," she said. "I've met no one like that. As a matter of fact, you're the only stranger I've gotten to know recently."

She let a wicked smile spread naturally. "Closely enough to matter, that is," she said.

Melino grimaced instead of reacting to the invitation. A *rather obvious invitation*, Hedia thought with a touch of pique.

"I know he's close by," Melino muttered. "He can't force the wards I've put in place around this house and he hasn't the strength to attack me directly, but he may try to reach you. If he does, you must reject him. Or. . . ."

His voice trailed off. His ring threw a bloody red reflection from the back of the mirror.

"This Lucinus wouldn't be the first man to try to make my acquaintance," Hedia said tartly. "He doesn't sound like the sort who would interest me, but I'll make the decision when I believe I have sufficient facts."

She was beginning to regret this excursion. Though . . . Melino's oddity, while irritating, added a degree of interest as well. She wouldn't second-guess herself just yet.

"That's why I brought you here," Melino said. "One of the reasons, I mean. To give you the facts about the man."

He turned the mirror so that both of them could see its face. To her surprise—concealed by an emotionless mask—the reflective surface wasn't of silver or highly polished bronze. Rather it was—

"This is a mirror of orichalc," Melino said. "Only the greatest of magicians have objects of this metal. It was the secret of the Atlanteans, and Atlantis perished a hundred Saecula ago, each of a hundred years and ten years!"

Hedia knew rather more about orichalc—and about Atlantis—than Melino seemed to realize. She saw no benefit in telling the fellow that. In seeming wonder, she said, "My! One could almost take it for gold."

"It's brighter than gold," he said smugly. "And much rarer. Now, look into it and I'll show you Lucinus."

He spoke a word. A reddish glow began to form on the mirror's face.

"Lucinus was the nephew of the magician Vergil," Melino said. "He was Vergil's apprentice and had been taught many of his uncle's spells."

Melino began to whisper verse, which Hedia heard only in snatches. "*Now take the path and complete the vision . . . ,*" he said, and the mirror's fiery surface brightened still more. In it objects appeared, at first wisps of smoke but gaining form and features.

An old man bent over a basin in a stone hall. The basin was flat, the shape of a mixing bowl for wine, but it was greater in diameter than the man was tall.

"That is Vergil," Melino said. "The greatest magician of all time, save Zabulon himself."

The old man straightened. He kicked off his sandals, then undid the sash of his tunic and pulled the garment over his head. He tossed it on the floor. Nude, he looked even older. He stepped to a marble bench and lay supine on it with the care demanded by creaking joints.

Hedia had known her share of older men.

A younger man appeared in the mirror beside the bench. He wore a breechclout and carried a cleaver with a broad, heavy blade.

"That is Lucinus," Melino said. "He is our enemy and the world's enemy. He hopes to gain Zabulon's *Book* and with it loose the Worms of the Earth. He thinks that he can control the Worms after he frees them, but he will fail. The Worms will destroy all things."

The image of Lucinus raised the cleaver high. "What is he—," Hedia said, her hands rising reflexively to her mouth.

Lucinus brought the cleaver down hard, beheading the old man and chipping a notch in the bench. The head rolled to the flagstones.

Blood pulsed three times from the stump of the neck, then oozed as the arteries emptied. What else could he have been about to do?

Lucinus tossed the head into the basin. Then, bathed in blood, he began methodically to joint the corpse. Each severed portion followed the head into the stone basin.

"He murdered his uncle," Hedia said. She had seen death outside the arena—and killed—before, but the cold brutality of this dismemberment shocked her. "To gain his uncle's power?"

"No, no, he didn't *murder* Vergil," Melino said in irritation. "He was to add the herb, the *moly*, to the basin to rejuvenate Vergil. Vergil had spent his last eleven years searching the Otherworld for the herb. When he found the place it grew, he plucked all there was and brought it back . . . but he couldn't prepare *himself* for the spell. His apprentice was to do that."

Lucinus dropped the last piece of the body, the left foot, into the basin. The liquid was beginning to boil, though there was no fire beneath that Hedia could see. He laid the cleaver on the dripping table and wiped his hands on a napkin that he took from a three-legged table. Only then did he pick up the small gold coffer that was also on the table.

"Instead of adding all the *moly* to the vat with his uncle as he was supposed to," Melino said, "Lucinus stole part of it for himself. See!"

What Hedia saw was that if Melino had wished, he could have convinced her—he could have let her convince herself—that Lucinus was a brutal murderer. Instead Melino was so focused on his business that he insisted that she know the truth about his enemy—even though her error had been utterly damning and perfectly believable to anyone not a magician herself.

It meant that Melino was rather a self-satisfied prig, but she'd already been aware of that. It also meant that the fellow was honest, or at least dealing honestly with her.

Lucinus opened the box, looked in, and dropped three pinches of the contents into the basin in careful succession. He closed the box.

The liquid boiled more fiercely. It began to change color from the original bloodred to orange, and then to yellow.

"He thought he could make himself immortal by taking the herb while he was still young," Melino said accusingly. "But the portion he stole only delayed his own aging, and it prevented his uncle's successful rejuvenation. The greatest magician since Zabulon has become a monster, because Lucinus betrayed him!"

Lucinus closed the coffer. Holding it in both hands, he stepped beyond the mirror's image. He was still covered with blood, and he left bloody footprints on the floor behind him.

The basin was at a rolling boil. The liquid was dark blue, but the color was changing to indigo as Hedia watched. Something—was it a hand?—gripped the rim from inside.

"Be closed!" Melino said. The image and the red haze vanished.

He staggered. Hedia caught him in both arms, then held him close with her right and took the mirror from his hand with the other. She set the mirror facedown on the strongbox from which he had taken it.

"Come," she said softly. "Isn't there a place we could be more comfortable?"

He looked at her, easing away. She couldn't read his expression.

"Yes," Melino said. "We'll go upstairs now. I think time is short."

Hedia smiled as she followed him to the stairs in a curtained alcove to the side of the office. One could have a great deal of fun in a short time, if necessary.

WHILE ALPHENA AND HER ENTOURAGE were still half a block from the house of Aulus Collinus Ceutus, the wife—Collina—rushed into the street with twenty of her servants, all wearing finery. Four maids under the direction of a corpulent steward began tossing flower petals onto the pavement.

"I was afraid . . . ," Pandareus said quietly to Alphena. "That our large troupe was going to frighten the poor woman. Apparently not, though I was surprised to see that we would have so many attendants."

Alphena heard the disapproval behind—though certainly not in—the teacher's comment. She smiled smugly and said, "I brought over a hundred, as many as I could scrape together here on the Bay. This is payment for her courtesy in receiving us."

The attendants began to shout, "*Sax*-a, *Sax*-a," as the head of the entourage reached the door of the Collinus dwelling. The cheers were ragged—too ragged to understand if you didn't know what they must be—but the enthusiasm was all that mattered. The households all along the street watched from windows and the roofs as the parade passed.

"I don't understand," Pandareus said. The cheering forced him to raise his voice.

"Collina will never forget that the daughter of a wealthy senator called on her at home," Alphena said. "And her neighbors would never forget it, either, even if Collina was too modest to mention it. Which she may be—you've met her."

"I don't think she is that modest, no," Pandareus said with a faint smile. "Your Ladyship, I appreciate your wisdom. And your courtesy."

"I learned it from Mother," Alphena said, swelling with pride but trying not to let it show in her voice. "How to think like this, I mean."

She smiled—at herself, really—and added, "I've learned a lot, since I started listening to her."

"The noble Lady Alphena, daughter of Senator Gaius Alphenus Saxa, Governor of Lusitania and former consul!" cried Balthus. "And her companion, the learned Pandareus of Athens!"

Balthus had been the Annunciator at the Carce town house. When age caused his voice to crack before he had announced half a dozen guests, he had been transferred to Puteoli as a sinecure. He still had the lungs for a task like this, though.

Alphena walked forward between the lines of servants. When Pandareus seemed to hesitate, she tugged at the sleeve of his tunic.

"Mistress Collina!" she said, taking the woman's plump hands in her own, then stepping back. *I won't be able to learn everything Mother has to teach, but I've learned some things.* "You're so kind to receive us on short notice. I hope to be able to repay your hospitality in the near future, after the business that brings me to you has been resolved."

Collina, a woman of forty who was trying without much confidence to look younger, seemed dazed at the attention. "Anything we can do for you, we're just delighted, my husband and I both. And Master Pan-dareus—"

She turned to the scholar.

"—when I wrote Ceutus that you might edit our letters for publication after all, he was so thrilled! He's at the estate that came from my family. I—"

She beamed at Alphena, suddenly looking five years younger and prettier as well.

"—well, why would one live on a farm when he has a house here? *I* think. But Ceutus is so proud to own an ancient Etruscan estate that he spends much of his time there, even though his ships sail from Naples."

"Are the documents still here, mistress?" Pandareus asked. "Or have they . . . ?"

"Oh, Venus, yes," Collina said. "They're mine, you see—my family. And if I'm going to live here, they move with me."

She clapped her hands in surprise. "Oh, but why are we standing out here?" she said. "Do come in. I'd love to offer you refreshment, but if you just want to read the letters, I understand. Whatever Your Ladyship wants to do, we'll help you, Ceutus and I, however we can!"

Collina turned. One of the maids still had a few flower petals left; she turned her basket over and shook it out on the front step, then hopped away. She couldn't have been more than eight years old.

"They're in the office," Collina said as she led the way through the entrance hall. The stewards—Balbinus had come himself to lead the contingent of Saxa's household; Collina's steward was already talking with him—would sort out what the escort was to do while Alphena was inside. "Ceutus had a new case made for them after you read the letters last year, Master Pandareus."

The walls of the reception room were frescoed with theatrical back-drops. On one side, porticos mounted over porticos until the one on top stretched off into the distance; on the other, painted Doric columns framed a plaza and a small, round temple—or possibly a well house—in the center of it. The work was bright and new enough that Alphena could smell fresh plaster.

"Here you are," Collina said, pushing aside the curtains in front of the office. "These are the letters, right here. Ceutus is talking about buying a librarian, but, well . . ."

"Do you have any books, mistress?" Pandareus said, kneeling in front of a cedarwood chest. A servant offered him a pillow; he nodded gratefully and slid it between his knees and the terrazzo of randomly mixed black and white stones.

"Well, no," Collina admitted. "Neither of us reads very well, to tell the truth. But Ceutus says we ought to have a librarian since we have valuable letters here."

She paused and added, "*I* have letters, I remind him. He has the money, and he took my family name when he married me, but the man who wrote the letters was my four-times-great-grandfather, not his. I'm just saying."

"Your husband is Illyrian, I believe?" Pandareus said, keeping his eyes on his work. He was removing small scrolls from the chest, reading enough of each one to determine the contents and then setting it on the floor as he took out the next.

"Yes, he is," Collina said. "He's really excited by being in an old family, though. Well, marrying into one. And he's a good husband."

Having watched the woman carefully, Alphena judged that she had wavered between a defensive response—"What of it? You're a Greek yourself, aren't you?"—and the neutral one she had chosen. With Pandareus, that was always the correct response: he was a scholar who gathered knowledge for the sake of knowledge, not to insult chance-met acquaintances.

Alphena wondered if neutrality wasn't always the correct response. Even if the question was meant as an attack, wasn't a calm smile better than showing the attacker that he'd gotten home? She would discuss it with Hedia. . . .

"I wonder . . . ," said Pandareus, gesturing with a letter he held partly unrolled in both hands. "It says here, 'I'm thinking of creating a water feature beside the Shrine to Inuus, but I will examine the hillside behind it first as there appears to have been a construction there in the past.' Would you would be able to identify that place? Identify the Shrine to Inuus, at least?"

"There's the shrine to the household gods on the wall of the reception room," Collina said. "We weren't very religious, I'm afraid. I don't know any Inuus. Who was Inuus?"

"Inuus is a very old—," Pandareus said. He caught himself before he had fully launched into his lecture and grinned broadly.

"Inuus is a herdsman's god," he resumed. "His shrine might have been close to the sheepfold?"

"I don't know anything about that," Collina said dismissively. "We didn't keep sheep when I was growing up, though Ceutus talks about starting a flock again."

She suddenly brightened. "I'm sure Ceutus'd be able to help you, though," she said. "What he hasn't learned about the estate I don't think there's to know. He's told me things my grandfather didn't know, all by talking to old servants and even the neighbors."

"That's very interesting," Pandareus said mildly. "I wonder how he checks the accuracy of what he's being told?"

"Oh!" said Collina. "Well, I don't know about that. He's a hard man to fool, though. He's been in the shipping business thirty years, and he knows about folks trying to lie to him."

"You know . . . ," said Pandareus. He set the letter back in the chest; the dozen or so others he'd looked at remained on the floor, but the servants could replace them easily. "That's very possibly true."

It didn't seem to strike him that Collina might take that as an insult. Nor, in fact, did she. Beaming at Pandareus, she said, "He'll be ever so proud to help you. A senator's daughter and a famous magician— why, it'll be the happiest day of his life!"

"I'm afraid I'm a scholar, not a magician, mistress," Pandareus said. He put a hand on the floor to help himself rise; Alphena bent down to offer her crooked arm, which he took. "Which may be a pity in this case, because it appears that magic may be involved in the matter."

"Are you really looking for a magician?" Collina said, frowning slightly. "Because there's one that my husband's been talking to. A priest, he calls himself, but he's really a magician. He does purification ceremonies and the like. His name's Paris."

"Does he know Quintus Macsturnas, who was just elected aedile?" Alphena said. "Because if he does, I met him the other day."

"Macsturnas?" Collina said. "I don't know him, but that's an Etruscan name, so I suppose he does. Paris is Etruscan himself. He's crazy—I call it—about anything Etruscan."

She grimaced. "I can't bear him," she said. "I don't like the way he looks at my husband. But Ceutus doesn't see anything wrong, so he's visited here a few times. Maybe at the estate too."

Pandareus looked thoughtful. "I wonder . . . ?" he said without finishing the question.

"Mistress?" said Alphena. "Would Paris accompany us to your estate if you asked him to?"

"Why, I'm sure he would," Collina said. "Why, I'll send messengers to him and Ceutus both, to say you're coming. Oh, my husband will be so pleased!"

Pandareus was looking at her without expression. Alphena nodded, then said to both her companions, "I didn't like Paris, either. But he knows something or he wouldn't have come along with Macsturnas. He may tell us more than the—"

How much did Collina know?

"—shrine or anything at the estate does."

"Yes," said Pandareus, smiling in acceptance. "Thank you, Mistress Collina; and again, Your Ladyship, I have reason to appreciate your wisdom."

"I'M HERE TO SEE MISTRESS BAUCIS," Corylus said to the man at the gate of the landscaper's yard. "I think she's expecting me."

His tunic was plain instead of sporting the two thin stripes of a Knight of Carce. He still felt out of place because his garments were new and clean. He was too young to be a landscaper or an architect but too well dressed to be a laborer. Those were the only classes of people who were likely to be calling on an establishment like this.

"Wait a minute," the gateman said, his eyes narrowing. "You're Cispius' boy, aren't you?"

Without bothering to wait for an answer, he turned and bawled, "Hey, boss! Young Cispius is here. You want me to bring him to the office?"

"I'm here, Blennius," said the blocky woman who came out from behind a row of three-year-old cypress trees in pots, ready to be transported to an estate that needed a windbreak. "Come on back to the office."

She looked Pulto up and down. "There's not a lot of room," she said, "but if you think the boy needs to be protected, you come right along too."

"That's Vibius over with the gang tending the roses, right?" Pulto said. "I knew him when he worked for the Old Man. Guess I'll go chew the fat with him until somebody tells me I'm needed."

He walked away. Looking after him, Baucis said, "I needed a supervisor, somebody to send out on big jobs or to watch the yard here while I was out. Your father let me have Vibius. It's one—"

She switched her attention suddenly to Corylus.

"—of the things I owe your father for. Come on back to the office, boy. What do I call you?"

"Corylus," Corylus said, falling into step with her. "Or 'boy.' Or pretty much anything else you want to call me. So long as I'm sure you don't mean some other dickhead."

Baucis burped a hoarse laugh.

A workman with a short-bladed knife turned from a row of fruit trees. "Hey, boss?" he called. "Want to take a look at these grafts?"

"Not unless you think I need to, Grammon," Baucis said. "And not now anyway. I'm busy."

Corylus didn't comment, but he viewed the yard with lively interest as they walked through. The laborers seemed cheerful, and the plants were well cared for. He even glimpsed a pair of olive sprites, hand-in-hand as they peeped out from trees in adjacent pots.

Baucis looked at him sharply. "Say, how do you like roses?" she said unexpectedly.

"Ma'am?" Corylus said. "I like them fine. Do you want a rose moved or something?"

She smiled. Her name meant "Very Modest." "Very plain" would have accurately described her. Baucis was now about fifty. She never could have been a beauty, and her right arm, right cheek, and the right side of her forehead were covered with a net of thin white scars. Perhaps she had fallen—or been thrown—into briars.

"We'll sit in the arbor," she said, "instead of the office. I don't mind work, but the work I have to do in the office is about my least favorite."

She gestured to the left; together they walked down an alley of fruit trees on one side, wisteria on the other. Corylus heard whispering, but no sprites showed themselves.

The semicircular arbor against the fence at the edge of the property was covered with pink roses. It wasn't part of the commercial layout.

The flowers were individually small, but they bloomed in homey profusion.

Baucis sat down and pointed to the seat facing her. "Now," she said. "Tell me what you want?"

"Well," Corylus said. This woman put him off-balance. He was tempted to treat her as he would a man, but he was pretty sure that would be as bad a mistake as patronizing her as a woman. Almost as bad a mistake. "You read my note?"

"I recognized Cispius' seal," Baucis said, flicking her left hand dismissively. "My secretary read the note to me. Your dad is as much of a scholar as you're going to find in this business, and *that's* because he needed to read to put together guard rosters. But I said, what do you *want?*"

"You provide the crews that take care of a fellow named Melino's gardens," Corylus said. If he had been standing, he'd have braced to attention. "I want to be on the next crew you send over. I can do any kind of gardening labor, certainly well enough to pass, and probably better than the man I replace."

"Let's see your hands," Baucis said. She leaned forward.

Corylus stretched out his arms and turned his palms upward. She took his wrists and peered closely at his hands before she released him.

"Your calluses aren't in the right places for gardening," she said. "But all right, you'll do."

"Nobody sleeps on Melino's property and leaves it," Corylus explained. "The guards are billeted in an apartment block a quarter mile down the road, and your people tend the garden on contract."

He coughed before proceeding to the awkward part. "I'll do my best not to involve you in any way," he said. "But of course there's a risk—"

Baucis laughed. She leaned forward, this time to pat Corylus' knee.

"You're Cispius' son," she said. "Of *course* you'll do your best to cover a friend. But to tell the truth, I don't much care."

"Ma'am?" Corylus said.

"I don't like Melino," Baucis said, turning her palms upward. "I couldn't tell you why—he pays on the dot *and* I'm socking him double the rate I'd charge most folks. But I don't like him, and if I lose his business—"

She gestured to the bustling yard without taking her eyes off Corylus.

"—I won't be begging in the street. That's the one side."

Corylus nodded to show that he was listening. He didn't speak.

"The other side is this," Baucis said. "My husband Gallus and I started this business. He was the business end and I was the plants, but we both picked up the other one's part pretty quick. But then Gallus died."

Corylus nodded again. He wasn't sure what he was about to be told, but he knew better than to interrupt.

"The rest of the nurserymen here in Puteoli decided it'd be a good idea to put the widow out of business," she continued harshly. "All but Cispius; he didn't think that was right. He helped me some with money, but mostly it was just him standing by me when I needed it."

She gave Corylus a lopsided smile. "Folks don't like to go up against your old man, Corylus," she said.

"No, ma'am," Corylus said, his voice suddenly husky. "Smart folks don't."

"So you tell me what you want," Baucis said, "and I'll see that you get it. I've got a crew going out this afternoon, and you're on it if you want to be. And don't worry about what it might cost, because that's been paid long since."

She stood up; Corylus rose also. He restrained his impulse to salute her.

"Have you maybe heard about the fancy woman Melino keeps upstairs?" she asked. "I can get you into the grounds, but for the house you're on your own."

"I don't know anything about that," Corylus said. "In truth, I don't know anything about Melino. That's why I'd like to get closer to him."

"Well, it's none of my business," Baucis said indulgently. "Show up here at the seventh hour, dressed for work. It's cultivation and watering today, nothing fancy."

She looked at him, again appraisingly but in a different fashion. "You're a handsome one, as I'm sure you been told. Handsomer than your father, that's for sure. But Cispius is a man."

She paused, then said, "Are you a man, Corylus?"

He was already standing straight. "Ma'am," he said. "I try to be."

Baucis laughed again. "I guess you'll do," she said.

CHAPTER VII

Melino turned left on the corridor at the head of the stairs. Hedia ran her hand gently down his back. As she had guessed, he wore nothing under the thin white robe.

He turned in apparent surprise and said, "What—"

Hedia embraced him as closely as her silk dress allowed and kissed him firmly.

Melino's arms came up as expected, and he pushed her away in horror. That was so far down the list of what she had expected that she could honestly say that it hadn't crossed her mind.

"What are you doing?" he cried.

"Embarrassing myself, apparently," Hedia replied coolly as she stepped back. "Well, making a fool out of myself. It takes more than that to embarrass me."

Her first thought was that Melino was one of the men who liked men, or boys, anyway. Her first husband, Calpurnius Latus, had been of that sort. But when rubbing her body against Melino's in garments so mutually thin, she had been *quite* sure that he found her attractive. So had Latus, if it came to that.

"Why did you invite me here?" she said. "Since it wasn't—"

Her hand twirled the air briefly.

"—what I assumed. What I think any reasonably attractive woman would assume."

"I . . . ," Melino said. He reached up as if to wipe his lips, then licked them instead. His eyes had the lambent glow she had seen before. "Your Ladyship—"

"'Hedia,'" she said, smiling at him. "As I was Hedia before, remember."

She had decided to be amused by the business, the way she had been amused by contretemps with other men. Though this was unique in her experience.

"Hedia . . . ," Melino said. He seemed to come to a sudden decision and went on, "If you'll come this way, I'll show you something. I wasn't going to . . . well, it doesn't matter. Come with me."

The upper-level rooms to front and back of the house had doors, not the more common curtains in the doorways of rooms within a private house. Melino turned and opened the door to the rear of the house instead of the front room toward which he had originally been headed. Hedia followed him inside.

When she was in a normal house—one of her own family or that of an acquaintance—she didn't notice the inevitable noise that the servants made. Here in a house with *no* servants, the silence was disturbing.

The room was divided by a sliding screen, a series of panels. It now reached from the middle to the back of the house overlooking the garden, but it could be telescoped against the internal wall. There was a dry odor that Hedia had smelled before but which she couldn't identify.

"I was going to show you this by another way," Melino said. "This may be better. You have to learn at some time if, if we're to succeed."

He pulled the cover off an upright object near the screen; it was a tall mirror. The support pillars were of black wood carved in the form of intertwined monkeys on the right side and crocodiles on the left.

The mirror itself was a sheet of orichalc.

Hedia wasn't precisely vain, but she was conscious of her appearance because she knew others would be conscious of her. She stepped in front of the mirror. Melino hopped aside as though she were a bar of glowing iron.

She saw nothing but the metal's sheen. The difference between gold and orichalc was the difference between a white topaz and a diamond. Diamonds and orichalc had an internal fire that the lesser materials lacked.

"I don't see anything," Hedia said, turning to Melino. "I don't even see a reflection."

"Watch," the magician said, holding out his left fist so that the ruby ring almost touched the metal. He said, *"Blazing with fire and blood they gain the land!"*

Hedia expected to see the brown girls dancing around the glowing egg as she had in the smaller mirror; instead she looked up an enormous sand slope. She knew without being able to look around that the sea was behind her.

Light spread across the sky. Sunlight was scattering from something beyond the dune; then the dune itself vanished into the maw of a crystalline hugeness, a great worm. It proceeded toward her, engulfing the earth itself instead of simply plowing across it. It was on top of her and—

The image vanished. She had not been looking into the mirror; rather, she had been a part of the vision itself.

She found that her knuckles were hard against her teeth. She lowered her arms deliberately and said, "Was that real? What I just saw?"

Melino had been smiling slightly, probably in pride at his success. His expression sobered under the impact of Hedia's cold anger. He said, "It will be real very shortly now, if Lucinus has his way."

He rubbed his face with the back of his right hand; sweat had beaded on his brow. What he had just shown her had cost him effort.

"This mirror," he said, looking at her. Pride swelled in his voice with every syllable. "It too is made of orichalc, which only the Atlanteans knew how to make. An artifact so large—"

He gestured with his right hand.

"—is only possible because I am such a great magician!"

Rather than discuss how much she knew about Atlantis, Hedia said, "The ancient Atlanteans? Why, that's amazing. I don't know how you men are able to keep such things in your head!"

She had learned early that you couldn't overdo dim-witted innocence when dealing with a certain type of man. Indeed, dealing with almost any man who was trying to impress you.

"It allows me to do great things that would be possible with no other material," Melino said. "This was my master's mirror. Now that he is dead, it is mine."

He paused, apparently considering his next words. "Are you familiar with the term 'Refulgence'?" he said.

"Reflection," Hedia said. "From a mirror or the sea or even the polished marble side of a building."

"That's one meaning," Melino said, smirking again. "In the Art it is used where another would use 'Nigromancy': searching to find the truth through black magic. But I prefer—"

He gestured to the mirror.

"—to say 'Refulgence.'"

Melino had gone pale from the vision of the Worm, but his color had returned to normal. "Now I will show you another thing," he said.

He turned to the mirror. Before he could speak, Hedia laid the fingertips of her left hand across his mouth. "Don't show me the Worm again," she said. "I've seen it once; that was enough."

She lowered her hand. "Not the Worms," Melino said. "Another thing. An island."

He held his ring toward the mirror again and murmured, *"The calm seas are silent, and a bristling forest hangs over the shore."*

At first the metal showed nothing but its own preternatural sheen. Then Hedia was again in a distant scene: a jungle of unfamiliar trees whose green bark was covered with hairs. The ground was thick with soft knee-high vegetation, though she could neither feel nor hear in the present vision.

She was looking at something that stood so still that for a moment she thought it was a brown rock in shadow, or perhaps tree roots growing from a gnarled stump. Then she realized that the glittering points were in a pattern, two large gleams on the edges and six smaller spots above and between them. They were the eyes of a spider, a spider the size of an ox.

All thought froze, since Hedia was bodiless in this vision. She had no more than the usual distaste for serpents, but she hated to have crawling insects touch her—and she was terrified of spiders.

I want this to stop now, she thought. She had no voice, and if she had, her dry throat would not have passed the words.

The vision ended with a silent *pop*. Hedia wobbled and gripped the hard, black wood of the mirror's support.

"That is Zabulon's Isle," Melino said. He didn't seem to have noticed how much the sight had disturbed her. "That is where we must go."

"*I* don't want to go there," Hedia said. She expected her voice to quaver and was pleased that it did not.

"Oh, but we must!" the magician said. "You see—"

He paused, looking toward the ceiling while his lips danced through alternate explanations. Meeting her eyes again, he said, "My master was a great magician, the greatest since Zabulon himself. He journeyed to the island where Zabulon was buried and brought back Zabulon's *Book* from the tomb, passing through the wards which Zabulon had set up to protect his wisdom."

"The spider?" Hedia said evenly.

"No, no," Melino said, flicking his hand as if to dispose of trash. "The spiders, the other insects—a magician can protect himself against them. But guarding the tomb itself is a dog who is a thing of magic and proof against magic, against most magic. My master forced that ward too, as no other could have done; but there is another way."

Hedia lifted her chin in a tiny acknowledgment; she even smiled, though one would have had to watch her very closely to be sure of that. She wasn't afraid of dogs.

Melino wasn't paying any attention to her, except as an audience. "When my master felt age on him," he said, "he returned the *Book* to the place from which he had taken it. The traitor Lucinus wants to get the *Book* for himself to loose the Worms. I must get it first, and you must help me."

"I'm not a magician," Hedia said. Memory of the crouching spider sharpened her tone. "And I don't care to go to that island."

"You don't think I can use the mirror as a passage," Melino said in resignation. "I understand. Well, you had better see this."

He reached for the catch of the sliding screen. Hedia remained coldly aloof. She hadn't the faintest idea of what Melino was talking about, but she had generally found silence to be the best response when someone began blurting secrets to her.

Melino walked the screen back with a series of clatters, opening the other half of the room. On a heavy wooden bed frame, fettered by coils of rippling reddish light, was another of the lizardfolk like the four Veturius had brought back from Africa.

This one was female. She hissed softly when she looked at Melino.

"You see?" the magician said. "With her to anchor us in the Waking World, we *can* pass through the mirror to Zabulon's Isle and then return."

He laughed in triumph. The sound came out as close to a cackle; Hedia wondered whether the strain was telling on him.

"I suppose you think she's a demon?" Melino said.

"*Is* she a demon?" Hedia said instead of answering his question, though he probably thought she had.

"Not exactly," Melino said. "She is the Princess of the Singiri, and she is a magician of great power. If she were free, she'd be a danger. Controlled like this, she is merely a tool and our guarantee of safety."

The lizardwoman looked at Hedia. Translucent membranes winked sideways across the serpent eyes.

Hedia met her gaze regally. *She is a princess. I wonder what she's thinking.*

"So you see, we can pass through the mirror and return safely," Melino said. "But we must act quickly to forestall Lucinus. Are you ready to come with me now?"

"I haven't told you that I'm willing to go at all!" Hedia said. Her normal response to a man pressing her to the edge of courtesy would be to ease back from him. Now, smiling, she reached out and stroked Melino's cheek, causing him to shy away instead.

"But you—," Melino said urgently. He stopped before he finished the sentence with, "—must!" or words to that effect . . . which was not going to help his case.

Instead he shook his head and said, "If you do not, the Worms will be loosed and will destroy the Earth, Hedia. What I showed you with the eyes of your mind will in weeks or even days engulf your body and the whole world with you."

His voice was soft, pleading. He held himself erect, and he met her eyes. Many men had tried to convince Hedia to do this thing or that thing over the years; she was confident of her ability to read the truth beneath any words.

Melino wasn't lying.

"The Princess . . . ," Hedia said. She was giving the magician information—and also giving herself time to decide how she would answer his request. "I saw four more of them. Lizardmen like her. At the port the day before yesterday."

"What?" said Melino. "You're sure of that? That they were Singiri?"

"What would I have confused them with?" Hedia snapped. "I was as close to them as I am to this one!"

"Yes, of course," Melino said. He rubbed his mouth as he thought, the way another man might have stroked his beard. She had felt no hint of whiskers when she touched his cheek. She wondered how old he really was.

"They were in a cage," she said when the magician continued to stand in silence.

"That won't matter!" he said. He looked at the Princess, then at Hedia again.

"They can't enter this house," he said. "My wards will keep them out. But they could hire human dupes; I'll be sure that my own guards are alert. I'll hire more if I need to. But time is *critical*."

He turned his palms upward, his eyes locked with hers. "Please, Lady Hedia," he said. "We *must* get Zabulon's *Book* before it's too late."

"I will need time to consider the matter," Hedia said, knowing that it wasn't really true. It was generally a good idea not to appear too willing, though, even when she really *was* willing.

She walked to the door back to the hallway, avoiding the pitiless eyes of the reptile princess. Melino followed, wringing his hands in silent desperation.

"I'll return tomorrow if I decide to accompany you," Hedia said, starting down the stairs.

She wished there were people with whom she could discuss the business, but there really weren't, not unless she wanted to say more than she thought was advisable even to her friends.

Especially to her friends.

The door opened untouched as she approached it. *Besides, I've always kept my own counsel.*

"THAT'S THE HOUSE UP THERE, Your Ladyship," the coachman called, pointing up the hillside with his whip when Alphena stuck her head out of the window. "D'ye want we should get all the way up to it?"

"No," said Alphena. "Master Pandareus and I will go to the door ourselves and bring Paris back."

She wasn't going to insult the driver by telling him he couldn't get the heavy carriage up a track so steep, but that was what she thought. It was almost certainly what the driver thought also, though she was sure that he'd have made a try.

She looked at her companion. "Ah, if that's all right with you, master?" she said.

Pandareus had reached for the door on his side to open it. The footmen whipped it open before his hand touched the lever. He smiled and said, "The road isn't as steep as the steps to the Capitol, which I climb most clear nights to view the stars. It will feel good to stretch my legs."

Servants formed around her and the scholar with the usual amount of shouting and argument. The coachman wanted them out of the way so that he could turn, which was going to be tricky even without leaving the main road. It curved around the middle of the hillside and, though the pavement was fairly level, the slope to either side—up to the right and Paris' farmhouse, down to the left and a small stream—was another matter.

She and Pandareus started up the track. A man and a woman—middle-aged, wearing worn tunics and looking worn themselves—watched over the courtyard wall, but they were obviously servants. There was no sign of Paris.

"Surely he must have heard us?" Alphena said. "Maybe Collina's messenger didn't reach him and he's not here."

"I suspect Master Paris is making a point," Pandareus said. He smiled again, very slightly. "I'm interested in seeing how he lives, so this may be fortunate."

Pandareus was having an easier time with the track than Alphena was. She realized that, just as he had said, he regularly tramped through the backstreets and defiles of Carce at night.

She was used to people saying politely that this or that wasn't a problem when of course it was. She smiled: Pandareus probably didn't do that. He was *very* unworldly.

Alphena had been considering how to rouse Paris if he continued to ignore his visitors when they reached the house. The Illyrian kinsmen Drago and Rago solved the problem by jerking the door open without orders.

"Hey, Your Ladyship!" one of them called. "Want we should haul him out?"

"We're coming up, Rago," Alphena said, hoping she'd named the right cousin. "We'll talk with Master Paris in his reception room."

To Pandareus she added in an undertone, "It'll take some time to turn the coach. I think we're better off up here where we can be sure it won't topple onto us."

A third servant was watching them from the olive orchard on the slope beyond the house. The building had three small rooms parallel to the road and a slightly larger one as the lower bar of its L shape. Even if Paris and the three visible servants were everyone living on the farm, quarters must be crowded.

The stone-walled courtyard closed the rectangle. There was a lean-to shed against it and an olive press under a thatched roof taking up most of the rest of the space.

Pandareus, apparently thinking the same thing, said, "This is the sort of cottage which a small olive grove—on rocky soil—would just about support. Given what the wealthy folk of Carce would pay to a soothsayer with the presence of Master Paris, it gives me to believe that he's honest. Although he's not—"

Pandareus smiled at Alphena. He was a remarkably good-humored man. That was despite being a foreigner in a society that didn't pay a great deal of money to real scholars, according to comments Varus and Corylus had made.

"—a man to whom I've warmed in our brief acquaintance."

They reached the door just as Paris came to it. The Illyrian cousins waited hopefully for Alphena to tell them how to react.

"This is what passes for courtesy when the self-styled master race comes calling, I suppose," Paris said.

"We'll go inside," Alphena said, "since we're here already."

She stepped forward. Paris hopped back out of the way so briskly that he must have understood at least some of what the Illyrians were thinking.

"I was rather surprised myself," Pandareus said conversationally as he followed Alphena inside. "I would have expected Rago and Drago to kick the door down instead of opening it. I suppose they were on good behavior in front of Lady Alphena."

The interior was cramped, dark—the small windows were under the eaves—and smelled as though cleanliness wasn't of much concern to

the occupants. There was a rectangular table, a low couch that probably doubled as a bed, and a single chair. The walls were mud brick without plaster or other decoration.

Indeed, there was nothing inside that was in the least decorative,
unless you counted the strings of onions hanging from along one sidewall. Alphena *didn't* count them, and she doubted that Paris did, either.

The Etruscan soothsayer was dressed for travel. Alphena said, "We'll
leave as soon as the carriage is ready. If that's all you're taking—"

She nodded to a cloak rolled into a bindle, probably holding a few
objects in its folds.

"—I can have one of my men take it down for you."

"I will carry it myself," Paris said. Her offer of courtesy seemed to
have made him angrier, though it was hard to say.

"I don't see any books, Master Paris," Pandareus said. "Is your library
in another room?"

"Books are the business of clerks," Paris said with a sneer. "A wise
man listens to the flow of the Cosmos instead of reading the words of
men who know *nothing* of reality."

"Indeed?" Pandareus said in a tone of mild curiosity. Alphena had
the sudden impression that she was watching a pair of gladiators,
though she suspected that neither man had ever held a sword in his life.

"And if I may ask out of scholarly curiosity . . . ," Pandareus continued. "Is yours a family name, or did you choose 'Paris' yourself from the
Iliad?"

"Your *Iliad*," said Paris, "is a lie told by a race of liars. This much is
true: My people were driven from their home by Greek barbarians and
settled here, only to be displaced again by even greater barbarians. The
Greeks called the prince of my people 'Alexandros,' but Homer knew
him by his real name too, Paris."

Alphena frowned. She had heard of the *Iliad*, but she thought that
it was very old.

"Do you mean that you're descended from the man in the poem?"
she asked. Another possibility struck her and she added, "Or do you
claim you're his reincarnation?"

Looking at Pandareus, Paris said, "She is completely without logic,
and she appears to be unable to listen. Yet I am to bow to her!"

Pandareus smiled in a fashion that restrained Alphena in a way that nothing physical could have done. He said, "Her Ladyship is, of course, a woman. She has therefore not been educated in logic and rhetoric—or in literature, for that matter. But I have found her withal to be intelligent and clearheaded in difficult circumstances. In addition . . ."

Alphena waited in anticipation.

". . . Her Ladyship has practiced swordsmanship with a degree of success which has impressed better judges than a Greek scholar like myself. She would not need the help of her entourage to end your earthly cares, Master Paris, and to set you adrift in your flowing Cosmos."

"Hey, Rago!" Drago said, ostensibly to his cousin, also in the doorway, but in fact loudly enough to be heard in the olive grove. "Archias got the wagon turned around down there."

Alphena smiled. Phalanthus, the understeward in charge of the present detail, was probably horrified, but the Illyrians' subterfuge served the purpose of informing her.

"We'll go on to the Collinus estate, masters," she said. "I hope we'll reach it within two hours, from what the coachman estimated."

She walked back outside and stepped away from the door so that Pandareus and the Etruscan could follow her. When Paris came out, carrying his bindle, she added, "And Paris? Master Pandareus was too polite to mention this, but I'll point out that it was his reading of books which has located the gryphon's egg we're all interested in seeing."

Alphena let her lips quirk, not *quite* into a sneer. Paris was glaring at her.

"Perhaps age," she said, "has deafened the ears you use to listen to the Cosmos. Reading books may be a better technique in the long run."

VARUS AND HIS ESCORT ARRIVED at dawn at a home on the Palatine Hill, coming from Saxa's town house nearby in the Carina District. He didn't know where Lucinus had spent the night, but he and one of the black goats were already standing at the gate with a thin, balding man.

"Lord Varus?" Lucinus said. "This is Lucius Trebianus, the owner of the house."

Trebianus made a half bow to Varus. His fringe of hair had probably been red when he was younger. Two servants accompanied him, but they were staring at the black goat. They looked terrified.

So was the trembling goat, tethered to the handle of the gate to the back garden. Its eyes rolled and it was too frightened to bleat.

"You promise that you can lay the spirits here?" Trebianus said, turning to Lucinus. He had a slight lisp and a tendency to put his nouns in the nominative case, whatever their position in the sentence structure. From his name, he was a Gaul from the Po Valley.

"I promise nothing of the sort," Lucinus said calmly. "But since you're not paying me and my colleague, I think I can promise that we will not cheat you."

He lifted the lid of the wicker basket at his feet, part of the slight luggage he had brought from his farm near the Bay. He took out a wooden boat wrapped in raw wool. It was flat bottomed and the length of Varus' forearm; there was a small cabin in the middle.

"Has your family been disturbed by spirits here, Master Trebianus?" Varus said. His escort, a dozen men directed by an understeward named Coccius, formed an arc around him and his companions; they narrowed the street as effectively as a builder's dray. More effectively: a wagon wouldn't club you senseless if you bumped it.

"Well, not that exactly," Trebianus said. "I've got a house on the Aventine; that's where I live. I bought this place for the lot, you see. This house—it's run-down, but mainly it's tiny. It's a hundred and fifty years old, here on this prime location! I figured to tear it down and build something big enough for folk nowadays to live in. Only—"

He licked his lips, glancing toward the gateway.

"You see," he went on, "the crew I brought in didn't like the feel of the place. They downed tools and the overseer wasn't any happier about sticking around to whip them than the crew was to keep digging like they'd been doing. And I—"

He glanced back again. Varus realized that the reason they were having this discussion in the street was because the owner didn't want to enter his own property.

"—don't like the place much myself. So when Master Lucinus said he was a magician, well, I was glad to meet him."

A wagon that must have hauled quicklime to a building site rattled along the street in a miasma of stinging white dust. The driver whipped his pair of mules along. Wheeled vehicles weren't allowed on the streets of Carce during the hours of daylight, but he was hoping to reach the apron of the Piling Bridge over the Tiber before the Watch stopped him.

Varus' escort drew together, shouting threats and waving their cudgels. They were probably concentrating on a possible normal danger so that they didn't have to think about the magic they might be about to witness.

"If I can ask you, lordship?" Trebianus said. "I was wondering just where you come in on this, you being a senator's son and all?"

He sounded suspicious rather than merely curious. *Perhaps he thinks I'm going to try to cheat him out of the property to build a house for myself.*

Suppressing a smile, Varus said, "This house was the property of Lucius Sulla during his dictatorship following the Social Wars. It was here that those whom he had proscribed as Enemies of the Republic were brought for identification."

Varus had dropped into the dry lecturing tone that he often used unwittingly. This time it was deliberate, showing himself to be the sort of pedantic scholar who might accompany a magician for no better reason than knowledge.

As I really am, he thought.

"That is, their *heads* were brought here, to this house," he continued aloud, "where they remained until either Sulla or one of his aides confirmed their identification so that they could be struck off the list. There were four thousand, seven hundred of them, forty-seven hundred severed heads, waiting here until they could be carried to the Forum and displayed to the populace at large."

Varus gestured toward the open gate like an orator. "It's scarcely surprising that this place should be the haunt of restless spirits," he concluded. "If malign influences exist anywhere, then surely it is here."

Master Pandareus would be amused at what I was doing with his rhetorical training, Varus thought. Then, *I wish Pandareus were here. His presence helps me believe in logic and the role of intellect, which I sometimes come to doubt.*

"Right, right, I see that," Trebianus muttered toward the ground. "It can't have been this bad all the time, though. Up to a couple years ago, there was people living here, and they couldn't do that if it was like it is now."

"I think we're ready to begin, Master Trebianus," Lucinus said. "Do you care to come into the garden with us?"

"Hercules!" the owner said. "Are you out of—"

He remembered who he was talking to. If fear of magic hadn't driven Varus' escort to a distance, one of them might have corrected him already.

"That is," Trebianus said, "I have no part in such matters, sirs. I'll leave you to it—and wish you Good Fortune!"

He started off, then paused and looked back at Lucinus. "I've given you the keys. When you're done, just lock up."

Trebianus turned, then turned back again. "Or leave it open, I don't care!" he said. "There's nothing to steal here, and I'm going to tear it down anyway. Only by all the gods, *cleanse* it, master. I'll pay more than the property's worth just to have the things here gone for good. And there *is* something here!"

"Then we had best be about our work," Lucinus said. He held the boat in one hand and the basket with the rest of his paraphernalia in the other. "Lord Varus? Will your attendants . . . ?"

"No," said Varus. He turned. "Coccius?"

The understeward was standing just beyond arm's length, facing outward. He spun and bowed to Varus.

"You have an idea of what we'll be doing here, Coccius," Varus said coldly. "You and your men will be a distraction for me, perhaps a dangerous distraction. I suppose it's already obvious that you're of no use?"

"Ah, yes, Your Lordship," said the understeward. He was a short man and from his accent a Sicilian. "We'd been wondering what you might want us to do."

"For my own safety, I want you to return to the house," Varus said in the same tone of haughty command. "I've told Agrippinus that I would probably do this."

If he didn't phrase his directions this way, there was a fair chance that the escort would refuse to leave. They were certainly afraid of magic, but that was an unknown quantity. They faced a certainty of crucifixion or being thrown to the beasts if they abandoned the young master in a dangerous situation, and *that* was a certainty.

"Agrippinus knows about this, Your Lordship?" the understeward said in relief.

"Yes," said Varus. "I gave him instructions in writing as we left."

"Right," said Coccius. He turned and said, "We're heading back for the house, boys! It's the master's orders!"

"Are you sure . . . ?" said one of the escort in a thick Thracian accent. He was a hand's breadth shorter than any of his fellows and slightly built; presumably he had been included for his enthusiasm.

"Look, d'ye want to take the place of that bloody goat, ye fool?" a comrade called. The Thracian looked blank, then trotted away with the rest.

Lucinus watched the escort leave with a sardonic expression. To Varus he said, "If you'll lead the goat, we can get to work. You'll probably have to drag him."

"All right," said Varus. He loosed the rope from the gate handle. The goat pulled backward but was too frightened to make a real effort to escape.

Varus wasn't sure how he would describe his feelings. He wasn't excited, certainly. It was more a matter of being resigned—and perhaps mildly curious about the outcome.

"There are shovels in the garden where workmen left them," Lucinus said. "Can you use one, Your Lordship?"

"It's a simple adaptation of an inclined plane, isn't it?" Varus said with detached amusement. "I should be able to master the principles involved, yes."

"Then if you'll close the gate behind us," Lucinus said, "we can get started."

Varus followed, smiling faintly. He found that he could drag the goat with reasonable ease if he lifted it by the halter so that its forefeet didn't touch the ground.

"Be philosophical, my caprine friend," Varus said. "You may well be the best off of the three of us before the day is over."

Lucinus looked back with an unreadable expression. Varus smiled a little more broadly.

"IT'S THE ONE WITH THE beige stucco," said Kurnos, the foreman of the three gardeners whom Corylus had joined as a fourth. Corylus grunted understanding: it was the house that Lucinus had shown to him and Varus in a vision.

The path to the back of Melino's house was more of a farm track than an alley. This far from the city, not all the houses had walls around their back gardens. A few servants were already at work as the crew passed; often there was an exchange of greetings.

"There's four guards outside and they got the gate closed," said No-thus, a one-eyed man who was missing the toes on his left foot. He looked at Corylus and added, "That something to do with you, kid?"

"I hope not," Corylus said. "But if I knew everything that was going on, I wouldn't be here."

He grinned: he wasn't doing anything unlawful, and he wasn't much worried about private punishment if Melino learned the truth about him. The crew carried hoes and shovels, and Corylus was pretty sure they'd stand beside a friend of Baucis against a few hired guards.

"Hey, Xerxes," Kurnos called. "What you all doing out here?"

"Hell if I know," said a guard. "Admetus and me are pulling a double shift, and there's supposed to be a whole extra crew hired from Ajax's gladiator school to take over at sunset."

"Roxolanus says we're supposed to watch out for lizards," said an-other guard with a puzzled expression. The guards carried light shields and six-foot spears intended for thrusting rather than throwing, as well as the swords Corylus had seen in Lucinus' vision. "I wonder if he meant snakes?"

"Well, we're here to water plants, that's all," Kurnos said. "Hey in there, open up!"

"It's Kurnos, Glabrio!" Xerxes called. "Let 'em in."

"Roxolanus is your captain?" Corylus said in a general fashion. He figured it was safe to show mild interest since the guards had brought the name up.

"If you ask him, he thinks he's god come down from Olympus," said Xerxes, lowering his voice slightly as the bar rattled on the other side. "Or wherever Sarmatian gods live."

Nothus spat in the dirt. It was probably a comment.

A guard inside pulled open the gate. He'd leaned his spear against the inner wall, but his shield was attached by a strap to the shoulder of his breastplate to take some of the weight off his left arm. He didn't speak as Kurnos led in the crew. Neither did the guard at the far end, near the door into the house.

Corylus swept an expert eye over the garden. It was of herbs, some of which were unfamiliar to him. Instead of piped water, there was a well with a basin below it; separate channels led from the basin to the eight planted rows.

Besides the herbs, there was a rose arbor against one corner of the house and an umbrella pine shading a bench at the other corner. Corylus tapped Kurnos on the shoulder to get his attention, then walked toward the pine. Kurnos opened one of the basin's watercocks, while the other two lifted water from the well and poured it into the basin.

Corylus glanced at the house, but there was nothing unusual about the outside. Louvered shutters closed the windows in the upper story. It might be possible to see out through them, but he probably couldn't view the interior even if he stood on the stone tie course between the floors.

There had been a row of trees down the middle of the garden, but they had been cut down within the past two years, probably when Melino rented the house and planted his herbs. The low stumps hadn't been removed. They had been fruit trees, but Corylus couldn't tell more without touching them. He thought of walking closer, but that would be too much like walking over a battlefield and closing the eyes of the corpses.

Trees die and people die; that was the way of existence. What was important right now was to prevent all trees and all people and all *life* from being swallowed down crystal jaws.

The pine's broad canopy would throw a dappled shadow over this corner later in the day. The marble bench was weather scarred; the relief of grapes and vine leaves was worn or covered by black corrosion. The tree must be older yet.

Corylus laid his palm on the trunk, his back to the house. His mind slipped into the tree the way water rose from roots to the topmost needles, permeating the wood.

An old woman waited for him in green silence. In a firm voice she said, "You're welcome here. But what has such a likely lad to do with an old woman like me?"

"I came to this garden to learn about the owner, a man named Melino," Corylus said. "He's a magician, and he's—he *may* be—planning to release the Worms of the Earth. I hope you may help us stop him."

The pine sprite laughed. "Loose Gaia's children, that one?" she said. "No, not him. He went to the Otherworld. He came back with a demon inside him and a greater demon on his finger, but he's no enemy to the world. Earth will take her revenge, but not through him, I think."

"I . . . ," Corylus said. "I had been told otherwise."

He had stopped himself from saying, "Are you sure?" which would have been insulting as well as foolish. Though dryads looked human to his eyes, they didn't feel the human need to lie.

"That one is no more a man than you are," the pine mused. Dryads considered names superfluous; few of those whom Corylus had met could remember—see any reason to remember—what one human called another. "He's as cruel as a man, though."

She looked at Corylus. He wasn't sure whether or not there was emotion behind her lined features.

"Are you cruel?" she asked.

"Mistress," Corylus said, bracing himself stiffly. "I'm not cruel by choice, but I've been trained as a soldier. In a hard situation, I'll act as I must."

The sprite laughed. Like her speaking voice, the sound was more mellifluous than one would expect from someone so gnarled and ancient.

"The lightning does the same," she said. "Shall I complain about the lightning? All things die. But that one. . . ."

Briefly behind her flashed a background of the garden in past years. Six fruit trees were in flower down the center, flanked by rows of hollyhocks and delphiniums.

"The apples and the pear, they were silly things, but they did no harm," the pine said. "I came to like listening to them chatter. That one had them cut down for no reason, just for another row of aconite and one of wormwood. He would have cut me down as well, but sometimes he sits on the bench and I shade him."

"You say that there is danger from the Worms, but Melino is not behind it?" Corylus said, wrenching his mind into the new direction. "Do you know who *is* behind it? Or what *is?*"

"Does it matter?" the old dryad said. "This one is afraid to die, but all things die."

She smiled again. In a more urgent tone she said, "The man approaching you is not your friend."

Corylus was back in the world that his body had never left. He

turned, ducking under the whistling spear shaft. The loaded butt hit
the tree trunk and bounced back. The huge Sarmatian swinging it
yelped as the shaft vibrated in his hand, stinging like a burning coal.

Roxolanus, the guard captain who thought he was a god. The Sarmatian was in full-length armor as though he were riding his horse toward
the army of Carce, as he probably had done in the past, and as Corylus
had watched his fellows do.

"Do you think Lord Melino pays you to stand around?" Roxolanus
said. His long coat was of scales of auroch horn sewn to overlap on a
backing of leather. The skirts fell to his boot tops while he was standing, but they were split in the middle so that he could fork his saddle.
"After I beat you to an inch of your life, I'll throw you out into the ditch
where lazy bastards belong!"

The gardeners were probably none of Roxolanus' business, but Corylus had met his share of officious officers before. He'd met Sarmatians
too.

The gardeners and the other guards were running toward the trouble, so Corylus had to finish it fast. "Your mother's too ugly for a whore
so we use her for a toilet!" he said in Sarmatian.

"What?" said Roxolanus. Corylus' Sarmatian was rusty and he'd never
been fluent in the language, but he'd clearly gotten his point across. "You
little worm!"

Roxolanus lifted the spear over his head, preparing to pin Corylus to
the pine tree. Corylus lunged forward, putting all his weight behind the
hoe whose blade he'd planted in the Sarmatian's crotch, through the
slit in his armor. He stepped aside as Roxolanus squealed, doubled up,
and fell forward.

"Keep away!" Corylus shouted. He tried to shout, anyway. He was
gulping air and too focused on his immediate enemy to care what else
was happening.

The Sarmatian wore a peaked cap covered with boars' tusks. It slipped
askew when Roxolanus hit the ground with his face. Corylus kicked it
away, reversed his hoe, and rapped the Sarmatian across the lower skull
with the handle. He could have cut the man's spine with the blade, but
he'd caused enough trouble already.

Roxolanus twitched and went still. *Hercules! Maybe I killed him
after all.*

Corylus backed away, gasping through his open mouth. He thrust the hoe into the ground to help support his wobbly knees. The whole business had taken only seconds, but it had taken *all* of him for those seconds.

His surroundings came into focus again. To his surprise, the gardeners and the remaining guards had stopped at a distance from him. Roxolanus was moaning, so he would probably live. He might sing at a higher pitch, but that was all right.

"And who are you?" said someone behind Corylus. "Since I don't believe you're a gardener."

Corylus turned and straightened. He had his breath back, or enough of it.

Facing him was Melino, whom Corylus had seen in Lucinus' visions. In the flesh Melino seemed older, though his face was even more boyish than Corylus had thought.

Melino wore a long shimmering-white tunic. On his left hand was a ring whose ruby flared momentarily brighter than the sun. His fist was clenched, holding the ruby toward Corylus like a shield—or the point of a spear.

"My name is Torquatus," Corylus said. "When I'm attacked, I respond. I'll leave your grounds now."

"Oh, no," said Melino. "I have a much better use for you."

CHAPTER VIII

C ome inside," Melino said abruptly, gesturing toward the door through which he had appeared. The back porch of the house was walled with a carved wooden screen; it allowed someone inside to look onto the garden while remaining in shadowed anonymity.

Corylus was still holding the hoe; he stretched it out so that Kurnos could take the hickory handle. He would have liked to keep it with him, but that would be impolitic, and he didn't imagine that it would help very much against the ruby ring. Whatever the ruby did.

Another man might have dropped the hoe on the ground. It had served Corylus well and deserved courteous treatment.

Melino glanced at Roxolanus, then said to Glabrio, "Get him out of here."

"Ah, Your Lordship?" Glabrio called to the magician's back. "Where should we put him?"

Melino laughed. "Throw him in a ditch, why don't you?" he said. "That was his suggestion, wasn't it?"

Corylus followed him onto the porch. Curved beams overhead had once supported grapes, but the vines were dead now; only gray tatters remained of the arbor.

Melino closed the slatted door and gestured Corylus onto a wicker couch. "I ask you again, Torquatus," he said, settling on the facing couch. "Who are you?"

"At the moment . . . ," Corylus said. He sat instead of reclining, and he was on the edge of the couch. "I *am* a gardener. My father had an estate in the Po Valley; we're Gauls."

Melino raised an eyebrow. "Your Latin is very good for a Gaul from the Po Valley," he said without inflexion.

"I had the best schooling," Corylus said. He had given some thought to what his story would be if he needed one, though he hadn't expected to use it. "I was taking lectures from Photius in Massilia when my father lost all his money."

Corylus shrugged. "My uncle Longus lives in Puteoli," he said. "I hoped he'd help, but he'd gotten angry over Father's dabbling in magic. He wouldn't talk with me."

"Your father is a magician?" Melino said. His posture didn't change, but he spoke in a slightly sharper tone.

"He thought he was," Corylus said. "It was all pretty harmless until he got involved with an Etruscan who called himself Teucer while I was in Massilia. That bastard took Dad for all he had—and all he could borrow from his brother, which is why Longus is so pissed off, I suppose. Then Teucer disappeared and our property disappeared—and I'm working as a gardener."

"Are you afraid of magic, Master Torquatus?" Melino said. "*Real* magic, I mean."

Corylus met his eyes. "I'm not afraid of anything," he said. "I guess your boy Roxolanus has guessed that too, by now. But let me tell you, if I ever meet Teucer again, *he'd* better be afraid."

"Roxolanus isn't my boy," the magician said mildly. He was no longer pointing the ring like a weapon; instead, he was rotating it idly with his right thumb and forefinger. "I have particular need of guards at the moment, and you have left me with no one to command them. Are you . . ."

He paused till Corylus met his eyes.

". . . interested in taking the place of Roxolanus?"

Corylus said nothing for a moment. If he had been here with no ulterior motive, he would have needed to know a great deal more about the job before he took it. Melino had started to frown with impatience before Corylus said, "What does 'take the place of Roxolanus' mean?"

"Commanding twenty-four guards," Melino said. "It was twelve until I got some troubling news this morning. I want half of them on duty at all times."

"If you want a full twelve, it'll take more than twenty-four total," Corylus said.

"Then hire more!" said Melino. "Half the gladiatorial schools in Italy are here on the Bay!"

"Go on," Corylus said calmly. That was the first break in Melino's facade of calm amusement. Staying calm was the best way to exploit it.

"I'll pay you five thousand coppers a month," Melino said, regaining control of himself. "You'll get a month in advance as soon as you accept the job."

"That's centurion's pay," Corylus said approvingly. In practice, a centurion—even a reasonably honest one—could double his wages through various perquisites, but this wasn't the time to quibble. "What are we doing to earn our money? Because if you want me to hunt lizards in your garden, you're out of luck. You can get an eight-year-old boy to do that better than I can."

"Who told you about lizards?" Melino said, deathly still.

"One of the guards," said Corylus, "and he got it from Roxolanus. Look, what *are* you worried about? You're offering too much money for anything I've heard yet, which makes me think that maybe I'd be underpaid if I took the deal after all. I'm still ready to walk out of here."

It was Melino's turn to pause. A staff of black wood leaned against a pillar of the house proper behind his couch; he took it in his hand. Corylus watched, but the magician's demeanor didn't seem threatening.

"You said you weren't afraid of magic," said Melino. Using his staff, he traced a wavy line on the ground between them. "People sometimes say things that they can't back up when they're tested."

"I don't," Corylus said. "Tell me what you're guarding against or I'll go back to opening irrigation channels. *I* don't care which."

A wraith of light—for a moment Corylus thought it was rosy smoke—spurted from Melino's ring and took shape as a nude female figure. The demon and Melino said together, *"Devour his helpless limbs in your maw!"* The wraith's voice was cold and sexless.

The line on the ground—across the marble chips of the path and the leaf litter and grass on the ends—squirmed and raised its horned head. It was a thick-bodied Libyan viper, about as long as a man's arm. It looked at Corylus, then rippled sideways toward him.

I should have kept the hoe after all.

Corylus leaned sideways with his left arm out, wiggling his fingers.

The viper stopped and focused on the movement. Its tail drew up under the rest of the body; its head cocked back.

Corylus grabbed it just behind the head with his right hand.

He didn't know what to expect—smoke, sand; perhaps his fingers slipping through nothingness. The reality was dry strength beneath a cover of pointed scales. He leaped to his feet shouting, *"Ha!"* and tried to snap the snake's body against the pillar behind Melino. The viper vanished from his grip.

Corylus was breathing hard. He remained standing, looking down at the magician. The wraith from the ruby had disappeared when the viper did.

"If you need me to kill snakes . . . ," he said, his voice harsh and unexpectedly loud. He didn't try to lower it. "Then I'll use a stick the next time, all right?"

"Yes," said Melino. His voice didn't quiver, but he had swallowed twice before he got the words out. "I apologize, Torquatus. I—that was unnecessary and I apologize."

Corylus stepped back. He had been standing over the magician and shouting at him. The viper had felt real and Corylus didn't doubt that its poison would have been real also; but it was over.

If I'd wanted a quiet life, I would have planned to stay in Carce as a lawyer. And very possibly I would shortly be swallowed there by a giant worm.

Melino lifted the lid of a small bronze chest on the table beside him; he took out five freshly minted gold pieces and placed them in an arc on the table. There seemed to be as many coins stacked within as there had been when the box opened.

"This is your pay for the first month," Melino said. He seemed to have regained his composure. "Now, if you'll come with me, Captain, I'll show you what your possible enemy is. I was afraid to do so with Roxolanus, so I tried to describe the danger to him."

He smiled faintly and added, "Unsuccessfully, it would seem. I believe your arrival this morning was providential."

Corylus followed the magician through the office and reception area, then up the stairs to the upper floor. He left the gold behind. He was a little embarrassed at being paid to spy on Melino, but he was beginning to wonder if he hadn't been wrong about the man.

He grinned ruefully. Except about Melino's connection with Hedia, which didn't endanger the Republic or the world.

Melino opened the door to the right at the head of the stairs and walked through. The slatted shutters dimmed the room even more than Corylus had guessed when he looked up from the garden.

Corylus saw the loops of quivering red light. It was a moment later before he realized they were bonds tethering a lizardman to a bed frame; Corylus grunted in shock.

It's a female. She's a female.

"This is a demon like those which a wizard is using to attack me," Melino said. "This is a female whom I captured and use as a tool to thwart my enemy."

He leaned forward and ran the ruby down his captive's thigh. She writhed, hissing: a welt sprang up as though the jewel had been a hot iron. The surface of her skin was lightly pebbled instead of being scaly.

"You see?" Melino said. "I control her completely. She's harmless so long as she remains in my power. If she should get free, though, she would help my rival to destroy the world."

"What do you mean?" Corylus said. He spoke in a carefully neutral tone, as though he was asking for clarification from his commanding officer . . . which in a manner of speaking was what he was doing. "Destroy the world, that is?"

Melino looked soberly down at his captive. "She is a princess of her people and a great magician herself," he said. "If her kinsmen were to free her, she would join my rival Lucinus and loose the Worms of the Earth."

Corylus said nothing. The pine nymph had told him that Melino wasn't planning to loose the Worms. He believed her. That meant part of Lucinus' story was false . . . and if the whole thing was false—

Has Lucinus tricked me and Varus into helping him destroy the world?

"My late master hid away a book of magic," Melino said. "If I can retrieve it, as I will if I have a little time, I can save the world. That's why I need you."

"You want me to find this book with you?" Corylus said slowly. He had entered Melino's grounds with a clear intention. Now nothing was clear. He was particularly puzzled about what *he* should be doing.

"No!" Melino said. Then, more mildly, "No, you're not a magician. I need you to protect the house against the Singiri who have come to free their princess."

"Lizardmen like her?" Corylus said. He looked at the female—the Princess. She met his eyes with an expression that hid some emotion. He had no idea what that emotion was, however.

"They'll be males," said Melino, "but there are only four of them. How many men will you require to keep this house safe?"

Corylus thought about the lizardmen he'd seen in Veturius' beast yard. Three of them were warriors; the fourth was old . . . but again, perhaps not to be despised. The guards Melino had hired while Roxolanus was captain seemed a decent lot from what Corylus had seen. And there were twelve on duty.

"I think we've got enough," he said, speaking as Torquatus, the squire from the Po Valley, who had just been hired. "If I change my mind, I'll tell you."

"Good," said Melino crisply. He gestured Corylus toward the door and the stairs beyond. "I have a place nearby where you'll sleep. Only men who are on duty stay on this property."

"I'll introduce myself to the men," said Corylus. "Then I'll take care of my personal affairs and return here."

"Don't worry about anything but guarding this house!" Melino said as they descended the stairs. "I am your only concern."

Corylus looked back over his shoulder. "You hired a guard, Master Melino," he said. "You didn't buy a slave."

He wondered what Varus was doing—and how Varus would advise him if they could discuss what he had just heard and seen.

Corylus stepped into the garden, facing not only the guards but also Kurnos and his crew. The magician had followed him down. He needn't speak, but his presence would confirm what the new guard captain was about to say.

"All right!" said Corylus. "I'm in charge, now. Anybody who doesn't like that can pick up his pay and leave. Or if they want to take it up with me, that's all right too. Anybody?"

In the silence that followed, Corylus glanced at the pine tree. He remembered that the sprite had called Melino cruel, and he remembered the cold brutality with which he had burned the leg of the Singiri princess.

If the world depends on such a man to save it, he thought, *perhaps the world isn't worth saving.*

VARUS STOOD ON TOP of the shovel to drive the blade's full length into the ground. The soil itself was soft—boggy, even—but the garden was badly overgrown. They were having to cut through roots, which was much more difficult than he would have guessed.

He was cutting through roots. Lucinus had scribed a six-pointed star on the ground and was writing in a circle just beyond the points. Varus couldn't read the words; in fact, he couldn't tell exactly where the star was despite having watched Lucinus mark it.

Ivy had overrun most of the raised beds and covered the gravel paths. Apparently the magician found it important to draw the symbol, but he didn't care that it be visible.

Lucinus straightened. "Is the trench finished?" he asked.

Varus tried to scoop up the dirt he had just loosened. Most of it spilled back when his shovel struck a root and the blade tipped.

"I suppose so," he said. "Is it long enough for you?"

Varus had joked when Lucinus asked if he could use a shovel. He now realized that there was a great deal more to it than he had assumed.

He had sometimes watched servants working while he was in one of the gardens of a house he was staying in. Varus preferred to learn from books rather than people. Still, because he *had* watched, he had known to use his weight to drive the shovel where the strength of his arm could not.

But he also knew that Attis, the gnarled, sixty-year-old chief gardener of the Carce town house, could cut a thumb-thick root with a twist of his shoulders. His young master couldn't manage that except by raising the shovel and slamming the blade three times in succession into the obstacle.

Varus smiled ruefully. *And* he was getting blisters in this interval of less than an hour.

Lucinus looked over. The would-be trench was three feet long, but it was ragged and no deeper than the length of a man's hand. Even some of that depth was loose dirt.

"It will do," he said. He used the hem of his tunic to wipe the scriber he had been using. Now that Varus had a chance to look, he saw that it was a knife whose blade of black glass was bound onto a deer-horn hilt.

Varus leaned his shovel against a terra-cotta planter that years of rain and occasional frosts had cracked into little more than an ivy-covered mound. He was mildly irritated that Lucinus hadn't been more impressed by the results of his work. He knew that was silly: it had been considerable effort, but only because he was so ignorant of proper technique.

"I could have brought our chief gardener with me," he said, smiling at himself. "I'm sure he could have done a much better job."

"Would he have been willing to do the work?" said Lucinus with a raised eyebrow. "He would have understood what we intend, I think."

Varus pursed his lips. "Attis would have done the work," he said. "But he wouldn't have been happy about it. And it would have been wrong to bring him, since what I could manage was sufficient to your needs."

Lucinus set the miniature boat on the ground parallel to the trench. He reached into his bag and came out with a pair of small scrolls.

"Is that a toy?" Varus said. He had expected Lucinus to set it in the center of the hexagram, but this seemed to be its final position. "The boat, I mean."

"It's a spirit boat from the tomb of one of the Libyan rulers of Egypt," Lucinus said. He untied the silk ribbons holding the scrolls closed. "It was intended to carry the soul of the Pharaoh to the Land of the Dead."

He gave Varus a hard grin and added, "Perhaps it did. We will use it for a different purpose, if all goes well."

Varus lifted his chin. "All right," he said. "What are my duties in this?"

"The spell I'm using is antiphonal," Lucinus said, handing one of the scrolls to Varus. "My uncle could have done this alone, but I need another magician."

I'm not a magician in that way, Varus thought. He didn't speak.

"We'll read the first stanza together," Lucinus said as he arranged spills of folded papyrus beside him. "I'll read the next alone, and then you'll read the third and we'll alternate. When I deem it to be time, I'll make the sacrifice."

Varus glanced at the goat. It lay on the near side of the trench, trembling and silent. Its eyes followed Lucinus.

"All right," Varus repeated. He put his left hand on the goat's shoulder, hoping to calm it. Varus' touch made no difference.

Lucinus picked up his copy of the spell. He stepped to what was probably the center of the hexagram he had drawn.

"We'll begin now," he said. Gesturing to Varus, he read, " *'This is our need.'* "

Varus noticed that though the magician held the scroll, he wasn't looking at it. He joined the reading, " *'This is our need.'* "

The words were coming to his lips without seeming to pass through his eyes. The morning sky seemed darker, duller, though there were no visible clouds; the change might have been his imagination.

Lucinus read, " *'We have a boat.'* "

Varus heard the wind sigh, then howl. The air was still. The sky was black, but he could see his immediate surroundings. *I am a citizen of Carce.*

" *'It is a fine boat,'* " Varus read in a clear, calm voice. No one listening to him would have imagined that he was frightened. His eyes were focused on Lucinus; everything beyond the edges of the magician's face had become a blur of gray in Varus' mind.

Motion beyond the trench drew Varus' attention. The funeral boat had swelled from a toy to something that stretched twenty feet from end to end, almost touching one wall of the garden. Instead of being solid, the crescent-shaped hull rippled with pale light. Varus thought he saw figures within the swirls.

"Our boat needs a crew!" Lucinus shouted. He threw down his scroll and grasped the goat by the uppermost horn; it bleated pitifully. The magician pulled the animal's head over the trench and cut its throat with the stone knife.

Blood gushed. The goat thrashed repeatedly, then went limp. Lucinus dropped the horn and lifted one of the hind legs to hold the goat upright over the trench as the rest of its blood drained.

"We will feed our crew," Varus said. He felt dizzy. The stench of blood and goat urine seemed overpowering.

The air thickened into ghastly wraiths, their features melting. One brushed Varus. He felt nothing, *nothing*; but the hair on his arm stood up straight.

The mouths of the wraiths were open. They moaned, pushing toward the blood-soaked trench but rebounding; they moaned louder, like the wind through a ruined temple.

"Our crew will row our fine boat to Zabulon's Isle!" Lucinus cried triumphantly. The wraiths swirled forward, merging as they filled the trench. The earth tossed and heaved as if children were playing in it, then became still again.

Varus saw motion, a thickening of the air, but the wraiths had vanished. The floor of the trench was dry, covered with fine dust. The six paddles bound to posts along the boat's side began to quiver.

"Come," Lucinus wheezed as he stepped out of the hexagram. He lifted his foot over the gunwale but wobbled there until Varus put a hand on his shoulder to steady him.

"Come . . . ," Lucinus repeated. He lurched aboard.

Varus followed the magician, standing near him in the bow. The paddles moved, and the boat began to move.

I am a citizen of Carce.

ALPHENA HAD ORDERED the sides of the carriage rolled up, though the roof still protected the right side from direct sun. The benches doubled as beds if the occupants wanted to sleep during the journey, so there was plenty of room for all three passengers to be in the shade, but Paris nevertheless sat opposite her and Pandareus. Paris wore his broad-brimmed hat, which at least shaded the back of his neck.

"I thought the Etruscans lived north of Carce," Alphena said. "But Collina's farm is closer to the Bay than to Carce, isn't it?"

She was embarrassed to speak because she didn't know a lot of the things—literature and geography and history—that her brother took for granted. She could identify a Thracian gladiator or a Gaul—but she didn't know or care where either of them came from.

"Which is why I doubt that there's anything to be discovered there," said Paris. "The Samnites ruled this region at the time you claim Collinus Laethius settled here. They were no friends to our people."

Alphena smiled in her mind. She knew what a Samnite gladiator was, and now despite herself she did know where Samnites came from. Not that most of the gladiators fighting with swords, large, round, shields, and helmets with grilled masks came from any particular tribe nowadays.

She didn't mind admitting to Pandareus that she didn't know things. He liked to teach, and he really seemed to appreciate Alphena's questions. She listened and either understood or asked more questions until she did; and she remembered.

"The letters of Collinus Balbo didn't address the question directly," Pandareus said. If he was aware of the priest's hostility, his tone showed no signs of it. "Based on his letters he was rather *nice* about his family's honor, though. He had found material belonging to his ancestor which distressed him and suggested that Laethius was in self-imposed exile in order not to face something worse if he had remained in Veii."

"If he was an Etruscan among Samnites . . . ," Alphena said. "How did he survive?"

She had only the vaguest notion of history. From what her brother had described to her, however, she fancied that the tribes of Italy during ancient times more resembled wild beasts in the arena than they did those jockeying on the Republic's distant borders in recent times.

"Balbo says that Ligurian mercenaries defended the Collinus estate," Pandareus said. "He was quite proud of the fact that his ancestor had paid them with unminted gold. He doesn't seem to have made the connection I did between the gold bullion and the practices which caused Laethius to leave Veii and his ethnic kin for what could best be described as a fortified outpost in savage territory."

Pandareus glanced at the Etruscan priest. "It would appear that whatever Laethius heard in the flow of the Cosmos . . . ," he said. "Brought material rewards with it."

Paris glared at the scholar as though the comment had been a personal attack. He said, "You can laugh at my people now, Greek. But soon neither gold nor any other material thing will be of value! Earth is preparing to wipe herself clean of life!"

Paris stood up and walked to the back of the carriage, gripping the struts that supported the roof. He remained there, looking over the tailgate at the countryside they had passed. His stiff shoulders were a mute rebuff to any attempt to continue the discussion.

Pandareus smiled again.

HEDIA GOT OUT OF THE sedan chair. The bearers—it was a hired vehicle; Venus only knew where they'd been born—didn't seem disposed to leave. Agrippinus must have paid them very well and they were hoping to get a refresher if they also brought Hedia back.

"You needn't wait," she said crisply to the man in front. She started up the short walk to Melino's house.

Hedia didn't know when she would be coming back, or if she would be returning, though that wasn't a concern she chose to dwell on. Every morning it was possible that she was awakening for the last time.

Six guards watched from the porch. The big Sarmatian wasn't there, though his Greek partner of the day before was on duty. He seemed less cocky now, though Hedia hadn't chosen to say anything about his behavior to Melino.

She felt, well . . . not frightened, but uncertain in ways that she usually wasn't. Hedia had gone to the houses of many men, more often at night than in the daytime, but by daylight as well. She had always had at least a maid with her, however. Leaving Syra behind had been unexpectedly difficult, though there was no reason to cause a very skillful maid the sort of difficulty that she would face if her mistress vanished—or was found dead.

If Alphena hadn't already left for Carce as directed, Hedia would have brought her. *I'm glad Alphena obeyed. But perhaps her honor wouldn't have been compromised if she'd stayed with her mother for just one more day. . . .*

The guards separated to either side of the door into a group of two and a group of four. They didn't speak to her, and only a blond fellow missing both ears—a thief or worse—would even meet her eye.

Melino himself opened the door. "Welcome, Lady Hedia. Welcome indeed!"

Hedia walked over the threshold and said curtly, "Close the door."

The door closed behind her. Melino hadn't touched the panels or even gestured, and no servant was visible. Well, she had known Melino was a magician, though she didn't find much interest in magic that did no more than an inexpensive doorman could.

Hedia would have preferred that her visit not have been announced to all the world. A slave who had done something similar when Hedia was visiting a gentleman would have been whipped to the point he couldn't walk—or couldn't breathe.

But Melino was a wellborn but very naive young man; Hedia was visiting for another purpose entirely; and at this point, her reputation could scarcely be blackened. There was an advantage to being notorious beyond redemption.

The last thought restored her good humor. She reached out and stroked Melino's beardless cheek. He yelped and sprang backward, startling the two baboons. They were already at the ends of their chains, trying to stay as far as possible from their master.

Smiling, Hedia said, "You're very serious for such a handsome young man. Are you really in such a hurry to find a book?"

He had offended her because he didn't understand proper decorum for a woman of her station. She had paid him back because she *did* understand *his* idea of proper decorum and thus could deliberately flout it.

"On us depends the existence or non-existence of all life!" Melino said in shocked amazement. "What could be more serious than that?"

If you have to ask that question, Hedia thought, *then it would be pointless to discuss the matter with you.*

"Then let's get on with it," she said. Her smile was brighter than the thought behind it. "Though it seems to me that reducing stress before a difficult task is a better plan than some."

Melino led the way upstairs with quick, mincing steps. He was wearing the same white robe as on the previous day, but this time he had cinched it with a sash of red fabric. Hedia wasn't sure what the material was—she didn't think it was silk, but it certainly wasn't one of the coarser cloths she was familiar with.

These are better things to worry about than more serious matters. Which I can't affect.

They entered the room where the orichalc mirror stood beside the frame to which the lizardwoman was shackled. Perhaps because she was expecting something, Hedia noticed an unfamiliar odor. The closest comparison she could find was that of hot sandalwood.

The lizardwoman watched Hedia rather than the magician. Hedia returned her attention coldly. The creature appeared to be securely fastened, which was the only thing that concerned Hedia.

"Now, there's no danger," Melino said in a forceful voice. "If there should be any difficulty when we reach Zabulon's Isle, all I have to do is speak one word and we'll return to this room."

In Hedia's experience, that tone of pompous certainty meant there was considerable danger. She had assumed there was danger from the beginning, so she merely smiled.

"With the mirror," Melino continued, "I can open a passage directly to the isle."

Hedia followed his eyes to the orichalc surface. She disliked the lack of reflection where her mind knew that she should be seeing herself, her companion, and the furnishings of the room from a different angle.

"The Princess isn't necessary for that," Melino said. The lizardwoman continued to watch Hedia, as though the magician did not exist. "What she will do is provide us with a tether to the Waking World. Her pain will draw us back no matter what our situation on Zabulon's Isle may be."

The decoration showed that this had been two separate rooms before an interior wall was knocked out. The portion to the right had pale walls into which were set black cartouches with gold figures of gods and goddesses; it had been half again as large as the other, which was frescoed with the teetering vistas of a stage set.

The sliding divider was in the center, not where the original wall had been. Melino obviously didn't care about aesthetics: he had made changes only for functional reasons.

Hedia looked at the lizardwoman again. Membranes flicked sideways across the creature's eyes, but its gaze did not waver. It wasn't hurting Hedia—she wasn't even sure it was hostile—but she found the implied judgment irritating.

"Pain?" she said. "It doesn't seem to be in pain to me."

"Do you want to see pain?" Melino crowed. He balled his left fist so that the ruby ring faced the lizardwoman. "Do you?"

A tiny voice chirped, *"Faster!"* Melino didn't speak the word; Hedia wasn't even sure she heard someone speaking and not wood rubbing wood somewhere close by.

The bands of light holding the captive were a red so dark that it would have passed for black in direct sun. The light became brighter with hints of orange.

The lizardwoman moaned softly. Her limbs quivered, but the movement didn't reach her torso. Her mouth opened, showing short, pointed teeth. A forked black tongue flicked over and past them.

"Is that what you wanted, Hedia?" Melino repeated. He had been nervous since he opened the door to her, nervous at least since she stroked his cheek. "Is it?"

It was, Hedia admitted silently. *And I regret it now, but no one will ever know that.*

Aloud she said, "You've convinced me, yes. Now, let her be so that we can get on to our business."

Melino laughed. "I can't let her be," he said. "Her pain is our lifeline, as I told you. But we can go now, you and I. You and I . . ."

He clenched his fist again. A mist rose from the ruby, twisted, and congealed into a nude female whose body had no blemish and no humanity despite its shape. The figure was the color of fire, and the same fire burned in Melino's eyes for an instant.

This is a demon, Hedia thought, and said nothing, because there was nothing to say.

"Let the ivory gate open a path!" Melino and the demon said together. Hers was the voice Hedia had heard in the ring. It was stronger and fuller now, but it had the cold timbre of stone striking stone.

The orichalc mirror changed from solid to a clear depth with highlights of blue. Hedia remembered a grotto on Capri, which she had seen when she was visiting one of the Emperor's advisors. This color was the same, but the light was as cold as the demon's voice.

Melino took his staff in his right hand. He and the demon chanted, *"Let there be easy access to the shadows!"* The mirror became a window onto a forest of strange trees. In the distance something monstrous stalked into sight and vanished again behind the trees.

"Let us cut a track to our goal!" Melino cried, with the demon singing a descant to the verse. The mirror was alive with flames whose heat made Hedia flinch back.

As suddenly as the flames had appeared, they were gone. Instead of a mirror, Hedia stood in front of an opening into another reality. A breeze with the odor of warm compost ruffled her tunic.

"Come!" Melino said. He gestured toward the window with his staff.

Hedia paused. The magician glanced over his shoulder. He didn't speak, but the demon piped, "Faster!" again.

The rippling light holding the lizardwoman shifted to a bright yellow. She gave a hissing moan and her body arched as though she had been poisoned.

"Sister Venus!" Hedia whispered. She stepped through the window onto soft loam. Melino followed her as the demon sucked back into the ruby.

Sister Venus!

CHAPTER IX

A hired porter followed with the bundle as Corylus returned to the rear of Melino's house. He could have used one of his father's servants, but keeping as close to his assumed identity—a Gallic gentleman in straitened circumstances—seemed better.

Leaving Pulto behind had been difficult. There had been a very loud discussion in which both parties had used the term "Duty" a great deal.

Corylus had won, but only by hinting at the thing he and his servant both wanted to avoid mentioning: Pulto's knees weren't up to the quick, silent movement a scouting expedition might require. Melino's house and grounds were just as uncertain and dangerous as the German side of the Rhine.

"Attention!" shouted Xerxes as the new guard captain approached. He and the other outside man—a fellow Corylus had rented from a gladiatorial school this morning—braced, though they handled their spears differently. Both had military training, but not in the same military.

"Stand easy," Corylus said. He paid the porter with a ten-bronze coin and took the bundle from him. "Has anything happened since I got my gear?"

"The four new hires arrived," Xerxes said. "One's inside with Glabrio; the other two's at the front with Admetus."

Corylus unwrapped his cloak from around a simple helmet of spun bronze, a breastplate of glued linen, and a sword with a dagger to balance it on the belt. The weapons had no identifying markings, but anyone who saw them would know that they belonged to an auxiliary cavalryman in the Republic's service.

Xerxes gave his fellow guard a nod and a knowing look.

"Want to say something, Xerxes?" Corylus said in a cool voice.

"I told Hicafrith here that the new captain knew his way around a battlefield or I missed my bet, sir," Xerxes said. "That's all."

"You don't miss your bet," Corylus said as he cinched the sword belt around his waist. "Carry on."

Glabrio had opened the gate a crack at the sound of Corylus' voice. Now he pulled it back to pass the captain into the garden.

"Anything new?" Corylus said, looking around as Glabrio slammed the gate behind him. Another of the gladiators hired this morning stood nearby; two more guards were at the porch. No one stood close to the umbrella pine.

"Just the reinforcements," Glabrio said. "Xerxes sent the other two around to the front. Ah—we don't go through the house, you know, sir? We take the path around the garden wall. Lord Melino didn't say anything, exactly, but . . . we just do."

"There should be four more recruits in the course of the day, and I plan to hire the rest tomorrow," said Corylus. "And you're wise not to enter the house."

He didn't add that anyone trying to leave through the front door would have to pass a pair of baboons. He might be facing the same problem. Because of where the baboons were chained, they guarded the stairs to the upper floor as well as the front door.

"Carry on," Corylus said without looking back at Glabrio. Eye contact would have given the guard an opportunity to prolong the conversation. Corylus walked to the pine tree, stepping carefully over the plantings. The guards were watching him, but none of them chose to— dared to—speak.

Corylus was as much on edge as he would have been while waiting for dark before he crossed the river on patrol. He wanted to talk with the pine sprite as much for her feeling of deep calm as for any information that she might have.

Information would be nice, though.

As before, Corylus laid his left palm against the rough trunk. The green coolness drank him in, absorbing the doubt and tension that had ruled him since Varus prophesied cataclysm in the beast yard.

The dryad smiled with the amused ease of several hundred years of experience. She said, "You fidget like a squirrel, Cousin. But you are as welcome as a squirrel also, because you remind me of how good the peace of my life is."

"If you're right about the Worms of the Earth destroying everything unless they're stopped . . . ," Corylus said. "Then your peace will end as surely as my fidgeting, Cousin. I want to stop them and save us both for our chosen lifestyles."

The sprite laughed. "The magician here wants to stop the Worms also," she said. "He has left the Waking World to halt them. But the Worms will come if it is their time, or they will not come. And if they do, well, all things die."

Corylus focused on the critical part of what the pine sprite had just said. "Melino isn't in the house now?" he said. "That is, he isn't in the Waking World?"

"The magician passed through his mirror," she said. Behind her spread a forest panorama, firs and hemlocks and pines. They grew so thickly together that when one died and tilted, its neighbors continued to hold the trunk upright. "Out of the Waking World, out of my world. I know no more, Cousin."

It hadn't occurred to Corylus that Melino would leave the house. Corylus wasn't sure what he should do with the opportunity, if it really was one. *I'm not sure of anything!*

"Do you know how long the magician will be gone, mistress?" Corylus said. He saw an elephant—a line of elephants covered with long black hair—walking through the trees behind the dryad. Despite the beasts' size, they didn't disturb the tightly sewn trees.

"Perhaps as long as a cloud takes to pass the sun," she said with a quiet smile. She shrugged. "Perhaps he will be gone until the sun burns out. I am neither a magician nor a prophet, and I do not care."

Corylus laughed in sudden realization. "I came here as a scout," he said. "Anyone listening to me would have thought that I was afraid to do my job."

He bowed. "Thank you, mistress," he said. "Perhaps we'll meet again."

His soul turned and stepped out of the pine tree. He stood in the garden again. The guards were all looking at him, but they glanced away as soon as he moved.

If people didn't offer you information, you went out and got it. That meant danger on the river frontiers, the Rhine and the Danube both; and if it meant danger here, what of it?

Corylus loosened his sword and dagger in their sheaths, then walked into the arbored porch of the house. He didn't acknowledge the guards' interest.

He stepped past two empty bedrooms and through the office to the reception room. The baboons sat, facing the front door. When they heard his step, they turned their heads to look over their shoulders at him. Their manes swelled as the individual hairs stood on end.

Corylus touched his sword hilt, then took his hand away. He continued toward the stair alcove with a firm stride. Aloud he said, "If you want a problem, I'll give you one."

Neither baboon moved in his direction, though one growled deep in its throat. Corylus took the stairs normally instead of backing up them so that he could continue to face the animals.

They had seen him with Melino, which was enough reason for them to have let Corylus go without violence this time. He gave a sigh of relief when he was sure that he was beyond the reach of their chains, though.

Of course, there was always the matter of getting past the baboons when he left. He grinned. It would be time enough to worry about that if he survived to leave.

Corylus had left his sword sheathed while he was downstairs so as not to show weakness to the baboons. At the head of the stairs he drew the long cavalryman's blade before he used his left hand to open the room where the lizardwoman was imprisoned.

He walked in behind the tongue of sharp steel. He hadn't seen any dangers when he viewed the room with Melino, but it would be only common sense for the magician to arm a trap when he left.

"There is no danger," said a voice. "Melino doesn't believe that anyone would have the courage to enter his domain uninvited."

The lizardwoman—the Singiri princess—had spoken.

Even though he knew she was present, it took Corylus a moment to see the captive. Her bonds of light were brighter this time, almost yellow, but the light drew and held his eyes instead of illuminating the limbs it gripped.

"Can all your people speak?" Corylus said. Those words replaced, "I didn't know you could speak!" before that, his—foolish—original thought, had reached his tongue. "There are four of you, males, in the harbor."

"Not all, n—*oh!*" the Princess said, arching suddenly in an apparent convulsion. Then she said, "Not all of my people can speak Latin, but a few can."

She closed her eyes momentarily; the lids were a soft reddish hue that contrasted with the pale beige—almost cream—color of her skin. Her limbs appeared swollen above and below the bands of rippling light.

She caught her breath and said almost in a whisper, "My people have come for me. I don't know how, but they have come."

Corylus felt silly with the sword in his hand. He understood now who he was guarding against—and why. He slid the round-tipped blade home in its sheath. "Are the manacles too tight?" he said, reaching for the band above the lizardwoman's right ankle.

"*Don't!*" the Princess said. She gasped and closed her eyes again.

Corylus by reflex gripped his sword hilt again, then took his hand away. He waited stone-faced for the captive to resume speaking.

She opened her eyes and said, "If you touch the gyres, they will burn you as they burn me. I would not have another being feel what I feel. But if my people have arrived to free me, I can continue to resist the pain."

"Why are you here?" Corylus said. He wanted to release her, but he had watched people suffer before. Sometimes that was necessary, as it was sometimes necessary to suffer oneself. He would know more before he acted.

"I found the wizard Melino trapped in the Otherworld," the Princess said. "I released him. When he was freed, he made me a prisoner as an aid to his own magic. He is a great magician."

But not much of a man.

And because the lizardwoman hadn't said that or made any other complaint, Corylus said, "How can I free you? *Can* I free you?"

"Iron will cut the gyres," the Princess said.

Corylus gripped for his sword. The hilt was hazelwood from the grove his mother and grandmother had tended when she met his father.

"No," said the Princess, as gently as a sudden gasp of pain permitted her to speak. "Not a good sword, a warrior's sword. The legs of the lampstand are iron."

Corylus took the adjustable lampstand in his hand. The shafts had been turned from delicately patterned walnut. The tripod legs were iron, as the Princess had said.

"Melino begged me to free him," the Princess said. "I do not beg you, warrior."

"Will you help Lucinus loose the Worms of the Earth if I free you?" Corylus said. It wasn't a real question, and anyway, he'd already decided that he wasn't going to leave the Princess to be tortured, by Melino, or by anybody else, but certainly not by Melino.

"I do not know Lucinus," the Princess said. She shuddered and her eyes closed, but she continued, "And I would not loose the Worms. We Singiri were happy on the Earth when we lived here. We would not destroy the Earth now, though we are in another place."

"Good," said Corylus. He tried to force the lampstand between the band of light and the bronze bedstead to which it clamped the lizard-woman. He planned to lever them apart—and when that failed, as he expected it would, try something else.

When the clawed iron foot touched the shackle, light spurted like a rainbow from a dolphin's blowhole. The gyre vanished, and the stump of the iron leg glowed a red close to orange.

The Princess gave a high-pitched cry. Her leg lashed out violently, but Corylus wasn't sure whether the movement was intended or a spasm.

He thrust the lampstand into the other leg shackle, this time creating a spray of white sparks as well as the rainbow mist. One of the floor tiles cracked at the touch of the blazing iron.

The Princess hissed like water pouring on a stove. Her lower legs were swollen, but her knees flexed and Corylus didn't see permanent damage. A little longer, though . . .

"Close your eyes," he ordered. "I don't know where—no, wait."

A piece of brocade covered the seat of Melino's wicker chair. Corylus ripped it off and laid it on the lizardwoman's face, covering her eyes.

Only then did he poke the lampstand under the bedstead and raise it into the bond holding her right wrist. There was an even greater gush of sparks this time, but none of the iron flew or bounced upward.

Half-rising on the bedstead, the Princess grasped the brocade herself and held it between the remaining gyre and her face. "Quickly," she whispered, "for I am—"

Corylus thrust, freeing her in a snarl of fire that devoured the remainder of the iron. He laid the paired shafts on the floor.

"I am very weak," the Princess said. She would have fallen backward if Corylus hadn't managed to get his arm behind her. "I am weak, and I might have died; but you saved me, warrior. You saved me."

"Where do you want to go?" Corylus said. Burning iron had seared the air to an acid dryness that ate at his throat. "You can't stay here."

"Can you take me to my people?" she said. She sat up with her own strength, allowing Corylus to step back. "If they have come for me, they will be able to take me back to our home."

"I think so," said Corylus. He looked for garments and found a robe of Melino's. It would do to get the Princess past the guards. After that it wouldn't be hard to get her to Veturius' compound. "Ah—but your fellows are in a cage."

The Princess got carefully to her feet. Corylus was ready to catch her if she toppled, but she managed to stand upright by herself and slowly relax. "They are bound as I was?" she said.

"No, it's an iron cage," said Corylus. "With a padlock, a lock that has to be turned with a key through a hole in the side."

The Princess burst into hissing laughter. "Oh, my!" she said. "Iron bars and a lock with a hole in it? I think they will be all right."

She sobered and patted Corylus on the shoulder, though she winced as her arm straightened. "You are a warrior," she said. "Those who have come for me will be warriors also . . . but did you notice if one of them was older than the other three?"

"Yes," said Corylus. Nobody likes to be laughed at—and he didn't see the joke in what he'd said—but the Princess obviously wished him well. "One certainly was older."

"That will be Tassk," she said, "as I might have known. Tassk will not find a lock difficult, my friend; and he can speak your language and many languages, though the younger warriors with him probably cannot."

"Put this robe on and I'll find you a hat," said Corylus. "And I'll take you to your friends."

He didn't know what he would do after he turned the Princess over to her fellows. *But it's like a long march,* he thought. *One step at a time.*

HEDIA STAGGERED AS HER FOOT plunged ankle deep in the loam. She braced herself against a tree trunk. Its green bark was smooth to the eye but felt like sharkskin to her palms.

Melino stepped out of the air beside her. He paid no attention to her. Instead, he clenched his left fist and said, "Open!"

The demon expanded from the ring; she was the same rosy hue as before. She seemed to be more solid than she had been on the other side of the mirror.

Hedia couldn't see the mirror from this side, not even as a shimmer against the forest background. She, Melino, and the demon were in a glade of waist-high grass through which grew strange trees like the one that had kept Hedia from falling.

"Which direction, demon?" Melino said. The demon pointed slightly to the right of the direction the magician was facing.

Hedia looked upward, then stepped back from the tree trunk to get a better view. Even so she couldn't see the branches except as wobbling silhouettes far above, still thrusting skyward. And there was something else. . . .

"The sooner we finish this, the better," Melino said. He started in the direction the demon had pointed.

"Wait!" Hedia said. "What's that? Just above the joint in the trunk?"

"It doesn't matter," said the magician. "Come along."

"I said *wait*," Hedia repeated. A rounded brown lump the size of a bear bulged from the trunk. She might have thought it was plant gall of some kind had she not seen the six golden legs that clamped the body to the tree.

"It is an animal drinking the sap of the plant," the demon said. She was looking at Hedia. "It is no danger to you unless it should fall, and its beak is sunk so deep into the stem that it probably cannot fall."

"It doesn't *matter*," Melino repeated. "Please come on. Delay may . . . anything may happen!"

Hedia realized that the magician was nervous, frightened even. The air was dead still, but shadows quivered when branches wobbled high above.

"Go on, then," she said harshly. She was nervous also, though thus far the island appeared strange but not frightening.

They set off through the forest. The demon led. She appeared to walk in normal fashion, but her legs passed through the high grass without making the blades move.

Hedia grimaced. She hadn't been sure about what to expect from Melino's invitation, but she'd been confident that it wouldn't be a dinner party. She had worn the heavy sandals in the knowledge that they would be preferable to fashionable footgear in anything *except* fashionable venues, but that was only one of many questions.

For example, she'd dressed in a knee-length tunic so that if she had to run it wouldn't tangle her legs as a longer garment might do. She hadn't thought about grass-blades sharp enough to tear her calves, though.

Perhaps I should have worn breeches like a Gaul, she thought. The image of herself as a northern rustic restored her mood and brought a smile to her lips.

They passed under a field of flowers a foot in diameter, dangling upside down from the canopy at the end of long vines. A few of the giant blooms were white, but most of them were pastels: blue, yellow, violet, and pink. There was even a green one, though the petals were hard to see against the forest background.

Hedia glanced at the branch from which the flowers hung. It seemed to span a pair of trees hundreds of feet apart, growing to both like a living bridge. On its underside was a pale green shape that she ignored as a leaf until it moved.

The triangular head turned toward her, and a pair of fanged forelegs lifted slightly. She was looking at a praying mantis. She saw them occasionally in the garden, but this one was over six feet long.

"Melino!" Hedia said. "Look up on the branch!"

The magician glanced upward. "We'd best get on," he said, resuming his course.

The demon looked up as she walked. "It is following us," she said without emotion.

The mantis kept pace above them to where the branch joined one of the trunks as they were passing by beneath. Hedia had forced herself not to look up, pretending that she needed to watch her footing, but she cocked her head now.

The mantis started down the trunk, walking head downward like a squirrel. Its four hind legs stepped one at a time, causing the long body to rock side to side as it proceeded. It moved deliberately, but it was clearly as fast as Hedia and her companions.

They walked on, passing a band of trees whose paired fronds stuck out at arm's length to either side. The demon drifted through them while Melino brushed them aside.

Hedia followed the magician. She disliked the touch of the fronds on her forearms; she wondered if they would raise welts the way nettles did.

She was becoming increasingly irritated with Melino's short answers and refusal to volunteer information. She started to ask him a question, then grinned and said instead, "Demon? How were you trapped in the ring where Melino holds you?"

They were walking through shorter foliage again, green clubs that unrolled upward as they grew. The tallest came to mid-thigh or perhaps a little higher.

Melino glanced over his shoulder and smiled. He didn't speak.

"The ruby protects me," the demon said. "It is not a trap; it is my refuge. The magician Zabulon drew me from the fires of the Underworld, then created this refuge in return for the help that I gave him."

"But you're helping—" Hedia's tongue froze on the word "Melino." Instead she continued, "You're helping us against Zabulon, though he protected you?"

"Zabulon is dead," said the demon. She didn't turn to look at Hedia during the conversation.

"The demon does as my spells constrain her to do," Melino said in a tone of satisfaction. "She has no soul and no feelings of gratitude."

The demon now turned her head. "Zabulon is dead," she repeated. Her eyes were unfathomable, but they were not empty. Hedia saw something in them, though she couldn't identify the emotion.

To the left ahead, a series of heavily veined dark green leaves grew from the ground. Each was the size of a ten-man squad tent, stretched out to dry.

On the underside of the nearest was a caterpillar marked green, yellow, and white in thin rings. It was three feet long and as thick as Hedia's thigh. It browsed the leaf in a short arc between two veins, backing in a ripple to devour another section when it had finished the one previous.

They passed the leaves. Hedia glanced over her shoulder to see if the mantis would pluck the caterpillar for its dinner. Instead the beast continued to stalk after them, coming slightly closer with each step of its four legs.

The demon reached a wall of vegetation shaped like so many six-foot sword blades. Each leaf had a green core and bright yellow edges. Instead of passing through, the demon stopped and turned around.

"Beyond is the cave," she said. "I cannot help you get closer."

Hedia pushed up to the yellow-green barrier, primarily so that she wasn't the closest of them to the following mantis. It crossed her mind that Melino might have brought her to throw into the jaws of danger and allow him to get on with his own business.

Her smile was tiny and humorless. If he tried that, he would learn that Hedia kept a small dagger in her sash. Its silver mountings were chased with delicate scenes of cupids farming, but the double-edged blade was as sharp as glass. It had already let out one magician's life.

The mantis was within twenty feet of them. It paused, its forelegs pumping minusculely in the air. It was about to act.

The ground beyond the wall of leaves was barren in a semicircle fifty feet in all directions from the cave in the outcrop beyond. The distant portion of the slanting rock was covered with plants ranging from patches of lichen to thick curtains of foliage from overhanging trees, but the portion near the cave was as bare as an iron pot.

If the mantis charges, I'm running for the cave no—

"Nodens take the creature!" Melino shouted. He thrust his left arm toward the mantis with his fist clenched.

The demon said, "Strike." Her voice showed a total lack of emotion, just as every other time Hedia had heard her speak.

A red flash from the ring lighted the insect and turned the surrounding foliage momentary shades of purple. The mantis scrambled forward like a bull in the arena. Melino stepped to the side, pulling Hedia with him.

Spurning clods and tearing shreds from the vegetation, the mantis plunged blindly toward the cave. It was barely its own length into the clearing when a dog the size of a pony charged from the cave, barking with all three heads. They slammed into one another.

The dog's jaws clamped onto the insect's right foreleg, its thin neck, and the middle leg on its left side. Choked growls and the crunch of chitin replaced the chorus of barking.

A thin chain—too thin to hold the monstrous dog, Hedia would have guessed, but from its shimmer it was orichalc—tethered the middle neck to a stake at the mouth of the cave. The rush stretched it as straight as a ship's mast.

The mantis slashed fiercely with its forelegs, but the toothed edges had no effect on the dog's iron gray fur. The insect's head came off and bounced across the dirt, the jaws still snapping.

All the limbs quickly separated from the mantis body, but the dog's jaws continued to worry what was left. The heads pulled against one another, ripping chunks of flesh apart and hurling them considerable distances. The sound was chilling, even to ears that were familiar with the carnage of the amphitheater.

Smaller bits spattered Hedia; then a ten-pound gobbet, shiny with clear ichor, landed at her feet. She could see muscle fibers in the white flesh, but she had no idea which part of the victim it had been.

She felt unexpected kinship with the mantis, though until a moment before it had been only a dangerous threat. *If I'd run into the clearing, that would be me.*

The noisy rending continued for minutes longer. The demon was still, and Melino made no attempt to intervene.

At last the dog finished its business and stalked stiff legged back to the cave. One, then the other, outer head glanced back at Hedia and her companions. Each time the throats growled counterpoints like three saws cutting stone.

The dog disappeared into the cave's interior. The mantis was spread over a wide area, mangled almost beyond recognition. Only the head and a few leg sections could be identified.

Looking around the clear area, Hedia saw fragments of previous victims: wing cases, bits of chitin, a giant stinger ripped from its place and lying forlorn with a portion of the poison sac still attached.

Hedia let out the breath that she had been holding unconsciously.

The stench of the carnage was unfamiliar. It was no worse than an afternoon in the amphitheater, but it was different.

She looked at Melino and said, "Well? Can't we just go around the dog? Keep outside the chain's stretch, I mean?"

The demon looked at her. *She would be smiling if her face ever changed,* Hedia thought.

"The cave is Zabulon's tomb," the demon said. "The *Book* is with Zabulon."

Hedia lifted her chin, showing that she understood the situation. She looked at Melino, expecting him to explain the next step. He said nothing; he even turned his face away to avoid meeting her eyes.

"Well, what are you going to do?" she said. Her voice was slightly strident. That wasn't deliberate, but she didn't attempt to polish away the overtones. "Strike the dog blind with your ring? Or kill him?"

Again it was the demon who spoke, saying, "Zabulon brought the dog to guard his body and to guard his *Book*. This one"—her eyes flicked over Melino—"cannot undo what Zabulon has done."

"Well, *what* then?" Hedia demanded. "You have some plan, so what is it?"

"The cave was Zabulon's workshop while he lived," Melino said in a low voice. He seemed to be gazing up the sloping outcrop, but Hedia was certain that the magician's mind was in a different place entirely. "It became his tomb when he died. He sits on the throne from which he worked his magic and his *Book* is in his lap. The dog which guarded the workshop while Zabulon lived now guards his tomb in death."

"And?" said Hedia. "What do we *do?*"

"Demon, tell her!" Melino said.

"The dog cannot be harmed," the demon said. Again Hedia caught a hint of something that convinced her that the demon was not so emotionless as Melino believed—or, anyway, as Melino stated. "Yet it is still a male dog. If a female in oestrus should run into the back of the cave, then the male would follow to the length of its chain. It would mate with the female for long enough that this magician could remove the *Book* from Zabulon's hands and retreat to safety with it."

Hedia looked from the demon to Melino. "You said 'a female,'" she said. "But a dog, surely?"

"I can change you into a dog," said Melino to the forest through which they had just passed. "For long enough, anyway, and change you back."

He turned and cried in a fury of anger and embarrassment, "You won't be harmed! It's a dog, and if you're a dog . . . Anyway, you won't be harmed."

Hedia looked at them both: the demon impassive, the magician wringing his hands in misery. She burst out laughing.

"I don't know how many times I've been called a bitch in heat," Hedia said, "but often enough, certainly. I suppose it's only fair that I should become one in truth!"

She continued to giggle as Melino and the demon prepared their spell.

VARUS WATCHED AS THE OARS dipped and swung back, sending swirls of bubbles through the clear water. The looms creaked in the rowlocks and water pattered as it dripped back into the sea. No one, nothing visible, was pulling the oars, but the boat slid forward.

Lucinus stood in the stern, holding the tiller of the steering oar. He didn't seem to be aware of what his hands gripped. He was murmuring softly, but Varus couldn't hear the words.

Varus didn't want to hear the words. Lucinus was a magician; Gaius Alphenus Varus was accompanying him because he too was a magician. The thought offended him as a rational man and as a philosopher, but because of magic—and in part his own magic—he was here on a sea that *could not* exist.

Varus sat amidships, just ahead of the shelter of linen cloth carried on hoops of reed. The few clouds were as sharp edged as blobs of clotted cream. The sun at zenith was redder and larger than what he was used to except at sunset on a misty day.

Varus rose to look out over the bow; he touched the shelter with one hand, but he didn't put his weight on the flimsy structure. Though he was careful to stay over the centerline, the boat wobbled.

Lucinus didn't seem to notice. If the oarsmen did—Varus smiled—their concern was as invisible as their bodies.

There was nothing on the horizon ahead, but now that Varus was standing he saw what might have been an island far to the left. *To port,* he corrected himself, recalling the technical term. The black smear might have been anything, even a shadow, but surf against the shore raised a lacey white froth.

Varus shielded his eyes with both hands, trying to make out details in what was a blur no matter how hard he strained, though perhaps a greenish blur instead of simply black. They were going to pass well wide of the island, so it didn't matter except as an object on which he could concentrate. Concentrating allowed him to trick himself into feeling that he was doing something productive.

Because his focus was so complete, it wasn't until he felt the boat rock that he looked down into the water. Swimming through the swells within twenty feet of the rail was an animal with tan fur, a dog's head, and a neck as long as a giraffe's on a bulbous body.

It looked back at Varus with warm brown eyes. Flippers at the front guided the creature like rudders, but broad hind flippers drove it forward in up-and-down undulations like a whale.

Varus resisted the reflex to *Do Something*. There was nothing he could do except possibly overset the boat; and anyway, there was no need to do anything. The creature looked so friendly that perhaps the greatest risk was that it would swim closer and try to nuzzle Varus like a friendly puppy.

The creature lowered its head and dived into the sea. It was visible in the clear water for over a minute, shrinking and blurring but never deviating from its arrow-straight line. Had it been a long-necked seal?

Lucinus continued to mumble in the stern. He hadn't noticed the creature, or at any rate he hadn't shown that he'd noticed.

The oars continued to dip and slant and rise. Their shafts were long and bisected the small semicircular blades. Nothing, not even shimmers in the air, indicated the oarsmen, but Varus remembered the mowing horrors that had guzzled blood from the trench.

Will I ever see Carce again? But that was a question anyone might ask while taking a sea voyage, and it was unworthy of a philosopher anyway.

The seal—the swimming animal, anyway—had seemed as real as the boat or as Varus himself, but the rock nearing to starboard had a misty outline and didn't kick the sea away from its shore. A woman sat in a niche on the slope. Her lips moved as though she were singing, but Varus heard only a faint susurrus.

The woman's mouth opened wider. Her teeth were blades with spikes at the corners of the upper jaw. Varus turned away. Even though he wasn't looking, the almost melody rippled like fingertips on his backbone.

Varus wanted to ask Lucinus about the boat, about the great seal, about the siren if she was a siren, about everything that was going on. He couldn't, because Lucinus was lost in a trance. If Varus *could* shake the magician out of his trance, the most likely result was that something undesirable would happen to the boat.

Varus grinned. The question of which particular undesirable thing would occur was at least as worthy of his attention as whether a rape victim should choose to marry her attacker without providing a dowry or if she should have him executed. That had been one of the subjects Pandareus had set for class debate a few weeks ago.

That world—the world in which Varus stood on the steps of the Temple of Venus the Ancestor and tried to convince his classmates of a point that he and they had no interest in—was a lifetime ago. It was farther from him now than this sea was distant from Carce and the Forum.

The sun was lower in the sky than it had been when they set forth from Sulla's garden. Varus wondered whether a day here was the same length as a day in Carce. He was in a kind of reverie also. It wasn't a trance like that of Lucinus, but Varus knew that his mind was in a state as unfamiliar as this sea.

Lucinus adjusted the tiller. Varus noticed that only because he happened to be looking sternward at the moment the magician's hands drew the bar slightly back. Lucinus continued to mumble. His eyes were empty, though he blinked occasionally.

They would be passing a wooded island close to port. It would be so close, in fact, that if Lucinus hadn't adjusted their course they would have piled up on the sloping shore.

Varus watched the island closely as they approached. There were bright flowers on the trees, some of them belonging to lesser plants that grew on the branches, and he thought he saw fruit as well.

The sun was touching the horizon. Even if the boat could continue through the darkness, Varus wasn't sure that Lucinus could. He was wobbling where he sat, as much supporting himself with the tiller as guiding it; his lips were barely moving. It would be risky to rouse the magician from his trance, but it might be more risky still to let him go on in this state.

Varus ducked to pass under the shelter so that he could put a hand on Lucinus' shoulder. He caught movement out of the corner of his eye. Straightening, he looked at the island again.

It crawled with serpents. There were thousands of them, wrapped around branches and writhing on the ground. Their wedge-shaped heads were lifted, and their eyes formed glittering constellations as they turned toward him.

"Ah!" Varus cried. He flinched back against the shelter and had to grab it to keep from falling over the rail. The boat wobbled, then steadied.

Varus got his breathing under control. Lucinus didn't seem to have noticed either the snakes or his companion's reaction to them, but Varus no longer doubted that the magician was aware of his surroundings.

The sun had set, leaving a red smear on the starboard horizon and smooth purple-blackness to port. Neither stars nor moon was visible, at least this early in the evening.

They were approaching an island covered with pine trees. As best as Varus could tell in silhouette against the dark sky, it was larger than the isle of serpents.

The magician was motionless. Varus pursed his lips and half-knelt, gripping the railings. He could only assume that Lucinus knew what he was doing. Certainly shouting in panic wasn't going to improve the situation.

The invisible oarsmen shipped their oars. The boat crunched up a shingle beach and stopped. Varus rocked forward, but the impact was gentle.

Lucinus let go of the tiller and slumped forward. Rather than crawl under the shelter, Varus climbed over the railing and splashed to the magician through the water. The sea was no more than knee-deep even at the stern.

"Help me," Lucinus whispered. His head and forearm rested on a thwart. "Carry me into the woods. . . ."

Corylus would be better at this, Varus thought as he lifted the magician as high as he could. He backed away from the boat. Lucinus tried to swing his legs over the railing, but in the event Varus simply dragged him.

Varus staggered upward, supporting the magician as best he could. The trees made a thick wall at the tideline, ten feet up from the edge of the sea at present. Varus pushed between what he thought were two of the smaller ones, crackling through branches that scratched his arms and calves.

He tripped over a tree root and fell. After panting on the ground for a moment, he lifted himself onto his elbows to take stock of the situation.

The magician's feet were into the brush, though barely. It would do.

The sky was purple velvet, but the sea was taking on a yellow-green phosphorescence. The boat rocked slightly now that the weight of its passengers no longer weighed it into the gravel.

I'll have to pull it higher up the beach, Varus thought. *In a moment.*

He was seeing images in the ship's hull. They were becoming clearer and beginning to move.

"YOU CONFER A GREAT HONOR on our ancient family, Lady Alphena!" said Aulus Collinus Ceutus, bowing as deeply as his paunch allowed. He was short, broad, and—despite having put on weight since the time he stopped commanding his own grain ships—looked impressively muscular. "Whatever your noble self desires will be done!"

Ceutus was his Illyrian birth name. He had tacked it onto the name of his wife's undoubtedly ancient family, while Aulus would be the first name of the citizen of Carce who had freed the slave Ceutus, or possibly the citizen who had freed the slave ancestor of Ceutus.

To receive a senator's daughter, Ceutus had dressed in a scarlet cloak with gold tassels, a toga—an uncomfortable garment that hardly anyone wore except in Carce, and even in Carce only on formal occasions—and cutwork sandals of red leather. The leather verged on orange and clashed with the cloak, which had a purplish cast.

Mother would say Ceutus looks vulgar—as of course he is, Alphena thought. She grinned. *I like the outfit. And so would most gladiators.*

"My father and I thank you, Ceutus," Alphena said, hoping to sound dignified if not regal. "I believe you already know my colleague, Master Pandareus? And Master Paris, of course."

Queenliness was for dignified beauties like Hedia, but Alphena had begun trying to act like a lady instead of a tomboy. Or like a gladiator, if she'd been having a bad day.

"Good to see you again, Pandareus," said the shipowner with a touch of reserve. "I'm glad you thought again about editing our family papers."

He paused and his eyes narrowed slightly. "That is in the plan, right?" he said.

Before Pandareus could decide how to answer, Alphena said, "My father has undertaken to publish the letters of Collinus Laethius. Master Pandareus will oversee the scholars involved in the project. But what we are here for, Ceutus, is the tomb."

"Yes, yes, of course," Ceutus said, bowing in agreement. "We can do this right now, if you like."

Alphena gestured with her left hand. They set off along the left side of the original house; a wing had been added to the other end. It stretched forward, turning what had been a rectangle into an L shape.

Women on the portico paused in their weaving to watch Alphena and her retinue with silent fascination. *I'm probably the first noblewoman they've ever seen. Most of them won't ever have left the estate.*

When she next talked with her father, Alphena would tell him that he was to pay for the editing of Laethius' letters. The money meant nothing to Saxa, and he might even find the project interesting.

She had a sudden vision of Saxa not as her aloof, disinterested father but as a would-be scholar perpetually saddened by his failure to achieve any respect from real literary figures, a later, equally laughable, version of Collinus Laethius himself. *He tries very hard, and he's unfailingly generous—with his money and with any other help he can give. I should be nicer to him.*

A dozen estate laborers carrying digging tools, and an equal number of Alphena's attendants, tramped along with them. Her escorts wore their swords openly here.

The open-fronted shed with a manger along the back was shelter for the oxen in bad weather, judging from the manure washing into the ruts in the road. Alphena's boots were better suited to the footing than the owner's expensive sandals, though he didn't seem disconcerted.

Paris walked separately, disregarding both the road and his companions. Ceutus had nodded acknowledgment, but Paris hadn't bothered to respond. The priest projected contemptuous anger at the world and at his presence in it.

"I'm really glad you told me about this, Pandareus," Ceutus said cheerfully. "I know right where you mean, but I wouldn't have thought of there being a tomb back of it in the hill. I just restored the temple, you know?"

Pandareus looked at him and raised an eyebrow. "You restored the Shrine of Inuus?" he said. "I didn't realize from what your wife said that anything remained of it."

"Well . . . ," Ceutus said. "There was a stone pillar that'd been built into the wall of the old sheepfold, you see. It said *Sacred to the God* on it, or anyway that's what my secretary puzzled out. So I figured the bits of old brick in the mud right there to the side was the foundation of a temple, and I built it back."

Ceutus led them past a pair of outbuildings. The hearth of the smithy was cold, but three men were repairing an ox yoke in the woodwrights' shop. They stared at the procession as fixedly as the weavers had done.

"That's a temple of Vesta," Pandareus as they turned to the right and approached a small, round temple. The building was so new that workmen were still plastering one of the six wooden pillars to give it the look of stone.

"Well, the inscription didn't say which god," Ceutus muttered defensively. "And, you know, I always liked that little round temple in the Forum, so I thought, 'Herakles, it mighta been Vesta, right?'"

Even Alphena knew that if the shrine had been to Vesta, the legend would have said *Sacred to the Goddess* rather than *God*. Alphena wondered if Ceutus could read and write in Latin. It wasn't a skill that an Illyrian shipowner was likely to need. His secretary wouldn't have tried to change his boss' assumption.

"Very sensible," Pandareus said in what sounded like approval. "And that may be the hillside behind it."

The hill was really a relatively gentle rise beyond a three-foot face of coarse limestone, sheer enough to be blotched but not covered by vegetation. A yew tree, ragged and gnarled, grew midway up the slope. Though the tree was only thirty feet high, its thick trunk and general appearance made Alphena guess that it had been growing on the poor soil for a very long time.

"I didn't have any notion of it till Collina's letter came, but we can chop back into this hill till we find the entrance," Ceutus said. "Do you think there'll be any jewelry?"

He looked at Pandareus and added, "Or pots, that'd be great! I'm going to build new cases into the office to hold whatever we find. The
ancestral relics!"

"That's blasphemy even to think!" Paris snapped. "Would you dese-
crate the tomb of a man who was a prince when *your* ancestors wore
skins and dressed their hair with sheep fat?"

"Well, I guess that's my business, isn't it?" Ceutus said, bunching his
fists as he turned to face the priest. "I been pretty lax with you and your
airs, Paris, you being a priest and all. But if you don't watch your tongue
I'll put you off the estate right now. And I won't need help to do it!"

He smacked his right fist into his left palm. Alphena didn't doubt
that Ceutus knew how to enforce his will: Illyrian sailors were pirates
whenever they thought they could get away with it.

"Lord Saxa greatly appreciates your allowing Lady Alphena and myself to pursue our researches on your family estate, Master Ceutus," Pandareus said quickly.

*A poor scholar who teaches the sons of noblemen learns diplomacy in a
hard school,* Alphena realized with a hidden smile. Pandareus had
learned well.

Aloud she lied, "Yes. My father commented on your generosity as we
were leaving this morning, Master Ceutus."

"Ah!" said the shipowner, smiling broadly again. "Well, that's very
nice, him thinking about little people like us. Most great men like him
wouldn't be so gracious."

He cleared his throat. "So, Master Pandareus. Have you got any special instructions, or shall we just start taking back the slope from, say,
here—"

He pointed to a point on the edge of the low escarpment. One of his
workmen, unbidden, notched the coarse stone with his mattock.

"—to there?"

Two men with picks followed the lead of their fellow, marking the
other end of the section their master had indicated. The ancient yew
tree grew twenty feet up the slope from the middle of the notches.

"Your practical eye . . . ," Pandareus said. "Has done a better job of
translating the information in the letter to the ground than anything I
could do, Master Ceutus."

"Then let's get on with it," the shipowner said. He turned to his foreman and said, "Harpax, keep cutting back till you find something that looks like a tunnel mouth. If you need heavier tools as you get deeper into the rock, we'll find some."

The laborers got to work with enthusiasm. This was a different and therefore more interesting job than their normal tasks, and they were under the eye of the master himself. Ceutus didn't seem the sort to let his men slack off.

While the owner watched his crew with satisfaction, Pandareus moved close to Alphena and said in a low voice, "Your Ladyship? There may be some objects or even a book in the tomb which bears on our concerns."

"Don't worry," Alphena said. "In Father's name I'm sure that I can offer Ceutus something that he'll find more valuable than the grave goods, whatever they may be. Or I suppose—"

She grinned to make it clear that she was joking.

"—I could have our escort massacre everybody on the estate so that we can make off with the loot unhindered."

"If I thought that were necessary to save the world, Your Ladyship," Pandareus said, "I would ask you to do it."

He smiled too, but he wasn't joking in the least.

CHAPTER X

Hedia sneezed. Half-burned foliage oozed bitter smoke, and pow-dered ash rose from the figures Melino was drawing on the ground with the tip of his staff.

Frustrated by the heavy undergrowth, the magician had clenched his left fist and nodded to the demon. She said, "Burn!" and his ruby ring sprayed a fan of scarlet light. The blast cleared a six-by-ten-foot hole and shriveled the vegetation at its edges.

When the light flared, the dog had stalked stiff legged from the cave. It paused at the edge of the semicircle it had trampled barren, glaring at Melino and growling in three different registers. The chain stretched tight behind the middle neck, but the dog didn't rush hard against its limit.

Hedia tried to meet the beast's stare for a moment but quickly turned away. It was disconcerting to be the focus of three sets of eyes, and the way the lips curled back from long teeth was stressful. She was mentally willing to face a vicious dog, but facing a pack of them was . . . well, it was unnecessary at present, so she chose not to do it.

Hedia glanced toward the demon and found that it—that she—was gazing back. *What if I told you to do something?*

But the demon would ignore her, and Hedia had nothing to tell the *being* to do anyway. She felt helpless and useless and frightened.

She quirked a superior smile toward the demon and immediately felt better. Pretending to be what you wanted to be—here pretending to be a gentlewoman fully in charge of the situation—was often the best way of becoming that very thing.

The demon smiled back and turned to face the snarling dog.

"There!" said Melino, straightening from his handiwork. Hedia couldn't tell what the symbols he'd drawn were. If she hadn't watched his staff moving, she would have passed off the markings as whorls left by a breeze.

Melino met Hedia's eyes for the first time since he had explained what her part in the enterprise was to be. He looked away just as quickly, though, before he said, "Take your place in the middle of the figure, Your Ladyship. If you're ready, I mean."

Hedia stretched very deliberately, reaching as high as she could, then bending her arms and torso backward. Settling back, she said, "I'm always ready, dear boy. Anyone could have told you that."

She stepped deliberately into the center of the burned patch, thankful for her sturdy sandals. Her calves felt the heat of the ground, but the thick soles protected her feet.

"Turn so that you're not facing me," Melino said in a peevish tone.

Without comment, Hedia presented her back to him. She suspected that he wanted her to turn not for any magical reason but because he would stumble over his spell if he had to look at her face. The thought made her smile.

Hedia was now facing the demon, who had somehow moved to the opposite pole from Melino. The demon was expressionless. Together, she and the magician chanted, *"Though her face be that of a young woman . . ."*

Hedia let her eyes drift away from the demon. She felt odd, though that might be from trying to hold still as she stood in this bitter atmosphere.

The dog had stopped barking; Hedia wasn't sure when that had happened. Nothing seemed *right*, neither time nor her surroundings nor her own body.

I know my body very well. I knew my body.

A thick-bodied snake lay in curves along a branch behind the demon. It watched Hedia. It must be twenty feet long. It didn't seem hostile or hungry, just interested.

"But her body is that of a savage dog!" Melino shouted. The demon's voice was a knife-blade echo to the magician.

Hedia fell into blackness and landed on all four feet. The three-headed dog began howling in frantic desperation. The world was shades of gray. The movement of a fly's wing or the antenna of a locust on a blade of grass was sharp beyond anything in Hedia's previous awareness.

She launched herself triumphantly past the guard dog, passing just close enough to brush his foreleg with her tawny flank. She yipped teasingly as she raced for the cave mouth.

A *greyhound*, part of her mind realized. *He's made me a greyhound.*

But that thought and all other conscious thought was submerged in anticipated delight. *Such a great, powerful male!*

The dog caught her before she reached the cave entrance—*He's so big!*—and shouldered her to throw her down. She ducked. He overran her, tripped, and tumbled with a chorus of startled yips. Hedia darted through the entrance.

He's so big!

She skidded to a halt to avoid crashing into the seated figure ten feet into what was a chamber rather than a cave. The walls were mirrors, but for an instant the dog perceptions overlying Hedia's human awareness were badly staggered.

Then she noticed the figure as something more than an obstacle in her path. It looked like a scowling man in dark robes with a beard that curled over its chest. It sat on a throne that Hedia perceived as an absence rather than a substance. Held by both hands in the figure's lap was a massive ironbound codex.

Figure, not man. It had no smell at all, not even the chalky dryness of marble or acrid tinge of bronze. It was not a man now, whatever it might have been at one time.

The guard dog burst through the entrance in a storm of yelps and growls. He bent toward her from the left. Hedia sprinted to the right around the figure. He caught her on the other side of the throne, nipping her neck with two of his three heads.

She rolled, onto her back and then to her belly again. The cave—the chamber—continued unguessably far back, but this was far enough. She lifted her muzzle and whined longingly.

Holding her neck now with all three sets of jaws, the great dog mounted her. She began to howl.

So big!

Hedia was vaguely aware that Melino had entered the chamber behind them, then scuttled out carrying the *Book*. She didn't care, not even the human remainder of her awareness.

So very big!

Hedia howled in mingled pain and delight, and the great dog bellowed above her.

ALPHENA'S STEWARD HAD BROUGHT skins of wine mixed with water, but the wagon was parked half a mile away on the graveled apron of the main building. Alphena had stepped toward Ceutus to ask if he had something to drink closer to hand when metal clinked on stone with a distinctly different note.

"Hey, we got something!" a workman cried. His pick had bit deeply and stuck when he tried to lever it back. "Master, there's a crack or something!"

"Bring a pry bar!" Ceutus said. "Zetes, there's a pair of boat pikes in the wagon! Get 'em over here now!"

Four laborers with shovels converged on where the pick had stuck, directly in the center of the forty-foot stretch Ceutus had chosen. They attacked the crumbling face of the slope and quickly laid bare a marble slab that had been inlet into a slot in the coarser living rock.

The boat pikes—ten-foot poles of stout oak with hooked iron heads—arrived from the wagon of tools at the back of the procession. Harpax, the foreman, placed both points behind the marble; then, with three workmen on each, they levered the slab out. The mortises that held it crunched into sprays of gravel.

The slab had covered a square opening. Beyond was as black as soot.

"Bring lights!" said Ceutus. "There ought to be lanterns in the smithy! Light them and bring them *now*!"

Paris began chanting in a high-pitched singsong. Alphena didn't recognize the language, but Etruscan seemed the likely choice.

Pandareus squatted to look inside. "Nothing," he said as Alphena stepped beside him. "I hoped if the Egg were glowing, you see . . ."

Paris, still chanting, crawled into the tunnel opening before anyone realized what he was doing. Ceutus yelped, "Hey! Get back here!"

Alphena turned to the nearest member of her escort, a Dalmatian named Vargo. "Give me your sword," she said. "Now!"

"You want I should go after him, master?" said Harpax, snatching one of the boat pikes from the trio who had been using it as a tool.

Alphena couldn't imagine a less suitable weapon for a cramped tunnel. Nor, for that matter, did she see why Harpax—or even she—should need a weapon to handle a frail old man. There might be something else in the tomb, though. . . .

"No, wait for the lamps or we'll bust up the treasures!" Ceutus said. "Buggering Hercules! What does that snooty little prick think he's playing at?"

Alphena followed Paris into the tunnel. The Dalmatian's sword hung from a belt that she tossed over her right shoulder. The scabbard was tin with a raised design picked out in black enamel. It was attractive, but it would be easy to replace if she damaged it bumping over the tomb's lintel.

Paris was chanting ahead. More people entered the tunnel behind her, blocking the light coming through the entrance. Because of that dimming and her eyes' starting to adapt, Alphena could see the Etruscan priest against the distant back wall, which glowed faintly blue. If it was a wall.

There was no sarcophagus or grave goods, nor was there any other sign of a tomb. Neither did a many-hued egg hang in the air as the old notebook described, though something was making the light farther down the tunnel.

Alphena caught up with Paris. He continued to chant, but he had stopped at a ladder of tree roots growing from both directions through cracks in the stone sides. The roots themselves looked natural, but the arrangement certainly wasn't.

Paris began to climb.

Alphena put her hand on the priest's leg; it was like touching the smooth, flaking trunk of a sycamore. She said, "Where are you going?"

Paris ignored her and continued to climb. She raised her hand, intending to grab the Etruscan's ankle and jerk him back into the tunnel, then changed her mind and began to climb also. Light came from above, not the eerie blue coldness from deeper into the tunnel but the warmer color of diffused sunlight. There hadn't been a visible opening up the hillside, but perhaps a crack . . . ?

Alphena heard Drago behind her on the ladder, calling to his cousin. Paris was close above, but he was growing dimmer and his voice had become faint. She sprang upward, climbing with her arms as well as the strength of her legs.

She touched the priest's bare heel. Paris stepped off the ladder and she followed him with a convulsive lunge, the sword banging against her thigh.

They were in a circular room perhaps ten feet in diameter. The walls and floor were wood. The floor was solid without the hole or trapdoor by which they had entered.

Paris had stopped chanting and was gasping for breath. His expression mingled anger and triumph.

"Where are we?" Alphena said. She touched the hilt of the borrowed sword to make her threat explicit.

There were doors in opposite walls, and midway between them was what looked like a casement window with four sections. The openings were empty instead of holding panes of glass, and the crossbars themselves were cut from the wood of the wall in which they stood.

"Are we inside a tree?" Alphena said. Paris had been leaning forward to breathe more easily. He straightened, though he was still breathing hard. "But the yew wasn't as big around as this!"

Paris steadied himself on the door behind him. "Look out the window," he said, pointing with his left arm. "Nothing else matters to you."

Alphena glanced through the crossbars, onto the rolling meadow beyond. She was not on the Collinus estate or anywhere familiar to her.

A man with the head of a bull came over the crest of the hill. He was twelve feet tall and carried a double-bitted axe over his right shoulder. His torso and limbs were covered with fine reddish hair, and there was no question at all about him being male.

The bull-man saw her looking through the window. He laughed thunderously and took the axe helve in both hairy hands. The blade looked the size of a warship's ram.

Alphena drew her sword. *He'll tear through the trunk, but if I'm quick I can chop his hands on the axe and—*

The bull-man opened his mouth and blew a ball of red-orange flame, blackening grass, daisies, and yellow flowers that Alphena couldn't identify. The vegetation was too green to sustain the fire, but the burned swath billowed white smoke.

The bull-man strode toward her, kicking up whorls of smoke and ash. Small flames curled from his nostrils, then sucked in again. He raised the axe.

Movement caught the corner of Alphena's eyes. She turned quickly. Paris had stepped through the door behind him. It closed and vanished before she could reach it. That section of wall was now as featureless as the patterns of wood grain to either side of where it had been.

The bull-man laughed again. He was almost close enough to swing the axe, or—

If he blows fire through the window, there's nowhere for me to escape.

Alphena pulled open the remaining door—it didn't have a latch— and dodged through behind the point of her sword. There was at least a chance of taking the bull-man from the side before he could shift the clumsy axe. Though it didn't seem very clumsy in his powerful hands.

Alphena froze. Instead of a meadow, she was in a circular stone room. She couldn't tell where the light was coming from.

The door closed behind her—and vanished, leaving nothing behind but air.

CORYLUS WENT DOWN THE STAIRS FIRST, then turned to watch the Princess. The long robe was opaque even though it was as thin as gossamer, and the broad, floppy brim of her hat hid her face from an ordinary onlooker; but she didn't move like a human being. The Singiri legs bent like a man's, but they seemed to have an extra joint in the ankles, which turned her gait into something instantly noticeable.

That disturbed Corylus, but it probably didn't matter. Puteoli was a port city, so it had more than its share of cripples and of foreigners with strange customs.

The Princess lifted the front brim of her hat. "Is there a problem?" she said. She not only spoke perfect Latin; she also had read the doubt in his expression.

Corylus grinned. Instead of taking off his sword belt, he'd tossed another of Melino's robes over him. He patted the hilt outlined beneath the thin fabric and said, "You probably won't rouse any questions walking to the harbor. And if some busybody *does* wonder, he's going to keep his mouth shut so long as you're with me. I'll lead, but you stick close."

The baboons watched as he and the Princess approached. One rose onto his hind legs, then fell back onto all fours with a whine.

The Princess hissed. Corylus stutter-stepped: the sound was as chilling as that of an unexpected arrow. The baboons shrieked and leaped away, their feet shooting out in front of them when they snubbed up at the limits of their neck chains.

"What did you do?" Corylus said.

"It wasn't magic," the Princess said. She had to raise her voice to be heard over the monkeys' frightened jabbering. "I just told them something that they didn't want to hear."

Corylus pushed the door open and stepped out, suppressing his smile. Admetus and the other three guards might wonder what it meant.

"Headman?" said Admetus, who seemed to be a Scythian. "Sir, I mean?"

"Carry on," Corylus said dismissively. "I expect to be back shortly."

The less he said, the quicker he and the Princess would get away from the house. He didn't want to be here—or have the Princess here—when Melino returned.

Corylus led the Princess across the porch and down the front steps. The guards didn't ask about the captain's companion. They probably didn't guess she was female, let alone that she was Singiri. He motioned her to his side as they started down the short pathway to the street.

In mid-step they crossed a barrier. It had been invisible until they were through it and into a jungle at sunset.

Corylus was so shocked that he snatched at the hilt of his sword, forgetting that he'd tossed a robe on to conceal the weapon in public. The fabric was so thin that he could have drawn the sword—but he certainly couldn't swing a blade wrapped in a garment he was wearing.

"Melino's trapped us," he growled, pulling the robe over his head and tossing it onto a bush whose leaves looked like a walnut's but were spiked like a holly. He drew the long sword now.

That could have gotten us killed. I've got to pay attention.

"Not Melino," the Princess said. "We stepped beyond Melino's defenses and fell into a trap laid by his enemy."

She had doffed her garments without the drama Corylus had put into the process. Her upturned hat lay on its low crown, and the white robe was folded over it. He grinned in amusement at himself.

"I don't know whether the trap was laid for Melino, or for us," the Princess said. "Or—"

With a solemn logic that Pandareus would have applauded.

"—whether some third party was the intended victim."

"Which way do we go, Princess?" Corylus said, looking about them without moving his body any more than he had to. "To get out of here. Because I'd *really* like to get out of here."

The sky was still bright, though the sun was almost below the red horizon. The leaves let only dapples of light through to the undergrowth and ground.

The plants weren't familiar. He and the Princess were in a stand of smooth-barked trees whose trunks were sinuous. Sometimes they rose braided in pairs, and there was even a triplet.

"I don't know where we are," the Princess said. Her wrists and shins were red and still slightly swollen, but she seemed to move without difficulty. "I will try to learn, and then I will try to learn how we can go elsewhere."

She plucked off a round, fleshy leaf the size of her face. It was so dark a green that it could pass for black in the red light of sunset. She held it before her with her left hand and began to trace patterns on it with her right index finger. She didn't score the leaf, and Corylus couldn't be sure that her finger even touched the surface.

Clouds shifted beyond the trees in the west, reflecting rosy light. Their movement made Corylus uncomfortable. He'd thought he was seeing birds, or something with red fur hunting birds, or something hunting him.

He shot the sword home in its scabbard, then touched the trunk of the nearest tree. "Neither of us will do you any harm," he said through closed lips. "We were placed here by an enemy, and we'd like to get out."

The dryad stepped into sight, seeming to come from behind a trunk too slim to conceal her body. She smiled uncertainly, clearly ready to vanish again.

Corylus smiled back, lowering his hand to his side. "Good evening, mistress," he said. "My friend and I are lost—in many senses. I hope you can help us find a path back to our own world."

"She's a Singiri, isn't she?" the dryad said, eyeing the Princess doubtfully. "Why has she come here?"

"We were both sent here by an enemy," Corylus said. "We didn't come by choice, and we'd like to leave as soon as possible."

It wouldn't do any good to press the nymph, a small, slim woman with skin the color of polished bronze. Her hair was straight and black and fell to her ankles.

The dryad gave him a speculative look. "*You* don't have to leave," she said. "I don't think the Singiri belong here, though."

Corylus glanced toward the Princess; her finger continued to move back and forth across the leaf. Nothing else had changed. Her mouth was open wide enough to display teeth like rows of tacks, but he didn't think that she was speaking.

"Is there a way out, mistress?" Corylus said. A bird—or was it a bat? The sky had become much darker—flew by, carrying something in its talons. There was a squawk from nearby, but it didn't seem to come from the flying creature which he'd seen. "I really think the Princess and I should leave."

"Why would you want to leave?" said the dryad. "*I* don't know how anyone would leave. Although—"

She frowned. "There are Ethiopes coming here, and they don't belong, either. If you brought them—"

She drew away, not so much physically as through a psychic chill.

"—then you should go. And take the Ethiopes with you, because they destroy everything. They're worse than elephants."

"I didn't bring them," Corylus snapped, drawing his sword. He no longer cared if he frightened this maddening sprite. "How many Ethiopes are there?"

The dryad spread her fingers and looked at them, pursing her lips. She shrugged and said, "I don't know. Many. Many many."

Nerthus knew what that meant, but it probably meant too many. Corylus would have chanced his luck with three and possibly with four of the horse-headed monsters, but more than ten—probably—would be suicide.

"Which direction are they coming from?" he said. "*Quickly,* now."

"You don't have to shout," said the dryad. "I don't think I like you very much."

Then, either because of a dryad's usual kindliness or because she correctly read his mood as approaching violence, she added, "From that way, I guess."

She pointed to brushes whose limbs rose nearly straight up. Their leaves were almond shaped and so bright a yellow that they stood out from the shadows even now at dusk.

"They're smashing everything, even when it's not in the way."

Corylus took the leaf away from the Princess with his left hand. "Mistress, Ethiopes are coming," he said, wondering if there was comprehension in her slit-pupiled eyes. "There're too many for me to fight, so we've got to run if we can."

"Yes, I can run," the Princess said. "For a time."

"Go ahead that way," Corylus said, gesturing in what he thought was the direction opposite to where the Ethiopes were coming from. "Unless you know a way out?"

The Princess set off at a lope around the trunk of a fallen tree that was being consumed by mushrooms the size of purple helmets. Corylus had sent her ahead to put himself between her and the danger, but she obviously had better night vision than he did.

"There is no way out from the inside," she said. Her steady pace didn't affect her speech, as it would have that of most human beings. "It is a trap like the one which held Melino until I freed him. We will be released from outside, or we will die here."

Or we'll be killed, Corylus added silently, but he supposed being killed was a special case within the general category "Dying." He thought of classes with Master Pandareus, and thought of the recent past, when his concern had been to decide with which legion to seek an appointment as tribune, the first step on his career.

They reached a creek. It was only about twenty feet wide and sluggish; motionless lilies floated on it, their flowers closed at nightfall. It couldn't be too deep or the plants wouldn't have been able to root in the bottom, but the Princess followed its bank in a gentle slant to the left.

Corylus didn't object. She seemed to know what she was doing, and he had no reason to believe that crossing the stream would bring any real advantage.

A pair of naiads watched from behind a lily pad, ready to hide if threatened. Corylus thought of calling to them, but he didn't have anything to say.

The Princess didn't seem winded and he was keeping up thus far without showing the strain, but they couldn't run forever. He couldn't at least. His sword dipped and bobbed, its long blade a lever that increased the effort of holding it across his chest. He would have liked to take the tip in his left hand, but he was afraid that as tired as he was, he'd manage to cut off his fingers on the naked edge if he tripped.

From the left a pair of horse-headed silhouettes stepped out from behind a tall shrub whose bi-colored leaves pointed stiffly upward. The Princess shied to the right with a hiss of surprise. Corylus thrust the leading Ethiope through the solar plexus, his blade horizontal. Momentum carried him around, slicing almost completely through his victim's torso.

The Ethiope's arms flailed sideways, one hand knocking his companion's spear aside and the other flinging his own stone-headed axe into the undergrowth. His mouth opened to a spray of blood. He couldn't shout because the stroke had severed his diaphragm.

As his sword came free on the other side of the falling body, Corylus raised the point as much as he could as he struck. The second Ethiope got his right arm in the way of the stroke, but the edge cut through one bone of his forearm and so deeply into the other that it cracked when Corylus levered his blade free.

The Ethiope bellowed and stabbed, but the weight of his own right arm weighed the spear down and the point slipped past Corylus' knee. Corylus lunged as though he were trying to tackle his opponent, but his point was forward. It split the Ethiope's breastbone.

Corylus straightened; he wobbled, then clapped his hand against a scale-barked tree with fronds like a palm dangling from branches. Except for the interruption he might have been able to continue running for another five minutes or so, but now he was finished until he got time to recruit.

Time that he wasn't going to get. Only those two Ethiopes had managed to flank them, probably cutting the chord of their swing to the left, but he could hear the rest of their enemies crashing through the woods nearby.

"Princess, keep running," Corylus said, breathing through his open mouth. "I'll hold them here."

The Ethiopes wore leather harnesses rather than proper garments. Corylus knelt and wiped his sword on the thigh of the one he had cut nearly in half, leaving parallel lines of blood on the mottled hide. He straightened.

"We will both wait here," the Princess said. She tugged the spear from the hand of the dead Ethiope. The shaft was heavy and had a noticeable kink, but it was better than nothing.

Corylus had reacted without thinking when the Ethiopes appeared, doing what training had conditioned him to do. He started laughing, despite the situation or maybe because of it.

"I knew I might die in the forest," he said without looking away from the approaching pursuit. "I just thought it would be somewhere in Germany."

Behind them was a screen of saplings whose branches curved toward the ground in showers of feathery foliage. Half a dozen Ethiopes burst through them.

Corylus didn't trust his legs for a rush, so he stepped back to the tree that had sheltered the initial ambushers. He felt the sprite stir in the darkness, a sturdy woman with almond eyes who was shivering at the violence.

Four Ethiopes charged the instant they saw him, calling in musical voices. They sounded more like huge birds than the horses their heads resembled. Each was at least seven feet tall, and one was nearly eight.

Corylus waited. It was like fighting Germans—but the Ethiopes were even bigger, even clumsier, and even stronger than Germans.

As he expected, the two in the middle collided because their fellows were crowding inward to get to their victim first. When the middle pair tumbled, they tripped the Ethiope on their right also.

The remaining attacker was raising his axe for a blow that would have split its victim to the crotch if it had landed. Corylus stepped forward and stabbed the Ethiope through the top of the thigh, severing the artery and bringing him down twisting onto the pile of his fellows. Corylus flicked the sword tip twice, breaking an Ethiope's spine and opening the neck veins of the fellow with whom he was tangled.

Corylus couldn't finish the last of the four because the pair who had hesitated were now galloping toward him. One leaped the pile of thrashing bodies, holding his spear like a vaulting pole. He had feet like a camel's, not horse hooves.

The Princess threw her spear, catching the Ethiope in the belly. The flaked point poked out from the Ethiope's back as he doubled up. Corylus didn't think he could have done better himself with so awkward a missile.

The other Ethiope came around to the left of the pile of his fellows. Corylus hoped he would collide with the survivor who had risen to all fours, but the attacker avoided that mistake. *My luck's been too good already. . . .*

The Ethiope had a long cudgel studded with chips of flint. He swung it horizontally, four feet up from the ground. Corylus ducked under the blow without thinking—there was no time to think, time only to observe and react—and thrust through the Ethiope's leading wrist.

The cudgel hit the tree trunk with a crash like nearby lightning. It bounced out of the Ethiope's remaining hand. He trumpeted in surprise at the blood spurting from his right wrist. Corylus thrust again, this time into the rib cage with the flat of the blade held parallel to the ground so that the steel wouldn't grate through bone and maybe catch when he tried to withdraw it.

The point slid in and slid out with no more trouble than stabbing a wineskin. Bright blood from the lungs gushed out instead of wine.

Which left the last of the original four—

The Princess swung an axe sideways, driving the edge into the Ethiope's temple with a hollow *thunk.* She stepped back as the Ethiope thrashed. The blunt stone blade remained buried in his skull.

"We've—," Corylus said/gasped.

More Ethiopes—a dozen or so; Corylus didn't have leisure for a proper count—crashed through the undergrowth hooting. *The dryad said many. . . .*

Too many.

Corylus was trying to breathe and praying not to fall over. His muscles burned, his lungs burned, and everything he saw was blurred and tinged with red.

The tone of the Ethiopes' cries changed. They were leaping, toppling as though a squadron of archers were shooting into them. Horse-headed hunters flopped to the ground in bloody confusion.

Two rushed Corylus. They were trying to escape rather than attacking, though it would amount to the same thing. He chopped to deflect the spear aimed at his torso. His sword bit deep into the spear shaft, but the Ethiope's point scraped his ribs as it passed under his raised sword arm. *Mithras, but these bastards are strong!*

The Princess threw an axe at the other Ethiope. It was good for line, but it struck handle first, staggering him without serious injury.

Corylus grappled with his own opponent. The Ethiope swung him aside, clearing the sword from the spear shaft. Corylus cut downward into the Ethiope's left ankle. It was a poor blow, but good enough to chip bone and cause the victim to bleat.

Instead of falling, the Ethiope shook Corylus off his right arm and raised the spear to stab him like a carp in a tank. Corylus tried to twist away. His right arm was numb and he couldn't raise the sword into even a pretense of defense.

The Princess was trying to tug free another spear, but the weight of bodies held it firm. The Ethiope whom she'd hit with the axe pitched forward, causing her to jump back. The back of his neck gouted blood.

The Ethiope preparing to kill Corylus fell like a windblown pine. Corylus managed to curl his legs so that the massive body didn't land on him.

Behind where the Ethiopes had stood was a pair of Singiri with short, serviceable swords of the sort that a beasthunter like Veturius kept in the arms locker of his compound. The weapons dripped with blood, as did the warriors holding them.

Corylus tried to stand. He got to his knees, but he couldn't rise from that posture. He let go of his sword hilt and gasped air on all fours, hoping to quench the fire in his lungs.

Two more Singiri appeared. One held a boar spear, while the other was the elder whom the Princess had called Tassk. These were Veturius' four lizard-monkeys.

Tassk didn't have a human weapon, but his fingers wore the clawed rings that had masqueraded as a necklace in the cage. He still had the loop of heavier chain around his waist.

"I hope your warrior doesn't mind us getting involved in a fight he seems to have had under control, Princess," Tassk said in Latin as well modulated as the Princess' own. His arms were red to the elbows, as though he'd been reaching into the chests of Ethiopes. That probably hadn't been necessary.

Corylus managed a smile. "The only thing I had under control," he croaked, "was the grass I was lying on. And that's pretty sparse."

He glanced at the ground, then lurched to his feet. A Singiri warrior stepped close but didn't offer help unless it were needed, which it wasn't, quite.

"We took the Ethiopes from behind," Tassk said. "Which was easy, because they were wholly focused on the warrior who had killed so many of them already. Perhaps another time we will all stand together."

The younger male Singiri faced outward around their leaders and the human, just in case there were other enemies, Ethiopes or otherwise. Corylus had seen too many ambushes to imagine that what these warriors had done was easy, though complete surprise had made it possible.

"Can you get us out of here, sir?" Corylus said. "You're a magician?"

Tassk's expression was probably a grin. "Not like my princess," he said, "but I can dissolve the maze which held you now that it's been breached from the outside."

"Corylus?" the Princess said, speaking for the first time since Tassk and his warriors had rescued them. "We will go back to our own world, which this no longer is. You are welcome to come with us, but I believe you have duties of your own."

"Right," said Corylus. He was starting to feel human again. He wasn't ready for another fight, but he'd be able to make a showing if one was forced on him. "If you need help, I think I can arrange a ship back to Africa."

He picked up his sword and wiped it on another corpse. The edges would take careful sharpening, and there was a chip out near the tip where he must have struck one of the stone weapons . . . or possibly a tooth.

"That will not be necessary," Tassk said, undoing the chain around his waist. "The other end of this is connected to the temple from which we came to recover our princess."

Corylus frowned, trying to make sense of the words. The chain wasn't connected to anything. Though . . . the end that had dangled loose when Tassk wore it was fuzzy, somehow, out of focus.

"Good Fortune to you, Corylus," Tassk said. "Perhaps another time."

The three Singiri warriors each gripped the chain with one hand. They watched Tassk silently.

The Princess took the last link of the chain in her hand. She smiled at Corylus and said, "I will not forget that you helped me, warrior, at my time of greatest need. There will be a time when your need is great also, and I will remember."

She did something with the chain that he didn't understand, then handed him a single link. "Keep this," she said.

Tassk hissed a syllable that may have been a word. The chain began to fade as though it were being hauled into a pipe, and the Singiri faded with it. When the Princess disappeared, the world in which Corylus battled the Ethiopes vanished like a soap bubble.

Corylus stumbled. He was at the edge of Melino's property, about to step into the street. His tunic and limbs were bloody, and the edge of his sword needed attention.

But the steel blade was clean.

VARUS SHIVERED IN THE WIND COMING off the water. He had felt no breeze while they were crossing the sea in sunshine, but darkness had chilled the air and was driving it hard enough to pick up scud from the surf. He and Lucinus lay among straggly cedars and knee-high shrubs with sparse, fat leaves the size of thumbnails; neither provided any shelter.

The magician moaned and trembled under Varus' cloak. He'd laid it over the older man, thinking he could better stand the cold himself.

Varus smiled wryly. That might be true, but it didn't mean that he was comfortable. It would be even less comfortable to spend the rest of his life on this island because Lucinus had died of exposure, of course; and a philosopher should remain unmoved by whatever his fate sent him.

It would be easier to remain unmoved if the air were a little warmer. He might be able to get to sleep then himself.

There were images in the hull of the boat. For the most part Varus saw only swirls of faint light, too dim even to have color. They reminded him of moonlight reflecting on a woodland stream. But occasionally—

Corylus stared out clearly. He was snarling and his face was speckled with blood. Behind him were bushes whose limbs wept down to the leaf litter on the ground.

Then Corylus was gone. The hull was a window onto lightless fog, and Lucinus gurgled as though he were choking. Varus glanced at the magician. There had been no change; the gurgle subsided into a whistling breath.

Varus looked out to sea again. Pastel lanterns approached in a line that stretched to right and left as far as he could see. They moved slowly but steadily just below the surface of the water, regardless of the movements of the mild surf.

Varus laid a hand on Lucinus' shoulder, wondering if they would need to flee deeper inland. He hoped that the magician would be able to move under his own power by now. Varus knew that he wouldn't be able to carry the older man any distance, and he wasn't sure that he would even be able to lift him into a standing position.

Brush crackled ten feet away. A creature pushed through the lower branches of a cedar, then rose onto its hind legs. It was an ape with a huge, shaggy head and deep-sunk eyes. It turned and stared at the humans.

Varus held still, praying that Lucinus would also. The magician moaned or mumbled something, but the sound was softer than the breeze. The only weapon they had was the knife Lucinus used as a scriber, and even that was still in the boat. Varus didn't imagine he'd be able to kill an ape so large even with a proper sword.

The beast resumed walking toward the sea; its feet curved inward. Other apes were shambling across the beach to left and right. A female with four teats passed close enough that Varus could have leaned across Lucinus and touched her. She ignored the humans as she strode awkwardly toward the water, occasionally dropping onto her knuckles.

The lights rose from the water as they reached the shore. They were fleshy bulbs on stalks growing from the heads of creatures that looked like dolphins or small whales. The sea animals waited in the surge and ebb of the water, raising their forequarters on arms that ended in flippers. Sometimes one opened its mouth to gulp air; the glowing lantern waved when that happened.

The apes took places on the shoreline, one or two facing each of the sea creatures. An ape raised his right foot and brought it down on the sand, the sound absorbed by distance and the faint burble of water. He raised his foot again and this time other apes drummed with him. Varus felt the vibration, though only because his eyes told him to expect it.

A sea creature tilted its head higher and bellowed like the wind blowing through a tomb. One after another, the remaining creatures took up the tortured call.

The apes were beating the sand in unison; the edge of the surf danced to their hammering feet. The drumming sound was lost in the tuneless bellows of the sea creatures. Their dim lanterns wobbled and swayed.

Varus didn't know how long it lasted. He awoke abruptly at a relative silence. *I must have slept after all. . . .* The inhuman but somehow meaningful noise had swaddled his discomfort like a cloak of down.

The sea creatures had left the beach. The lights of a few were visible far out to sea.

The apes were retreating from the shore with the same clumsy certitude with which they had arrived. The two that passed close to the humans again ignored them. Varus couldn't be sure whether or not they were the same two that had come near going the other way.

Lucinus was silent. Varus thought he was still breathing, but—he grinned tiredly—there was nothing to be done about it now if the magician had died.

Varus lay on the gravel and pillowed his head with his arm. He slept till dawn, however long that was, and roused the groggy Lucinus for the next stage of their voyage.

HEDIA SAUNTERED OUT OF THE CAVE, twitching her tail. It hadn't been cropped, and its long, feathery hair snapped to and fro like a flag.

The dog followed her but sprawled at the entrance, all three heads flat on the ground. One of his throats whined. Hedia looked over her shoulder, yipped, and flicked her tail as she walked away.

I haven't had a night like this save once in my life, and that time there were six men involved. I think it was six.

She paused and stretched, her forepaws scraping straight out in front of her until her deep chest rubbed the ground. Her tail was straight up in the air, fluttering in triumph; her tongue lolled from her long jaws.

Melino stood just back from the edge of the clearing. His left hand held the leather-bound book from the dead man's lap; in his right was his staff.

He pretended to look to the side, but Hedia's keen vision noted that he was watching her from the corners of his eyes. Her tongue waggled in silent laughter.

Beside the magician stood a figure of glowing red light in the form of a Saluki bitch. It watched Hedia approach with an air of cold unconcern.

Hedia paused again and growled. The demon didn't react.

Hedia tossed her head and walked proudly out of the clearing. She laid her cheek on Melino's knee and rubbed it firmly in a gesture of ownership. The demon watched, showing no emotion. She had no soul, but the greyhound Hedia sensed as surely as the human Hedia did that the demon was more than an automaton as Melino claimed.

Instead of using the *Book*, which he had been at such pains to get, Melino pointed the ruby ring at Hedia. The demon spoke what was for a moment mere human gibberish.

Hedia felt herself slipping through a crimson membrane. She came out the other side as a human being, nude and—she stretched again, rising onto her toes and pointing her fingers upward—aching.

But that would pass. As it always had before. She grinned.

"Your clothing is there on the ground," the magician said. He gestured with his index finger. He was staring into the jungle in the opposite direction.

Hedia pulled on her tunic, the silk inner one and then the other of soft but tightly woven wool. She would have to untie her sandals before she put them on again; her dog feet had stepped out through the straps.

"I'm terribly sorry for what you had to undergo," Melino muttered. "If there had been any other way . . ."

Hedia looked at him. The demon was in human form again, smiling sardonically.

"You're a sweet boy," Hedia said, patting Melino's cheek. "It's really all right."

Melino grimaced but said nothing further.

Hedia finished awkwardly retying her sandals. It was normally a task for a junior maid under the watchful supervision of Syra. As Hedia rose, she felt a flash of cold as though someone had suddenly showered her with water.

Melino cried out in horror. Hedia looked around for a cause, but nothing appeared to have changed. The demon's smile was impassive.

"What happened?" Hedia said. "I felt a chill."

The magician fell to his knees. He was making sounds, but Hedia wasn't sure whether he was muttering or blubbering in terror.

The demon looked at Hedia and said in her cold, precise voice, "The Singiri princess has died or has been freed. We no longer have a connection to the Waking World."

Melino was certainly blubbering.

CHAPTER XI

Varus stepped into the stern so that the boat's bow lifted as they ground onto the shore. The beach was of head-sized rocks, coarsely volcanic. They were black except where the sunset picked out a fleck of included mica or of quartz and turned it into a bloody ruby.

Lucinus collapsed forward. This time Varus was ready to catch him. The boat's hull was soft wood and not overly thick; but bad as it would be if they ripped out the bottom on this harsh shoreline, it would be even worse—for Varus at least—if the magician broke his neck as they landed.

Varus pulled Lucinus' right arm over his shoulders and gripped the wrist, putting his left arm around the magician's waist to take some of the weight. It would take effort that he couldn't maintain more than a few steps to lift the fellow's feet high enough not to touch. They would have to lie at the edge of the water until Lucinus regained enough strength to at least move his legs. These rocks would in an instant flay to the bone whatever part of a man was dragged over them.

The island where they had landed the first night had been a waste of scrub and beasts. Their present landfall was a cone of volcanic cinders, lifeless and featureless save for a fallen statue near the peak.

Varus got Lucinus out of the boat and tottered two steps up the shallow slope, then laid him down as gently as possible. After some moments' thought, Varus rolled his short cloak into a pillow for both their heads.

Lucinus seemed to be comatose, which was a mercy. There was no way to level the ground, and no leaves or twigs to use as a cushion between the rocks and their bodies.

Varus tried to settle himself. He thought of trying to sleep in the boat, but that would mean curling up between the thwarts. Even so, it might be a better choice than these rocks.

If he'd had more energy, Varus would have investigated the fallen statue. It was the hundred-foot-tall bronze figure of a warrior in armor, holding a long spear. The statue hadn't broken into pieces when it fell. It lay at length on its back, its head at the top of the cone.

Varus wondered why the figure had been erected. *How* it had been managed was even more puzzling, because the whole island appeared to be volcanic cinders like those he and Lucinus were lying on. A statue weighing tons would have to be anchored with an equally heavy base of concrete or solid masonry.

But although Varus did nothing but sit or stand during the voyage, he was exhausted when he disembarked in the evening. He wasn't used to heavy labor, of course, but he didn't overeat and walking to the Forum and elsewhere in hilly Carce kept him in good condition.

Nevertheless, he was as tired and achy as he might have been after spending the whole day sparring with Corylus. He looked down and realized that Lucinus did nothing physically strenuous during the voyage, either. It might be that something besides the invisible oarsman drove the boat across this sea. In any case, Varus didn't have strength to climb the slope in pursuit of mere knowledge.

He smiled grimly. He never before had thought of knowledge as "mere." He had never been so tired before, either.

Varus lay back, hoping to find a way to compose his body so that he could sleep. The sun was fully down, though the western sky was still red.

He heard a creaking sound. He looked up the slope to see if perhaps a huge bird had risen from the interior of the volcano.

The bronze warrior was sitting up. It was an automaton, not a statue.

Varus reached for Lucinus to shake him awake, but he probably wouldn't be able to accomplish that even if it was necessary. It might not be necessary, after all.

And the god Saturn might return to Earth and impose a second Golden Age of peace and plenty. Hope would be a fine thing. . . .

The bronze warrior got to its feet with squealing deliberation. Its great spear was butted in the cinders as a brace. Lifting the spear into a slant across its breastplate, it began to tramp sunwise around the cone.

It took no apparent notice of the humans near the shore nor of the boat they had arrived on.

Varus watched the huge automaton circling the peak. It moved with the regularity of a water clock. By the third circuit he was sure that it was moving down the slope, though he couldn't be sure how long it would be before the warrior neared him and Lucinus.

Varus chuckled. He wondered if he was feverish.

There was nothing to be done until daylight, when they could launch the boat and set off on the next stage of the voyage. Varus laid his head beside the magician's on the improvised pillow. He could feel the faint steady tramp of the automaton's feet through the fabric of the island.

Before long, Varus slept.

ALPHENA WAS STANDING in front of a low porphyry basin in which liquid roiled without bubbling. She thought she saw images beneath the surface, but she didn't have time for that now. She scanned the hall in which she stood.

The ceiling was about ten feet high here in the center and curved down for fifty feet to sidewalls that she could probably reach the top of on tiptoes. The floor and walls were gray stone blocks fitted without mortar. The dome was smoothly white. Alphena would have thought it was plastered were it not for the fact that it glowed faintly, the only light in the windowless hall.

The basin was six feet in diameter. Across it from her was a short figure—a wizened child rather than a little man—who glared at her in fury.

"Who are you?" he shrieked. "Who? *Who?*"

Alphena drew up to her full height, which, slight though it was, made her taller than the Child. She sheathed the borrowed sword with a *sring!* clink against the lip of the scabbard. She didn't need a weapon for this little fellow, and showing contempt helped her state of mind.

She wasn't afraid of the Child. She *was* afraid, though: afraid of the unknown, which was most of her present situation.

"I am the Lady Alphena," she said. She tried to project a ringing tone, but the hall seemed to drain her voice to a querulous squeak. "I am the daughter of Gaius Alphenus Saxa, Governor of Lusitania and former consul, and the Lady Hedia."

She paused, then added, "And who, sirrah, are you?"

The Child rocked back on his heels and buried his face in his hands. For a moment Alphena thought he was going to cry.

He lowered his hands and looked at her again but without the anger that had flared so brightly when he first saw her. "Who indeed?" the Child said bitterly. "A halfling, an abortion. I was the greatest magician of all time, and I am *nothing!*"

He stared into the basin. The liquid contents suddenly cleared. As though through a high window, Alphena looked down on a village of grass shacks. She saw no living humans, but corpses sprawled among the huts.

In the central plaza was a small wooden idol. On the ground around it were the skulls of human beings and crocodiles.

"Where . . . ?" Alphena began, but she swallowed the rest of her question because the scene had changed.

She saw Hedia and Melino, but they were in a jungle of strange trees and huge, bright-colored flowers. The magician had the staff and ring with which he had worked his illusions at the dinner party, but he was also carrying a leather-bound codex closed with iron latches.

Hedia looked regal and so unconcerned that she *had* to be exerting all of her control. Only a terrible situation could bring her to that fierce resolution. Beside her and Melino, apparently with them, was a column of flame, orange and hungry.

Alphena swallowed. The Child made stirring motions with his left index finger; the images began to succeed one another more quickly. Some she didn't recognize, but she saw her brother, Varus, on a boat of some sort, which was being rowed by—

By horrible things, worse than demons. There were six of them, voids of aching hunger without shape or being. Varus ignored them, as did the older man in the stern at the steering oar.

Alphena's mouth was dry. She was no longer afraid for herself. She imagined a world without Varus. He had been the only thing stable and constant while she was growing up with a father who ignored his children and their birth mother, who was even more distant.

Again Alphena might have spoken, but the scene became flat, yellow thornbush in which stood a tree with a huge trunk and limbs like roots thrusting into the air. The leaves were in sprays at the tips of tiny branches, completely out of scale on a trunk fifty feet in diameter.

Beside the tree danced the three brown-skinned girls. In the center of their circle was the glowing Egg that Alphena was seeking. *The way to it was here in the tomb after all!*

"There!" she cried. "Who are the women? And what's that in the middle of them?"

The Child sidled around the basin toward her. He cackled and said, "They are the Daughters, and that is the Egg. Some call them the Daughters of the Egg, but they call themselves the Daughters of the Mind."

"Is it a gryphon's egg?" Alphena said, pointing.

She jerked her arm back. She'd almost touched the image. She suddenly realized that she didn't know what would happen if she did. She had a feeling that it wasn't merely an image.

"The Daughters do not think that it is a gryphon's egg," said the Child slyly. "But time will tell."

Alphena was so engrossed in the dancers that she wasn't aware of what the Child was doing until he put his arm around her waist. She cried out and jumped away.

"What are you trying to do?" she shouted. If she hadn't been so shocked, she would have slapped him.

The Child looked away, grimacing, and wrung his hands. "I don't know what you mean," he muttered.

Meeting her eyes again, he said, *"Wholly a goddess, her white arms drew him in though he tried to resist!"*

"I want to go back to—" Alphena then thought again. "I want to go to my mother. You showed her to me. Can you take me there?"

The images in the basin were shifting, changing, but they no longer had her attention. She clasped her arms before her.

"You see this body, the result of treachery," the Child said. His expression was meant to be wheedling, though the result was ugly beyond Alphena's previous imagination. "But this is not me—my genius remains. My verse makes me a god! You should feel honored at the chance to become the consort of a god!"

Whatever happened to his body, Alphena thought, *must have damaged his mind too. But he's my best hope of escaping.*

"I don't care about poetry," she said, flicking the fingers of both hands contemptuously. "My brother is a poet too. If I wanted to listen to poetry, I'd listen to his. I want to get *out* of this place. If you help me, my father will reward you."

"You heifer!" the Child shrieked in berserk fury.

He lunged forward, shoving Alphena hard. She reached for his ear to twist him away, but the lip of the porphyry basin behind her caught her knees.

She tumbled over backward. As she plunged into the basin, she saw the village around the hideous black idol. The corpses scattered on the ground had decayed to skeletons.

CORYLUS TURNED AND WENT back up the walk to Melino's house. He wasn't running, but he strode as quickly as his tired muscles let him.

Corylus wasn't sure he *could* run. He had pushed himself pretty hard following the Princess through that jungle.

He grinned. He wasn't exactly out of condition, but he didn't have the edge he'd gotten when he lived with his father on the Danube. There had been very little to do *except* keep in shape in the barracks town of Carnuntum, of course.

"Headman!" Admetus said. He'd lifted his spear, and the three men with him also had their weapons ready. "What Hell did you drop from?"

Hecate take me if I know, Corylus thought, but he didn't let the words come off his tongue. Even his grin seemed to take the nervous guards aback.

Aloud he said, "Has Master Melino said anything to you?"

"What!" said Gittus. "What would he say to us?"

That was as informative an answer as Admetus' own, "No, sir, we haven't seen him all day."

He took a better look at Corylus. "Sir," he said, "did you just hack your way through the Dacian army? What's going on here?"

"There may be some trouble," Corylus muttered. "Ah—it's not my blood."

Mostly it wasn't his blood. The jagged pain across the right side of his ribs reminded him that some of it certainly was his blood.

Corylus had been thinking about his strained muscles and the amount of work it would take to sharpen his sword back to fighting condition. He hadn't been concerned about the state of his skin and clothing, because those weren't important concerns. They *were* fairly important if he was to be seen in public.

"Do you have a cape?" he said, glancing around the detachment. He could wash his arms and legs in the watering tank, but his tunic was more clotted red than its creamy natural wool color.

The men looked at him blankly. They were ill at ease, doubtful about what had happened, and worried about what would come next. Rather than shout pointlessly, Corylus said, "Never mind; I'll check the troops in the garden."

He went around the side this time. He didn't know what the baboons would do about someone who stank of blood and didn't have the escort of a magician.

Corylus grinned. *And* whose sword needed sharpening, though he'd make do if he must.

The detachment in back was if anything more surprised than Admetus and his men had been. They didn't recognize their captain. Xerxes shouted, "Look alive, Glabrio!" through the gate, and drew his short, incurved sword.

The blade had gold inlays, suggesting that Xerxes had been a man of some significance before circumstances caused him to leave his home in the East to see what Carce offered. Corylus suspected the main thing Xerxes had found in the Republic was a lack of death warrants with his name on them.

"It's all right!" Corylus said. "I need to wash off. But keep an eye out; there may be trouble that I haven't already taken care of."

He slipped into the garden—Glabrio had opened the gate to see what was going on—without further discussion. By warning the guards to watch for something coming after him, he hoped to avoid a long discussion.

Instead of washing off in the trough, Corylus strode past it to the umbrella pine. He laid his left hand on the bark and leaned against it as before.

"Captain?" Glabrio said at his shoulder. "What—"

"Not now!" Corylus said. "Don't disturb me or it's all our lives!"

The snarl chased Glabrio back toward the gate; none of the other guards showed a willingness to pursue the matter. Corylus hoped he was lying, but the chance the statement was true was better than he liked.

Corylus slipped into the green coolness. He felt . . . it wasn't peace, though that was the first word he might have used. Rather, he was aware of time and of the length of time . . . and of the insignificance of everything except the sun and the rain and the earth itself.

"Mistress," he said to the old woman waiting for him. "I feel better just for seeing you. Thank you."

"We are cousins, after all," the dryad said, matching his gentle smile. "Should I not greet a cousin? Even your human relatives would do that."

"Lady, I freed the Singiri princess," Corylus said. He grimaced, frustrated with himself for saying what the pine already knew. "Do you know—can you tell me, I mean, what Melino will do when he learns that I released her?"

"The magician is on Zabulon's Isle," the sprite said. "I cannot say what he is doing, for when you freed the Princess you broke the magician's bond with the Waking World and with me. I suppose he will try to leave Zabulon's Isle, but—"

Her smile had an edge.

"—without the Singiri to bring him back here, the only place he can go is to the Otherworld from which the Singiri freed him. He has no friends there and many enemies, so he will hesitate to do that."

She smiled more broadly and added, "He is cruel, even for the cruel race of men. I do not trouble myself with human matters generally, but I am pleased with what you have done, Cousin."

"He can't come back, then?" said Corylus, trying to keep the surge of hope out of his voice. Even if Melino wasn't the danger to the world that Lucinus had claimed he was, Corylus didn't mind the thought of never seeing the fellow again.

"The female with him is no magician," the dryad said. She shrugged. "They will stay where they are or they will go to a worse place, but they will not return to the Waking World unless a great magician helps them again."

Smiling more broadly, she added, "I do not think the Singiri princess will help this magician again, now that you have freed her."

Because it was so unexpected, it was a moment before the dryad's offhand reference to "the female with him" really sank in. Corylus swallowed and said, "Who is the female? You hadn't mentioned her before."

"I don't pay attention to humans," she said with another shrug. "And why should I have mentioned her? I told you she isn't a magician, so she doesn't matter."

Corylus felt a jolt of fury, but the dryad was right. He was angry because he hadn't bothered to ask for information that a pine tree wouldn't see any reason to volunteer. Pines scatter thousands of seeds every season, so to them the concepts of kinship and family were broader and much more shallow than they were to humans.

And of course he might be wrong to fear that Hedia was the woman with Melino. There were many other women. . . .

"Thank you, mistress," Corylus said as his spirit withdrew from the dryad's world. "I have work to do now, and perhaps a mistake to repair."

If it could be repaired.

Corylus shook himself as his soul and body merged. The bark was a rough presence under his left hand.

The guards were staring at him; he still held his bare sword. He sheathed it with care, using both hands. Heavy use had warped the blade slightly as well as dulling it.

"Glabrio?" he called over his shoulder as he bathed his arms to the shoulders in the irrigation tank. He splashed water on his legs, but if he moved fast enough nobody was likely to ask him about what looked like blood. "Did a woman come by this gate to see Master Melino this morning?"

"No, sir," Glabrio said. "But the same one that came to the front yesterday was here again today, only she didn't have her servant this time, Admetus says. I guess she's still in there."

I'm afraid you guess wrong, Corylus thought, but he nodded assent and went out through the gate to jog around the house. He felt cold in the heart as he rejoined the guard detachment in front.

"Admetus, did a woman visit Master Melino this morning?" he asked.

"Yeah, that's right," Admetus said. "He let her in himself. I guess she's still in there, right?"

"Captain, she's real class," volunteered Magnus, one of the newly hired gladiators. He had a thick German accent, but that was nothing new to Corylus. "I seen her last year, watching us train with some fancy friends of hers. She keeps covered up when she comes visiting here, but her name's Lady Hedia."

"All right," Corylus said. His mind put together a course of action, just as he would have done if the transport in which his patrol had crossed the Danube ripped its bottom out on a snag. "I don't know when I'll be back."

I'll go back to Father's house to clean up and talk with Pandareus. Lucinus is a magician, so maybe he can help us rescue Hedia, but I need to talk with Pandareus to settle my mind, because it was my error.

He started for the street. A mule cart was rattling up on the way from town. Corylus paused to let it go by, then realized the driver was Lycos and that Pulto was the passenger with him on the seat.

Pulto levered himself heavily to the ground. Lycos waited with the reins, ostentatiously not listening to what the servant had to tell Corylus.

"Master," Pulto said, "we got a message from Pandareus. He was with Lady Alphena up to the estate of some Aulus Collinus Ceutus. He's still up there, but Lady Alphena went into a tomb with that priest Paris and Pandareus says they both vanished."

He cleared his throat. "It was Ceutus sent the courier," he added. "I don't guess Pandareus runs to that kinda money himself. If Ceutus isn't scared shitless about what's going to happen for losing Lady Alphena like that, he ought to be."

"Yes," said Corylus. "I'll give you a leg up."

He made a stirrup of his hands and said, "Lycos, do you know where the Collinus estate is?"

"Yep," said the driver. He grinned. *Dear gods, he's ugly!* "Is there going to be trouble?"

Corylus hefted his servant onto the seat. As he mounted beside Pulto, he said, "I wish I thought there was going to be something for us to fight when we got there, but I doubt it."

"Well . . . ," said Pulto, unwrapping the belt from around the sheathed sword he'd carried in the back of the cart. "Maybe we'll get lucky. And I brought an extra sword for you, which looks like a good thing."

HEDIA WAS IGNORANT of what was going on, which meant she might be about to be overwhelmed by any sort of lurking future. All she would effect by badgering Melino and the demon with questions would be to delay the chance of them finding a real solution, so she said nothing.

Her uselessness made her angry. That was perfectly foolish, but it was harmless so long as she kept her mouth shut. Which made her even more angry.

She grinned and stepped away from the argument, though she continued to listen to Melino and the demon. Hedia had never been very interested in nature, and there didn't seem to be anything on this island other than nature, except for the guard dog, so she watched him.

The dog perked up an ear, then three ears. Two of his throats began to whine.

If I let him come over here, he'd lay a head in my lap, Hedia thought with satisfaction. She smiled at the dog, but she had no wish to go beyond idle speculation, at least until the swelling had gone down a little.

"She can't have died!" Melino insisted. "She was in good health, and I didn't raise the pressure on her bonds enough to really hurt her. The worst they could do is lead to gangrene, and that would have taken *weeks* to kill her, long after I was back safely!"

"The Princess is dead or she has been freed, master," the demon said. Her voice was perfectly flat, but there seemed to be a smile in it. Perhaps Hedia was projecting her own cold humor onto the thing of orange fire.

"Only a magician as great as myself could have freed her," Melino said. "Lucinus couldn't get through the wards I placed on my dwelling, any more than I could break the defenses of his farm. Who else is there, save the Princess herself? And she is harmless as long as she's bound!"

"She is no longer bound, master," the demon said. "She is free or she is dead. Either way, she will not draw you back to the Waking World."

The foliage nearby quivered, drawing Hedia's eye. An ant wriggled through clumsily. Its six legs seemed to be controlled by six different minds as each picked its own direction.

Hedia would have giggled, but the ant was very large. The jaws alone were the length of her hand with the fingers outstretched; when they closed and opened, they gave her the impression of large shears.

"I have Zabulon's *Book*!" Melino said. "There must be a path that will take me back to the Waking World. I have the power of the *Book*!"

The demon said nothing. In fury, Melino snarled, "Tell me how best I'm to return to the Waking World!"

He is her master, Hedia thought, *but she is not his friend.* The demon would answer the magician's every question and carry out any command;

but if he didn't use the correct form of words, the demon might choose to smile at him and do nothing.

If she were my servant, I would have her whipped for dumb insolence, she added silently.

She smiled at the pair of them. Aloud she said, "My son once told me that 'a man has as many enemies as he has slaves,' though I think he was quoting some philosopher or another."

"What do you mean, woman?" Melino said. Irritation had apparently worn away his embarrassment, because he looked directly at her for the first time since her interlude with the guard dog.

"She knows," Hedia said, turning up her left hand in a gesture to the demon. "But right now, if you don't deal with this ant—"

She gestured again.

"—we'll have to move."

Then she said, "These ants," because two more ants—and now a third—were following the first through the moss-like shrubbery.

"Nodens!" Melino swore, and thrust his fist toward the insects.

"Burn!" the ring piped in the demon's voice, and the yellow-orange light incinerated a cone of vegetation including the ants. A leg twitched as though it were trying to walk. It was still attached to a scrap of the armored body.

Melino sagged back. He wiped his brow, using the crook of his elbow because both his hands were full. Turning to the demon again, he said, "How can I return to the house I left without first dropping into the Otherworld? *How,* demon?"

"There are more ants," Hedia said. "Come, let's move away from here and discuss it where we're not in their way."

At least a dozen were in sight. The cleared ground might still be hot, but that didn't appear to disconcert the insects crossing the patch.

"They are forager ants," the demon said to her. "They are already on three sides of you, and they will close the fourth before you can escape their cordon."

She turned to Melino and went on, "With the *Book,* you can go to the Waking World or to anywhere else through the Beginnings. I know of no other path, and the Beginnings is in the Otherworld."

The magician swore in a desperate undertone. He pointed his fist as the demon watched with what would have been a smirk in a human being. The ring said, "Burn!"

This time the magician swept his hand in an arc as the light blazed from it. The vegetation was too juicy to sustain the flames, but steam screamed under the fiery lash. Several of the higher trees wobbled when their trunks were severed, then began to topple.

Hedia stepped to the side because she thought one was coming down too close to her. It slammed into the ground and bounced slightly. Melino could have reached out and touched the trunk, but he hadn't moved as it fell. From the look of him, he had barely enough strength to stand.

Hedia could see parts of ants at the edge of the boiling devastation. One victim was still alive, lying on its back with three legs flailing the air. The legs on the other side had been seared off.

More ants were approaching, their antennae twitching and their saw-toothed jaws scissoring closed and open. Hedia looked over her shoulder in a wild surmise.

"They're all around us!" she said.

"If you do not leave here," the demon volunteered coolly, "you will die. I am not alive, so it does not matter to me."

Melino moaned wordlessly. He held the *Book* in his right hand and used his left thumb to throw it open. Hedia expected him to read out a spell. Instead the *Book* itself boomed an inhuman word in a groaning bass voice.

Hedia fell out of the world just as the jaws of an ant clamped shut on where her right ankle had been.

VARUS HAD AWAKENED when the automaton made its most recent circuit, striding massively past, twenty feet up the slope from where the humans lay. The creature's sandals struck sparks from the rocks: their soles must be iron, not bronze. The huge spear—it was longer than a ship's mast when viewed from this close—might be iron also.

Varus smiled. If he had been here with Pandareus or Corylus, he would have mentioned his observation. Lucinus wouldn't care.

Very few people seemed to care about knowledge for its own sake, and perhaps that majority was right. Regardless, if Varus didn't launch the boat before the automaton returned, his knowledge would die with him. He might be able to dodge the iron-shod feet, but the boat would not. Starving on this wasteland would be a worse fate than being pulped into its black rocks.

It *might* be a worse fate. At any rate, he didn't intend to try either alternative.

Although Varus planned to get up immediately and to force Lucinus to get up, it was so hard to move that he found himself lying in a grim reverie when the vibration of the automaton's feet reached him again through the ground. The creature was still out of sight; but it was coming, and it would arrive soon.

Varus rose as carefully as he could. The irregular lava was poor footing at best, and if a block turned under his weight he would scrape an ankle if he didn't sprain it.

He lifted Lucinus by the shoulders. The magician seemed to awaken, but he remained a weight as dead as a hog's carcase. By the time they reached the shore, Lucinus was able to stand upright while Varus muscled the boat back into the sea. He couldn't have gotten it over the stones with Lucinus' weight already aboard.

Varus collapsed with his head in the boat when it started to bob freely, but his torso and legs were still in the water. The eastern sky was bright. When he lifted his head from the gunwale, he saw the sun was already painting the upper slope of the island. Bronze flashed bright, and the helmet of the automaton appeared above the black rock.

"Lucinus!" Varus said. The magician was facing Varus, but there was no recognition in his eyes.

The automaton tramped inexorably toward them; most of its great body was now visible. On its breastplate was molded the fall of Phaethon, blasted from his father's sun chariot before the boy could scorch the world to a cinder.

Varus saw a variety of bad choices, but unquestionably the worst would be not to act at all. He splashed back onto the dry rock, seized Lucinus by the arm, and staggered toward the boat with him. It wobbled outward as they approached.

With a final desperate grab, Varus caught the gunwale in his left hand. The water was already at his lower chest. He half-lifted, half-shoved Lucinus into the belly of the boat, then stood gasping, unable to follow the magician.

The automaton strode along the shore, rattling thunder with each slow pace. Its head creaked around and its empty eyes stared down at Varus.

He dragged himself over the side. Lucinus was already at the steering oar, mumbling a spell.

Varus lay gasping, looking back at the island because his head was turned in that direction. The automaton had halted. It watched the boat for a moment, then lifted its spear in what might have been a salute.

The automaton turned and began climbing back toward the peak where it had lain as a fallen statue when the vessel approached on the previous evening. It walked directly up the slope instead of reversing its winding progress to the shore. Varus continued to watch until the island sank below the eastern horizon.

CHAPTER XII

Alphena hit the ground hard enough to bruise, but the village clearing was no farther beneath her than the bottom of the basin would have been if it were stone and not magic. She rolled to her feet, drawing her sword with only a faint ring of steel against the lip of the scabbard.

Alphena felt as though she were in the steam room of a bathhouse. It had rained recently, perhaps within the past few minutes. Water stood in pools on the bare ground, but it was evaporating quickly in the heat.

She looked around, then up, hoping to see the opening through which she'd fallen. Just as the door by which she entered the Child's chamber had vanished as soon as she was through it, so there was nothing now beyond the huts save trees and the vines hanging from them.

Something chattered angrily from a tree, but she couldn't see it. The creature could have been anything—bird or monkey or for that matter a frog. In any case, it probably wasn't dangerous, or at least immediately dangerous.

Alphena was sweating already. The stone chamber had been cool and dry. She hadn't paid much attention to it at the time, but the contrast with this muggy, muddy jungle was overpowering. Of course the temperature and humidity weren't the things she should be worrying about.

There were twenty or so huts, arranged in a rough circle. They all had roofs of leaf thatch on pole frames that were walled with wicker for about three-quarters of the way up. The eaves were so low that anyone taller than Alphena would have to duck to go through the doorways. Most had originally had doors of wicker, but many of those had been wrenched off.

The huts were beginning to fall in, though that might happen in a short time in these conditions. The corpses—Nubians, apparently, unless the scraps of skin still clinging to the bones had darkened after death—lay all about. They had variously been stabbed or battered to death; a broken flint spear blade was wedged in the spine of one.

Alphena had never been good at counting. There didn't seem to be much point in knowing the exact number anyway. There were several, maybe more, for each hut. From the way bodies were disarranged, wild animals had been feasting until the flesh became too rotten for anything but the blowflies.

The jungle already bursting through the stockade walls stank of rot also, a heavy vegetable odor that Alphena found more oppressive than that of the human corpses this long after the slaughter. *I may have to spend the rest of my life in this stinking place,* Alphena thought.

In the center of the clearing was the idol she'd noticed when she stood beside the Child, looking down on the basin's visions. She walked over to it, her sword out. She was ready for any excuse to use it.

Killing something wouldn't help get her home, but at least then she could feel that she'd stopped being a marker on somebody's board game. *I wish I'd killed that Child when I saw him!*

The idol was of naturally black wood. It was about two feet tall, but its tapering base had been forced into a crack on the top of a block of field-stone. That base allowed the idol to glare back at Alphena eye to eye.

It was even uglier close up than she had thought while looking from above at the vision. Branches springing nearly straight up from the trunk formed its arms. On their ends were crudely carved hands.

The almond-shaped eyes were inlaid with clamshells drilled to indicate the pupils. The nose was as flat as a pig's muzzle. From the snarling mouth protruded a tongue that had been a knife blade of hammered iron. The blood that had been smeared on the lips and mouth had dried black and was scaling off.

When she looked at the image in the basin, Alphena had seen skulls ranged around the idol—two human and two of large crocodiles. The bones had been carefully cleaned, either by boiling or possibly by being set on an anthill so that the tiny insect jaws could pick off the flesh and sinews.

With the skulls were now the heads of a pair of lizardmen like those in Veturius' compound. These had not been properly cleaned. They sat in pools of their own liquescent decay, and their pebbled skin was slumping away.

Did the lizardmen slaughter the villagers? But surely they wouldn't have left their own dead to rot here if—

A man with the head of a horse stepped out of one of the less-damaged huts, tearing off half the roof instead of bending low enough to go through the doorway. He was seven feet tall and naked except for the sash over his right shoulder. From that hung a stone axe and two flint-bladed knives.

His spear was longer than he was tall. Its shaft was a three-inch sapling that still had the bark on.

The Horsehead laughed like sewage bubbling. "The Master was right to leave me in this wet hell!" he said in guttural Greek. Alphena could barely make out the words. "Now I will kill you and rejoin my herd."

He stalked toward Alphena with the spear raised to thrust like a harpoon. His feet were split into two fleshy toes.

Alphena instinctively stepped to the side to put the idol between her and the Horsehead. She immediately recognized her mistake: the length of the Horsehead's spear and his great reach meant he could easily drive her back, but it would prevent her from closing with him to use her sword.

At least I know who massacred the villagers.

She grasped the bottom of the idol and pulled it upward. It didn't come out of the crack into which it was wedged. She jerked harder, lifting the fieldstone base from the ground for an instant before its own weight pulled it from the wood.

Alphena danced away, holding the idol out in her left hand. It was the best choice she could see for a shield.

She wouldn't have thought she could lift the stone base left-handed. Her huge opponent had brought out the best in her.

The Horsehead laughed again. He shuffled forward with his legs splayed widely apart, so that he could follow instantly if she tried to circle him.

Without signaling his intention, the Horsehead made a mighty overarm thrust. Alphena sidestepped to the right but interposed the idol to the blow in case her opponent tried to hook his weapon into her. The spear struck like a battering ram, rotating Alphena widdershins, but the flint head shattered without scarring the black wood.

Alphena stabbed the Horsehead through the lower chest. Her unintended pirouette added force to the blow. The sword drove so deep that she felt its point crunch into the giant's spine.

The Horsehead lurched backward. His bawl of pain turned into a wheeze. Alphena came with him because she wasn't giving up the sword. Her grip was more a spasm than conscious thought; her mind was a blur of light and motion.

She tried desperately, mindlessly to free the blade. It slid out ahead of more blood than she had ever imagined could come from a wound.

The Horsehead's arms flailed convulsively. Alphena saw the spear shaft coming at her through the corners of her eyes, but she was toppling and couldn't dodge it.

She felt the blow as a burst of white light. Then she felt nothing.

"ALL RIGHT," SAID Corylus to the assemblage. "Where was Alphena when she disappeared?"

He was working at keeping emotion out of his face, hoping that he didn't look too grim. All those milling around—Alphena's entourage, workers from the estate, and most particularly Collinus Ceutus himself—gabbled and twitched like a henyard immediately after a hawk has snatched its dinner.

"Lady Alphena entered that cave," said Pandareus. He not only pointed his right arm but also took a step in the direction of the hillside that had been eaten back by the recent excavation. "The tunnel, I suppose it is. Paris went in and she followed. The rest of us were behind her."

Except for the old scholar, those present were behaving like surviving villagers in the wake of a German raid: terrified, unsure of what just happened; mourning their losses and nervously certain that the disaster would be repeated as soon as they turned their backs.

Corylus gazed around the crowd. He knew that what these people were most afraid of was him: Gaius Cispius Corylus, the young representative of the wealthy senator whose daughter had disappeared while in their company.

In his heart of hearts, Corylus was glad they were afraid. They *had* let something happen to Alphena. His anger was irrational, so he would never let it show—but it pleased him that they were feeling the lash of the blame he was too reasonable to voice.

"Sir, I was right behind her," said Drago, who with his cousin led the escort. "The old guy—"

He nodded to Pandareus.

"—tried to get in ahead of me, but I dragged him back. He didn't have a sword, and he didn't look like he'd be much use with his bare hands, so I got him outta the way. Then I went in after her."

"Correct on all points," said Pandareus. "Frankly, I wasn't thinking of the possibility of danger."

"All right," Corylus said. "How close to her were you, Drago?"

"Dum near run up her ass, I was that close," the Illyrian said, shaking his head. "I didn't know how big the cave was inside and I was afraid I'd lose her in it. I went barreling in and there she was. She was following the priest close enough I could hear him mumbling something. Though I couldn't see him at first."

"This was nothing to do with me," said Ceutus, wringing his hands. He sounded desperate rather than defiant. "I didn't even know that the tomb was there till Pandareus told me about it. *I* didn't go in."

Corylus looked at him and said, "If you know nothing, then be silent until I ask you to speak."

The landowner cringed away. Corylus had sounded—even to himself—as though he were about to pronounce sentence of death. *Ceutus isn't at fault, but if he insists on calling attention to himself . . .*

Drago waited through the interruption with his mouth open. Corylus turned toward him again and said, "Did you have a light? Did anybody in the tunnel have a light or did it all come through the opening there?"

"That's a funny thing," said Drago, frowning in concentration. "There wasn't a light at first—that's how I near run into Her Ladyship—but then the *ceiling* started to get light. Like there was a hole in it, but there wasn't."

"That's how it appeared to me as well, Master Corylus," Pandareus said formally. His present attitude was that of a student to his teacher rather than the reverse, as it would have been during class. "I saw Lady Alphena and even Paris in silhouette—when I could see past Master Drago, that is. I was following him."

Pandareus pursed his lips as his eyes turned briefly toward his memories. Then he said, "It did seem to be coming from the tunnel roof. I couldn't see the rock above Paris, just a glow. It was very faint at first."

"All right," Corylus said as he digested the information. "We'll go into the cave, then."

He glared around him. "Just the three of us, Drago and Pandareus with me. The rest of you keep away from the entrance. And—"

To one of the estate servants.

"—give me that lantern."

Corylus took a deep breath, then drew his dagger instead of the long sword. With that in his right hand and the lantern in his left, he said, "Drago, you first. I'll follow you. You'll follow me if you please, Master Pandareus."

Corylus had been afraid that the whole tunnel would be so low that he had to crawl, but he could stand upright once he was beyond the entrance. The ground level outside had risen with erosion from the slope above, but the stone door had kept all but seepage from entering the tunnel.

The walls were coarsely finished, showing adze marks and a few drill holes, but there was no doubt that the tunnel was artificial or at least largely artificial. It was cut through living rock; an opening, even if blocked off again, would have been obvious from the shadows the lantern threw when Corylus held it close to first one wall, then the other.

"Look, it was about here," said Drago, squeezing against the side of the tunnel so that the lantern illuminated one wall and the floor ahead of him. He squiggled his broad, sickle-shaped sword toward the ceiling. "I know it wasn't much farther in—"

He was standing about ten feet from the entrance.

"—and anyway, how much farther is there?"

He waggled the sword again, this time toward the solid rock that ended the tunnel. It was closer to him than the entrance was.

"You, old guy?" Drago said, bending to peer back past Corylus. "Don't it seem about this far to you?"

"Yes, it does, Master Drago," said Pandareus. Only someone who knew the scholar as well as Corylus did could have heard the smile in his voice. "The light in the ceiling seemed brighter and there were tree roots growing out of the right sidewall."

He leaned forward and rubbed his fingertips over the stone.

"Which is not the case now," Pandareus said, straightening. "Master Corylus, I clearly saw Paris climb upward, using the roots as the rungs of a ladder. Lady Alphena followed him very closely—so closely one of her hands was on the same root as one of his feet, it seemed to me. They both faded as they went upward, but I thought they must be lost in the light."

"Sir, I *tried* to follow her," Drago said. His face was beaded with sweat, the result of emotion, despite the tunnel's relative coolness. "Zeus bugger me if I didn't, I was afraid, but I *tried*. Only my hand couldn't feel the roots and then the roots wasn't there. And the light went out and Her Ladyship was gone and I *tried!*"

Corylus lifted the lantern and ran his dagger lightly over the ceiling, hoping that the point would find a crack that his eyes had not. Like the walls, it was nothing more than roughly carved rock.

"All right," he said. "Master Pandareus, we'll go back outside now."

Everyone was acting as though Corylus was here as the agent of Senator Saxa. Corylus hoped that Saxa would approve of what he was doing, but that was secondary to the need to act immediately. Corylus was the best person present to take charge; and on the frontiers, you learned not to wait for an order before doing what was necessary.

The scholar turned and started back. Over his shoulder, Corylus said, "Drago, you and your fellows won't be punished. I'll assure Lord Saxa that there was nothing you could have done. The same thing would have happened if I had been there in your place."

Except that I would've been leading, he added silently. Though—as strong-willed as Alphena was, that might not have been possible even for him unless he'd been willing to grab her around the waist and carry her out of the tunnel.

Corylus smiled wanly at that thought. He was fairly sure that Alphena's escort would have killed him immediately even if they agreed with his decision. Saxa was a kindly man, but he would have had his servants crucified if he learned they had permitted a commoner to manhandle his daughter.

The sunlight outdoors was a pleasant change, though Corylus had been sunk too deeply into the problem to think about the tunnel and its darkness as anything but factors to be considered. He handed the lantern back to the servant from whom he'd taken it, still lighted.

For a moment, he stood in grim silence while everyone stared at him. *If they're expecting wisdom, they may have a long wait.*

He grinned in sudden realization and glanced up the slope. There *was* another witness: the ancient yew tree.

"All right," said Corylus. "Master Ceutus, get your men back to the house proper. At any rate, I don't want you or any of your people any closer than that."

It didn't matter to him whether the estate workers stood around watching, but it might matter to the dryad.

"Rago and Drago, take Lady Alphena's escort back to the carriages," he continued. "Be ready to come if I call for you."

There was absolutely nothing useful that a gang of toughs could do in the present situation. Saying that to men like the cousins would invite the reply that they didn't work for Corylus.

"Pulto and Lycos, I want you fifty feet from the entrance to the tunnel," Corylus said. "Don't let anyone come past you, all right?"

"You're going into the tunnel again?" Pulto said, his hand on his sword hilt. There was a growl of challenge in the question.

"No, I'm not going into the bloody tunnel!" Corylus said, feigning irritation that he didn't feel. Pulto and Lycos would do what they thought his father would wish. They would be pretty sure that allowing Corylus to walk unaccompanied into danger would *not* be what the Old Man expected of them. "I'm going to go up that hill—"

He pointed.

"—and stand beside that bloody yew tree. There's no danger at all, but I don't want a bunch of yobs disturbing what I'm trying to do. And if you wonder if I mean you when I say a bunch of yobs, I bloody well do!"

Lycos chuckled like pottery breaking. "Yes, *sir,* Prefect," he said. He plucked Pulto's sleeve with the hand that didn't hold his narrow-bladed spade. "Come on, trooper. You heard *that* tone before, same as I done."

Pandareus watched the two old soldiers moving away, talking to each other in low voices. "I don't understand what your driver meant," he said.

"Lycos told Pulto that I remind him of my father," Corylus said, also watching the men. His eyes were threatening to go blurry. "Under the circumstances, there is no greater compliment."

He blinked and focused on Pandareus again. Before he could speak, the scholar said, "Master Corylus, I realize that I can't help in what you plan to do; but if it were possible, I would like to walk to the tree with you. For knowledge's sake."

Corylus paused. He'd planned to send Pandareus away also, but the scholar had nothing in common with anyone but him of the hundred or so people in the immediate vicinity.

"Of course, teacher," he said. "I'm not sure that there'll be anything for you to see, but your company is welcome."

They walked up the slope together. Corylus chuckled. Before the scholar could turn and raise an eyebrow in question, Corylus said, "I feel safer having you with me now than I would having Pulto. Than I would with the whole Third Batavians."

"While I agree that the army is unlikely to be much help in the present circumstances," Pandareus said with a dry smile, "I fail to see that I'm any better. I asked to accompany you for my own purposes, not because I could imagine my presence being of any benefit."

"Master?" said Corylus. "Are you afraid?"

Pandareus looked puzzled. "Well, I don't wish to die, if that's what you mean," he said. "But I'm not a young man, so my death is inevitable in the not too distant future no matter what I do."

They had reached the yew tree. Corylus grinned at his teacher and said, "Master, you probably live too much in your own world to understand how refreshing your example is to someone who is of a less philosophical bent. Someone like myself."

Pandareus pursed his lips. "So long as you don't count on me to stop a charge of screaming Germans," he said. "Or, in the present circumstances, Ethiopes."

Corylus reached for the tree trunk, laughing for the first time since they had arrived at Ceutus' estate. Before he quite touched the thin, ragged bark, the dryad stepped into view.

She was smiling, but Corylus noticed that she kept him between herself and Pandareus. "I suppose with all the magic from the priest's spell," she said, "your friend can see me as easily as you can, Cousin?"

"Yes, mistress," the scholar said, bowing. "I am Pandareus of Athens.

In normal times I teach rhetoric to Master Corylus, here; but more recently, he has been teaching me."

"Taxus," Corylus said, using the dryad's name, "Pandareus is my friend and a friend to all those who wish to preserve life on Earth's surface. We wish to find—to rescue—the young lady who vanished recently with the priest whom you mentioned. Can you help us?"

Because the tree was over fifty feet tall and six feet in diameter, very large for a yew, Corylus had expected the dryad to be as aged as the spirit of the pine behind Melino's dwelling. Instead, Taxus looked to be only a few years older than Hedia—and equally beautiful, though in a lusher, riper fashion. Her hair was a flowing black, and her lips were a red as vibrant as that of Serian lacquerware.

Yews are very long-lived trees, Corylus thought. Then he thought, *I wonder if her lips would poison me if I kissed them?*

Taxus gave him a slow smile. She reached out with her right hand, running her fingertips over his cheek as lightly as the touch of a butterfly's wing. "You are a *very* pretty boy, Cousin," she murmured.

Corylus took her hand between both of his. He squeezed it, then firmly lowered her arm to her side again.

"Please, Cousin," he said. "The girl is the sister of my closest friend. Can you help us find her?"

Dryads were whimsical, even beyond what Corylus had learned to expect from human women, but this yew spirit had an apparent presence that set her apart from her sisters. *She could be cruel,* he thought, *but as a matter of cold deliberation—not whim.*

Taxus licked her lips as she considered him. "I don't know where the female went," she said at last. "I'm not a magician myself. But I can take you to a magician's garden, and from there you can go to him. He can help you further—if he chooses."

A number of questions ran through Corylus' mind, starting with, *Who is the magician?*

He didn't ask them, because it didn't matter. The dryad had offered a way of—possibly—reaching Alphena. That was more than he had expected, and much more than he would wind up with if he tried to press Taxus.

"Thank you, Cousin," he said. "I would appreciate that kindness on your part."

Taxus laughed. Her expression chilled. She said, "Does your friend come too?"

"Yes, mistress," Pandareus said. "If I may."

He looked at Corylus and added with a crooked smile, "For the same reason as before, of course."

"I don't know a better reason than the pursuit of knowledge," Corylus said. "Yes, Cousin. Both of us will go."

The dryad smiled again. She took each man by a hand and with them walked into a greenish fog.

VARUS HUDDLED IN THE BOW as the boat trembled through the dusk. They were nearing another island, but he felt as though his brain had turned to sludge; he had no interest in what would happen next nor in what was happening now. He was very tired.

Varus didn't feel hungry or thirsty, though he had eaten only his usual slight breakfast of bread soaked in wine lees before he joined Lucinus three days ago. He should be ravenous by now if they really had been at sea that long.

Was this a dream while his body slept in Sulla's garden? Or lay dead in Sulla's garden? In the latter case his soul might journey for eternity like a more literate version of Tantalus, in search of an island and a book that it would never reach. Varus smiled at the speculation.

The island was forested down to the sand beach, rosy in the sunset. The foliage of the trees themselves was ragged and dangling, like that of cypresses, but vines and other plants and even other trees grew on the branches. Fruit hung from some of the vines, rotating slowly in a breeze that Varus couldn't feel.

Those weren't fruit: they were human heads hanging by their long hair. They stared at Varus with empty eyes.

"Lucinus!" Varus cried. He stood and immediately toppled to his knees because his feet had grown numb while he hunched motionless. He crawled to the stern through the hooped deckhouse. He had previously avoided the shelter for no reason he could explain, but he had no time to waste now.

The bow crunched up the beach, throwing Varus backward. Perhaps there was still time to get to another island.

"Lucinus, look at the heads in the trees!" he said. He grabbed the magician by the shoulders and shook him to keep him from lapsing into unconsciousness. "We've got to get out of here while we still can!"

Lucinus looked at him with a dull expression. His lips moved.

"What did you say?" Varus said. "I can't hear you!"

"They won't bother us . . . ," Lucinus whispered. He went limp in Varus' arms.

Varus carried him up the sand to just below the trees. He chose a location at the base of a palm. The scattered palms didn't seem to have hanging heads, perhaps because they didn't have proper branches.

Lucinus should know whether the heads were dangerous. At any rate, there was nothing Varus could do about it if the magician was wrong.

Varus pulled the boat a little farther up the beach. Seeing the hanging heads at least had the benefit of shocking him into greater alertness than he had risen to since boarding the vessel in Carce a lifetime ago.

The faces had no thought or even life in them, but their sightless eyes followed him as he moved. A heliotrope followed the sun, of course, but that didn't mean the flower had any hostile intent.

It was a pity that there was no one with whom Varus could discuss the wonders he was seeing. Perhaps after they had found Zabulon's *Book* and returned he could question Lucinus about the heads, about the bronze giant, about the sea on which they traveled, and about so much more.

And perhaps one or both of them would be dead.

Varus lay on his back beside the magician, sharing the rolled cloak again as a pillow. As the sunset faded, stars began to come out.

Varus wasn't a real astronomer, but he had as good a grasp of the heavens as anyone who didn't depend on the stars for his livelihood or for his life: a farmer, say, or a sailor. To his surprise he recognized the constellations. They were the normal ones of home—but they were the stars of early spring, not the fall in which he had left Carce.

As he pondered the sky, Varus felt another existence slowly envelop him. He was at the base of a hill. He began climbing the rocky path, knowing who he would find at the top.

The old woman had been facing the other way as Varus reached the top, but she immediately turned to greet him. She wore a long white tunic without ornamentation, under a blue wrapper that covered her head like the hood of a cape. She said, "Greetings, Lord Varus."

"Greetings, Sibyl," Varus said. He walked across the narrow crest of the ridge to stand with the old woman on the other side. "Mistress, why have you called me to you this time?"

The Sibyl laughed in a cracked voice. "I cannot call you, Lord," she said. "I am only a whim of your mind."

She looked over the precipice before them. Though she did not gesture, Varus followed her eyes as he was meant to do. Below was the beach on which he had landed.

The stern of the boat was still in the water; he thought he had drawn it onto dry sand. It probably didn't matter, because this sea appeared to be tideless. And in any case, he had done the best his body could manage at the time.

Varus examined his own wan, lifeless face. It reminded him of the heads hanging from the trees, not the pleasant features he was used to seeing when he looked into still water or the polished bronze surface of a mirror.

A scum of foam and flotsam bobbed minusculely at the edge of the sea. A shadow rose from it. Farther down the beach, a similar shadow rose or perhaps coalesced from the air.

The shadows had no form. To the eye of Varus' mind, they were merely palpable darkness.

"Sibyl?" he said, trying to keep his voice calm. The darknesses were drifting slowly in the direction of the sleeping men. "What are those things? The mist, the blackness."

"They are Elementals," the Sibyl said. "They are ageless and soulless, and they hate men."

"What are they doing?" Varus said as the Elementals drifted toward the sleeping humans.

He wondered how his mouth could become dry. After all, his body wasn't really here. He wasn't sure it was below on the sand, either.

"They have sucked existence out of men who landed here in the past," the Sibyl said with the same calm certainty, "and they have hung the heads from the trees. They will do the same with newcomers, if they can."

"I've got to wake Lucinus!" Varus said. By now the blurs of foulness were on either side of the sleepers. "He must not have known about the Elementals when he said the heads wouldn't harm us!"

"Lucinus is a magician," the Sibyl said. "He knows the Elementals will not try to harm magicians."

Varus shouted, "*I'm* not a magician! What do *I* do?"

"Are you not a magician, Lord Varus?" the Sibyl said, her voice rising into a cackle of laughter. "Are you not?"

"*Let a burning power come through the sea to the land!*" Varus said. There was a flash of light so intense that for an instant the water and sand were transparent.

Varus' spirit spiraled back into his body; he lurched upright.

Lucinus still slept. The Elementals had vanished without a trace. Strands of hair dangled from a few branches when Varus looked around, but the heads were gone.

I hope they've found peace.

Varus lay back on the sand. He slept like a dead man.

HEDIA WAS SO SUDDENLY in another place that she swayed, though she hadn't moved in any fashion that should make her stumble. She spread her left leg wider, as much to steady her nerves as for any physical need.

Melino bent forward, bracing his wrists on his bent knees for support. Because he still held both staff and *Book*, he couldn't use his hands. The demon ignored him and Hedia, facing the surrounding forest of what seemed to be giant grass stems. She wore an expression of either disdain or disinterest.

The landscape was grayed out; the sky glimpsed through the vegetation was as featureless as a coat of indigo paint. Daisies wobbled twenty feet overhead, but there were monstrous trees as well. The ground was littered with dead leaves six feet long and chestnuts the size of grain baskets, some still in their husks.

Hedia could hear music, but at first she couldn't see where it was coming from. She jerked quickly around at seeing movement in the corner of her eye, but there was nothing but a giant fern where she looked.

Frowning, she turned back. On a log that had been empty sat a youth with a feathered cap and a long smock, playing a coiled horn. Beside him sat a man-sized grasshopper with the head of a fox. It plucked the strings of a lute whose sound box was the shell of a river turtle. They were the source of the music Hedia was hearing. The turtle's limbs, still attached, wriggled.

The horn player watched her; the fox eyes did not, not openly at least. The notes of the lute ran around and through the soft waves of sound from the horn.

People began to step out from around grass-blades or rise from behind pebbles. They wore all manner of clothing, generally pleated skirts for the females and breeches held up by shoulder straps for the men. Their headgear was invariably ornate, running to feathers and furs and metal spikes or sheets of foil.

They looked odd without quite being grotesque. They gave the impression of being normal humans who had gone about all their lives with stone blocks on their heads, slowly flattening them into shorter, broader beings.

"Where are we?" Hedia demanded. She spoke because the newcomers were making her nervous. If she simply stood and waited for others to act, she might show that fear.

There were twenty-odd of the strangers. The tallest was shorter than Hedia and probably not even as tall as Alphena.

"We are in the place from which I went from this world to the Waking World," Melino muttered.

He opened the *Book*. As before, it spoke a word. Hedia felt existence shudder like a sheet of water sweeping over rocks.

Melino tottered. Hedia put out her hand to steady him, but at the last moment she hesitated.

The magician opened his eyes. He nodded toward two inward-arching grass-blades. Hedia could follow the opening between them for as far as her eyes could reach.

"That way," Melino said, closing the *Book*. He started forward.

A short man in red breeches and a puffy white blouse stepped into the magician's path. He wore a hat with a low crown. Tiny chariots appeared to race around its wide brim.

"One moment, sir," the little man said. "This can be a very dangerous place for those who don't know its foibles. My family and I will guide you."

When Melino said nothing, the stranger said, "It would be very dangerous for you to attempt to proceed without our help."

Melino sniffed. To the ring demon he said, "Deal with him."

The demon's expression might have been a smile. She said, "Pluck," and extended her left hand. A dusting of ruby sparkles drifted from her fingertips toward the strangers' spokesman.

The little man backed away, but the sparkles encircled him and closed in. "Please, good master, you must have misunderstood me!" he said.

The sparkles pulled back from the little man's torso, tearing his blouse and trousers away in shreds. His torso was ridged, and a third pair of limbs had been concealed under his clothing.

"We meant no harm!" the little man squealed, though he wasn't a man. His fellows had vanished. "You must believe—"

The sparkles pulled away the three limbs on his left side as they had done his clothing. He fell to the ground, shrieking wordlessly. He began to wriggle in a circle, but he couldn't rise.

"That should be enough of a lesson," Melino said. He was breathing hard. "Come along, though, before something worse finds us."

He started in the direction he had indicated, walking around the crippled spokesman.

"Are you going to finish him?" Hedia said, skirting the writhing thing a little wider than Melino had done.

"He's no longer a danger," Melino said. "He can squirm as long as he wants to. Although—"

He looked at Hedia.

"—are you hungry? They taste like crabmeat."

"Thank you," said Hedia, "but I don't care for shellfish."

They walked briskly through the forest. The demon was leading.

Sexual bondage with the right partner could be pleasant, but Hedia had already decided that the magician would *not* be the right partner. The business behind them merely reinforced that opinion.

The lute was still playing. The turtle's feet plucked the strings.

CHAPTER XIII

The haze cleared, and Corylus could see the ground on which he walked. The sky remained featureless: evenly lighted, but with the same greenish cast as the atmosphere that had formed the curtain between wherever this was and the Waking World. The yew sprite released his hand, but she moved slightly closer to him.

He leaned forward to look past her and said, "Pandareus?"

"Yes, I'm quite all right," said Pandareus. "But I'm interested in the ground cover. Have you noticed it?"

Only to the extent of making sure that we're not stepping off a precipice, Corylus thought, but he didn't expect the scholar to be concerned with the possibilities that Ethiopes—or Germans; there was no end of potential enemies—would momentarily charge over the horizon.

"No, master," Corylus said. "It looks like mushrooms, but I don't think they're dangerous. Unless we eat them, perhaps."

"Fascinating," Pandareus said, his eyes on the ground. "I almost hate to step on them, they're so lovely."

The mushrooms covered the ground for as far as Corylus could see. The only difference when he looked back was that their three sets of footprints—paired trails rather than prints because their toes had dragged through the fragile growth—started in the middle of the plain.

Their colors differed, mostly in the form of soft pastels but with occasional vivid splotches of red. Corylus instinctively avoided those last. Some varieties of fungus clumped together or formed streaks across the multi-colored background, occasionally forming patterns that seemed to have meaning.

Corylus wasn't in a mood to consider beauty. Something was a threat or it wasn't; and at present, nothing seemed to be a threat.

"The footing's all right," he said. The mushrooms gave only the slightest resistance to his heavy sandals, pulping as he touched them but sometimes coating his foot with dust or slime as he tramped on. It was like walking across thin mud on top of ground that was still frozen beneath.

Corylus was irritated that Pandareus was behaving like a scholar, not a fellow soldier on a dangerous reconnaissance. He chuckled at the realization. He would have gripped his teacher's hand in friendship if the dryad hadn't been between them.

"Corylus?" Pandareus said, responding to the laughter.

"You remind me that there are things beyond the present, teacher," Corylus said formally. "And that if life has any meaning, those things are the only ones that are important."

"We could have walked within the forest," said Taxus, glancing toward Pandareus. "You would not have damaged the mushrooms then, nor damaged the ones who live within the mushrooms. But—"

She looked now at Corylus; her fingertips caressed his sword scabbard.

"—they might have damaged you, some of them. And besides, you are a short-lived race and might not have lived long enough to reach the garden."

"I doubt that the color patterns would be as attractive at that scale," said Pandareus. "Although if I was forced to make them my life's work, I'm sure I would find a great deal of interest in them. I'm a philosopher, after all."

Corylus laughed outright. The most amusing aspect of his teacher's statement was that though he said it in a tone of dry humor, it was literally true, every word. And Pandareus knew it was.

"There," Taxus said, gesturing ahead of them with her right hand. "The garden of Vergil."

"The poet Vergil?" said Pandareus, his voice unnaturally flat.

"He may have been a poet," the dryad said. "He was a magician, surely."

She looked at Corylus and added, "I'm not good at human names, you know, Cousin. But he marked this garden as his own, and no one forgets that."

Corylus supposed that he shouldn't have been so surprised. Lucinus had spoken of his uncle Vergil's magic, after all. It remained a shock to learn that the man who wrote, "I sing of arms, and the man who first driven by fate fled the shores of Troy to Italy," used that same skill with words to twist the Waking World to his wish and to build a garden here in the Otherworld.

The garden ahead was extensive, though Corylus couldn't tell how far back it stretched because the terrain was dead flat. The rows of olive trees might reach into the infinite distance from all he could tell.

He glanced at Pandareus and said, "The ground is unnaturally flat." They both grinned at the joke.

"I'll leave you here," said Taxus. "You'll have to make your own way through the wall . . . though I don't think that you'll find that difficult."

She smiled knowingly. "You won't, at least, Cousin."

"I don't see the wall," said Pandareus. "Ah. But I'm not a magician, so I shouldn't expect to see a barrier built by a magician."

"Thank you, mistress," Corylus said, bowing to the dryad.

She stepped back but eyed him with speculation. "May your roots always find water, Cousin," she said. "And perhaps we will meet another time."

Instead of walking away, she vanished. There were now only two tracks across the colored fungus, those of the humans; the dryad might have been a dream. Corylus and his teacher stood at the edge of the garden.

The cultivated ground stood out from the mushroom forest as sharply as a volcanic vent raising its cone in a pasture. There was a row of olive trees on the outside edge and individual olives were scattered deeper within the garden to shield and support grapevines. Corylus could see flowers and vegetables in furrows beyond—

And workers as well, all of whom were automatons. Some hoed and pruned, and two were gathering ripe olives into the handbarrow in which they would transport the olives to an unseen press.

"They don't appear to see us," Pandareus said.

"Be thankful you don't look like a cabbage worm, then," said Corylus. "My concern is the form the barrier takes."

He reached out with his left hand. He thought of using the toe of his sandal, just in case the barrier was a sudden sheet of flame, but he decided that would be cowardly. Nonetheless, it was with his extended little finger that he probed—nothing, but a nothing as solid as polished granite. Only air protected Vergil's garden, but that air was impenetrable.

"Well, that could have been worse," Corylus said, feeling a rush of relief. "Mind you, it doesn't get us any closer to entry."

One, then a full dozen olive nymphs appeared and walked to where Corylus and his teacher stood outside the wall. The nymphs looked mature—certainly not in their first youth—but were radiant with health.

The first to step from her tree stood arms akimbo, smiling at Corylus; her sisters stood just behind and to the sides. They wore gray-green tunics so thin that they were transparent except when they caught the light.

The first dryad said, "We've waited a long time for visitors, but you're worth waiting for, Cousin."

"The other one's cute too," another said with the back of her hand across her mouth to hide her lips' moving. She and the nymphs closest to her giggled.

"Mistress," Corylus said, "we've come to find a way to rescue our comrade, who was stolen away by a magician. Your cousin who guided us here—"

"He means the yew," a dryad whispered hoarsely.

"Such *prickly* things," another said/agreed. "I can't imagine why *anybody* would keep company with a yew."

"—said that there's a passage in your garden by which we can follow her," Corylus said, keeping his eyes on the leading dryad. He had to hope that she at least would stay focused for long enough to help him. "But now that we're here, we can't enter the garden."

He patted the invisible wall with the flat of his hand.

The dryad laughed and took him by the wrist. "Of course you can come in," she said, drawing him firmly toward her as though the barrier did not exist—which it didn't, so long as she was holding him. "We're glad to have *you* visit."

"Here, you come too," said another olive nymph. She reached through the barrier, if it really was a barrier to the sprites. Their feet didn't pass beyond the point that his finger reached in the other direction, though. Before her hand touched Pandareus, three of her fellows also snatched at the scholar's tunic and left arm.

"Mistresses!" Pandareus said as he fell off-balance into the garden. "I'm quite willing to enter. You don't have to pull."

Corylus smiled as he stepped through. He'd expected the dryad to move back and give him room, however. Instead her arms wrapped about him and she kissed him hard.

Corylus lifted the dryad off the ground, returning her kiss, then set her down at arm's length when her hug slackened. He continued to hold her at a distance. "Thank you for your courtesy, Cousin," he said, "but our friend may be in great danger. Can you guide us to the passage which leads us to where the magician has taken her?"

Corylus didn't know where Alphena was, let alone what sort of route would take him to her. This was as bad as wandering in darkness through the Hercynian Forest, hoping to find a soldier who'd gone missing.

Corylus grinned. There might well be worse things lying in ambush here than there were across the Rhine—but at least for the moment the olive nymphs didn't pose a life-threatening danger.

Pandareus was in the garden also, almost hidden by the clot of giggling dryads around him. "Please, mistresses!" he said in as agitated a voice as Corylus had ever heard him use. "I'm not a eunuch, but I don't find this in the least congenial. For one thing, there are far too many people—"

Corylus thought he heard a minute hesitation as the teacher chose the word.

"—around for me to be in the least titillated by your behavior."

"Such an old silly!" said a nymph. She winked at Corylus. "That's half the fun!"

"Please, Cousin," Corylus said, his eyes on the dryad whom he held. Though other nymphs hovered close, he wasn't being mobbed the way his teacher was; perhaps his nymph had authority of some sort over her sisters.

She made a disappointed moue, then backed out of his grip. "Not this time, girls," she said. "I'll take them to the master's bridge. Perhaps we'll be luckier when they return."

"I think they'd be luckier too," said one of the sprites stepping away from Pandareus with a look of disappointment.

Pandareus straightened his tunic. "Thank you, mistresses," he said.

"I truly appreciate your enthusiasm, but I fear that I'm too staid to match it."

The dryad Oliva took Corylus by the hand and walked through the garden. Pandareus quickly fell into step on his other side, and the whole grove of olive nymphs followed in a chattering group.

The automatons tending the plants were made of untarnished silvery metal. Close up their limbs and torsos appeared slender, but they weren't as skeletal as they'd seemed when Corylus first saw them. Highlights from their highly polished surfaces hid their lines.

"Ah!" said Pandareus as they passed an automaton trimming a rosebush with a large pair of secateurs. "That's interesting."

Corylus raised an eyebrow toward his friend. *He* hadn't noticed anything unusual.

"The gardener slowed the rate at which it was circling the bush with its shears," Pandareus explained. "Now that we're past, you'll notice—"

He glanced over his shoulder.

"—that it is pruning more quickly again. If it had continued at the same rate, I would have collided with it. Therefore, it *is* aware of our presence."

"Does that matter?" Oliva said with a puzzled frown.

Pandareus chuckled. "No more than any other information does, mistress," he said. "And while there are other opinions on the matter, my philosophy has always been that *nothing* matters in the greater scheme of things."

Flowers and vegetables didn't appear to have a fixed growing season here. Spring-flowering plants bloomed in the shade of trees that were already dropping nuts that should not have ripened until fall.

They passed a beehive-shaped kiln. Two automatons were shoveling fuel into the furnace underneath it. As Corylus and his companions passed, another pair arrived with a handbarrow of waste to burn: dried clippings and the bitter sludge of skins and pits after the final olive pressing. Faint blue-gray smoke rose through a roof vent.

"What are you firing, Cousin?" Corylus asked. It was a scene that might have occurred on any estate in the Republic, except that it was being performed by slender, silvery laborers.

"Jugs for the wine and oil," Oliva said. Pensively she added, "They'll need to build another shed soon."

"What do you do with the produce, mistress?" Pandareus asked. "That is, what does the owner do with it?"

"The servants store it in sheds," the dryad said. "I don't think anything happens to it after that, but I don't pay much attention."

She frowned and added, "When I was young, I think our master took the oil away, but I didn't pay much attention then, either. Why should I? And anyway, our master hasn't been back in . . ."

She made a circle in the air with her left hand as she concentrated.

"Time," she said to conclude her statement. For an olive nymph, that was a respectable intellectual achievement.

They reached an open-fronted shed with a sloping roof. Inside were four rows of ordinary terra-cotta transport jars, amphorae. Their narrow bases could have been dug into sand to stand upright, but here they were just tilted back against the previous row and ultimately the back wall.

There were about two hundred jars in this shed. Behind it was another shed—and so on, for farther back than Corylus could see. Presumably the file came to an end somewhere, since Oliva had talked of building more.

"There," she said, pointing to a marble structure similar to the base of an altar. Instead of a platform for sacrifice and the altar itself, it framed a corridor sloping down into the earth. Similar tunnels—cryptoporticos—were common features of extensive gardens.

Corylus mounted the six steps of the base and crouched to look down the corridor without entering it. There was light—daylight, apparently—at the end, only twenty feet away.

He rose to see if there was a window or opening of some sort in the ground to explain the light. He couldn't see anything.

"This is our master's bridge of air," the dryad said. "This is the way he entered his garden."

She frowned and said, "I don't think he ever came from outside the way you did."

Pandareus squatted to look down the tunnel himself. "There's a wall niche near the end," he said. "I think there's a statue in it, but—"

He leaned to the side, supporting himself with his hand.

"—I can't be sure without going closer."

Corylus pursed his lips. The walls of this garden proved that air could be solid, but he would have preferred some other material for a bridge he was going to walk on. Though it couldn't really be worse than some of the rain-slicked tree trunks on which he'd crossed gullies on the frontiers.

"What is at the other end of the bridge, Cousin?" he asked, more to give himself time before he made what he already knew was the inevitable decision. They couldn't stay here in the garden, after all.

The dryad ran a hand gently down his spine. "I don't know," she said. "Nothing as nice as you'd find here, I'm sure. You can stay, you know."

The—negative—echo of his thought made Corylus smile. "I'm sorry, Cousin," he said, "but we can't stay and still do our duty. Master?"

Pandareus rose carefully to his feet and nodded.

"Then let's go," Corylus said, striding down the sloping corridor. The stone of the passage was polished gneiss glittering with mica and bits of quartz. Wet, it would have been dangerously slick.

Something moved in the wall niche ahead. A bronze automaton eight feet tall stepped out to confront them. It held a curved sword in each of its four arms.

"I am Talos!" it thundered. Its swords danced before it in an impossibly intricate pattern. The blades never touched one another, but Corylus doubted a finger's breadth of the area before Talos would have escaped their keen edges.

"I will kill any who attempt to pass me," the automaton said, "saving Vergil, my master!"

Talos stepped forward.

Corylus had drawn his long sword, but he had seen too many battles to doubt how he would fare against the automaton. "Run, teacher!" he shouted. As soon as Pandareus was clear, Corylus sprang out of the tunnel himself.

He waited to see if Talos would follow; the ramp's slope gave the man at the top some advantage, though a slight one. Instead the automaton returned to the niche in which it had waited. Its bronze feet clashed against the stone, and its throat gurgled with laughter.

ALPHENA KNEW THAT SHE WAS DREAMING, but she couldn't wake up. She had no body; at least she wasn't aware of her body as she watched a giraffe drink from a clear, shallow stream while another kept watch. The one drinking had spread her forelegs to twice the width of their hind legs, reducing the distance that her neck had to slant down to the water.

Across the creek, the Daughters of the Mind were dancing. Whose mind? All Alphena knew about them came from the Child, and she wasn't sure she should believe anything he said. Though there didn't seem to be any reason he should lie about the three figures who circled the glowing Egg.

If the dreaming Alphena had had a face, her lips would have smiled. *Perhaps the Mind is a rhetorical device like the ones that my brother and Master Pandareus get so worked up about.*

The female giraffe raised her neck; the male that had been watching kicked his forelegs sideways and bent to drink in turn. Suddenly both the giraffes straightened and turned, bolting back through the forest. They didn't call out, but their hooves slammed the sod like mauls, spurning back huge clods.

A cloud of scarlet butterflies rose into the air. Alphena hadn't noticed them until now.

A lens of air blurred. Through it walked Paris, the Etruscan priest she had followed into the tomb. He was chanting.

Paris stepped to the side, making room for the first of what became a long line of horse-headed giants like the one Alphena had killed. They spread to either side as they advanced toward the Daughters, their weapons ready.

The young women didn't take obvious notice of their danger, but the pace of their dance quickened. The Egg brightened and dimmed as it spun, never remaining a single color long enough for Alphena to identify it.

Alphena had believed that the Egg was within the circle of the dancers. From her present vantage point, she was no longer sure. Though the Daughters were clearly dancing around the Egg, it appeared to be infinitely far away.

It faded and they faded, vanishing from the plain. Grass and the dust from which it grew were disturbed where the Daughters had danced.

The Horseheads stopped where they were and trudged back to the portal from which they had emerged, lowering their weapons. One by one they passed through the portal. Paris followed them, and the portal closed.

Alphena's dream changed to a steep slope above a vividly blue lake. Lobelias and cabbage-topped trees with shaggy trunks surrounded her.

The Daughters were dancing across the lake on a bare, fairly level patch on a slope similar to that of the dream Alphena's vantage point.

She wondered if this was a volcanic vent, because the only similar terrain of her waking existence had been a cleft in the side of Vesuvius. That had been raw and steaming, the very rocks flayed by sulfur fumes oozing from cracks in the sides. The vegetation here was strange but thick, so any eruptions must have been in the far past.

As the dancers circled, there was sudden commotion in the nearby forest. A trio of giant apes with shaggy fur shouldered their way through the vegetation, occasionally glancing over their shoulders and hooting.

Moments later, a portal opened in the air not far from the Daughters. Paris emerged, then the Horseheads just as before. They tramped down the slope, moving as deliberately as the surface permitted.

Alphena was reminded of dogs hunting in the arena. Instead of springing violently toward their prey like cats, canines paced around the enclosure in a seemingly leisurely fashion. Eventually even the swiftest antelopes would begin to stumble and the pack would close in.

The Daughters merged into another place, as before; again the hunters returned to the portal from which they had emerged. Alphena knew she was dreaming, but it seemed to her that the Horseheads had come nearer to their prey this time.

The hunt continued, scene after scene. The landscapes were all different and all unfamiliar, but occasionally Alphena recognized an animal from the arena.

Once she saw a herd of elephants. They were giants like the one from deep in Libya that Veturius had brought back along with the lizard-monkeys, the Singiri. These were placid in the presence of the Daughters, but when the portal formed, the herd fled through a belt of bamboo, splintering the tough grass that Alphena would have expected to stop even such great beasts.

How long . . . ? Alphena wondered, weighed down even in her dream by the number of images.

And then she was watching from the village where the Horsehead had attacked her, but while it was still a bustling community. The Daughters danced in the plaza in front of the ugly black idol. Villagers looked on with wonder and delight, but they were no more frightened by what they saw than the wild animals of previous scenes had been.

From the air, between the circle of dancers and the outer circle of spectators, appeared a pair of Singiri. Instead of being naked except for chain collars like those in the animal compound, these wore vests from which tools and weapons hung. Each held a small, round shield of dark bronze in his left hand and brandished a curved sword of the same material in his left.

The spectators' skins were much darker than those of the Daughters, and they were taller as well, as tall as Germans. The Singiri shouted to them in a language that the Nubians understood but Alphena did not. The village males ran into the huts for weapons; the women snatched up children, gathering their offspring around them.

The village was surrounded by a wall of poles woven into a fabric that would have stopped a herd of bulls, but the gates suddenly burst open. Horseheads burst in, a larger number than Alphena had seen before. They were six wide in the gateway and more came through for as long as the vision lasted.

The only reason there was a battle at all was the stand the two Singiri made, slowing the onslaught for long enough that many of the villagers could arm themselves. Even so it was a massacre for all but the first minute or so.

The Daughters and their Egg melted away, but it had been very close for them this time. *If the Singiri hadn't been present* . . .

Instead of leaving as soon as the dancers escaped, the Horseheads took time to kill every animal in the village. A few women threw their offspring over the walls, which had become a trap rather than protection.

Almost at once the little corpses were flung back inside, impaled on stone spears. The village had been completely surrounded before the attack began.

When everything was dead, the attackers shambled back toward the Etruscan priest and the portal. The last thing they did was place the crudely hacked-off heads of the Singiri in front of the idol where the skulls of men and crocodiles already rested.

"Well, have you had a long enough nap?" rasped an unpleasant voice in Alphena's dream. She opened her eyes.

She was staring at the wooden idol that she had used as a shield. "Who spoke?" she said, sitting up. Her head throbbed.

The idol licked fresh blood from its face with its iron tongue. It grinned at her.

"I did, Alphena," it said. "Who did you expect?"

VARUS LOOKED OVER THE BOW of the boat, then off to either side. Looking back would mean seeing Lucinus, whose face was as dead as the Egyptian mummy that Saxa had once bought for his collection.

That specimen had quickly begun to rot in the humid atmosphere of Carce. Saxa's fastidiousness had overcome his collecting instinct and the mummy had gone onto a pyre like many less august personages, but Varus had first unwrapped it out of scholarly curiosity.

The mummy had been interesting to Varus' intellectual side, but it was disgusting to him as a human being. Thinking of that centuries-old corpse in parallel with the magician on whom his life depended verged on being frightening.

Varus grinned. He couldn't avoid weaknesses; but so long as he could smile at them, they were under control.

On previous days, the boat had regularly passed close to islands that provided subjects about which Varus could speculate. This blank, blue sea had nothing for his mind to fasten on, though there were specks in the heavens that might have been interesting if they had been close enough for him to see details.

Given that the specks were extremely high, well above the occasional cloud, they must each be bigger than the boat. Varus decided he would rather be bored than learn just how interesting a flying creature of that size could be on really close acquaintance.

He looked into the sea again. The water was so clear that sometimes Varus thought he saw ripples on the sea bottom. Once, far to the left side, he saw a cloud of fine sand settling back over a stretch at least a furlong across, though he couldn't tell what had caused the disturbance.

The voyage should have been a perfect time to sleep, and it wasn't the risk of danger that kept Varus awake. On consideration, he decided that he would rather be asleep as he slipped down the throat of a gigantic seagull than awake to savor every excruciating moment of that final experience. The thought made him smile again.

But Varus wasn't being given a choice. He felt the same sort of nagging discomfort that he once had after he cracked a tooth. He was somehow involved with the effort of driving the boat, and it kept him from sleeping.

He remembered the gaunt, ravenous wraiths that he had seen taking up the oars in Sulla's garden. *If those creatures are feeding on me . . .*

His smile returned, but with a wry quirk. If the wraiths were feeding on him—and certainly *something* was draining his energy—then he could only hope that he was fit enough to permit them to row until the boat reached Zabulon's Isle. Desiccating here at sea because the crew had starved was not the end that Varus hoped for himself.

Though I'll try to be philosophical about it if that should eventuate.

Something moved in the sea, a shadow paralleling the boat's course but a furlong to the left. Varus squinted, but he was unable to see any details in the long blur.

Abruptly a lizard-like head as long as a man's body lifted and turned toward the boat. The eyes faced forward, the gaze of a hunter which focuses on its victim not prey which searches for threats in all directions; powerful teeth were set in the long jaws.

The creature dived. Varus caught a glimpse of paddles like a turtle's and a heavy, turtle-like body as well. It had no shell, just tiger stripes on a dark gray base, and those teeth were meant for tougher victims than the jellyfish that sea turtles dismembered with their beaks.

The boat's hull had been pegged together from billets of soft sycamore wood. The creature's teeth could crunch through it easily.

Varus caught movement forward in the corner of his eye; he glanced over the bow. There was an island dead ahead, the first that he had seen since they set off that morning. It was barely midday, rather than sunset when they normally landed, but the boat would run aground if they didn't change course abruptly.

The sea lizard edged closer, effortlessly pacing the boat. It was watching them intently. Though Varus couldn't pretend to read the mind of the silent creature, he was willing to bet that it was about to attack.

Vegetation covered the island to the shoreline. From the present distance—about a quarter mile—it looked like giant grass. Either the tide didn't rise here or the plants were resistant to salt water.

"Lucinus!" Varus called. It was the first time he had tried to rouse his companion while on shipboard. Viewing the magician's corpse-like appearance was less troubling than the imminent threat of being devoured.

Lucinus ignored the summons. He didn't seem to be aware of the world around him, though his eyes were open and his lips were miming the words of his chant.

"Lucinus, the lizard is going to—"

The lizard drove toward them in churning foam. Its forepaddles moved in paired figure eights, and its deep breastbone raised a spray of mist. The hind paddles acted as steering oars, guiding the creature toward an intersection with the boat.

"—catch us before we reach the shore!"

Varus thought of grabbing an oar to thrust at the lizard, but its teeth would splinter the pine as quickly as they would human bones. Better to keep his dignity.

Reaching the shore wouldn't mean safety. Though the lizard was well adapted to swimming, its powerful paddles would allow it to lurch some distance on land. It could hop along faster than Varus could run in his present condition, certainly.

Lucinus continued to mouth inaudible words. He didn't turn his head toward the lizard.

Varus crossed his arms, then regretted his Stoic pose as the boat rocked in the swell of the lizard's approach. *Toppling into the water on my back would not be a heroic way to meet death.*

The lizard's jaws opened, expelling a miasma of decayed fish. Its bite would shear the hull to well beyond midpoint. Varus braced himself mentally.

The lizard crackled bright blue. The air bit the inside of Varus' nostrils and rasped the back of his throat. The lizard blackened and shrank; bits flaked away like ashes blowing from a funeral pyre.

The boat ran up on the shore, throwing Varus sideways into the bow. He grabbed a thwart with one hand and managed not to knock himself silly on the gunwale, but that was more luck than skill. He'd been so focused on doom rushing toward him that he'd forgotten about the island.

Varus rose and helped Lucinus to sit up. The magician looked at him with dead eyes and said, "We've arrived. This is Zabulon's Isle."

Then he collapsed again into Varus' arms.

· · ·

THE BRIDGE LOOKED EXTREMELY FLIMSY. In fact, Hedia didn't realize it was a bridge until the demon stepped onto it.

Canes four inches in diameter and thirty feet long were fitted into one another end to end to walk on. Pairs of similar canes were tied in X patterns, with the lower ends thrust into the bed of the river. The floor pole was supported in the upper angle of the frames.

There were dozens of frames to cross the furlongs of flowing water. The downstream leg of each was splayed out much more than the upstream legs. Thinner canes tied to the tops of the upstream members formed a handrail.

The demon stepped onto the central cane and began to cross, ignoring the railing. Though her feet appeared to touch the pole, Hedia wasn't sure that the glowing body was truly material.

"This isn't safe!" Hedia said. What she really meant was, *I can't walk on that!*

Melino turned his head. "Of course it's safe," he said in a tone of irritation. "The bamboo would support the weight of an ox."

If you could get an ox to walk on it, perhaps, Hedia thought. But she had control of her emotions again, or her tongue, at any rate. She nodded curtly. She allowed the magician to get ten feet ahead of her, then followed him.

I wonder if I could walk it without the railing, she thought. The only reason to attempt that would be to prove that she was just as capable as the demon leading them. The demon presumably couldn't drown, so it wouldn't be a fair test.

Hedia smiled wryly. She had just tricked herself into a justification of sensible behavior . . . and not for the first time. Nevertheless, if she hadn't been willing to push boundaries, she would have had a much more boring life.

The narrowness of the path wasn't as much of a problem as she had expected. The cane had been worn—and by what feet?—rough if not flat, and Hedia had been trained to walk with grace from the time she took her first steps.

She *hadn't* been trained to walk on a length of bamboo that gave under her foot and bounced upward as her foot rose after each step; there were continuing shudders from Melino's steps as well. *This is a task for a ropedancer!*

Hedia grinned as the thought brought up memories. Ropedancers, like mimes and flute girls, often performed at dinner parties. They were all generally expected to provide additional services later in the evening.

At least I can handle that *as well as any professional.* Touching the flimsy railing with the tips of her fingers, Hedia walked forward at a stately, regal pace.

The demon didn't weigh down the springy cane, but her feet seemed to move with it as though they had real substance. Varus and his teacher would doubtless have made learned observations about what was happening, and perhaps Publius Corylus would as well.

Hedia wished Corylus were here, though his strength and sword wouldn't be of any obvious benefit in the present situation. The young man was a comforting presence; someone who she could believe could handle anything fate threw at him . . . even if she couldn't imagine how, and probably he couldn't imagine how, either.

Hedia glanced down into the water, a sign to herself that she was feeling more relaxed. She expected it to be muddy brown; instead, the stream was faintly blue and as clear as good glass.

A crowd of little men and women—two or three feet tall, had they been standing—with fish tails instead of legs were peering up from the water. When they saw Hedia look at them, they pointed, giggled, and began to chatter among themselves. She didn't recognize their language.

Nor did she care to be mocked by dwarfs with tails. She considered spitting, then reconsidered. Facing forward, she walked on—she smiled coldly—at a stately, even regal pace.

She and Melino had fallen into a rhythm, their steps syncopating each another. It wasn't comfortable, but at least it didn't change and throw her off-balance.

The river's far bank sloped steeply upward for twenty feet, then became sheer bluffs that shot up hundreds of feet—close to a furlong, Hedia thought, though she had never been skilled at estimating distance. "Melino?" she said. "Are we to climb the cliff?"

The alternative was to walk left or right along the side of the river. The slope rose a foot for every foot inward from the river and was sprinkled with brush growing among the coarse scree that had flaked from the bluffs. Hedia wasn't sure that was the less appealing alternative, particularly since the brush appeared to be thorny.

"The *Book* is leading us," said the magician. He glanced over his shoulder and added, "If you don't want to go on, then stay. Otherwise, don't disturb me. I have the *Book* now."

"I see," Hedia said without inflection. Her lips wore a faint smile.

In her experience, men thought in the short term. They generally had the physical power, so perhaps they could afford to. Women had to take a longer view or they would find themselves discarded as soon as they lost their youthful bloom.

Hedia had a very good memory. More than one man had found that Hedia wasn't disposable after all, and then had repented something he had said while momentarily sated.

Bees rose from the bamboo. One circled close to Hedia's face. She felt a flash of anger at the servants whose job it was to keep insects away from her. She didn't try to control the absurd reaction, because it prevented her from thinking too much about the bee, which she now saw had a woman's head.

"You are discourteous!" Hedia snapped to the insect. It moved off to a less pressing distance, though it and its fellows continued to watch her.

Hedia hadn't swatted at the bee because inexperience would have made her awkward. Irritation was better than looking silly.

There were holes in the canes, though they looked like dark blemishes except when a bee was crawling in or out of one. The insects had human—female—heads. She wondered whether they stung, though they seemed inoffensive except in the social sense.

She was used to boorish behavior. There was no lack of humans who wanted to be closer to her than she wished to be to them.

Bees followed Hedia briefly, then curved back to where they had first appeared. More bees flew up from the framework, however, and followed her for another ten feet or so before returning to their holes.

After the first, none came too close to her. Had they understood her objection? She wondered if what she had taken for buzzing was really the sound of high-pitched voices.

Twenty feet ahead, the demon stepped onto solid ground at the far end of the bridge and began to climb the slope. Her glowing body pushed aside branches, but the thorns didn't seem to affect her. Hedia grimaced, well aware that her skin would not prove as durable.

She briefly considered wearing leather breeches like a Celtic cow-

herd. *If I went about it the right way, I could turn it into a fashion statement. . . .*

On the other hand, breeches would be uncomfortable any time Hedia
wasn't traipsing through brush, which she hoped would be the whole
remainder of her life. And breeches would be ugly even when they were
useful. Tunics were a better choice.

The demon was walking straight up the slope. Melino followed her
as best he could. The *Book* in his left hand was a serious handicap, but
he was often able to use the staff in his right for support.

As Hedia had expected, thorns gouged her bare legs and gripped her
tunic. She had chosen a sturdy fabric when she dressed to visit Melino
this morning, and it didn't tear badly when she tugged it loose. As for
her skin, well, it couldn't be helped.

She wondered if it still was morning, then wondered if the concept
of time had any meaning in this Otherworld. But those were questions
for Pandareus and his learned pupils.

*What are Varus and Corylus doing now? And Alphena, who needs a
mother's guidance more now than ever before . . . and I am not there?*

Hedia had been concentrating so completely on her footing that it
wasn't until Melino cried, "What?" that she looked up. At the top of the
slope, their demon guide was vanishing into the vertical basalt cliff. The
heel of her trailing foot was a rosy glow as it disappeared into the stone.

Melino stepped forward and rapped the basalt with the end of his
staff. He must have been expecting the cliff to be an illusion, because
his smug expression blanched. He reached out with the tip of his index
finger to no better effect: the black stone was just as solid as it appeared
to be.

Hedia hid her amusement, but she was pleased to see the magician
discomfited. In the longer term, it wasn't a good result for her; but in the
longer term, she would die of old age unless something took her away
more quickly. Something quicker looked probable at the moment.

Hedia stopped beside Melino, then moved a bit to the side for better
footing. Rock had scaled from the cliff in irregular chunks. Even the
larger slabs were apt to shift when she put her weight on them, so she
had learned to be careful.

She didn't comment on the situation, since she had nothing useful
to say. She hadn't forgotten the magician's dismissive response to her

recent question, but she suspected that her faintly supercilious smile was as cutting as any verbal insult she might offer.

Melino looked at her; for want of any other companion, Hedia suspected. "I'll have to use the *Book*," he said miserably.

She raised an eyebrow slightly higher. "Well?" she said. "That was why you got it, wasn't it?"

Hedia smiled. "As I recall . . . ," she added, stretching. "I carried out my part of the business."

"Nodens bugger you!" the magician said in sudden anger. "Do you think that magic of this level comes without cost?"

Hedia let her smile broaden. "I've never met Nodens," she said. She was speaking for effect; in fact, she *had* heard her son and Pandareus discussing that British god, along with his Thracian, Carian, and Galician equivalents. "If you'll introduce us, though, we'll see how things develop."

Melino started to raise his staff with an expression of fury. Hedia said, "Don't," and gripped the hilt of the dagger hidden in her sash.

If he lifts that thing higher, I'll grab his arm with my left hand and keep stabbing until he goes down. . . .

The magician swallowed and turned to face the cliff again. He used the short end of his staff—the portion above his grip—to flick the *Book* open. Hedia relaxed, but she didn't remove her hand from the dagger for the moment.

The *Book* boomed a syllable. It wasn't a word in any language Hedia knew, and her mind wasn't even sure in retrospect that it had been a sound that her ears heard.

The world shivered. For a moment there were a hundred separate Hedias, occupied in a hundred different fashions. Then the Cosmos was whole again, and Hedia stood in front of an entrance whose framing pilasters and pediment were carved from the living rock.

Melino staggered. Hedia supported him and didn't even smile with satisfaction. She was so relieved at the renewed chance of escape that she was able to forgive the magician's contemptuous dismissal as they crossed the bridge.

The demon waited ten feet ahead of them in a square-sided tunnel. Her glowing figure was the only light. She looked over her shoulder at the humans, smiled, and walked on as she had ever since they entered the Otherworld.

The demon's smile reminded Hedia of the one she had given Melino when he realized that the basalt would resist anything but the *Book*'s powerful spell. She wondered if the magician had the same knack for irritating other men as he did the females who had come in contact with him.

Although the demon walked at her previous measured pace, she was clearly drawing ahead. The tunnel's floor felt slippery despite seeming solid enough.

Hedia gestured. "There's something wrong with the ground," she said.

She glanced to the side. The coarse black stone was barely visible in this light, so she touched the wall with her fingers. "Melino," she said. "We're moving backward."

"This isn't right!" the magician said—or moaned, better. It was a foolish statement unless you thought that whoever was punishing you might be moved by pity. In the present case, Hedia wouldn't have wasted her breath.

Melino opened the *Book* as before. This time the word no mortal lips shouted made colors reverse themselves: the demon became a deep indigo and the tunnel walls were a white as opaque and featureless as the blackness of an instant before.

The light returned to normal, what Hedia supposed was normal when one was being guided through a tunnel by a glowing demon. The temperature dropped abruptly, making the floor feel cold even through the soles of Hedia's heavy sandals.

Melino was wobbling again. Hedia caught him.

"Come," she said, putting her right arm around his torso. She tried to lift his left arm over her shoulders, but the magician clamped the *Book* to his chest. She wasn't sure he was aware of her presence.

"*Come*," she repeated more urgently. The demon wasn't waiting as she had when they were blocked by the sheer cliff. The glow of her flesh would be visible for a very long distance, but the details of her figure were already blurring.

Hedia began walking with quick, short steps, half-pushing and half-dragging Melino. She wouldn't be able to carry him, at least not for long, but he fell into step after a period of stumbling and grunts.

Hedia lengthened her strides, forcing the magician to keep up with her. They had almost caught up with their guide by the time Melino straightened and shrugged out of her grip.

"I'm all right," he said. He sounded like a man on his deathbed. "I can walk by myself."

Until the next time, Hedia thought, but she shifted away from him. Only now did the demon glance over her shoulder and smile—but this time at Hedia, not at the magician.

Hedia smelled fresh blood, an odor familiar from the arena but unexpected here. The floor had been bare stone when they entered the tunnel. Now it showed cracks crawling across a rime of hoarfrost. They oozed a thick fluid whose red color might simply have been the demon's glow, the only light in the tunnel.

Judging from the smell, the ooze was surely blood. Still tacky, it clung to the soles of Hedia's sandals. She smiled coldly.

She was probably spattering her lower legs with every step, but she wouldn't be fit for polite company until she had bathed and changed her whole wardrobe anyway. It was unlikely that she would be meeting polite company until she returned to the Waking World, so her appearance was well down the list of the problems that concerned her.

She wondered how far they had to walk in this tunnel, but she didn't ask. She would walk until she got to where they were going—or she dropped. She wouldn't be ready to drop for a very long time yet.

Hedia laughed. To her surprise, the demon looked back at her and chuckled pleasantly.

Melino glanced from one of them to the other without speaking. Hedia and the demon laughed again.

They walked on.

CHAPTER XIV

Alphena sat up carefully. Her head throbbed, but mostly that was bearable. Once a flash blinded her, and she felt as though her skull were being ground between millstones. It was just a flash, though, gone as suddenly as it came.

She turned her head and threw up, leaving a splash of bile on the baked earth. Immediately she felt better. Enough better—she smiled at herself—that she began to wonder when she next would get a chance to eat.

On the ground before her lay the idol she had used as a shield. She rotated it so that she could look at its remarkably ugly face, but she didn't pick it up.

"You may call me God, mortal woman," the idol said. Its iron tongue licked, but it had already cleaned as much of its face as it could reach. "So long as you provide me with regular sacrifices, I will continue to spare you."

Anger, then amusement, danced through Alphena's mind. Between them, the emotions brought her back to full alertness.

"I won't call you God," she said. She curled her feet under her, but she wasn't quite ready to rise yet. "And since I'm not staying around here—"

Though she didn't have any better place to go that she knew of.

"—you'll have to find someone else to sacrifice to you."

Alphena leaned forward, preparing to get up. The horse-headed giant was already bloating. Dead on the ground, it looked even bigger than it had while she was fighting it.

"Wait!" said the idol. Alphena thought she heard desperation in the raspy voice. "You need me, Alphena. You won't be able to do anything without my help."

That was pretty much Alphena's opinion too, but she wasn't sure that a talking stick would help much. She said, "What sort of help?"

"Will you call me 'First'?" the idol said. "Or perhaps 'Chief'? It means the same thing in Ashangi."

Alphena made a production of considering. "I'll call you First," she said. "If I have any reason to speak with you in the future."

Having made the threat clear, she added in a milder tone, "What's this horse-headed thing?"

Instead of nodding, she gestured with the sword.

"And why did it try to kill me?"

She needed to wash the blood off her sword; mere wiping wouldn't be enough. And she needed to bathe, because she was as red and sticky as the weapon.

"A magician set the Ethiopes, your Horseheads, to hunting the Daughters of the Mind," First said. He sounded relieved and cheerful. "He left one of the Ethiopes behind to kill any of the Daughters' allies who were following them. And you fed the Ethiope"—he was crowing in triumph—"to me, gracious worshiper!"

Alphena wasn't a grammarian, but she couldn't have grown up around her brother and not found herself noticing the details of words. In sudden realization she said, "First, you said 'worshiper,' singular. If I go off and leave you, how long will it be before your Ashangi come back here?"

"Surely you would not leave me, Alphena?" the idol said. She heard fear, not assurance, in his tone. "I will help you."

"How long?" Alphena demanded in a louder voice.

"They will never come back," First muttered. "This place will be accursed ground until all things have rotted and the jungle reclaims it. All things, even me."

Alphena lifted the idol in her left hand. It felt heavier than it had when she jerked it loose from its base. She rose to her feet slowly, thrusting the sword and idol out in front of her to balance the weight of her torso until her legs straightened. Her head throbbed with the effort, but not unbearably.

"First," she said. "If you don't do what I tell you to, I'll leave you here. Do you understand?"

Standing, Alphena felt the presence of the Daughters dancing about her. They weren't visible, but in the corners of her eyes she sensed them moving.

"Lady Alphena," the idol said in a hurt tone. "I am a just god. I would always help my worshiper to the best of my ability."

"All right," said Alphena. "Then take me back home. To Carce or to Puteoli, I don't care which. I want to go home!"

The catch in her voice took her by surprise. She had gone through so much today! She just wanted to be in her own room with her mother. She *so* wanted to see Hedia again.

"But Alphena . . . ?" First said. "Where is Carce? Where is Puteoli? Show me where these places are and of course I will take you there."

Alphena sniffled with despair. She started to hurl the idol away, but the control she was learning from Hedia stopped her. If she was ever to get out of this jungle, she needed the idol's help even more than she needed the sword in her other hand. There was no chance that she was going to throw away the sword.

She hid her face in the crook of her right arm and cried. Nobody was here to see her. If somebody did appear, Alphena would be so pleased that the embarrassment wouldn't begin to bother her.

She lowered her arm and faced the idol. She swallowed. "I don't know where Carce is," she said. "I don't know where *I* am now."

She hoped the idol might speak. He didn't volunteer anything, and she was pretty sure that he wouldn't have an answer to a direct question, either. She didn't ask, because she wasn't ready to handle more disappointment.

Alphena itched and ached all over. Flies were buzzing around her and the dead Ethiope. Both the fresh corpse and the blood caking on her own body were beginning to reek in the hot sun.

"First," she said. "Do you know where water is? I need to get this . . . I need to clean all this blood off me."

"I'll guide you, Alphena," First said brightly. He really *was* afraid of being left to rot. "The village is a little back from the river for safety's sake—the Ashangi travel by canoe. I'll take you right there."

The idol twisted in her hand as though someone were gripping the other end. She remembered the impression she'd had of the wood shifting by itself into the path of the Ethiope's thrust—and the way the flint spearpoint had shattered on contact. There'd been too much going on at the time for her to have paid attention to the details of her survival. Now, though . . .

She began to realize that First had been a friend to her even before she became aware of him as a person. Well, as an individual.

The idol pointed to the gate through which the Ethiopes had burst. "Ah, Alphena?" he said. "You'll want to keep your sword with you while you bathe. There are crocodiles in the river."

"I'll keep the sword with me," Alphena said as she walked out of the ruined village. She wished Hedia could have heard her. Not long ago she would have screamed, "Do you think I'm an idiot? Of course I'm not going to leave my sword behind!"

She still felt that way, but—First had saved her life, which was one thing; and First was her best hope of surviving and possibly even getting out of this muggy pit, which was an even more important thing. Hedia didn't seem to temper her—low—opinions of other people, but she had taught Alphena that she didn't always have to say what she thought.

New growth was already re-covering the trail. Mostly it was leaves flopping over the track from both sides, but there were also vines dangling down from branches and a blotch of striking purple mushrooms— which Alphena decided to hop over instead of striding through as she started to do. Mostly she brushed by, but once she hacked off a thorny stem leaning across the path.

She thought of what the idol had said about rot and burial in the returning jungle. The same would happen to her bones unless she managed to get *out* of this place.

She came out onto the river unexpectedly, though when she saw brown water through the gap in the undergrowth she realized that she had been hearing its deep whisper even back at the village. The bank was a slope of red mud, partially covered by vegetation. Mostly the foliage trailed from plants rooted above in the jungle floor.

The opposite bank was only forty feet away, a solid mass of greens and of blacks scarcely darker than the greens. Alphena tried to walk down—and slid instead, because the clay was so slick. She splashed into the dark water and felt immediate relief.

"You don't have to keep holding me, worshiper," the idol said tartly. "Dig my base into the bank so that you have a hand free."

Suddenly concerned, he added, "But you mustn't leave me. You won't leave me, will you, Alphena?"

"Of course I won't," she said, putting as much assurance as she could into the words. The idol's base tapered almost to a point, and the wood was as hard as metal.

Alphena looked at the river. There could be a pack of crocodiles hiding under water that was as dark as the forest floor. "First, will you warn me if something is creeping up on me?"

"Of course, Alphena," the idol said. His voice no longer grated on her; she must be getting used to it. "And I will watch when you sleep. I am generous to my worshipers, you see."

Alphena ducked her head under the surface. The river was surprisingly cool. Even its grittiness felt good as she rubbed her bare palm over her legs and torso to scrub off the blood.

Sleep—real sleep, not throbbing unconsciousness—sounded blissful. Though—

"First, is there anything I can eat around here?" she asked.

"The Ethiope brought seed cakes to sustain him while he watched," the idol said. "The food the Ashangi had gathered will have rotted by now. But—"

With a suddenly hopeful lilt.

"—can you catch fish?"

"No," said Alphena. "And I wouldn't know what to do with a fish if I did catch it. But I'll try the seed cake when we go back."

One thing at a time. One step after another to the end, whatever the end was.

But after this bath, Alphena was feeling more optimistic about at least the next few steps.

BREATHING HARD AT THE TOP of the ramp, Corylus faced the sunken entrance to what he hoped was a bridge to the Waking World. He could no longer see the bronze man, but he heard his laughter and the clash of his feet on the stone floor. Though Talos had not followed Corylus and his teacher, neither had he returned to the niche where he had been waiting motionless when they arrived.

"He never behaved that way before," Oliva said, her brow furrowed with surprise. "I wonder if there's something wrong with him?"

"You knew Talos was guarding the passage?" Corylus said, keeping a rein on his temper. His blood was up for a fight, and running back a few paces hadn't been enough to calm its surges.

"Yes, he's always been there," the dryad said, still trying to work out what had happened. "But he didn't move ever. The other automatons tend the garden."

"Thank you, mistress," Pandareus said calmly. "You've given a very clear account of the situation from your viewpoint."

Corylus laughed and sheathed his sword. Pandareus had provided a neutral summary of what had just happened. It was the sort of thing that the master's students should have been able to do instinctively themselves.

Corylus looked at his teacher. "My body reacted without waiting for thought," he said, "which is good, since it saved our lives. My body was also talking without thought, which is the sort of thing I should have known to avoid even before I became your student, master."

He bowed to Pandareus, then to Oliva. "I apologize to you both."

The dryad's brow wrinkled still further. "Why . . . ?" she said. Brightening like a sunrise, she said, "Oh! You mean you do want to have fun with me after all? Oh, that's wonderful!"

"I regret that I have forbidden my student to have fun in the fashion you imply . . . ," Pandareus said in magisterial tones. "Until he has completed the duties which the present crisis have placed on him. Perhaps afterward."

He cleared his throat. Oliva blinked, again out of her intellectual depth. From the way she was beginning to pout, she had at least guessed that she and Corylus were *not* about to make love.

Corylus was trying to keep a straight face. He bowed to Pandareus and said, "Of course, master. My duty comes first."

The problem was that he didn't see any way of getting past Talos. Unless there were potential allies here in the garden, Corylus and Pandareus would have to find another way of following Alphena.

"Mistress Oliva?" the old scholar said. "How do your automatons light the fire in their kiln?"

"*I* don't know," the dryad said, wrinkling her nose. "I don't *like* fire!"

"Of course," Pandareus said, nodding. "I should have realized that.

Well, I trust they will allow me to snatch a brand from the kiln itself. That's probably a better choice anyway."

Corylus stood quietly. He didn't have a plan of proceeding, but his teacher clearly did and would deliver instructions in good time.

Pandareus turned to him and said, "Master Corylus, can you bring a jar of oil here? I want to pour the oil into the passage and ignite it."

"All right," Corylus said. "I'll bring a jar."

"And while you're doing that . . . ," said Pandareus as he set off in the direction of the kiln. "I'll look for a torch."

Pandareus gathered an entourage of dryads as soon as he stepped away from Corylus, but they didn't seem to be pestering him any more than a flock of chickens might have. Corylus grinned at Oliva and said, "Would you lead me to the sheds where the oil is stored, Cousin?"

He didn't need her help finding the sheds that they'd passed only minutes before, but it was a friendly thing to say. Besides, he might well have other questions.

"Oh, I can do that!" the dryad said, beaming out of her pout. "Come along!"

She took his hand in hers and skipped off with him. Her grip was firm and hinted of more strength than her appearance suggested.

"What are you going to do with the oil?" Oliva said. "Are you hungry?"

Yes, now that you mention it, Corylus thought. Aloud he said, "I believe that Master Pandareus intends to try to burn Talos so that we can reach Vergil's bridge. Talos won't let us pass, as you saw."

"Here's the shed," Oliva said. She pursed her lips, thinking.

Corylus bent, gripped the end jar in the outer row, and straightened his knees as he lifted it to his shoulder. It was heavy, but it wasn't a real test of his strength.

The automatons nearby didn't appear to notice what Corylus was doing. They probably did, as Pandareus had shown, but it wasn't a problem so long as they didn't interfere.

"How will fire make Talos let you go past?" Oliva asked when she had finally formed the question. "He's not made of wood, you know?"

Corylus was taking shorter steps than he usually would have because he wanted to keep the jar centered over his feet. There were plenty of

others if he happened to drop this one, but he—he smiled at himself—
preferred to do things right the first time.

"I know that," he agreed. He also knew that olive oil didn't burn hot
enough to melt bronze, at least without a bellows. "Master Pandareus is
a very wise man. He has a plan."

Pandareus *was* very wise, but he didn't necessarily have enough
practical experience with metals to know how much heat was required to melt bronze. Corylus didn't have a better idea. Rather than
carp at the scholar's plan untried, he was going to do his best to exe-
cute it.

Pandareus was waiting with a branch sawn to the length of his arm,
burning at one end. It was from a fruit tree, not an olive tree; Oliva
eyed it with no more than a dryad's normal distaste for fire.

"Ho! Humans!" Talos called from the base of the ramp. His four
swords danced in an inhumanly graceful pattern before him, then stilled.
"Come down and let me cut you to collops! You cannot pass me!"

"If you'll unstopper the jar," Pandareus said, "the oil will run down
the ramp. Then we can light it."

"If you want me to . . . ," Corylus said. "I can pitch the jar to the bottom of the ramp. You can throw the brand into the oil when the jar
breaks."

The base of the ramp was only ten feet away and downhill besides.
Corylus wondered what would happen if the jar's weight hit the bronze
man—and also whether more than whim prevented Talos from coming
up the ramp to close with the humans.

"Yes, that would be ideal," Pandareus said. He spoke in the same approving tone that he would have used in class for a pupil's well-turned
phrase.

Talos was laughing again. Corylus leaned back, then pitched the jar
outward with both hands. He didn't run toward the opening to add to
the inertia of the throw, because a stumble would take him down the
ramp into the swords. The only question then would be whether the
bronze man killed him quickly or by slices.

Talos met the jar in the air with the point of one outthrust sword. If
the blade really was bronze, it was of a harder alloy than Corylus had
ever seen. The terra-cotta shattered in a spray of oil, but the sword neither bent nor broke. Talos didn't even rock backward.

"Do you plan to drown me?" Talos said. "It will take more jars than one, and I cannot be drowned anyway!"

Pandareus threw the branch awkwardly. It bounced off the ramp's sidewall and caromed into the passage below. Talos' swords chopped it into bits despite the bounce and spin, though that just meant the missile fell on the oil in a dozen blazing fragments instead of one. Low yellow flames spread across the surface like reflections dancing from a pond.

"Do you think I will burn?" said Talos. He bent and scooped up oil on the flat of one blade. It ran down his arm and shoulders as a lambent tongue. "Come down and die!"

"I can bring more oil," Corylus said to his teacher. "We have as much of that as we want."

"This should be enough," Pandareus said calmly. "If it works at all, that is."

Talos continued to laugh. He bent down to scoop up more burning oil.

Light, as sparklingly bright as an eruption of Vesuvius at night, erupted from the bronze man's left heel. The sizzling jet carved into the polished granite wall behind him.

Talos cried out and tried to straighten. Instead he toppled to the floor of the passage, still bent over.

The blaze from his heel spluttered and ceased. By contrast the flames of the remainder of the olive oil were scarcely visible.

"Well!" said the dryad. "He never did *that* before, either."

"What happened, master?" Corylus said. He grinned and added, "Master indeed."

"Well, I don't consider Apollonius a trustworthy source," said Pandareus. He kept his tone measured where a lesser man—almost any other man—might have crowed in triumph. "But according to Alexo, Thales also claimed that the essence of life was sealed into Talos with a lead plug. While the oil flames could at best soften bronze, I was altogether more hopeful about their effect on lead solder."

He smiled broadly. "Correctly hopeful, I'm glad to see."

Corylus hugged the older man. "Master," he said, "you are living proof of the value of a rhetorical education."

He stretched, releasing the tension that had built up ever since Talos had appeared.

"And when the flames burn out," he said, "we'll see where Vergil's bridge leads us."

HEDIA HAD BEGUN TO SEE FACES peering from the walls of the tunnel as they walked past. They stayed close to the demon, the only source of light now that the entrance was what seemed a mile behind them. Hedia's eyes were getting used to the dim glow.

"Melino?" she said. "Look at the stone. It's carved into faces."

"No," said the magician without turning his head. He was hunched like an old woman carrying firewood, though he no longer needed Hedia's help to keep up with the demon.

"Look at it!" Hedia said sharply. It didn't really matter, but she resented having the man dismiss her statement without bothering to check it.

She touched the wall to emphasize her demand. Her fingers brushed flesh rather than basalt. She yelped in surprise and skipped sideways, bumping Melino.

He stumbled but recovered by clicking his staff down. He chuckled in a cracked voice, but he still didn't turn to look at her.

"Others have come this way," said the demon over her shoulder. "Some of them remain. They are not dangerous, but what caused them to remain is as dangerous to you as it was to them."

The faces were turning so that their eyes could follow Hedia and her companions, but they moved slowly and their expressions were agonized. They reminded her of bandits crucified outside Carce at the gate to whichever road they had infested, husbanding all their remaining strength to keep from suffocating when their arms could no longer hold their chests high enough for them to breathe.

Hedia swallowed. She focused her eyes straight ahead and crossed her hands in front of her. She would like to wash them, wash the one that had touched the wall, at least.

It was the changing echo of her and her companions' feet on what again was a stone floor that alerted her, not anything she saw immediately. The demon halted. The tunnel beyond branched to right and left.

Doesn't she know which way to go? Hedia thought, but she didn't speak aloud.

A deep shadow lifted itself like a cloak of filth at the mouth of the left branch. It opened huge yellow eyes; it was a toad larger than an ox. Its tongue licked out and back.

Melino was shivering and his face had no color save that of the demon's rosy light. He said, "You must let us pass, Paddock." He sounded like a dying beggar.

The toad's laughter gurgled like oil at a roiling boil. "Must I, wizard?" it said. "*I* do not think so."

Melino raised the *Book* in his left hand. "Paddock," he said, his voice stronger. "You *must*."

The toad grunted. Its dark mass quivered; Hedia poised to run.

Instead of attacking, the toad slopped to the side in a series of awkward motions. When at last the way was clear, the demon walked down the left-hand branch.

Melino staggered after her without hesitation. Hedia waited until her companions were far enough ahead that she could sprint past without risk of bumping into them.

The toad didn't move until they were some distance down the passage. Behind them in the darkness Hedia heard broad feet slapping the stone as the guardian resumed its post.

The magician looked like a walking corpse. He had drawn Zabulon's *Book* close to his chest again; he clung to it like a drowning man clutching a float. Even the threat of using the *Book* seemed to have drained him.

Hedia wondered how many times more Melino would have strength for the spells this place required. She wondered what would happen to her if he collapsed, dead or hopelessly weak.

And she walked on.

VARUS AND THE SIBYL STOOD beside the two exhausted humans sleeping on the shore near their boat. In the water thirty paces up the beach was a crab whose shell was ten feet across and whose claws were paired scythes. It was in restive motion, sidling two paces toward the sleepers and then one back. Its body barely broke the surface.

"Sibyl?" Varus said. He felt more alive in this world of his vision than he had since he boarded the boat in Sulla's garden. Exhaustion had worn his physical body to a gray shell during the voyage. "*Is* this Zabulon's Isle?"

"This is the island to which Zabulon retired, bringing his *Book*," said the Sibyl, turning to look into the jungle close behind. "This is the island where he died and where his body remains."

The crab continued to edge closer. It was clearly interested in the sleepers. Varus wondered how fast it could move in a rush.

"The *Book* will not confine the Worms," the Sibyl said in a musing tone, "nor will the *Book* destroy the Worms if they are released; but if a magician of sufficient power holds the *Book*, the Worms could be confined or even destroyed."

The crab stopped ten feet from the sleepers, but its stillness was as threatening as that of a crouching leopard. Water shivered above its gills.

"Sibyl, can you drive away the crab?" Varus said. He wondered what would happen to his present self if his physical body passed down the gullet of a giant crab.

"Why do you ask me, Lord Magician?" the Sibyl said with a cracked laugh. "If you want it away, send it away yourself."

And how do I do that? But the best way to learn was to try. . . .

Still in the vision, Varus stepped toward the crab. "*Raging fire will flow!*" he said, and waved his right hand in a gesture of dismissal.

To his surprise, there was a *crash!*

A blue glare enveloped the crab. Water sizzled and the crab leaped back the way it had approached, then scuttled into deeper water. One of its legs wobbled at the shoreline; the severed joint was noticeably charred.

Varus tingled. He felt exhilarated.

"If the Worms proceed undisturbed," said the Sibyl, "they will cleanse the Earth."

Varus turned to her. "They'll destroy all life!" he said. "That's what you mean, isn't it?"

The Sibyl shrugged. "Perhaps," she said. "As you destroy the molds and tiny creatures living on your body when you bathe. When you cleanse yourself."

She looked eastward, as if by chance. Varus followed her eyes and saw that dawn was beginning to brighten the sky. Lucinus moaned softly, but Varus' body was as motionless as a stuffed dummy.

Philosophically, he could accept the view that the Earth had as much right to clean itself as he did. He could also accept the view that to a philosopher a gentleman of Carce was neither better nor worse than a tattooed savage from Britain.

That said, the Briton was going to be thrown out on his ear if he tried to barge into the Alphenus town house—and Varus was going to stop the Worms if there was a way to do it. Even at the cost of his life.

"It's time for me to return," he said.

The Sibyl nodded and said, *"Now join those who go forth!"*

Varus shook his body awake on the shore of Zabulon's Isle. The air breathed a mixture of spice and composting vegetation, and a creature wailed in the far distance. The Sibyl's voice still rang in Varus' ears.

He put a hand on the magician's shoulder. "Wake up, Lucinus," he said. "We're here."

Varus' muscles ached, but he was exhilarated from loosing the blast that had seen off the crab. If that had really happened . . .

He glanced toward the shoreline. The burned leg floated where he remembered it from his vision. That much at least had been real.

Lucinus awakened more easily than he had on previous mornings during the voyage. He rubbed his eyes in normal fashion, then brushed the cheek that had been lying against the sand.

His eyes lighted on Varus. "You're ready, then?" he said. "Good."

Lucinus got up from the sand. Each joint moved separately, like those of a marionette. He looked at the vegetation before them, then said to Varus in a haughty tone, "The world depends on my power and on your ability to help me."

Varus lifted his chin in recognition of the statement, but he didn't trust himself to speak. The voyage had been physically and mentally difficult, so his control was wobbly. A farmer from the Campania should not be patronizing a noble of Carce.

It was a thought unworthy of a philosopher, but it was quite proper for Lord Gaius Alphenus Varus. If Lucinus persisted in arrogance, he was likely to meet the other half of his companion's personality.

The thought renewed Varus' good temper. He smiled, then gestured to the older man. "Lead then, Master Lucinus," he said. "We will both attempt to act as befits our stations in life."

The magician strode into the vegetation. The soft-stemmed brush near the beach bent away before he could have touched it, but it sprang back at once.

Varus smiled wryly and elbowed the foliage aside in normal fashion. During the voyage he had worried that Lucinus might not be in condition to act when they reached Zabulon's Isle. That concern was obviously misplaced, but the magician in his full health and strength posed other problems.

A creature with a black, shiny body stepped in front of them. It was the size of a bull. Great eyes covered most of its face with myriad separate lenses.

A *cricket*, Varus realized, and therefore probably not interested in them as food. But if it stepped on them—

Lucinus held out his left hand with the fingers spread in a fan. Red sparks popped and crackled from his fingertips, wilting the foliage that they touched. The cricket gave a spastic leap and landed on its back thirty feet away. Two of its legs had shriveled, but the remainder were thrashing violently.

The magician stalked on as if following a paved track; Varus followed. The shriveled vegetation eased the younger man's progress somewhat, but his arms already itched from contact with the plants.

Lucinus led them into a forest of hairy-trunked trees. There was enough room to walk between them comfortably. Varus glanced upward: they were in a stand of sunflowers hundreds of feet tall. The multiple bright yellow blossoms on each stem were in motion, turning their eyeless faces slowly toward the humans below.

The flowers didn't seem hostile, but he was glad when the magician led him into a bed of ferns larger than palm trees. Attention from objects that should have been inanimate was more disquieting than Varus would have guessed without the experience.

He wished he could discuss matters with Pandareus now. The voyage with Lucinus was providing Varus perspectives on life that books and lectures would never have given him. Of course the same would have been true if he had become an officer on the frontiers the way Corylus planned to do, or had been enslaved by the Sarmatians and trudged across the plains behind a squealing wagon.

To a philosopher, all forms of experience were equal. Varus felt on consideration, however, that he preferred books and lectures.

Lucinus halted at a band of grass that grew higher than his head.

The blades were as close together as the palings of a fence. They were bright yellow on the edges, but their cores were green.

The magician lowered himself carefully to sit cross-legged on the ground. "We have reached our destination," he said. "Beyond this—"

He nodded to the grass.

"—is the tomb of Zabulon."

Varus had been a pace behind the older man. He moved slightly to the side and examined the grass. It grew in a band four feet deep and as sharply bordered as if it were in a rich man's garden. He wondered if the bed was artificial or if it had grown in this fashion by the whim of nature. Nature on this island certainly was whimsical.

Something had burned a swath into the grass. Fresh growth was poking up from the roots, but the original stems were black and shriveled.

Lucinus was taking colored stones from his satchel and placing them in a pattern on the ground. Varus watched him for a moment, then stepped into the burned place. He shifted the remaining grass to the side with his arm so that he could look through.

The ground beyond the curtain of grass was trampled and scarred, bare except for fragments of giant insects. It stank like the mudflats fringing the Tiber when the river was low.

Across the semicircle of bare ground was a limestone bluff, steep though not quite vertical, and in the middle of that a cave or tunnel. Varus stepped forward.

Lucinus looked up from his preparations. "Don't, you fool!" he shouted.

A huge dog sprang toward Varus from the cave mouth, barking savagely from all three throats. It covered half the distance in its initial leap and stretched to spring on top of its prey.

Two years previously a lightning bolt blew the doors off the temple Varus had been about to enter. The blast had driven him back, though he hadn't been injured except for a tingle all over his body. This was the same: he backed a step from the sheer violence of what was happening.

And stopped, crossing his arms before his chest. He couldn't outrun the dog, and he wasn't willing to give up his dignity. *I am a citizen of Carce.*

The dog reached the end of the chain that Varus hadn't seen. The shock jerked the dog's forequarters high—the collar was around his middle neck—and his hind legs skidded out in front of him. His hind claws flicked up, fanning the grass between him and Varus.

The dog hit the ground on his back. Everything shook as though a building had collapsed. *He weighs as much as an ox,* Varus thought.

The dog scrambled to his feet, whining but uninjured. Being slammed to the ground didn't seem to have affected him beyond silencing his barking. He paced off to the end of his chain, not straining against it but keeping the thin flame-colored links off the ground. No wonder the ground was trampled bare.

Varus turned away. The magician was staring at him.

"Are you insane?" Lucinus said. He sounded amazed, not angry. "You just stood there."

Varus looked at him, trying to understand what point Lucinus thought he was making. "My friend Corylus would have noticed the chain, I suppose," Varus said. "I just realized that I couldn't get away. The rational choice was to stand where I was; I wasn't being brave."

"Don't take insane risks," Lucinus growled as he returned his attention to the pattern of stones he'd laid before him. "I need you to enter the cave and bring back the *Book* while I hold the dog. I *can't* do both."

He touched his temples with his fingertips, apparently concentrating. He looked at Varus and said, "Now, don't do anything until I have put the dog to sleep with my magic. *Especially* don't distract me. As soon as I've held the dog, run into the cave and bring the *Book* from Zabulon's lap."

"All right," said Varus. The great dog continued to pace back and forth at the edge of the clearing. Whichever head was on the outside focused on Varus and the magician, but the other two kept watch on the jungle and the sky above.

Lucinus had his *athame* out again. As he chanted, *"Let peaceful calm relax your limbs,"* the obsidian blade dipped from one stone to another. The motions were not in a particular order that Varus could identify, but he was sure that there was a structure beyond his awareness.

"Let peace come from the stars on light breezes."

Varus had watched spiders building webs. Their movements seemed random also, but the pattern of each finished web proved that the tiny creature was working as precisely as Pheidias had when he designed the Parthenon.

"Put your head down and rest your twitching eyes."

The dog was becoming logy. It wobbled as it paced, and one or another of its heads nodded.

Suddenly it lunged with all its remaining strength toward the seated magician. The chain snubbed the dog up as before. The snarl from the middle head choked to a squeak. The dog lowered all three heads to the ground.

Red light flashed around the dog and clung to his fur like a spray of water. The beast lay where he was, paws outstretched. The chain reached back to the cave mouth like a trickle of fire.

Varus glanced at Lucinus. The magician seemed as stiff as the dog. Barely moving his lips, he said in a rasping whisper, "Quickly! The *Book!*" Varus pushed through the grass and quickly skirted the beast.

Though it was as motionless as a statue, the dog gave off a definite animal odor and radiated heat. Varus had been doing some physical exercise since he and Corylus became friends, but he wasn't fit enough to outrun the monster if the magician's control slipped. An Olympic sprinter wouldn't be able to do that.

Varus grinned. He was focusing on details to avoid thinking about the chance that he would suddenly cease to exist. Given that his mind could comprehend athletes running a two-furlong course but it could not comprehend non-existence, this showed good judgment on his part.

He took one step into the cave, then paused to let his eyes adapt. A tall man sat on a throne facing the entrance: Zabulon. His hands were open and empty in his lap.

Varus climbed the three-step pedestal on which the throne stood, then moved his hand over Zabulon's hands in case the *Book* was invisible. *It has to be here.*

It wasn't there.

Zabulon glowered in frozen fury. Varus avoided touching him, touching the body, he supposed, but it would have been easy to imagine that Zabulon was still alive and about to breathe out again.

Knowing that Lucinus might lose his hold on the dog at any moment, Varus stepped down from the throne and went farther back into the cave. There were apparatus whose purpose he could not guess and apparatus whose purpose was all too obvious, including a complex and horrifying rack. A tapestry hung against the cave wall without hooks or a framework, and balls the size of chickpeas danced by themselves in the air.

There were no books nor any chest or basket that looked as though it could hold a book. *I didn't ask whether Zabulon's* Book *was a scroll or a codex . . . but I don't see either one.*

He heard a dog whine. *The* dog whine. It was breaking free of Lucinus' control.

Varus sprinted from the cave toward where Lucinus sat. If the dog was already loose, he was doomed. At that point he would turn and meet his fate, as he had done earlier. Until he was certain that there was no escape, however, he was going to do everything possible to survive.

There was nothing undignified about physical effort. Vergil himself had said that brutal labor overcame all things. . . .

The dog wasn't fully awake, but his right foreleg was pawing the air. He saw Varus come out of the cave and his roan right head turned and howled mournfully toward the interloper.

Varus ran across the barren ground. Through the green and yellow curtain, he saw Lucinus swaying. Varus crossed his forearms in front of him against the edges of the grass-blades.

The *athame* dropped from Lucinus' hand and he began to topple forward onto the pattern he had laid out. Varus leaped as though he were diving into the water. He felt the slam of the dog's feet as his own left the ground.

Varus fell through the grass curtain and sprawled bruisingly onto the ground. The shock of the dog crashing down at the end of its chain bounced Varus up and flipped him on his back. He lay panting, unable for a moment to turn his face away from the bright sun.

He rolled over slowly. He was dizzy from effort and emotion. As he'd flown through the air, he had been sure that the dog was going to rend him among its pairs of jaws.

Lucinus was already sitting up. Angrily he said, "Where is the *Book*? I don't see the *Book*!"

Varus carefully got to his feet. The dog was slavering on the other side of the grass, hopeful that his prey would come just a little bit closer.

"Where is the *Book*, boy?" Lucinus shouted. "Didn't you bring it?"

"Zabulon's *Book* wasn't there, Master Lucinus," Varus said. He was too weary to be angry. "There were no books in the cave, not on Zabulon's lap and not anywhere else I could find. There didn't seem to be anything deeper into the cave than I got, but I couldn't have seen a book without more light anyway."

"It was there, you fool!" said Lucinus. "The world is going to end because you're blind!"

Varus felt something change. He still wasn't angry, or at least he didn't think he was, but he was very cold, and he shivered with the power that filled him.

"Come then, little man," Varus said. He didn't shout, but the ground trembled. The great dog yelped and backed a step. "*Come*, I said."

"What do you mean?" said the magician. "Are you mad?"

Varus took Lucinus by the shoulder and dragged him into the trampled area. Blue fire danced about them. The grass flattened, and the leaves of nearby trees stood stiffly away as though caught in a violent storm.

Lucinus was wailing something, but his words were lost in the dog's triple fury. The beast didn't attack, but it bent so close to the humans that all three heads spattered them with slaver.

Varus watched both through his own eyes and from a place outside himself. He felt no emotion.

He tried to slap the dog with his open hand. He didn't connect, but a blue flash lifted a cloud of dust from the ground and tumbled the dog end over end. It yelped pitiably and slunk to the most distant edge of the clearing.

Varus pulled Lucinus to the mouth of the cave. It took the older man a few paces to get his feet under him so that he wasn't being dragged, but that made no difference to Varus in his present state.

Varus threw Lucinus into the cave. "Look, then!" he said. "There is no book!"

The world shook with each syllable. Pieces of apparatus clinked against one another, and the stiff figure of Zabulon fell off his throne.

Varus turned and walked away. Light sparkled about him and vegetation bent away.

His disembodied viewpoint noted that he was heading for the shore where they had beached the boat. A great tree in their path shattered and fell to the side, carrying with it a great swath of the jungle. Winged things, some of them birds, lifted away from the coming ruin.

The hull of the boat showed Alphena asleep in a ruined village, surrounded by corpses. Varus stood beside the vessel for a moment, then collapsed. As he sprawled on the sand, the detached viewpoint through which his soul had been watching went black.

CHAPTER XV

Alphena was dreaming. Beside her stood a black figure with harsh features and white eyes. His pupils were tiny. The world beyond was faint and grayed out.

"Well?" said the figure. "What will you do now, Alphena?"

His iron tongue clicked against teeth as white as his eyes. He was not the idol, but he was what the idol represented. He was First.

Alphena swallowed. She didn't say either the first thing that came into her mind: *I don't know!* or the second: *I want to go home!* because neither was an answer to the question. She didn't have an answer to the question.

She looked about her. Everything but First was blurred, seemingly by distance rather than fog. The Daughters of the Mind danced about her, but they were fainter shadows among the slightly sharper scenes—which were also of the Daughters.

Alphena viewed the women in separate moments and settings. They didn't blur into one another, though there was no separation. When she focused on them dancing on a waste of sand dunes with no other life visible, the adjacent images—a forest so deep that the treetops shaded out the undergrowth, and the mud shore of a lake too broad to see the farther bank—faded into near transparency.

"You are viewing the past and the present," said First. His head turned stiffly, but his arms remained crossed on his chest. "When what you see ceases to be the future also, the world will end for living things."

In every scene, the Ethiopes appeared—spreading out, marching stolidly toward the dancing women. Just beyond thrusting distance of an Ethiope spear, the Daughters vanished. With them went the Egg in the center of their pattern."

"Why would it change?" Alphena said, trying to keep desperation out of her voice. "Why shouldn't they just keep dancing?"

"Even the Mind . . . ," First said in a terrible voice. "Grows tired."

Alphena saw the same scene in each of the hundreds of segments about her. The Daughters danced on dunes of red sand; to the west the surf broke and broke again, dozens of times in total, before it crawled up the shore. Pieces of driftwood, some of it ripped from the hulls of ships, lay here and there as half-buried monuments.

An arch of rosy light, a portal, appeared on the next dune inland from where the women rotated about the Egg. The Etruscan priest Paris stepped through. His lips moved in an inaudible chant. Ethiopes followed him. They paced toward the women, their feet scattering sand ahead of them.

The Daughters continued to dance. The Ethiopes reached the valley between the dunes and climbed toward them, though the sand slipped and gave under their weight. There were scores of Ethiopes already, and more continued to appear through the portal. The leaders were nearing the ridge of the dune.

"They're going to leave now, aren't they?" Alphena said. The horse-headed giants had come closer to the dancers in previous images, but there was something different this time.

"They cannot," said First, "so they will not. The Mind is tired, so the Daughters of the Mind will die; and the world will die."

"They can fight!" Alphena said. The women couldn't fight. They were naked except for belts of eggshell. "They can do something!"

"They will die," First repeated. "And because they die, the world will die."

The Ethiopes surrounded the dancers. The giants paused, then surged in like the sea reclaiming an island. They looked awkward, but Alphena had seen their strength. They stabbed and slashed. When the stone heads of their weapons rose again, they slung fresh blood in connected strings of droplets.

Paris was cackling in triumph. On the horizon beyond him, two great crystalline worms twisted toward the dunes. Their open maws engulfed the ground itself, leaving behind them a surface as smooth as that of the jet pendant on a woman's throat. The Ethiopes continued to hack at the bloody sand.

"Stop it!" Alphena cried. She didn't know if she was talking to First or to the Cosmos, but in any case the images vanished. She stood in grayness with the black figure. The dancers were only a hint of motion, and there was nothing else.

"First," Alphena said, forcing herself to meet the statue's eyes of polished shell. They had a sardonic glint as they returned her gaze. "Two lizardmen fought the Ethiopes so that the Daughters could escape in your village. That's right, isn't it?"

"Two Singiri fought the Ethiopes and died," said First. "Why must I tell you what you watched yourself, worshiper?"

Alphena's hand clenched on her sword hilt, then released it. There was nothing in this limbo to use a blade on. There was no purpose for *her* in this place.

"Can you take me to the Daughters?" she said. "Wherever they are!"

"They are with us now, Alphena," the statue said. His tongue licked his carven lips again. "If that is what you choose."

"I choose it!" Alphena said. "I can buy them some time. I can do something!"

"There will be much blood," said First with satisfaction.

As he spoke, Alphena felt the world shifting into a grassland beneath a towering basalt knob.

VARUS WATCHED HIS FRIEND Corylus walking unsupported among the stars. He carried his sword bare against unguessable threats.

Pandareus followed, looking about with wonder and delight—a sharp contrast to the set, hostile expression with which the younger man faced the empty cosmos. They seemed real enough to touch, but Varus knew that when he opened his eyes he would find that he had been dreaming.

"Lord Varus?" Lucinus said.

Varus started. His eyes *were* open. He was sprawled on the beach of Zabulon's Isle, watching his friends in the hull of the boat that had brought him here.

Varus sat up and at some greater length regretted having moved so quickly. His vision blurred.

He closed his eyes and braced both palms on the coarse sand because he was afraid of toppling over if he didn't. He seemed to have fallen flat without injury the first time, but he wasn't sure that his luck would hold if he repeated the experience.

"You're all right, aren't you?" Lucinus said. He sounded concerned.

"I think so," Varus said. "I'm not going to stand up for a while, though."

He reopened his eyes, then turned his head carefully to look at the kneeling magician. *He's not* worried *about me*, Varus realized. *He's frightened.*

"I was wondering if you would explain how you controlled the guardian, Your Lordship?" Lucinus said. "As one adept to another, that is? I, ah, didn't hear you intone a spell, though of course I was distracted at the time."

"I don't know what I did," Varus said, looking away. He felt uncomfortable talking about what had happened. He was uncomfortable even *thinking* about what had happened. "I didn't do anything that I remember. I'm not sure that what happened had anything to do with me."

"The dog was afraid of you, Lord Varus," Lucinus said. "It was afraid of you even before you drove it back with a wave of your hand. The guardian should have feared nothing save Zabulon, and Zabulon was dead; but it feared you."

"I said I don't know what happened!" Varus said. "I don't want to talk about it!"

He closed his eyes, then opened them and looked at the scene before him. There was a purple clamshell between his hands, no larger than his thumbnail. The shell opened slightly and thrust out two tiny legs. On them the clam ran down the beach and into the sea.

"I see," said Lucinus, who clearly didn't see. He continued to watch Varus warily.

"What do we do now?" said Varus, who was coming to himself again. It was a necessary question; and besides, it sufficed to change the subject. "Do we return to Carce?"

He wasn't sure it was possible to return to Carce. At best, the voyage would be as grueling as the voyage here had been. Still—if needs must, they must.

"We have to find the *Book*," Lucinus said in an attempt to sound positive. "The *Book* is necessary if I am to save the world. I've recovered enough that I can work a—"

He paused and looked at Varus. Licking his lips, he resumed, "Ah, that is, unless you wish to carry out the exploration, Lord Varus?"

"No," said Varus with a jerk of his head. He tried to control his anger. "Do as you see fit."

Lucinus had set up another array of stones—stones and a tiny figure of orichalc—on the sand while waiting for the younger man to come around. Varus couldn't identify the statue because reflection from the bright metal hid the details.

Lucinus raised his *athame* and pointed with it as he intoned, "*Let the spirits send to me—*"

Varus sank into himself. He clearly remembered slapping back the dog and dragging Lucinus into the tomb. He had watched it through his own eyes and from a disembodied viewpoint that was still his own . . . but he had no idea of how he had done it or even why he had decided to do it.

Yes, of course—he'd been irritated when the magician accused him of cowardice and stupidity. If someone had asked Varus at that moment what the result of stepping within the guardian's reach would be, though, he would have said that the dog would tear him to bits.

Even so, he hadn't been courting suicide. Some part of Gaius Alphenus Varus had known exactly what he was doing.

"*—truth through the membrane of black horn!*" Lucinus shouted. Into the air before him lifted a spiral of sand that caught sunlight and formed itself into images:

Melino scuttled from the cave, bent over something that he held to his chest.

Lucinus was breathing deeply. He no longer chanted, but his *athame* continued its complex rhythm as though his arm's motion wasn't connected with the deathly fatigue Varus saw in his eyes.

A bitch came out of the cave, whisking her tail in wide sweeps. The three-headed guardian followed her, but she ignored its fawning attempts to attract her attention. It snubbed up at the end of its chain; the bitch continued through the curtain of grass and rubbed against Melino's leg.

Melino spoke a word, unheard in the vision. Hedia rose from where the

*bitch had stood, slender and startlingly beautiful. Her garments lay on the
ground; she donned them with her usual grace.*

*Melino lowered his arms to look at the thing he had brought from Zabu-
lon's tomb. It was a codex bound in black leather, with iron mountings.*

Lucinus gave a stifled groan; the vision collapsed into a cascade of
sand without form or meaning. He wailed, "We've lost. That woman
gave Melino the key to Zabulon's *Book*. With the *Book* he will destroy
the Earth, demon that he is. There is no hope for the world, and there
is no hope for us except that we stay here on the island which Zabulon
took out of space and time."

Varus frowned as he considered what he had just seen. "I don't believe that," he said. "My mother would never help destroy the world.
There's some other thing going on."

"You saw her, you fool!" Lucinus cried, too miserable and desperate
to choose his words. "You saw her, didn't you? She distracted the guardian and Melino has the *Book*!"

Varus got to his feet. "That is bad logic," he said, as coolly as though
he were addressing another member of Pandareus' class. "Even if the
vision is to be trusted, and I don't think we *can* trust the vision. We've
seen other things in this place which indicate that it has its own laws."

"Your mother is a fool and you are a fool, boy!" the magician said.
"Melino tricked her. It's obvious that she was helping him!"

Another man—his friend Corylus among them—would have reacted a different way. Varus laughed.

"Little man," he said, drawling his words like the most affected
member of his noble circle. "Fooling me would be easy enough. Fooling
my mother would be quite another thing. You would more easily trick me
with a forged stanza of Sappho than you or *any* man would mislead my
mother regarding his intentions."

Varus thought for a moment. He was fully himself again. He noticed
at the back of his mind that he was beginning to feel thirsty. There
hadn't been food or water on the vessel, but he hadn't been aware of
their absence during the voyage.

"Unless Hedia and Melino are still on this island . . . ?" he said to
the magician, raising an eyebrow.

"No, no!" Lucinus said peevishly. "They're gone and the *Book* is gone. Don't you understand? Zabulon's *Book* has given Melino *all* power."

The magician could know if Hedia—or at least the *Book*—was still on the island, though Varus hadn't seen him do anything to determine that fact. Varus accepted the statement for now. He wasn't going to spend the rest of his life searching a jungle that probably contained nothing of interest to himself. Which meant—

"Since our purpose for coming here is now moot," Varus said, "we'll return to Carce. If nothing else, my friends there may need my—"

He twitched at his unconscious arrogance when he heard the words.

"That is," he said, "they may be in a situation in which I can help."

Varus felt a wave of relief now that he'd examined the choices and determined the best course of action under the circumstances. He gestured to the magician.

"Come," he said. "Get in the boat and I'll push it off the beach."

His tone was peremptory, that of a nobleman speaking to a commoner. It wasn't Varus' normal way, but Lucinus became an unpleasant companion whenever he thought he was in a position of power.

"We must stay or we'll die!" Lucinus said. "You have no choice. You have *nothing!*"

He extended his left hand toward the boat and said, *"Go your way; your work is finished."* A cloud of tiny red motes sprang from his fingertips.

Varus turned. Light covered the boat; its lines softened. In the hull Varus saw his sister standing with her sword out. Toward her strode horse-headed Ethiopes, brandishing their weapons. Corylus and Pandareus appeared at her side.

"You have nothing!" Lucinus repeated.

I have friends. Varus bent low and dived into the vision.

"I'LL LEAD, MASTER," Corylus said, walking down the ramp with his sword lifted. A breeze blew from his back, carrying the smoke away. A few puddles of olive oil still burned.

Molten lead had cooled to a bright silvery smear on the stone at Talos' heel. There was a sparkling sharpness in the air that reminded Corylus of the odor of a nearby lightning bolt.

"I would have liked to learn how Talos was powered," said Pandareus, bending over to examine the frozen figure. "I don't suppose he could have told me, even if he were willing to."

Corylus looked back over his shoulder. "Ah, master . . . ?" he said, hoping he sounded less concerned than he felt. "Ah—Talos is dead, I'm sure. But if your foot slips on the oily floor, those double-edged swords look awfully sharp."

The swords looked sharp enough to cut sunbeams. If Corylus was any judge, there had been as much magic in their forging as there was in animating Talos.

"Ah," said Pandareus. He straightened and edged carefully around the automaton. "Yes, I see what you mean."

"Perhaps we'll have another chance to look at him," Corylus said. He winced to hear himself. *That's the sort of nonsense a nurse tells a child!* "But I hope we don't, now that I use my mind instead of letting my mouth talk by itself."

"I'm fairly sure that we'll see other things just as wonderful as Talos," Pandareus said. The automaton half-blocked the passage. When they passed him, Pandareus had begun walking alongside Corylus. "I'm less certain that the experience will be as survivable as this has proved, but I've never been concerned about personal existence."

They passed the alcove in which Talos had waited for interlopers. It was just that, a shallow niche of the sort that might have held a statue in a rich man's house. Corylus walked on, wondering when he would come to the bridge. He saw a glint ahead, but it was too distant to have shape.

"I don't believe we're in the material world anymore," Pandareus said in his usual tone of polite interest. "The floor and the walls aren't—"

He brushed his left hand through what had seemed to be gray stone before that moment. His hand was fully visible.

At his touch, the walls grew fainter, melting like fog in the sunlight. The gray was replaced by crystal nothingness sparkling with points of light that must be stars in the infinite distance. Both men stood frozen.

The ground—the floor of the passage—began to dissolve also. Corylus could see the stars through where it had been, just as far away as they were in all other directions.

"Oh dear," said Pandareus. "I'm very sorry, Master Corylus. I fear that my curiosity has killed us both."

"The bridge is still here," Corylus said. "Even if we can't see it."

He tapped his foot down. The unseen surface was as hard as diamond.

"There was a light in the direction we were going," he said, focusing his eyes on that point. "You follow directly behind me and we'll continue on. There won't be a problem. Ready? We'll go, then."

Corylus strode on with every appearance of confidence. All he was sure of was that if he dropped into nothingness Pandareus would have warning enough to stop. Perhaps the scholar would be able to crawl back to the garden on all fours, keeping one hand on the edge. As for Corylus himself—

Well, he would have time to think about that if it happened. Probably a great deal of time.

They walked on. And on.

"I think the light is coming closer," Corylus said. "That we're coming closer to the light, that is."

He'd thought that for . . . actually, he wasn't sure for how long. He hadn't been counting his paces, and with no external markers—neither sun nor scenery—he didn't have a feel for time.

"I've been thinking that myself," said Pandareus. "I was afraid to say anything, though, because I knew my mind might be tricking me into seeing something I want to be true."

Corylus risked a glance over his shoulder. Pandareus was slightly to his left instead of directly behind as Corylus had clearly ordered. He was thus able to see things ahead of him besides the back of the younger man.

"Master," Corylus said, grinning. "I thought of saying that you would make a terrible soldier, but I decided that I would be better saving my breath to discuss the question of whether water is wet."

"Certainly a matter worth consideration in the unusual circumstances in which we find ourselves," Pandareus said, nodding. "And Master Corylus? Allow me to congratulate your teacher, from whom you have gathered such skill in the use of *praeteritio*."

They were both laughing as they reached what they had been approaching, an archway curtained in opaque light. It stood in the midst of nothingness.

"I'll go through first," Corylus said after an instant's consideration.

"Follow me immediately. I don't know that I'll be able to return to tell you what's on the other side, and I suspect there're risks to standing out here also."

He grinned. "If you step through into molten lava, I'll apologize now," he said. "Because I probably won't have time later."

"Your apology is accepted," Pandareus said with a smile of his own. "If all my students had been like you and Lord Varus, my teaching career would have been as uniformly joyful as these past few months have been."

Corylus stepped into a broad stone room covered with a low dome. In the center, a child-sized man bent over a basin. He was very ugly.

"Welcome, sir," the little man said. He reminded Corylus of a wax figure that had started to slump in sunlight, but he turned with a pleasant smile. "Welcome, gentlemen, I should say since I see there are two of you. I get few visitors, so I'm glad to see you."

Corylus felt mildly embarrassed to have entered with his sword ready to thrust. *I'm not so embarrassed that I'm going to sheathe it until I know more about this place, though.*

"Pardon us for this intrusion," he said formally, walking to the center of the hall but angling his approach to keep the stone basin between him and the little man. That made the bare sword less of an overt threat; or anyway, Corylus hoped it did. "We're looking for a friend of ours, a young girl: Lady Alphena. We were told—we were told by a dryad—that this might be a path—"

He happened to glance into the six-foot-wide basin. Instead of liquid, he saw Alphena standing on a prairie. Beside her were the three short Nubian dancers he had seen in previous visions.

"Hercules!" he shouted. "There she is!"

"Oh, *that* poor girl," the little man said. "Yes, she was here. I lost my temper and sent her away. I'm terribly sorry; I was sorry the very moment it happened. Though really, she didn't know *anything* about poetry."

The vision of Alphena had drawn a sword, not a surprise for anyone who knew her: she practiced in the family gymnasium with the determination of a gladiator whose life depended on his skill. Her life and those of her friends, Corylus included, *had* depended on her skill.

Alphena was small and a woman besides, with less strength than an equally trained man of the same size. That said, she was *very* skilled for a woman, better than many soldiers who assumed their rear-area billets kept them safe. Every once in a while, a German raid would prove that some quartermaster's clerk should have been spending more time on the practice field than in the wineshops of the Strip.

"I wonder, gentlemen?" the little man said. "You appear to be cultured fellows. I'm trying to remember a line—"

Switching to Greek, he said, "'*The boy is only a baby . . . .*'"

"Yes, of course," said Pandareus. "'*Your son and my son, his mother and father both doomed.*' Andromache is speaking to the corpse of her husband Hector before his pyre is lighted."

"Yes," said the little man. "Yes, of course. I—"

Unexpectedly he began to weep. For a moment he covered his face in his wizened hands, but then he thrust them down at his sides and faced his visitors.

"I had the world," he said, making a broad gesture. "Now I am a ruin and will never be anything more than a ruin. If I leave this room, I will die. *I*, who was ruler of poetry and of the unseen world!"

Pandareus watched the speaker with consuming interest. Corylus instead surveyed the hall now that he was sure the little man didn't have a weapon or, apparently, any wish to harm them. There were no doors or passages in the walls. The arch by which Corylus and Pandareus entered was blank stone from this side, identical to the rest of the walls.

"You see my body, crippled!" the little man said. "But my mind, that's the horror. That's crippled too, stunted. I who was the greatest of men and more than a man, look at me now! I should better step out of this place and crumble away entirely, body and mind."

"We were discussing Lady Alphena," Pandareus said. He opened his left hand toward the vision in the basin. "You said she was here and you sent her away, master?"

The little man slid up from his grief like a casement suddenly opening. "Yes, that's right," he said. "She must have been a magician herself to have come here. I wasn't; I shouldn't have. . . ."

He began to cry again. Corylus wondered what had happened to bring the fellow to his present state. Age alone would not have been enough.

"Can you summon her back from where you sent her, master?" said

Pandareus, gesturing again to the basin. "My friend and I have come to return Lady Alphena to the Waking World, you see."

"Really?" said the little man. "There was a time I would have been able to do that, you know. I was powerful; I had *all* power, except over time. I tried to become young again, but it all went wrong, so badly wrong. . . ."

He's about to cry again, Corylus realized. He put his left hand on the little man's shoulder and said, "Master? Can you help us with Lady Alphena? Can you help our friend, please?"

The little man shook himself free of Corylus. "No, no," he said querulously. "I can't; and anyway, why would I want to? She's a fool! She didn't respect poetry and she didn't respect me!"

He looked into the basin and added, "She knows to respect me *now*, though!"

Ethiopes, the horse-headed giants whom Corylus had fought when he fled with the Singiri princess, were advancing on Alphena and the Nubian dancers. Scores of them were visible already and more appeared with every breath at the misty edge of the vision.

Corylus considered the twisted little creature who had sent a young woman into the hands of monsters. His mind bubbled with cold anger.

"If you cannot return Lady Alphena to us . . . ," Pandareus said, ". . . can you send us to her?"

The teacher's clear, calm voice brought Corylus back to . . . not his senses, because he had never lost either awareness or control. Rather, it put him back in the mind of a scholar, or of a soldier. Not of a skin-clad barbarian looking for a chance to kill something because he was in a bad mood.

"What?" said the little man. "Of course. Or you can simply go, step into the image yourself. That's all that's required."

"Then if you will give me a hand, Master Corylus . . . ?" Pandareus said, putting his left foot on the lip of the basin—it was almost knee height above the floor—and holding out his right hand to his younger friend. He smiled.

Corylus smiled back as he mounted the lip, then braced the older man to stand beside him. The teacher's calm good sense made him a better companion in this business than any number of additional swordsmen would have been.

"Ready?" he said.

"But wait!" said the little man. "Do you have to—"

"Yes," said Pandareus. Together he and Corylus stepped into the vision of another world.

THE CLIFFS ON EITHER SIDE of the chasm glowed faintly red. The color put Hedia in mind of the magic Melino worked, but this was none of his doing.

The bridge they were crossing was very like the structure of cane over which the demon had led them into the Underworld in the beginning. This time the "floor" was a hawser of silk as thick as Hedia's thigh and the "handrail" was a wrist-thick silken cord. Whatever would the Serians who sent fine silk garments to Carce think of this *industrial* use of their luxury fabric?

Hedia walked without difficulty along the hawser. It didn't spring upward when her foot or the magician's lifted, though it always quivered with a high-pitched vibration of its own.

She kept her right hand above the lighter rope in case something unexpected happened. "Unexpected" in this place meant "even more horrible than everything else is." Hedia had decided that being ready to grab the handrail did not cause her to lose her dignity, or at least not an unacceptable amount of dignity.

Smiling wryly at the mental games she was playing with herself, Hedia said, "What is the name of this gorge, if you please?"

"Be silent, woman!" Melino said from immediately ahead of her. He didn't turn his head.

"The gorge has no human name, Hedia," said the demon, leading the procession. Her voice was emotionless, but Hedia was sure that there was a note of dry humor in the words. "No human who crossed it returned alive."

After a step and another step, the demon added, "Not all of them were alive to begin with, of course."

Hedia giggled. The situation wasn't funny—she had no doubt that the demon had stated the literal truth—but Hedia was amused at the way she and the demon were baiting Melino in response to his surly arrogance.

Hedia was used to men assuming they were her superiors, generally for no better reason than the fact they were men. She had never come to like the experience, however. She found the game she and the demon were playing to be deeply satisfying.

Hedia had kept her eyes trained along the course of the bridge in a conscious attempt to keep from looking downward. Movement drew her glance reflexively: something as large as a warship under sail had swept under them. She couldn't tell what it was, but she had the impression of scales rather than feathers.

"Nothing will attack you while you are with me," the demon volunteered. "If you fall from the bridge, something may catch you in the air. You will fall for a very long time unless that happens."

The magician hunched lower. He clutched the *Book* to his chest with his left arm but kept his right hand and the staff firmly over the upper line.

Hedia laughed. Speaking so that the demon could hear also, she said, "You should have been taught to walk gracefully the way I was, Master Melino. My teacher was Narcissus, the most esteemed pantomime in Carce during my childhood."

She lowered her right hand to her side. She was no longer afraid of falling. The echoing hiss she had noticed when they began crossing the gorge might come from water running somewhere in the depths, but in this place it might not be water; and it didn't matter anyway.

They had been walking uphill since before the winged thing flew under them: the hawser sagged under its own weight. Ahead of them were a gleaming metal arch and double doors of the same bright metal. Hedia thought it must be orichalc, but she couldn't be sure in this dim red light.

The demon halted in front of the doors. Melino moaned something, a prayer or perhaps merely a groan, and raised Zabulon's *Book*. The doors groaned inward even before the *Book* spoke.

White light flooded from the opening, turning the demon into a crimson silhouette of herself. She walked through the doorway; Melino followed; and Hedia, squinting so that she could see in the sudden brightness, followed also. Behind her the great metal valves closed with a sound like souls in torment.

They had entered a domed vault, flooded with light from the floor and the domed ceiling. Hedia couldn't be sure how big the space was because the material was so dazzling. It glittered like clear white sand, but at least what she was standing on was solid and as smooth as a bronze mirror.

They stopped twenty feet or so from the door by which they had entered. Hedia looked back, but the metal valves were lost in the light. At any rate, she couldn't see them.

Melino began to laugh. He was standing straighter now. Entering this place had given him back both strength and confidence.

"Now!" he said. "Who but I could have come here? We *can* return to the Waking World from this nexus. It will cost me the ring, but what of that if I have Zabulon's *Book?*"

He raised the *Book* in his left hand. Hedia looked at the magician sharply, considering what he had just said. The demon remained impassive.

Melino's lips moved. The *Book* rumbled a word. The vault and the world beyond trembled to the echo.

A vortex formed in what had been a solid crystal floor. It spread outward and downward, eating into the stone. Melino backed a step and knelt.

The demon did not move. "It is not the rock that is dissolving," she said, her eyes on Hedia's. "The Cosmos itself is dissolving in this place."

Hedia looked down. She had not retreated when Melino did, because the demon had remained where she had been standing. The edge of the cavity stopped just short of her toes. Though it continued to expand away from her, they were in no more immediate danger than they had been when they entered the huge chamber.

At the bottom of the slanting pit was a flickering point of light, blue and so intense that Hedia's head jerked back reflexively from its impact. She felt as though shards of ice had been jabbed into both her pupils. Her head ached, and she saw floating orange afterimages even after she massaged her eyes with the heels of her hands. Her vision cleared slowly.

The magician had knelt, supporting part of his weight on the staff, after the *Book* spoke. He didn't get to his feet yet, but his features were still animated and his face hadn't lost its color as it had when he used the powerful spells in the past. This light-filled cavern strengthened him or at least made his recovery quicker.

"He will smash the ruby," the demon said, speaking to Hedia. "Then he will order me into the Underworld unprotected; and I will obey, because he is my master. My agony will anchor the spell which he speaks through Zabulon's *Book*. It will open his passage to the Waking World. His passage and yours."

Hedia looked at Melino. He took the ruby ring from his left hand and placed it on the crystal floor in front of him, then lifted himself upright with his right hand on the staff.

She had started to say, "Is that true?" but the demon hadn't lied— couldn't lie?—yet and there was nothing in what she had said that didn't fit with Melino's previous behavior.

"Stop," Hedia said. "We can't do that. She's one of us."

"What?" said Melino, looking more dumbfounded than angry. "Are you insane?"

He positioned the butt of his staff over the ruby and prepared to bring it down. The blow would shatter the jewel into dust. The demon watched.

"No!" said Hedia. She bent and snatched the ring away with her left hand. "She's one of *us*!"

"You slut!" Melino said. "Well, your pain will do as well as hers!"

He stepped toward Hedia with the staff crossways, pushing her toward the edge of the pit. She tried to claw his eyes. He blocked her with the *Book* in his left hand.

I'm going over, Hedia thought. She was beyond fear. *This is how life ends.*

The demon's lips moved. Zabulon's *Book* boomed a word that froze time. A force set Hedia back on the crystal floor.

Melino screamed in sudden awareness. Spinning, he plunged into the tunnel he had opened into the Underworld.

Hedia didn't follow him with her eyes—she remembered the pain of her first ignorant glance—but the screams continued as though they would never stop. She swallowed. The demon was watching her with a slight smile.

"What do I do now?" Hedia said, knowing that she was on the edge of more than a passage to eternal torment.

"Whatever you wish, mistress," the demon said. "Zabulon's *Book* gives you all power."

"I want to go back to the Waking World!" Hedia said. "But I can't; I'm not a magician. I can't use this—"

She hefted the *Book.*

"—because I can't work magic!"

"Then it's fortunate, mistress . . . ," the demon said with the same cold smile as before. "That your servant *can* work magic."

Her expression changed slightly. Hedia remembered Melino saying that the demon had no emotions. She had thought him a fool to believe that. *A fool indeed, and now a damned fool.*

"There are other ways to focus a spell than by agony," the demon said. "But agony is fitting, since that was the method my former master preferred."

Her lips moved silently. The *Book* in Hedia's hand opened and thundered a word.

Melino's screams redoubled, seemingly louder than if he were standing beside them instead of by now far below. The pit slowly began to close as a similar cavity rotated into the wall of the chamber behind Hedia.

She looked at the ring in her left palm. "Demon, what do you want?" she said.

The demon had no expression. "My will is your will, mistress," she said.

"Hecate strike you barren!" Hedia shouted in frustration. "My will is that you tell me where you want to be! Do you want to remain in this place? What do *you* want?"

"If the ring that protects me were dropped into the Underworld," the demon said, "then it would keep me safe from the rigors of that place; and there I would be safe also from magicians of the Waking World who would use me for their ends. But I have no will but your will."

"Then go!" said Hedia, and hurled the ring into the pit. The demon's form sucked into the ruby like a wisp of smoke an instant before the ground closed over it.

The *Book* spoke again. Hedia stood on packed red sand. The sun was rising. It was already bright enough to dispel the chill fog that had come in from the sea.

CHAPTER XVI

Hedia's first thought was, *This isn't Carce. Why did the demon send me here?*

Her second thought was that she was back in Atlantis—from which she had escaped either weeks ago or eleven thousand years ago, according to the figure Master Pandareus had given for when the island had been destroyed.

But this wasn't Atlantis. At least it wasn't Poseidonis, the capital where Hedia had been imprisoned, and the distant black cliffs cutting the bay off from the interior of the land were nothing like the Atlantean terrain she had seen.

The ruins she stood among, though, were unquestionably Atlantean: crystal pillars worn to a rough milky texture, and even bits of orichalc that must have come from the swags and finials of the buildings. The remains were being engulfed by the coarse red sand that now filled the bowl within the rocky hills.

The other side—the west side—was surf drifting lazily from a sea without apparent end. Hedia had no way of knowing how far the water stretched, but in her heart she was sure that this was Ocean: the great stream that circled the rim of the world.

She smiled faintly. At any rate, the sea was as uninviting as the rough black rocks to the east. Tufts of knee-high grass sprouted from the sand dunes, but the rocks had no vegetation that she could see. Perhaps if she got close enough, she would find lichen in some of the cracks and on shaded surfaces.

Occasionally driftwood stuck out of the sand where the surf had deposited it. There were branches and whole tree trunks, and once there was a curved timber that might have been the keel of a ship.

Hedia's smile became colder still. An old wreck was no more helpful than the trunk of a palm tree. Reefs streaked the sea with foam for as far out as she could see. She didn't imagine that a ship could reach this shore safely though them. She had thought that this might have been a port, but no vessels—

Hedia grimaced with sudden realization. She wondered why she hadn't seen the obvious immediately. No *seagoing* ship could reach this place, but the ships of Atlantis flew through the air. This had been a colony, protected on both the land and water sides.

The Atlanteans spoke Greek, and it seemed that like the Greeks they had sent colonies to distant shores. This had been such a settlement. Though it had not been caught in the destruction of its motherland, it could not survive long by itself in this inhospitable place.

Something was moving along the line of surf. A dog? Or perhaps a shaggy brown wolf with vertical stripes. It was prowling the margin, making occasional snaps into the water and tossing whatever it had caught higher up the beach, then pouncing on it. Fish, Hedia supposed, or more likely crabs, when she thought about it. The dog was big enough to be dangerous if it wanted to be, but for the moment it seemed to be as harmless as the gulls screaming overhead.

Thirst and starvation were more likely to kill her than the dog. If nothing else happened, thirst and starvation were certain to kill her.

Why did the demon send me here? I was better off in the Otherworld!

But that wasn't true, as she knew as soon as the words formed in her mind. She would rather die in the Waking World than live for however long in the Otherworld. For that matter, from what she had seen of the other denizens of that place, "however long" was likely to have been a very short time.

It was still surprising that the demon, whom Hedia had considered an ally and perhaps a friend, would have sent her here. Well, there was no reason to expect that a human being would find a demon's humor to be funny or even survivable.

The sand at her feet wriggled. A breeze she couldn't feel? She looked down; a bright lizard eye looked up at her for an instant before vanishing. The ripple continued down the face of the dune as the lizard burrowed away.

Hedia looked about the ancient ruins and considered her choices. She had only the clothes she wore and Zabulon's *Book*. The clothes were of sturdy construction, but they were already considerably the worse for the time she had spent hiking through the Otherworld.

Though—thank Venus!—she had learned from previous experience and was wearing garments that were appropriate for hiking across a wasteland. Or, better, thank her own common sense.

As for the *Book* . . . it was of no more use to her than her gold bead earrings, the only jewelry she had worn when she went to meet Melino in the guise of a commoner. Even her maid Syra wore earrings, though they were merely gilded iron. She might just as well set the *Book* on one of the fallen pillars. A loaf of bread would have been much more valuable.

Still, the *Book* wasn't heavy enough to be a real burden. If she kept it, there was always the possibility that someone would offer to trade her a loaf of bread for it.

Hedia carried a little knife hidden in her sash. At the moment she saw no better use for it than to open a vein when thirst grew unbearably oppressive. Still, the knife had saved her life—and had taken lives—in the past; it might do so again.

She had been facing the sea, watching her shadow on the sand shrink as the sun rose higher. She turned, wondering if there was a path eastward that she had missed earlier: to safety or at least to life.

Something shimmered in the air near a block that might once have been the sacrificial altar standing before a temple. For a moment, Hedia thought she was seeing a mirage; then she realized that real figures were forming out of the air.

Her hand reached into her sash.

ALPHENA, GRIPPING THE IDOL in her left hand and the sword hilt in her right, stood in a plain of wild oats, waist high in the sunlight. A few thorn trees were the only green vegetation visible in the sea of russet grass. A mile or so to the north was an escarpment of bare rock climbing by a series of steps to a considerable height.

The Daughters of the Mind sat resting on a knob where the stunted oats were no more than a palm's breadth above the ground. Alphena guessed that there was a boulder buried under such a thin layer of soil that the grass didn't get enough moisture to grow to normal height.

The Daughters rose when she appeared. The Egg was a glowing presence in the center of their group, throbbing with light that didn't color even the ground that should have been shaded by its presence.

This was the first time Alphena had seen the Egg directly rather than in a vision of some sort. She couldn't focus on it; she couldn't guess how large it was or even *where* it was. The women stood within six feet of one another, but the Egg seemed to be much farther away—farther even than the cliffs to the north.

"Greetings, sister," the Daughters said. They spoke together, their words as perfectly synchronized as those of the chorus of a mime. Alphena heard Latin, spoken with an upper-class accent, but the movements of their lips didn't match the sounds. "We are pleased to have your company, but you should know that you are in great danger so long as you are near us."

"Two Singiri visited us recently," the Daughters said. As before, all three spoke, but what Alphena heard was in a different trio of voices. "They were killed by those who wish to kill us."

"They were killed by the Ethiopes," the Daughters said in a third voice. "The same who killed King Ganges and who wish to destroy the Egg which we guard."

Alphena heard—or rather felt—a humming. It might have been coming from the Egg, but she couldn't understand *anything* about the Egg.

"The Singiri who visited the Daughters were students, come to learn," said First. "They stayed to fight the Ethiopes instead of returning to their people. As they could have done."

Students like my brother and Publius Corylus, Alphena thought. *But lizardmen.*

"The Singiri said they wanted to learn from us," the Daughters said in unison. "But we have nothing to teach. They were brave, though."

In a different voice they added, "Are you a student, sister?"

Alphena swallowed. "No," she said. "No, I'm not. But I have a sword, and I hope I'm brave. As brave as a lizardman, anyway."

The wooden idol laughed. One of the Daughters looked at him.

Together they said, "Greetings, First. I hope you have kept well since we left you?"

"Very well indeed, children," the idol said. "My new worshiper has fed me and will feed me again. You need not be concerned about her courage."

At the base of the northern bluffs, red sparks crackled into an arch of rosy light. A man came through it—the priest Paris, whom Alphena had followed into the tomb and by stages to this place.

Paris stepped aside. Ethiopes followed him through the portal one after another. They loped through the oat grass, holding their weapons. Alphena watched, wondering if there was an end to their numbers or if the horse-headed giants would continue to appear for as long as there was something for them to kill.

She took a deep breath. She had to die somewhere, sometime. Perhaps here she could make a difference. A minuscule difference.

The three women resumed their high-stepping dance around the Egg. Alphena could hear their chant, now: *"The most ancient of things is God, the uncreated."*

"Go on," Alphena said. "I'll hold them for as long as I can."

First laughed again. "Not yet, little worshiper," he said. "Take us with you, Daughters—one time more. *Then* I will feed."

The women made no response, but Alphena felt darkness close off the world. She could see nothing, not even the sword and the idol that she held in front of her.

Nothing but the Egg, spinning in the infinite distance.

"The swiftest of things is Mind," chanted the Daughters of the Wind. *"For it speeds everywhere."*

CORYLUS WAS BRACED to step into the high grass in which Alphena had been standing when he looked down on the vision in the basin. Instead he was on coarse red sand in the midst of wind-worn crystalline blocks that seemed to have been part of buildings in the distant past.

One environment wasn't better than the other—though perhaps these packed sands would be firmer footing for a swordsman than grass, which might hide gopher holes or the roots of shrubs. He was shocked not to be where he had expected to be, however. The unexpected was always a jolt when you were in hostile territory . . . which this certainly was, despite the presence of Alphena, the dancers whom the little man called the Daughters of the Mind, and Hedia.

Hedia being here was an even greater surprise to Corylus than it was to find himself standing in a mountain-fringed half bowl on the shore of a great sea. She looked worse for wear, as he had seen her in the past at moments of crisis. This time her tunics were whole, though muddy and plucked into tufts by thorns, and she was wearing sturdy sandals.

She was also carrying a book, a black-leather codex. Corylus wasn't sure that he had ever seen Hedia holding a book before. She looked calm and unruffled, disdainful, in fact, of the situation in which she found herself.

Jupiter! What a commander of a legion she would make. Especially for a legion which was facing ten times its number of howling barbarians!

"My goodness," Pandareus said. "Surely these are Atlantean ruins! Do you suppose there are Atlantean settlements which might still survive? On the coast of Lusitania, perhaps?"

Hedia gave him a cold smile. "I'm more concerned with our own chances of survival, Master Pandareus," she said. "Which I don't rate as very high at the moment."

"First brought me here because I asked him," Alphena said. "I didn't know you were coming, Mother. Or y-you, Publius Corylus." She swallowed, looking upset.

Corylus scanned the rocks that formed a distant rampart for the enemies who he was sure were coming. He had come seeking his friend's sister in order to get her back to the Waking World, which now seemed to be impossible. He wasn't interested in what the girl thought or wished or wondered.

"Who is First, Daughter?" Hedia said. From the approving look Pandareus gave her, he would have asked the same question if Hedia had not.

"First—," said the carved wooden cudgel in Alphena's hand, making Corylus jump and breaking his concentration on hidden enemies, "—is the god whom Lady Alphena worships. If you are wise, you will become my worshipers as well."

"First, when we return to Carce," Hedia said, "I will ask my husband to build you a temple commensurate with the assistance you have been to my daughter and to the rest of us. If you return us to Carce immediately, we will build you a temple as large as that of Jupiter Best and Greatest."

Pandareus looked puzzled. "Would the Emperor allow a private citizen to do that, Master Corylus?" he asked in an undertone.

Corylus didn't know whether to slap the scholar to silence or hug him in delight. Facing probable death in an unfamiliar place, Pandareus was focused on the minutiae of a negotiation. And if Varus were here, he would have had the same first concern.

Surely the human race was of some merit if it included individuals who were more concerned with the truth than they were with their lives or anything else. More concerned with truth than with the continued existence of life on earth.

Corylus chuckled. Everyone looked at him. He said to Pandareus in a normal tone, "Not everyone would share my appreciation of your quest for absolute truth, master."

"What?" Pandareus said. "Oh, I see what you mean. I'm very sorry; I wasn't thinking about, well, where we are."

"I came here to defend the Daughters against Paris and his Ethiopes," Alphena said, speaking loudly and with deliberate clarity. "Because I couldn't go home, I mean. I was going to fight them so that the Daughters can escape again, because if the Ethiopes destroy the Egg they're caring for, the world will end."

She was blushing. Alphena was young and not particularly cultured, but she must have realized that what she was saying sounded exactly like a boastful senator extolling his courage upon his return from a lackluster campaign.

The carved stick in her hand laughed like crows cackling. First said, "The Daughters have stopped running, little worshiper. They will meet Paris in this place. The priest and his savages cannot harm the Egg; not even the Worms can harm the Egg. But the Worms which Paris loosed will devour all things on the surface of this Earth, and there will be no one to summon the Egg when it must hatch."

Corylus saw light moving at the edge of the surrounding escarpment. It was reddish, the wrong color to be sunlight reflected from black rock. As he by now expected, the glitter formed itself into an arch of light. The priest Paris stepped through it.

Ethiopes shambled after him. Their uncouth forms had become as familiar to Corylus as the antelopes that were regularly butchered in the arena of Carce. He visualized archers protected by a grill shooting arrow after arrow into the horse-headed creatures, laying their corpses in windrows on the sand.

Corylus didn't frequent the arena—he'd seen too much of slaughter done for real on the frontier—but he might make an exception for that event. It wasn't going to happen, though; and even if it did, he wasn't likely to be around to watch it.

"Well," he said to his companions. "Whether or not these women intend to flee—"

He nodded toward the Daughters.

"—it appears to me that Lady Alphena's plan of fighting the Ethiopes is better than any alternative I can come up with."

He had sheathed his sword when he and Pandareus found themselves among friends. He drew it again and walked toward the oncoming Ethiopes. He didn't want to slash one of his companions if he cut broadly in the violence of the moment. Not that it would matter for anything but the very shortest time: the time it would take for more Ethiopes to lumber past his body and massacre all the other humans present.

Corylus heard commotion behind him. Varus had just dived into their midst from *somewhere*. It pleased Corylus to see that his friend tucked his head under and rolled to his feet instead of sprawling full length as he would have done before they started practicing gymnastics together in Saxa's private exercise ground.

The Ethiopes were getting closer. They were as inexorable as the sea, and like the sea they would grind down all before them.

VARUS WAS SO PROUD of his perfect tuck-and-roll that it was several heartbeats before he realized that not only had he joined his sister and mother, as he expected, but Corylus and Pandareus were present as well. "Master!" he said in delight. "I'm very glad to see you. I've so often in the past days—"

Has it been "days" in the Waking World? Are we in the Waking World now?

"—wished you could see what I was seeing!"

"I'm sure we both have things to tell the other about," Pandareus said, beaming in obvious pleasure. "Although—"

He looked up at the Ethiopes, still a mile away. They were spreading to left and right as they approached, obviously planning to come at the humans from all the land sides.

Varus couldn't imagine why they were bothering to be so careful. Did they—or the Etruscan priest who commanded them—think that any of this group were going to run for the hills?

"—it seems unlikely that we'll have time to discuss matters. I suppose under the circumstances I shouldn't even name her. I'm pleased to see you, Lord Varus."

Varus shrugged. He said, "From what I've been told"—by the Sibyl, though he didn't say that aloud—"if we don't save these Daughters of the Mind—"

He gestured like the orator Pandareus had trained him to be.

"—the Worms will wipe all life from the Earth. I would prefer to be with friends if that happens."

As it seems very probable that it will, though he didn't say that aloud, either. He was scarcely the only one having the thought, however.

The Daughters seemed unconcerned about what was going on, though they watched the Ethiopes with the interest one might give to the entrance of unusual animals into the arena. Pandareus looked in their direction and said, "I can't see the Egg clearly. I wonder whether it has material existence or if it exists only as an idea, as Plato speculated."

One of the Daughters smiled at him. All three said, "The Egg is real, master."

"But it is not in this world until the time comes for it to hatch," the women continued in a different voice.

"If we die," they said in a third voice yet, "then it will never hatch. But the world will be no more, so there will be no purpose for the Egg."

"When I heard you chanting before . . . ," Varus said. He directed his comment to the Nubian women out of courtesy, but he was really speaking for the benefit of his teacher. "You were quoting Thales."

"Of all things, the most ancient is God," the Daughters said. The two looking in his direction were smiling. "Thales visited us, friend. But he did not teach *us.*"

Varus tightened his lips in embarrassment. "I was reversing causation, master," he said to Pandareus.

"An easy mistake to make under stress," the scholar said. "And *I'm* certainly feeling stressed."

Varus looked in the direction of the Ethiopes. His sister and Corylus had moved ten feet out from the rest of the group. Alphena put a fallen pillar behind her. It was worn to a milky spindle that only memory suggested had been six feet in diameter and as clear as the sea at Baiae.

"I suppose I could throw rocks at the Ethiopes," Varus said. "Judging from my performance in ball games in the baths, I'm afraid that I'd be more likely to hit a friend, though."

"Do you suppose our enemies there are the reason Herodotus refers to Ethiopians as wearing horse skulls as helmets?" Pandareus said.

Varus felt a surge of fellowship. He and his teacher were scholars. Though they might not be able to prevent their own slaughter, neither did fear of death keep them from being scholars.

"According to the Sibyl," he said, "these horse-headed savages were wiped out when the Singiri left this world long ago. I thought perhaps that the Ethiopians of Herodotus' day may have adopted the fashion from legends they preserved."

Pandareus chuckled. "It is an honor to have been your teacher, Lord Varus," he said. "And now to be your colleague."

Hedia had been looking in the direction of Paris. He was walking toward them behind the first few hundred or so Ethiopes. Grimacing, she stepped to Varus and his teacher.

"Your pardon for interrupting, Master Pandareus," she said. "I need to speak to my son."

She held out the codex she was carrying, using both hands now that the ironbound weight wasn't cradled against her body. "I think this will be of more use to you than to me, Varus," she said. "I'm told that it is Zabulon's *Book*."

HEDIA RUBBED HER LEFT BICEPS, feeling the hard weight of the *Book* now that she had passed it off to someone who might possibly have some use for it. She would have given it to Varus immediately on his appearance if she hadn't simply forgotten that she was holding it. Quite a lot was going on.

She had gone to a great deal of effort to get the *Book,* so it was good that it had gone to someone who would appreciate it. She and Melino together had invested effort, to be accurate. She thought of Melino with some regret, but only for what he had turned out to be. She didn't regret the end his behavior had brought him to.

Things that had happened recently suggested that Varus was a magician of some sort, though Hedia hadn't had any inkling of such interests on his part in the past. His father—poor dear Saxa!—had made quite a production of studying what he called the Hidden Arts and what Hedia called being fleeced by every mystical charlatan who passed through Carce. She had been mildly irritated by that: Saxa was a sweet man who didn't deserve to be taken advantage of.

But then Saxa had become involved with a real magician, and that was *much* worse. That was very nearly the end of the world . . . and the world was not safe yet. This present business was all part of what had started then.

Hedia sniffed. This might very well end it. Not in the fashion she would have wished, but a woman living in a man's world learns quickly that her wishes rarely matter to anyone else.

She looked fondly at Varus. Whether or not he could use a book of magic, he certainly was the proper custodian for a book. That was particularly true if these were his last moments and heralded the end of life on earth.

As for Alphena . . . Hedia glanced toward the girl, standing ten feet away from Corylus and constituting with him the entire defenses of the party. In all likelihood, the entire defenses of the life on earth.

Gaius Alphenus Saxa had known what Hedia was when he asked her to marry him. All Carce knew what Hedia was: she was notorious. All that she had promised was that she would be a dutiful wife and a mother to his children. She took her duties as seriously as any of the famous women of ancient Carce had taken theirs.

There was little she could do for Varus, but boys were relatively easy. Varus was intelligent and had no bad habits; his bookishness was probably his worst flaw, but Hedia was too wise to imagine that she could cure him of that. His friendship with Corylus was the best antidote she could imagine against the risk of the boy becoming a humorless prig with no companions save his books.

Alphena was a more difficult problem. She was just as strong willed as her brother, and her personality was even more different from Hedia's. If the girl had been a tramp, it would have affected the kind of marriage Hedia could make for her. If Alphena got a reputation for being a man wearing a woman's body, though, it would make marriage within her class almost impossible. Even well-born spendthrifts otherwise lured by a large dowry would shy away from becoming laughingstocks.

She smiled wryly. It appeared that the girl's unladylike interest in swordsmanship was more of a benefit than not; and marriage didn't appear to be in her future, either.

Hedia sighed. Alphena *wasn't* boyish; she was just rebellious and athletic. At some level she had probably decided to be the son Varus was not, out of a kind of family pride. Family pride was something that Hedia understood very well.

Corylus twisted as though someone had grasped the side of his tunic. A lizardman—the old one whom Hedia had seen caged in the dealer's yard in Puteoli—appeared beside him.

Hedia picked up a block of crystal at her feet: a chip broken from a pillar when it fell against the base of another pillar. It was worn more or less round, and was just of a size for her to grip firmly in her right hand.

Three more Singiri stepped into sight. Corylus clasped the old one's left hand with his own instead of attacking. "Tassk!" he cried. "I wasn't expecting *you*!"

Hedia didn't exactly relax, but she felt a marginally positive change in her attitude. The lizardmen had been Melino's enemies, but that didn't necessarily mean they were *her* enemies—or Mankind's.

"The Princess gave you a link of chain, Lord Corylus," the old lizardman said. "So that you could come to us, she said; and that is true. But the chain connects at both ends."

Tassk spoke better Latin than most of the servants in Saxa's household did. He slurred his words slightly, but no worse than guests midway into the drinking after a dinner party.

He, the leader, was naked except for the bits of hardware that he had worn in the cage. His three younger companions might be the same individuals who were his fellow prisoners at that time, but now they wore dark bronze body armor and carried curved swords. They had small shields of bronze also; one of them carried an extra shield.

Alphena seemed just as surprised as Hedia—or as Corylus himself, come to that. Hedia walked toward the group, leaving Varus and his teacher with the Daughters. She didn't see much point in standing with them, so she might as well learn what their defenders—the ones with swords—were discussing.

"But what are you doing *here?*" Alphena said, coming immediately to what Hedia thought was the real point.

"Our princess thought that a few warriors might be of service to Lord Corylus, little one," Tassk said. "Though she was concerned that he might be embarrassed to accept help."

"I'm the son of a soldier," Corylus said with a snort. "I've never seen an army that was too big to win a battle, and I'm *sure* not worried about that being a problem now."

A younger lizardman had been staring at Alphena. He said something to Tassk in a language of clicks and sibilants, still looking at the girl. Hedia moved closer to her daughter, suddenly reminded of the rock in her hands.

Tassk bowed to Alphena and said, "My colleague has noted that you and the older female—"

He dipped his head to acknowledge Hedia. The motion was more sideways than up and down, as though his spine differed from that of a human being.

"—visited us when we waited in the port. As did the two males who are not warriors, I believe. We do not know what their purpose is in this place."

"At the moment," Hedia said, "our purpose appears to be waiting for slaughter by those Ethiopes."

"I do not know the future, honored lady," the old lizardman said. His little finger—the Singiri had four, not five, fingers and toes—pointed in the direction of Hedia's block of crystal. His forked tongue lolled out in the expression that Hedia had thought in Puteoli was laughter. "But I honor your spirit."

The lizardman with two shields tossed one to Corylus, who caught it by the crossbar handle. Tassk said, "I'm sorry I did not think to bring a shield for your young companion, Lord Corylus."

The club named First made a rude noise. "My worshiper has no need for a metal plate which doesn't care if it's fed or not. *I* will appreciate her offerings."

I'm not sure that's an adequate reason to reject a proper shield, Hedia thought. But Alphena was a better judge of weapons than her mother was, and the shield wasn't available anyway.

Corylus glanced from the Singiri to the Ethiopes, then back again. The leading enemy was only about a furlong, six hundred and some feet, away.

"Master," he said. "I suggest that we wait till the leading beasts have come three-quarters of the way toward us, then rush them and kill the first dozen or so. Then retreat to here. It's what a squad of Batavian Scouts would do with a straggling column of Sarmatians."

"My princess sent us here to aid you, not to command you, warrior," Tassk said. He spoke in rapid syllables to the others. In acknowledgment, each ticked the boss of his shield with the flat of his sword.

To Corylus Tassk added, "We are pleased that you are willing to accept our aid."

Corylus grinned broadly. "There are no men of any race," he said, "whom I would rather have with me in this business than you and your warriors."

Tassk translated that to his fellows. One of them responded. Tassk said to Corylus, "He says that since he saw you use your sword in defending the Princess, he is willing to accept that you are a man also. As for me, I will stand with the old one."

He flicked his little finger toward Pandareus. "It is good for aged men to have companions."

"It's about time to open the proceedings," said Corylus. "Alphena—Lady Alphena? I'd appreciate it if you kept close to me."

Alphena nodded and walked behind the three Singiri warriors who were spreading to the left. She gave Hedia a glance with no obvious meaning in it.

Venus aid you, Daughter, Hedia thought. Her face showed nothing, either.

The Etruscan priest had halted in the ruins of a small, round building, probably a temple, a tholos. It might never have had a roof. In any case, all that remained now were the bases of six columns. He was chanting.

Hedia eyed Paris and eyed the Ethiopes. Corylus' attack would probably draw those who had slanted off to encircle the humans back to the direct line of approach. Hedia balanced the rock in her hand and started walking in a curving course. It would take her to the tholos if nothing intervened.

ALPHENA WAS FRIGHTENED. Not of death or injury, at least not those things at the top of her mind. What concerned her was that she would be fighting at the side of Corylus and three Singiri and that they would be depending on her to keep her end up.

Even without the respect Corylus showed the Singiri warriors, Alphena could see by the way they moved that they were veterans. Though the five defenders didn't have a chance of success against the Ethiopes—even the ones already present—she didn't want to let down her friends and allies as her last act in life.

"You needn't worry," First said in a rasping, cheerful voice. "With you as my helper, worshiper, we will amaze them all. Amaze them! Oh, I will drink *so* much blood!"

Alphena blushed to hear the bragging. It was like listening to gladiators before a bout.

"Don't talk like that," she said in a low whisper. It was so *plebeian*! What if Corylus should hear?

Alphena glanced at her mother, who was walking away from the group. Was she going off to die alone?

Alphena felt a flash of insight: *I'm as much a lady as Hedia is. I don't want to be a gladiator; I just want to have the* right *to become a gladiator. I'm a lady of Carce and I should have the right to do* anything!

First's ugly face twisted upward. The shell eyes were looking at Alphena, and the iron tongue quivered with laughter. "That's not a very enlightened view, my worshiper. What would your philosopher friend think of it?"

"I don't care what Pandareus thinks!" Alphena snapped. As the words came out, she knew that they weren't true: she respected the scholar, though it would be hard to imagine a human being with whom she had less in common.

"And anyway, Varus feels the same way I do," she added, defensively, though with more truth. "He just wants different things. *He* doesn't want to plow fields or whatever plebeians do!"

"You are my worshiper, little one," First said through gales of grunting laughter. "Why should I care what you do with those who do not worship me? Cut the throats of all of them if you like, so long as you feed me their blood!"

The nearest Ethiope was still two hundred feet from the point at which Corylus had said he would order the defenders to attack. She risked looking over her shoulder.

The Daughters were chanting again. This time the words Alphena heard were, *"Of all things, Time is the wisest, for it brings everything to light."*

The old lizardman and Pandareus squatted on their haunches, facing each other. They seemed to be chatting. Varus had walked closer to the Daughters, holding the book that Hedia had given him.

The Egg was brighter and sharper than Alphena remembered seeing it before, but she still wasn't sure how far away it was. Even more than before she had the impression that it was spinning very quickly, faster than motes of dust in a windstorm.

"The Daughters are trying to bring the Egg into the Waking World so that it will hatch," the idol said. "But they are the Egg's servants, not magicians. They will not be able to hatch the Egg before its time."

"But the Egg will be safe where it is, won't it?" Alphena said. "The Ethiopes won't be able to smash it, will they?"

"The Ethiopes cannot harm the Egg," First said. "But when it *is* time for the Egg to hatch, there will be no Earth for it to hatch onto."

Then, in a softer, almost wistful voice, First said, "I will drink well today. But when the Worms of the Earth come, I will perish as all things will perish, for the Worms have no blood. But that will be a later time. Now I will feast."

"Ready!" Corylus called. Alphena faced around.

VARUS SHADED HIS EYES as he watched the Ethiopes advance from the east. It would be very hot on this shore soon, though he and his companions would probably be dead before the heat became oppressive. He wondered how the Atlantean settlers had dealt with the problem.

He didn't know what he ought to be doing. Everyone else appeared to have a purpose. Hedia was walking away from the main group. Varus couldn't imagine what she had in mind, but he understood his mother too well to doubt that she was planning *something*.

Even Pandareus watched the proceedings with bright enthusiasm for new information and new experiences. He was focused on learning: the use of what he learned and the length of time he survived to savor it weren't his concerns.

I'm not enough of a scholar myself to take that attitude, Varus thought. The teacher's greater age was part of the difference but, on reflection, not the whole of it.

Pandareus was the son of a successful farmer on Melos, an island noted to history only because the Athenians had massacred its entire male population five centuries earlier. By contrast, Varus was the heir of one of the greatest families in Carce, a city that through the drive and determination of its citizens had risen from rural obscurity to rule most of the known world. He and Pandareus were equal in intelligence and in their love of learning, but differing heritages shaped their attitudes.

The leader of the Singiri, Tassk, wasn't facing the Ethiopes with his fellows. He approached Pandareus, nodded politely to Varus, and said, "Since both of us are too old to fight, master, I wonder if you would help me with a spell?"

"A spell?" said Pandareus. "I'm not a magician, I'm afraid. Perhaps you were thinking of my colleague here, Lord Varus?"

"Lord Varus has more important business than the small things that old men can accomplish," Tassk said, flicking his forked black tongue toward Varus. *I suppose that's a friendly acknowledgment.*

"I am not a magician, either, merely an old warrior who has learned certain sounds," Tassk continued. "But if you can repeat sounds after me, our voices may be able to help where our limbs no longer can."

"My limbs never could have helped, I'm afraid," said Pandareus, smiling. "But sounds are another matter. I am pleased to join you, Master Tassk."

They squatted facing each other. Tassk began to speak syllables that sounded to Varus like chickens settling in for the night. After he completed a phrase by flicking his little finger, Pandareus repeated it with a skilled orator's ear for inflection.

Varus presumed they were speaking words, though not in the Singiri language and not necessarily in the language of any living thing. He grimaced, wondering what Tassk meant by the "important business" that Lord Varus had, since at this moment the most important thing Varus appeared to be doing was casting a shadow on the sand.

The fog was growing thicker. It was a moment before Varus realized that this was not the sea mist that must drench this coast nightly. He was drifting out of the Waking World into the Sibyl's realm, while hundreds of murderous half men poured down on him and his companions.

Varus smiled in his dream vision as he started up the familiar trail. He would do the cause of his friends and humanity just as much good if his soul were here as if it were in his physical body at the moment it was smashed with a stone axe.

The climb seemed steeper than on some previous occasions, and the shapes half-glimpsed through the fog were threatening even if they were only odd-shaped rocks. He wondered if he would feel pain if his psychic body was devoured by the elephantine creature with the head of a lion that seemed to be watching him as he passed.

If the situation arises, I will try to be philosophical, he thought, and smiled more broadly. He was sure that his friend Corylus would face such a death with perfect courage, but he might not find as much humor in the prospect as Varus did.

The Sibyl was sitting on a bench cut from coarse volcanic tuff, much like the seat Varus had seen in what was called the Grotto of the Sibyl in Cumae. He had always suspected that the grotto was of recent construction, but perhaps he did the current priesthood an injustice.

"Greetings, Lord Magician," the Sibyl said. He thought she was smiling, but her wrinkled face had any expression the viewer thought he should see.

"Greetings, Sibyl," Varus said, looking down the other side of the ridge, toward the half bowl in which his body and his companions waited for death. Foreshortened and viewed from such an apparent distance, the Ethiopes looked like a column of ants swarming from their nest. "You have said that you are a creation of my mind. What will happen to you when my body dies there below?"

The Sibyl cackled. "Not all men die, Lord Magician," she said. "Perhaps you will be one of those who never die."

"Like Tithonous?" Varus said bitterly, thinking of the wrinkled grub to which the Dawn's lover had shrunk because she gave him eternal life but not eternal youth. "That's a myth."

"Or like Herakles, who became a god," the Sibyl said. "What is myth, Lord Magician? Can there be no truth in myth?"

"I'm not Herakles," Varus said curtly. He was embarrassed to have implied that it was a fact that myths were meaningless rather than that he *believed* they were meaningless. That was bad logic, though he still believed he was correct in his assumption.

He could see the Egg more clearly than his physical eyes had done in the Waking World. It wasn't spinning as he had thought, but something was moving inside the translucent shell. It cast sparkles of light like an array of polished jewels.

The Sibyl gestured toward the mountains forming the alcove. Varus followed her hand.

The sky changed. Two huge crystal forms, the Worms of the Earth, writhed beyond the black rocks, gnawing at something unseen. The beams of the rising sun passed through them unimpeded, but their bodies blazed with a foul internal light.

"They are not of the Waking World," said the Sibyl. "Yet. But the magician Paris will break the barrier soon."

"But why?" Varus said. "He'll die too, won't he? Won't everyone die?"

"His Etruscan tribe had its time in the world," said the Sibyl. "But that time is past. He knows he cannot return his people to greatness, and he chooses to destroy all men and all life rather than accept that reality."

She laughed again. "The Etruscans were never as great as he imagines," she said. "I well remember when their scouts reached the valley of the Tiber and found my kinsman Evander already there. But the destruction he envisages, that is real enough."

Paris raised both arms as though praying to the mid-sky. To Varus' present eyes, a ghost image of the round temple surrounded the Etruscan priest.

The sky cracked. The Worms, each a river of living crystal, flowed through. Plumes of dust rose from the desert beyond the black rocks as they began to eat their way toward the Egg. In the basin, Corylus was leading his band of defenders into the oncoming Ethiopes.

"Then I will be with my friends when that happens," Varus said.

"Let the blessed man come down from the expanses of Heaven!" cried the Sibyl.

Varus staggered as his spirit returned to his body. He could already see the glittering backs of the Worms above the surrounding cliffs; the shouts of the fighters came to him over the sea breeze.

The Daughters were chanting. Suddenly aware of what he should do, Varus walked toward them, holding the *Book* in his left hand.

It fluttered open by itself. All sound ceased. The Daughters became faint shadows as though Varus saw them from within a globe of smoky quartz. With him were the Egg, brilliant now, and, across the Egg from Varus, a slender female member of the Singiri.

"I am Princess of the Singiri," she said, speaking Latin with perfect inflection. "Your friend the warrior Corylus saved me from torture. If you are willing, Lord Magician, I will help you save him and save your world, though it is no longer our world."

"Your help is very welcome, Princess," Varus said, remembering how Corylus had accepted the help of the Singiri warriors. He raised the *Book* a little higher.

The *Book* thundered words in two separate voices. The world beyond the globe shuddered with their power.

CORYLUS HAD PLANNED to launch his sally when the leading Ethiope reached a particular protea growing about a quarter furlong in front of him. The plant was a clutch of fat green leaves on top of a stem that rose knee-high from the sand: it even looked like a marker flag.

The straggling Ethiope column plodded forward, reminding Corylus of a line of Sarmatian ox wagons rather than a squadron of cavalry. It was maddeningly slow. He remembered that the Ethiopes had two horny toes like cows, not a horse's single hoof.

The leading enemy was still ten feet short of the protea when Corylus shouted, "Ears for Nerthus!" and launched himself toward the enemy. He didn't want to wear himself out—and wear out his "troops"—before the fight even started, but there was a point at which the cost of watching danger amble closer outweighed the physical exertion of a few extra strides.

Tassk was the only one of the Singiri who spoke Latin, but that didn't matter much in the current situation. They were warriors. When their leader charged, they were going to charge right along with him—even if they thought he was shouting, "Run for your lives!"

And in truth, few regular legionaries would have understood the particular words that Corylus had shouted. The 3d Batavian Cavalry, his father's command on the Danube, were Germans. Individual soldiers each had his own favorite deity, but the squadron's scout section as a unit worshiped Nerthus. Their camp was at a little distance from the main squadron fort at Carnuntum, because they generally operated in darkness and needed to avoid noise and bother when they set off for the river and boats that would carry them to the Sarmatian side.

In the center of the Scouts' camp was a thick oaken pole—a length of trunk, stripped of bark but not smoothed: it was the shrine of Nerthus. To it were nailed the right ears of enemies whom the Scouts had killed across the river.

Corylus was ten when his father took command. He had tried to count the trophies when he first saw the pole, but he had given up before long: there were over a thousand ears.

By the time Corylus was fourteen, he was accompanying the Scouts on raids, without his father's knowledge, at least at first. Their war cry was a promise, not a boast.

If I were already in the army, I'd be a junior tribune on the commander's staff, carrying messages to and from the centurions who led the troops into the fighting, Corylus thought. His experience with the Scouts would have been unimportant. Here, however—

I know what to do because I've done it. Thank Nerthus, or Father Jove, or Good Fortune.

He had been running parallel to the course of the Ethiope column, a little to the right. Ethiopes who had spread to the sides were moving back inward at a heavy lope. One of those turned and raised her spear overhead like a harpoon. She didn't carry a shield.

Corylus hunched down and stopped in a spray of sand, bracing his right foot against a block of crystal sticking up from the ground. His cleats sparked on the stone. If he'd tried to remain upright, he would have pitched forward on his face.

The Ethiope stabbed downward like a battering ram. Her spearhead shattered into flint needles: she must have struck another fragment of ruin just under the surface. Even without a point, the shaft would have crushed through a human body in its path.

Corylus rose, thrusting past the quivering spear and through the Ethiope's diaphragm. She doubled up and slid slowly down the spear shaft, which she still held in both hands.

Two more Ethiopes were approaching from twenty feet away to

Corylus' right, but he ignored them and ducked toward the main column. An Ethiope with his shield raised was facing in the opposite direction. Corylus stabbed him through the kidneys. The Ethiope's huge body followed his spear. He had been jabbing toward a Singiri warrior who easily avoided it.

The next Ethiope was turning toward Corylus when the Singiri lopped through his knee. The warriors' bronze swords must be extremely sharp. The joints were cartilaginous, but a quick cut at an angle like that must have clipped solid bone both above and below.

And the Singiri must be extremely strong despite their slender limbs. That wouldn't change the outcome of a battle at odds of fifty to one—and rising every time another Ethiope stepped into the Waking World—but it would help humanity survive longer, if only by a matter of minutes.

Ignoring the falling Ethiope—he would bleed out before he could crawl to the Daughters on three limbs—Corylus thrust for the ankle of the next. His sword crunched home, but the Ethiope's axe was already swinging down. Corylus lifted his borrowed shield to meet it, knowing the Ethiopes' strength and wincing mentally before the physical shock.

The axe only *ticked* the rim of his shield and sailed off into the sand. Even so, Corylus' left hand quivered on the handles—it was a buckler, not a larger target supported by loops for his left forearm. Alphena had slashed through the Ethiope's wrist so that only inertia guided the climax of the stroke.

"Behind you!" she said. The flanking Ethiopes whom Corylus had bypassed in the initial rush were closing like bulls charging in the arena.

Farther down the line, half a dozen Ethiopes were on the sand. Some thrashed, some merely bled, and some had already bled out: the Singiri warriors knew their business. None of the enemy was close enough to be a threat as Corylus turned to meet the flankers.

Alphena shifted left, away from Corylus. The nearer Ethiope angled to follow her, crossing the path of his fellow. Corylus was on his left side, but the Ethiope held his shield low and Corylus' long sword licked over it.

The high, pointed ear flew into the air in a spray of blood. The Ethiope bellowed, twisting as he fell sideways. The stroke had cut deeply enough into the skull to stun, but it wasn't immediately fatal.

The following Ethiope jumped his sprawling fellow. Alphena lunged, stabbing him through the groin while he was still extended in the air. The idol in her left hand blocked the flint knife with which the Ethiope on the sand tried to stab her.

Corylus chopped through the base of the fallen Ethiope's spine, as high as he could reach while he was off-balance. The Ethiope's legs went limp, but his arms and torso spasmed, throwing Alphena clear.

Hercules! Alphena's ugly carved idol hadn't *blocked* the knife thrust, it was gripping the flint blade. It cackled with high-pitched laughter as it threw the knife aside. Its iron tongue was licking off the blood that had spewed from Alphena's disemboweling stroke.

I'm the commander. Corylus glanced across the battlefield. His vision blurred and he thought for a moment that he might vomit. His stomach and eyes settled.

The Ethiopes were now charging toward the fight, throwing up plumes of dust. Because of their great weight, they plunged deep into the sand when they ran, making their advance much more tiring than their previous stolid walk had been.

Every little bit helps. But it was time now to fall back. The Scouts used whistle signals—they didn't usually have a trumpeter with them across the river. Corylus didn't have a whistle, and they hadn't set up calls ahead of time anyway.

"Recover!" Corylus shouted. His throat was as dry as if he'd been trying to swallow sand instead of just fighting on it. What in Hades' name was the Singiri signal to fall back?

"Recover!" he repeated, waving his sword overhead. The tip slung drops of blood.

One of the warriors glanced over his shoulder. Corylus pointed toward the rear with his sword, then started jogging back.

The Singiri clicked something in his own language, and the others turned also. One was limping.

"We'll wait for them back where we started," Corylus muttered to Alphena through panting breaths. "Then we'll do it again."

And probably a third time. But it wouldn't be very long before he and his companions were too exhausted even to raise their weapons. Then they would die and the world would end.

But until then the Horseheads would be in a fight.

CHAPTER XVII

The sky had turned a color like unmixed wine viewed through a glass tumbler. Hedia gave it a glance of haughty dislike.

The shade ought to cool this niche in the hills. Instead the clouds overhead were a swirling purple-black lid that cut off the sea breeze and the atmosphere was sweltering. Hedia didn't suppose it really mattered, but it was as irritating as being groped by a dinner guest who she knew was too drunk to perform if she *did* give him an opportunity.

She walked at a measured pace, watching her footing more intently than she did what was going on around her. There were soft patches in this sand; she'd almost fallen sideways once already.

Loose sand rasped between her soles and the sandals despite her having tried to shake it out. Well, she'd compromised her fashion sense as far as she was going to by wearing heavy sandals when she visited Melino. There had been no possibility that she would wear cavalry boots against the possibility of having to cross deep sand.

When Hedia set out on her personal mission, she had been afraid that an Ethiope would leave the main column to dispose of her. The half men were capable of running, whereas she was not, certainly not on these dunes.

In fact, the Ethiopes had paid no attention to her. She supposed that one of them would have knocked her head in if she stumbled into its path, but they barely looked at her as she angled off well to the side of their line.

Corylus and the lizardmen had drawn the flanking Ethiopes inward as Hedia had expected, so there was nothing in her way. She suspected that the half men would ignore all the others in the basin, human and Singiri alike, if they simply moved away from the little Nubian girls.

The Ethiopes were as mindless as ants; but also like ants, they were inexorable. They were carrying out the orders they had been given. Death would stop an individual, but there were too many individuals for that to be a practical answer.

Disposing of Paris, the wretched Etruscan *farmer*, who was responsible for the whole trouble, probably wasn't an answer, either. Things had gone too far by now.

The Daughters of the Mind, as somebody had called them, were sprawled on the sand. Nearby the air around their Egg was rippling. A mirage? That, or something else was going on, which seemed likely enough in this place and this time.

Through the distortion Hedia could see Varus and a lizardman on either side of the Egg, but the images were smeared as though she were looking through a thick sheet of mica. She couldn't identify the lizardman. Tassk was talking with Pandareus. The three warriors who had come with Tassk were fighting alongside Corylus, but she looked again to be sure.

Alongside Corylus and Alphena. The thought made Hedia cringe mentally, but nothing showed on her face. No doubt Alphena was making herself useful, as indeed the girl generally did, now that she was being herself instead of reacting against others.

Here, though, it would make no difference to the final result, and Hedia had a mother's natural desire that Alphena would die a lady.

Hedia smiled wryly. Alphena would at least die a virgin. Hedia found that she didn't take as much satisfaction from that fact as a more proper mother would. A girl's purity was important for a good marriage, but marriage seemed as unlikely now as Hedia herself becoming a Vestal Virgin.

Paris had been kneeling before symbols he had drawn in the sand before him, tapping his wand over them while he chanted. As Hedia approached, he rose to his feet and stretched both arms toward the dark sky.

Hedia had assumed the wand was ivory or pale wood. She saw now that it was a shinbone, probably human, though perhaps from a deer.

Paris shouted to the heavens. In Etruscan, most likely, but Hedia had never learned the language. She could carry on a conversation in Oscan if she needed to, since one of her nurses had been from the Samnite backcountry.

A crash louder than lightning snapped Hedia out of her reverie. The purple sky cracked open to north and south. Sunlight reached through, but beyond the sunlight and crawling closer were the glittering immensities of the Worms of the Earth. She could see their backs above the black rocks, and the rocks themselves were being ground into their maws.

Paris lowered his arms. "You are too late, woman!" he said. "The Worms are loose on the Waking World! They will scrape all human foulness from the Earth!"

He waggled the wand toward Hedia. She was only ten feet away.

"Do you know what this is?" he said. "It's a bone from Romulus. I have used the founder of Carce to destroy the race of Carce and all life with it!"

"My husband would be fascinated," Hedia said, walking forward. "And I daresay that Varus might be interested also. Men have to be younger and in better condition before I pay much attention to them."

She swung her block of stone at the priest's face. He threw a hand up to parry it. Hedia's arm was stronger, and the crystal's own weight gave force to the blow.

Paris fell sideways. He had saved his skull for the moment, though his broken hand crumpled when he tried to support himself on it.

"It won't help!" he shouted. "You're doomed! Your whole race is doomed!"

"That," said Hedia, "is a problem for another time."

She struck at the priest's face again. This time bone crunched.

Paris sprawled. Hedia toed his head so that she could see his face. His eyes were open. She hit him again in a spray of blood.

Hedia would have struck a fourth blow, but she had lost her grip on the stone. She was trembling from reaction.

She was afraid that if she bent over to pick up the stone she would fall. Besides, it was filthy with blood; and anyway, there was no need.

The Worms were devouring a path through the hills. The grinding roar of destruction made her think of surf driven by an impossibly huge storm.

Hedia, wife of Gaius Alphenus Saxa and a noblewoman of Carce, walked regally back toward her son and their friends. Her face was calm. She clenched and unclenched the stiffness out of her right hand.

ALPHENA WAS BREATHING through her open mouth. She'd never before in her life been so tired.

I've thought that before, she realized. Well, perhaps she'd been right before also.

She and Corylus were fighting as a pair. An Ethiope charged them, snorting through flared nostrils; a second was not far behind. Alphena shifted left as usual.

More often than not her movement would draw the attack on her, but this Ethiope lifted his huge spear and went straight for Corylus. Alphena slashed for the Ethiope's raised right elbow, clipping the bone.

If she hadn't been exhausted, she would have thrust with the point, but she didn't trust her timing. In fact, the stroke was perfect, but if she'd been off a little the edge would still have jolted the Ethiope's arm and thrown off his thrust.

He bellowed and turned his head toward Alphena. Corylus stabbed upward past the Ethiope's shield—he'd dropped it slightly at the pain in his other arm—and withdrew his sword in a spray of arterial blood from the Ethiope's neck.

It was as neat a piece of swordsmanship as Alphena had ever seen in the arena, but she didn't have time to savor it—let alone to congratulate her partner. "Ware front!" the idol shrieked, and the second Ethiope was on her almost before she could react.

The Ethiope's pounding hooves kicked a curtain of sand before them. Alphena lifted the idol with her eyes slitted against the dust. First twisted into the path of the point and shattered it on his wooden breast.

He's a better god for a warrior than any Olympian would be, Alphena thought. She couldn't stand against the power of the thrust, but she let it spin her widdershins, hoping to thrust her huge opponent through the body as his rush carried him forward. Instead the Ethiope's shield hurled her backward like a feather-filled paddleball hit squarely.

Alphena slammed into the sand. Corylus stabbed the Ethiope through the kidneys, spilling him on the ground beside her with a despairing howl. She cut off his right hand with a quick stroke, though the agony of the kidney wound would probably have paralyzed the creature for the few minutes before it bled out.

There was another lull in the fighting. The Ethiopes had bunched up when they ran toward the defenders' sally. When the defenders fell back, Ethiopes arriving through the portal had resumed their amble toward the battle.

When the later-comers reached the defenders, they wouldn't be as blown as those previously dealt with. Without this pause, though, Alphena wasn't sure that she would have been able even to get to her feet.

She rolled onto all fours, still gripping both the sword and the blood-smeared idol. First was licking himself and chuckling with glee. From training, almost mindlessly, Alphena wiped her sword blade, one side and then the other, on the harness of the Ethiope sprawled beside her.

She gasped to bring in air. She seemed to be able to breathe more deeply in this posture than she could while standing.

The Ethiopes were enormously strong. Even the accidental blow from the Horsehead's shield had thrown Alphena more than her own height backward. Neither she nor any other human could actually stop the creatures' rush any more than one could stop a ramming warship.

But despite their strength and their numbers, the Ethiopes fought as individuals. They were more likely to get in one another's way than they were to support a comrade's attack. The Singiri worked as a team, and so did Alphena and Corylus.

The idol looked back at her, though she hadn't spoken aloud. "Am I not fighting beside you?" First asked. "Would you rather have a disc of bronze like your other companion?"

"Your pardon, sacred companion," Alphena said, and meant it. Most of her business with gods in the past had been to watch when the host at dinner offered a crumb and a drop of wine to the household gods.

Alphena would personally burn incense to First if she returned to Carce. Which seemed extremely unlikely at the moment.

She would have worn armor if there'd been any that would fit. Now she thanked Hercules that armor *hadn't* been available. A helmet and corselet wouldn't have delayed by eyeblinks the strokes of the Ethiopes' weapons, but they would have slowed her and confined her breathing. It was difficult enough to suck in air as it was.

Alphena stood up carefully. Corylus was leaning forward slightly to give his lungs more room also, but he looked ready to fight again. Alphena wasn't sure that she was. The upper rim of Corylus' Singiri shield was dented, so perhaps he had gotten some benefit from it after all.

Hedia was walking back from some distance into the desert. For a moment Alphena couldn't imagine what her mother was doing; then she traced Hedia's course outward and saw the body of the Etruscan crumpled among the ruins.

Alphena felt sudden warmth. *Mother isn't one to forget, friends or enemies, either one.*

Farther away still was a dazzle of gray light reflecting over the ring of hills. The roar that Alphena had ignored in the stress of battle reached her consciousness: *The Worms. The Worms of the Earth.* Doom, eating its way toward them from the south and—she turned her head—north as well.

The next wave of Ethiopes approached at a measured pace. More were appearing through the portal; the priest's death had changed nothing. The sand of this beach had once been solid rock, but the waves had ground it down.

Alphena glanced behind her. The Daughters lay on the ground, exhausted or perhaps dead. It probably didn't matter which.

Pandareus and Tassk were deep in conversation. Surely they weren't having a philosophical discussion at *this* time?

But again, it probably didn't matter. The old men were as useful talking about the nature of the firmament as they would have been with swords. Indeed, in the long run their talk would be as useful as anything Alphena and Corylus were doing with swords.

Within the circle of the slumped Daughters, the air was gray and metallic. Alphena could see two figures through the translucence, but she didn't know who—or what—they were. She hoped one was her brother, because otherwise she didn't know where he was.

The Egg, instead of being dimmed by the barrier of air, was as brilliant as a jewel in sunlight. Alphena looked away instantly, but she still had to blink at afterimages dancing across her vision. What was going on?

But that didn't matter, either. All that mattered for the moment, and probably for eternity, was the line of horse-headed giants. The leading Ethiopes broke into a clumsy trot as they neared.

"The next course of the banquet!" First chirped. "Oh, never has a god been fed so well by his worshiper!"

I'm glad someone is happy, thought Alphena. She shifted to the left to draw the first Ethiope's attention away from her partner.

A wind from the sea was picking up. It sent stinging whips of sand across her calves.

THE SIBYL AND GAIUS Alphenus Varus watched from a high ridge. Below them humans and Singiri fought horse-headed savages, while the Singiri princess and Gaius Alphenus Varus chanted spells through Zabulon's *Book*.

"I don't understand what is going on," Varus said.

He didn't remember joining the Sibyl this time. Half of him thought—imagined—that rather than looking down from their usual detached viewpoint she was standing beside him as he faced the Princess across the glowing majesty of the Egg.

Of course none of it was real. But what *was* real? Was anything real?

"You are great magicians, Lord Varus," the Sibyl said. "You are bringing the Egg into the Waking World before its Saeclum of Saecla is accomplished, and the *Book* is your lever."

A *saeclum* was a period of either one hundred years or one hundred and ten years; the best sources that Varus had found didn't agree. An insistently pedantic voice at the back of his mind wanted to ask the Sibyl which figure was correct.

The Worms were already larger than the basalt escarpment that they were devouring from north and south. They scoured a hundred feet deep, well into the bedrock. Their heads cast sideways, back and forth, in arcs like those of maggots in dead flesh.

Rock, the flesh of the Earth, vanished down the crystal maws. The immense forms grew with each pass, and the jaws swept deeper into the basin where Varus and his companions fought.

Sunlight glanced off them, refracted into shades of gray instead of rainbows. It reminded Varus of feathery variations in smut that rotted wheat while it was still alive.

Varus looked at the Egg. He was even less able to judge its size now than he had been earlier. It *must* be huge, but his body could have reached across it and touched the hand of the Princess whose lips moved in silent synchrony with his own.

Varus glanced at the Sibyl. "Lady?" he said. "Shouldn't I be below? Shouldn't I, my spirit . . . shouldn't it be with my body?"

"To do what, Lord Varus?" the old woman said. "Are not you and the Princess, your fellow magician, already doing all that mortals can do to save the world?"

Varus shook his head, trying to clear it of the fog that seemed to be clogging his attempts to think. He said, "I'm not doing anything! I'm just watching!"

The heads of the Worms continued to sweep side to side, deeper into the basin. The . . . things, creatures, *cancers,* however you described them. They didn't so much crawl forward as grow outward, absorbing more of the Earth and expanding by that ever-increasing amount. The range of hills had vanished except for the nub remaining between the arcs that the two Worms had devoured.

"A *saeclum* is not an age of years," the Sibyl said, "but an age of the Earth, a period of the Cosmos. You are at the close of one *saeclum* and the beginning of the next. In one age—"

She gestured. Varus saw from an enormous distance but with perfect clarity the Worms of the Earth writhe and absorb and grow until there was nothing to absorb but a bead of fire like the heart of a volcano, over which the pair of foul crystal Worms twitched untouched.

"And the other age—," the Sibyl said.

The Egg was blue light and all light and all colors, resting in the basin on the edge of the sea but greater in another sense than all the Waking World. The Egg *was,* and then it cracked open, spilling light that expanded without any more boundary than sunlight itself.

For a moment, Varus thought he saw the form of a bird, splendid and perfect.

Then, as his spirit reentered his body on the sand, he heard the Sibyl say, "Well done, Lord Magician. You have hatched the Phoenix."

WINDBLOWN SAND WAS TORTURE on the back of his calves, his arms, and especially his neck. *I'll be bleeding tomorrow,* Corylus thought. He started to laugh but gagged on an incoming breath, so he had to thrust for the Ethiope's upper thigh while off-balance.

His sword went home anyway. He withdrew the blade. Blood from the creature's femoral artery gushed as though the valve of an aqueduct had opened. The Ethiope turned toward his slayer but crumpled before he could raise his spear for a stroke.

Alphena had been ready to put in a finishing blow, but there was no need for that. Earlier in the fight she would have stabbed the Ethiope through the kidneys as soon as he turned away from her. Now, neither she nor Corylus had energy for any unnecessary movements.

The wind was punishing to the defenders, but it blinded the Ethiopes who were attacking into it. Stolid though the half men were, they could not look into sand that literally wore their eyelids away and then ground their corneas opaque. They advanced with their shields lifted to cover their eyes. The first they knew of their opponents was when a sword licked below or beside their shield, dealing a lethal blow.

Corylus and Alphena had been retreating slowly, driven back by the bodies piling into a windrow before them. Their worst danger was that they would be hemmed in by the twitching dead and unable to avoid a wild swipe from a stone axe or a spear as thick as a ship's jib.

The next danger—the one they wouldn't be able to avoid—was that they would become too exhausted to raise their swords. The Ethiopes could slaughter the Daughters and anyone else in their way just by falling dead on top of them; their massive bodies weighed hundreds of pounds apiece.

"Corylus!" Alphena shouted. She pointed outward with the blood-covered stick in her left hand. "Look! Look!"

For a moment, Corylus couldn't see what she was pointing to. *There are no Ethiopes close enough to—*

The head of a Worm swept by sunwise with the slow majesty of a waterfall. It towered above them, higher perhaps than the escarpment that it had devoured.

The ocean followed the Worm's body. At the far end of its stroke, the Worm had gouged deep into the seabed, and the water rushed to fill the new embayment. Eventually the Worms would between them drink the seas as well as the land, but for now the ocean laughed thunderously at its new conquest.

The Worm didn't *eat* the land the way a caterpillar did sections of a leaf. Rather, its dark-glimmering head passed by, absorbing all that had been in its path. Rock and sand fell, no longer supported by the ground beside it, but the process of destruction itself was as silent as thought.

The Worm continued on—toward the remaining mountains and into the desert beyond. It did not seem a swift process, but Corylus realized that a galloping horse could not have kept pace with the Worm's head. Only the creature's enormous size concealed the speed of its movements.

Corylus looked for the Ethiopes. There were none nearby except the scores of sprawled corpses. Survivors loped clumsily back toward the portal by which they had entered the Waking World. Over the ocean's gurgle, Corylus heard the Ethiopes hoot and bellow.

Varus said that the Ethiopes had been wiped out in their own time, so their return would bring them doubtful safety. That was a matter between them and their gods, however, if they had gods.

The wind stopped. Corylus sprawled backward—as did Alphena. He—they—had been leaning against the pressure without being aware of it. Normally they would have been able to catch their balance without falling down, but Corylus wasn't sure for a moment that he would be able to stand again ever.

At least not before the nearer Worm absorbed another devouring arc of the landscape, which would, this time, include Publius Cispius Corylus, Knight of Carce.

Corylus scrambled to his feet, wobbling slightly. *I'm not going to die on my back.* He leaned carefully over the Ethiope he had just killed and wiped his sword on the black fur of the creature's shoulder.

Corylus' blade was not only dull but twisted. Even so, it had come through the test better than anyone would have predicted. It was a standard product of one of the army shops; but then, the army of Carce manufactured weapons in the expectation that they would see hard use.

I'll hang it as an offering in the Temple of Mars the Avenger, Corylus thought. *If I return to Carce. If Carce continues to exist.*

The Singiri warriors hadn't lost their footing when the wind ceased to blow. Two of them now sat on their haunches, watching the Ethiopes flee.

The third lay on the sand between them. An axe had crushed his head to a smear of blood and bones connected by skin. One warrior had been limping before the wind rose. Even the blind thrusts and swipes the Ethiopes made when they couldn't see could be devastating to anyone who was slow to dodge.

Had been devastating.

Alphena was still on the ground. She didn't appear to be injured. When Corylus walked toward her, she rolled onto all fours and managed to get to her feet. Corylus would have offered a hand, but she was obviously determined to rise without help, or at least without his help.

Tassk and Pandareus had been hunching in a swale. It was slight, but it had been enough to keep them out of that murderous wind. Corylus smiled grimly.

Alphena must have been thinking the same thing, because she said, "The wind saved our lives. It flayed my bare skin, but if the Horseheads had been able to see, they would have killed me."

"Killed us," Corylus said. He walked toward Pandareus, hoping that the scholar could tell him where Varus was.

"Corylus?" Alphena said, walking beside him. "How long will it be before the Worms come back?"

They both wobbled, but they were keeping their feet. Corylus dropped his shield onto the sand, but Alphena kept her wooden club as well as her short sword. Its blade was as warped as that of his longer weapon.

Corylus looked at the deep inlet from the ocean and, on the other side of it, the shimmering crystal cliff. The Worm's flank trembled as the head cut eastward, inland. When it reached the end of that arc, probably at the Worm's own side, it would begin to swing back for the deeper cut that would engulf the humans and Singiri here in the basin.

"A quarter hour, I suppose," he said. "I wasn't paying a great deal of attention to what the Worms were doing."

In a battle you learned to prioritize. The first thing you dealt with was the enemy who would kill you in the next instant. After that you could worry about the mission.

"I'm going to see Mother," Alphena said. "She may need . . . I'm going to see her."

Hedia was picking her way past the final pile of Ethiope corpses. She was blood spattered but regal. Her face was as calm as though she had been watching her husband burn a pinch of frankincense on the altar of Jupiter Best and Greatest.

Hedia didn't need any help Alphena could bring her, but her icy strength was exactly what her daughter needed after the murderous battle just concluded.

Tassk and Pandareus had clasped hands as they sat facing each other. They seemed to be supporting each other.

"Master," Corylus said. "Do you know where Lord Varus is?"

"I'm afraid not," Pandareus said. He was looking down at the sand between himself and Tassk, apparently too exhausted to raise his eyes. "I have been . . ."

He looked up after all. He smiled and said, "Master Tassk and I have been chanting a spell, I believe. It was a unique sensation, and one I hope never to repeat."

"Your friend Varus," Tassk said, his voice soft with weariness, "and my princess are saving your world. But especially Lord Varus, who has Zabulon's *Book*."

"Saving the world?" Corylus repeated, feeling as though his mind were clogged with scum. He looked toward the Worm, a shivering cascade of glittering gray horror. The other Worm was visible also, in another arm of ocean lit by the morning sun. "I don't understand."

Tassk gestured toward the three Daughters, now standing together. Beyond them was a steely distortion that completely shrouded whatever was inside it.

Corylus couldn't be sure how large the distortion was. It was as confusing as the Egg had been. And where was the Egg?

"There," whispered Tassk.

The distortion vanished. For an instant Corylus saw Varus, holding a black codex in his left hand, and the Singiri princess. Between them was the Egg.

Where the Egg had been was suddenly light, and the light, a rainbow as bright as the sun, filled the basin and the world.

There was a plangent cry, sweetly musical but so loud that Corylus thought the cells of his body were melting. For an instant, everything was joy and peace.

He again stood on sand at the sea's edge with his friends nearby. The sky was rainbow light. A spike of that sky stabbed down into the nearer Worm, lifting it as a starling does a grub.

The Worm was unthinkably huge. Corylus for a moment imagined that he saw the frozen Danube hanging in the air, thrashing wildly. The Worm vanished by portions—by gulps, or so it seemed. The massive grayness merged into the blaze of rippling colors and was gone.

Pandareus raised an arm; Corylus braced it so that the older man could rise. The last of the Worm disappeared, though water sloshed and chuckled in the channel it had eaten in the Earth. The sweet cry repeated. Pandareus' hand tightened on his.

The sound died out. The second Worm flicked into the air as the first had done. It began to disappear as well.

"I wish my friend Atilius Priscus were here," Pandareus said in a wondering tone. "He loves music above all things. He would give his life, I'm sure, to have heard that sound."

"We're still alive, master," Corylus said. "For however long the gods grant us, of course. But that's always been true."

The last of the Worm was dissolving into the light. The Princess walked toward them—toward Tassk, most likely—but Varus stood as motionless as a statue. He had lowered the *Book* and held its weight against his chest, but Corylus was sure that his friend's mind was in another place.

The Worms were gone. The cry sounded a third time. The radiance sucked itself into the high sky and vanished in its turn.

"I was never in doubt that we were on the correct side," Pandareus said musingly. "But I'll admit to doubting until just now that we would be on the side which survived."

"Yes," said Corylus. "I doubted that too."

He bowed to the Princess as she joined them.

Epilogue

Tassk stood when he saw the Princess approaching. Corylus offered an arm, but though Tassk moved carefully, he didn't need help.

"You fight well, warrior," Tassk said. He looked toward Alphena's back and his tongue lolled out in the Singiri equivalent of laughter. "As does your little friend. The females of my race are not warriors."

"Nor are most of ours," Corylus said drily. "I'm fortunate that Lady Alphena is an exception, because I wouldn't have survived without her watching my left side."

He tried to sheathe his sword but stopped in sudden stupefaction. The blade was too damaged to have fitted the scabbard anyway, but that was secondary: his scabbard and belt were missing, and there was a deep gouge across his ribs from what must have been the same flint-headed spear that had ripped off his equipment.

"Hercules!" he gasped. He'd been so wrung out generally that he hadn't noticed that particular wound. When he did, the pain hit him like a shower of hot coals. *"Hercules!"*

"Is the injury serious?" Tassk said, tracing it with his long fingers but not quite touching either flesh or the scraps of tunic that were now glued to the wound.

"I don't suppose so," Corylus said, trying not to wince. There wasn't a great deal of blood, all things considered, though it continued to ooze out in brighter red whenever he moved and cracked the scab. It was deeper than the similar injury to his right side during his fight while trapped with the Princess. "I don't recall it happening, is all."

Even trying to cast his mind back didn't help much. An Ethiope had thrust a spear at him—and missed. That had happened at least a score of times in the past quarter hour, but most of them hadn't come anywhere nearby.

Or anyway, he hadn't thought they did.

Which reminded him . . . "Master Tassk?" he said. "Do we have you to thank for the wind? Because it saved our lives."

"Master Pandareus and I raised the wind," Tassk said, nodding. The scholar stood with them but seemed to have drifted into a separate world. He wore a dazed expression.

"When one grows too old to fight," Tassk said, "one must find other ways of serving the Princess. I will never be a magician, but by effort and the help of a very skilled partner—"

He glanced at Pandareus again, this time with obvious respect.

"—one can help real warriors like yourself and my younger brethren."

Corylus looked at the surviving Singiri warriors, squatting beside the body of their comrade. They hadn't moved since the Ethiopes fled.

"I didn't have much time to watch what your men were doing," Corylus said. "I was busy myself at the time. But I can see the bodies of those they were fighting. I'm glad Alphena and I were facing Ethiopes and not your warriors."

Tassk burst into hissing laughter. "Oh!" he said. "Oh, that would be a delight to watch, yes."

He sobered and went on, "But yes, your world is fortunate that you and your female were fighting on its behalf rather than against it."

The Princess joined them. She must have slowed in order to let Corylus and Tassk speak to each other privately, man-to-man.

Corylus gave a hard smile. Tassk might have scales, but he was a man by any definition that mattered to Corylus.

The Princess nodded sideways to Tassk, then turned to Corylus. "Warrior Corylus," she said. "I and mine have tried to repay your kindness to me."

"You have done so, Lady," Corylus said. "My help was just a personal thing, but you've saved my world."

The Princess made a gesture with her hand, dismissal, Corylus thought, but he might have been imposing human meaning on a Singiri action.

Tassk said, "The difference may be less than you think, warrior. Regardless, we all acted in a fashion that will make our offspring proud when others speak of this day."

"Do you wish to return with us, Warrior Corylus?" the Princess said. Her tone made him think of Hedia in her formal guise.

"No, Princess," Corylus said, trying to equal her formality. "I will stay with my friends, though I'll admit that this—"

He looked around him.

"—isn't the most attractive part of the Waking World."

Tassk laughed again. The Princess said, "You and your companions will return to Carce, if that is your wish. But for you, Warrior Corylus? Keep the link of chain which I gave you. It may be that someday my world will seem a refuge from the place in which you find yourself. You will be welcome."

She nodded to Tassk and said, "It is time that we return."

The Princess walked toward her three warriors. The survivors rose to their feet, lifting the corpse of their fellow between them.

"Tassk?" Corylus said as the old Singiri started to follow his princess. Tassk turned again and faced him.

Corylus nodded toward the warriors. "I'm sorry about your Theta," he said, using army slang; *Theta*, the first letter of "thanatos," dead, was the roll-call marking for fatalities. "Please offer my condolences as a warrior to his mate. Ah, if he had a mate."

Tassk laughed again. "Oh, Sele was a great hero, Corylus," he said. "Else he would not have been here, where few could be brought. There will be many females to mourn him. I will tell them that you honor Sele in memory."

Tassk looked at the Singiri warriors, waiting for him with the Princess. Very quietly he said, "Sele will never grow old. His fellows think that he is unfortunate, but they are young too. When they reach my age, they may see things in another way."

Tassk trudged toward his fellows, looking older than he had at any time since Corylus first saw him in the shipping cage in Puteoli. The Princess was holding out the chain that had taken her and the warriors home after her rescue.

Varus suddenly shouted something, the first sound he had made since the Phoenix appeared. Corylus walked toward his friend.

When he glanced back, the Singiri were fading like mist in the sunlight.

VARUS LOOKED DOWN on the fan-shaped patterns eaten from the surface of the Earth below his viewpoint. "So much damage in only a few minutes," he said. "Such deep scars."

Beside him the Sibyl said, "The sea has already softened the cuts. In a year, they will have blurred together. In fifty years, sand drifting from the desert to the east and sand brought in by the sea will have made the bay indistinguishable from any other on this coast of Africa."

"The Phoenix saved us," Varus said.

"The Phoenix hatched," said the Sibyl. "And saved the world."

Varus understood the difference in emphasis, but he wasn't willing to accept the implication that *he* had helped save the world. *I watched everything happen from here in a dream!*

Below, the Singiri were joining hands at a slight distance from Corylus and Pandareus. Varus' own body stood by itself, and the women—his mother and sister—were making their way slowly toward the men.

"What will you do with Zabulon's *Book?*" the Sibyl said. Her voice was as calm as the surf.

"What?" said Varus. He looked into the crook of his left arm where he supported the codex. It was closed and the iron clasps latched the covers together. "I'd forgotten I had it."

He thought for a moment, then said, "I won't do anything with it. If Vergil thought it should be taken out of the world, then I have no business with it. Do you want it, Sibyl?"

He held the volume out in both hands, suddenly aware of the weight.

"I have no existence outside your mind, Lord Varus," the old woman said, smiling like a whorl in the bark of a desert tree. She lifted the *Book* from him. "But it can return to Zabulon, who created it and who is dead."

She touched the back of Varus' wrist with a fingertip as light as a butterfly landing. It was the first time he had been in physical contact—or so it seemed—with his vision.

"You are wise, Lord Magician," the Sibyl said. "You are wiser than you are powerful, and you are more powerful than you dream. You did not need the help of the Princess, though it speaks well of her and of the Singiri that she came."

"I don't want to be powerful!" Varus shouted. "I want to read my books and learn things and maybe someday complete a survey of the ancient religion of Carce!"

"Your wishes and my wishes do not control the Cosmos," said the Sibyl. "While we are here, we have our parts to play in its workings."

She raised her right hand and continued in the same cracked voice, *"Under the pleasant sun—"*

"—*I take delight!*" Varus cried, and his body staggered as he reentered it on a ridge of sand. He no longer held Zabulon's *Book*.

Corylus clasped him, arm to arm, in friendship, Varus was sure, but also to catch him if he collapsed after his reverie with the Sibyl. Varus was more alert than he often was after his visions, but he appreciated his friend's foresight and kindness.

Varus appreciated it even more when Corylus gasped and bent toward his left. Varus glanced down and saw that his friend's side was bloody beneath a scabbed black gash.

"By Mercury!" Varus said. "We've got to get you to a surgeon!"

"It's not as bad as it looks," Corylus said, twisting his grimace into a smile. "The Princess said that we'd be able to return to Carce, though I'll admit that I don't see how that's to happen. If she was right, I'll have Pulto look at it."

"Yes," said Varus, thinking about what the Sibyl had said. "The Princess told me she came to help us because you had helped her. I don't think she'd lie."

Pandareus joined them. He looked tired but oddly ebullient. "Master?" Varus said carefully. "You look as though you've gained great knowledge."

What he really meant was, *You look as though you've had a religious experience.* That was the sort of thing silly women did when they joined barbarian cults, and the thing barbarian madmen did by baking their brains out in the Syrian desert, and a thing barbarians did generally.

It was not something that a scholar steeped in the philosophy of Greece did. To suggest otherwise was an insult that Varus cringed even to have admitted into his mind.

"I've gained the greatest kind of knowledge," Pandareus said brightly. "I know now that there's a kind of knowledge which I previously did not believe to exist!"

"Ah, master?" Varus said. "Do you mean the gods are real?"

"Oh, by Holy Wisdom, I certainly *hope* not!" Pandareus said. "I will have wasted my entire life if they are—though that in itself raises the question of the meaning of life, doesn't it? But I can see that there really is something to magic, though I can't see what it is."

"Well, I've watched . . . ," Corylus said, then stopped in embarrassment. He looked at Varus, shrugged, and resumed, "I've watched Lord Varus work magic. What must have been magic. And you've watched him."

Varus lifted his chin in minuscule acceptance of the statement. It didn't matter how he felt about it. He couldn't fault the accuracy of what his friend had said, and the truth was the truth.

"Yes," said Pandareus, grinning wryly at the illogic of what he was saying. "But I wasn't able to believe what I saw. Not the way I could believe in the perfection of Hector's final words to his infant son, which I could understand even though I could never have created them."

Pandareus beamed again like a religious convert. "Thanks to Tassk, I was able to see the mechanism that was at work," he said. "I once watched bull tendons wound into springs for a catapult, and it was the same feeling of revelation. I didn't become a mechanic who could build catapults then, and I'm not a magician now—but I understand the principles which allow others to act."

Varus pressed his hands to his face to hide from the inquiring looks of his friends. "*I* don't understand," he said. "I know what happened, I know what I *did*, but I don't know how I did it."

"I wonder . . . ," said Corylus, thinking about the scene from the *Iliad* that Pandareus had used as an example. "If Homer knew what he was doing."

"Homer was a genius," Varus said, shocked to the core. "Homer was the greatest poet of all time!"

"Yes," said Corylus. "He was. I'm sure he knew he was a great poet, because he could hear the other poets of his day. We probably have the best of them still—"

He looked toward Pandareus, who lifted his chin in agreement. The scholar was smiling at something that Varus didn't see, or at least didn't see yet.

"—and they're at best curiosities, while Homer had genius, *is* genius. But I wonder if Homer knew why he was a great poet and the others weren't, any better than you know how you just saved the world, my friend."

Varus turned away. He understood now. He didn't want to meet his friends' faces while he tried to decide whether Corylus was correct.

Varus' mother and sister were coming toward them. Both were splattered with blood. *Alphena was fighting beside Corylus and the Singiri, but whatever was Hedia doing?*

The answer quirked Varus' mouth into a grim smile: *whatever she thought was necessary.*

He went to meet the women. Corylus and Pandareus walked to either side of him.

ALPHENA WAS ALMOST COVERED IN BLOOD. It was sticky and uncomfortable, especially when it glued her clothing to her skin and pulled out hairs when she moved—but it wasn't her blood. She was sure of that, because if any significant portion had been from her own body she would have been dead.

"Ah, did ever a god feast as I have done today?" said First. "You are twice fortunate, little worshiper, because you have me to worship, and also because your mate is such a man of blood. Would he also worship me, do you think?"

"He's not my mate!" Alphena said, jolted into fury. She lifted the idol, meaning for an instant to smash it against one of the worn crystal pillars.

She calmed immediately. The mental image reminded her of the number of times in the past hour when flint points had shattered against the black wood. First, uncouth and ignorant though he undeniably was, had saved her life repeatedly.

It also reminded her that slamming First against the crystal would probably just numb her hand. She grinned. First, who she already knew could listen to her think, giggled.

Aloud Alphena said, "Gaius Corylus is a sturdy example of the yeomen who guard our borders." She was trying to be both stilted and didactic, in part because that tone infuriated her when somebody used it on her. "He's a fine fellow in his own fashion, of course, but *I* am a lady of Carce. You might as well suggest that I mate with a dog."

"You should ask your mother about that," First said. He giggled again.

Alphena looked up, saw Hedia directly in front of her, and blushed furiously. Hedia raised an eyebrow, and the idol laughed even harder.

Alphena had to turn away. *How much did she hear?* she thought. And, far worse, *Is it true?*

"Alphena, dear?" Hedia said. She didn't make the question more explicit.

If I asked her, she would tell me—no matter what the truth was, Alphena thought. *And it doesn't matter, not to me or to Father or to anybody else.*

"I'm very glad to see you, Mother," Alphena said formally. She suddenly realized both her hands were full.

Hedia stepped close and hugged her anyway, saying, "I must say the same."

"Oh, I'll get you all bloody!" Alphena said, trying to jump back.

Hedia laughed and let her go. "Well, bloodier, perhaps," she said. "When we get back to Carce, that will be easy to cure. And of course if we don't get back to Carce, it won't matter."

"You'll go back," First said, gesturing with one of his tiny wooden arms. "Look at the temple where your enemy was opening the sky. A friend of yours, Lady, has given you passage."

"What friend?" Alphena said, following the gesture toward the remains of the round temple where the Etruscan priest lay. Around it and around him had formed a ball of hard, red light. It could not have been confused with the pinkish glow of the portal through which Paris had pursued the Daughters and the Egg.

"Not yours, little worshiper!" the idol said sharply. "Your mother, who does not worship me yet. Though perhaps . . . ?"

Hedia sniffed. "I said my husband would build you a temple if you got us back to Carce," she said. "While you personally weren't responsible for that, neither Saxa nor myself is a pettifogging clerk. And the fact that our daughter came through the fighting and is still able to walk—"

"I wasn't touched, Mother!" Alphena said. "And First really did help me!"

"I'm sure he did, Daughter," Hedia said. She reached out with her left hand and caressed the idol's bloody, ugly head as though First were a puppy. "He will have a temple and an endowed priesthood in Carce."

"And blood?" First said.

"And blood sacrifices," Hedia agreed, but with a hard edge to her voice. "Though our acquaintances will think we've become barbarians, if they ever hear about it. And doves, I think, rather than larger animals. No matter how much we appreciate you, First, you are a very small god."

She and First exchanged oddly similar smiles. The idol giggled again.

Hedia looked beyond her; Alphena glanced over her shoulder and saw that the three men—Pandareus and his students, though thinking of them in those terms *now* made her smile—were walking toward them. Corylus limped and his side was bloody, which she hadn't noticed before.

"We'll join our friends," Hedia said. "And we'll all go to the temple where we see the red arch, because I think that will be our way back to Carce."

She looked toward the sea, but Alphena was sure that Hedia's mind was much farther away than that.

"The color of the light," Hedia said, "is the same as that of a ruby which belongs to a recent acquaintance. A friend, I would say."

Her face shifted into its public expression. She smiled a greeting to Varus and his companions.

WE LOOK LIKE SURVIVORS OF A SHIPWRECK, Hedia thought dispassionately as she watched her companions trudge toward the circle of column bases. She was at the end. She had taken charge of their return simply by force of will, and this was where she chose to be.

The arch of red light was mostly transparent, giving jewel-bright radiance to the scene beyond: desert and the remaining escarpment, the portion between that engulfed by the two Worms. Occasionally, though, Hedia thought she glimpsed the back garden of Saxa's town house in Carce. She might be letting her wish to go home trick her into seeing something that wasn't there, but—her smile was cold—why not?

Walking was uncomfortable, because blowing sand had rubbed the outer skin off her legs. Hedia had borrowed a sturdy woolen tunic from her maid before going to Melino's house at the start of this business, but she had worn a silk tunic beneath it for comfort.

When the wind rose as she walked into it, she had lifted the skirt of the outer tunic to shield her face. Her legs felt as though she had the worst sunburn of her life, and the inner tunic was reduced to a shredded train.

I've had my clothes ripped off in more pleasurable circumstances, she thought. Her smile was so dry that it didn't reach her lips.

Corylus was limping more noticeably. Hedia didn't think the boy's wound was serious, but it was stiffening and he couldn't have much reserve of energy after the battle with the Ethiopes. Hedia hadn't watched the fighting—it would only have distressed her—but the flashes she had seen, and the straggling piles of horse-headed corpses, showed how fierce it had been.

Ethiope weapons were strewn along the track Hedia's group was following. Fleeing, the creatures had passed close to the ruins where Hedia had met Paris, and where Paris remained.

"Corylus, let me help you," Alphena said, moving close to the youth's left side. "Here, you can lean your weight on me."

"Lady Alphena!" Hedia said. "Please step back. Varus, please go to the aid of Publius Corylus."

Her use of "please," particularly the first time, was merely a tuft of silk on a sword blade. Hedia intended to be obeyed, and nobody who heard her tone could have doubted that. Alphena stepped aside without looking back, though not very far aside.

"I don't need help," Corylus grumbled. The weakness of his voice belied his claim.

They all paused as Varus put his friend's arm over his shoulder, then resumed shuffling forward. Together the youths were moving no faster than they had been separately, but there was less chance that Corylus would fall on his face.

Pandareus dropped back beside Hedia. He said, "If you don't mind, Your Ladyship?"

"So long as everyone keeps moving, Master Pandareus . . . ," Hedia said. By now they were within fifty feet of the temple ruins. "I'm glad of your company."

That was a polite fiction rather than the truth, though Hedia didn't mind the scholar's presence. She felt that she should be concentrating on the remaining details of their return—but there *were* no details.

Her mind was spinning like that silly *aeropile* that Varus had built on the instructions of some Greek from Alexandria. Steam from heated water flowed into an egg with angled arms and squirted out, making the egg rotate pointlessly. You could get the same result with less effort by giving a pet squirrel a wheel to run in.

"I wonder if you could tell me anything about the passage we'll be following here," Pandareus said, gesturing with his left hand. "Master Corylus and I arrived in a very different fashion, by stepping into a vision which a dwarf who had been Vergil created in a basin."

"I don't even know if there is a passage," Hedia said. "My daughter's idol, First, tells me that there is and said that it was opened by the demon which Master Melino controlled. Well, First hinted that."

She smiled at a memory. "Melino insisted that his demon had neither personality nor emotions," she said. "He was wrong about both; and in the end, he appears to have been wrong in believing that she was *his* demon."

Because she was with a man, Hedia reflexively glanced down at herself. "I look a fright," she said ruefully. "My maid will be horrified."

"I trust you'll be able to clean up before your husband sees you, Your Ladyship," Pandareus said mildly.

Hedia laughed cheerfully. "Saxa won't worry," she said. "Saxa seems to think that nothing can really hurt me."

"Your husband is a very wise man," Pandareus said.

Hedia stared at him in surprise. She didn't reply, but only a lifetime of control kept her from blurting, "Are you joking?"

"I realize that Lord Saxa has foibles," Pandareus said. He was obviously serious. "Underneath them, though, he has remarkable understanding of character, understanding of the heart, if you'll allow me to use a term which I believe is more accurate than a more scientific one would be."

"I think you are correct, Master Pandareus," Hedia said after she had taken the necessary time to consider the statement. "And I thank you for an observation which had escaped me."

The two youths and Alphena had reached the temple. The arch of light was a solid ruby wall, no longer transparent or even translucent. It seemed to burn with internal light.

The girl turned in horrified realization. "The Daughters!" she said. "Where are they? I promised I'd defend them!"

"The Daughters are with the Egg," chirped First. "Where would you expect them to be, worshiper?"

"The Egg hatched," said Varus in what for him was a hard voice. He was frowning at the discourtesy to his sister. "Where are the Daughters now?"

"The Egg hatched and the Phoenix fed and lived its *saeclum*," First said in a singsong. "And now the Daughters again guard the Egg of the Phoenix, *Lord*."

The last word was obviously a sneer.

Varus had no expression for a moment. Then he chuckled and said, "Thank you for enlightening me, little godling."

I'm not sure he learned that sort of response from me, Hedia thought. She felt a surge of pride. *But he might have.*

"Well, aren't you going through?" First said. "There's no point in building me a temple here. Though I suppose having lizards sacrificed to me is better than nothing."

"I'm going through," said Corylus, lifting his arm clear of his friend's shoulders. He strode into the pane of light and vanished. Alphena and then Varus stepped after him.

Hedia's eyes fell on the body of the Etruscan priest. There were bubbles of blood at his nostrils. As she focused in surprise, she saw his remaining eyelid quiver.

The sun will finish him off before long.

She thought of Melino, and thought of the little insect man that Melino had left half-legless in the Otherworld.

"Go on through," Hedia said to Pandareus. "I'll follow in a moment."

The scholar lifted his chin in acknowledgment and vanished into the light. Another man might have protested the brusque order, but Pandareus seemed to have quite a good grasp of character himself.

Hedia walked back a few paces to the spear that an Ethiope had thrown down. It was like dragging a tree, but she didn't have far to go.

Hedia set the point against the Etruscan's chest and tilted the shaft into an upward angle. "Since you believe in gods," she said, "go to whatever place they choose for you."

She leaned forward, but the weapon's own weight did most of the work. The needle-sharp flint crunched through bone and gristle; the eyelid ceased to flutter.

Hedia, wife of Gaius Alphenus Saxa, stepped into ruby light and through, to her companions and to the Waking World.